T0012696

MEETING
HER
MATCH

Books by Jen Turano

LADIES OF DISTINCTION

Gentleman of Her Dreams:
A LADIES OF DISTINCTION
Novella from *With All My Heart Romance Collection*

A Change of Fortune

A Most Peculiar Circumstance

A Talent for Trouble

A Match of Wits

A CLASS OF THEIR OWN

After a Fashion

In Good Company

Playing the Part

APART FROM THE CROWD

At Your Request:
An APART FROM THE CROWD
Novella from *All for Love Romance Collection*

Behind the Scenes

Out of the Ordinary

Caught by Surprise

AMERICAN HEIRESSES

Flights of Fancy

Diamond in the Rough

Storing Up Trouble

Grand Encounters:
A HARVEY HOUSE BRIDES
COLLECTION *Novella from Serving Up Love*

THE BLEECKER STREET INQUIRY AGENCY

To Steal a Heart

To Write a Wrong

To Disguise the Truth

THE MATCHMAKERS

A Match in the Making

To Spark a Match

Meeting Her Match

THE MATCHMAKERS | BOOK 3

JEN TURANO

a division of Baker Publishing Group
Minneapolis, Minnesota

Published by Bethany House Publishers
Minneapolis, Minnesota
BethanyHouse.com

Bethany House Publishers is a division of
Baker Publishing Group, Grand Rapids, Michigan

Printed in the United States of America

Library of Congress Cataloging-in-Publication Data
Names: Turano, Jen, author.
Title: Meeting her match / Jen Turano.
Description: Minneapolis, Minnesota : Bethany House, a division of Baker Publishing Group, 2024. | Series: The Matchmakers ; 3
Identifiers: LCCN 2023049988 | ISBN 9780764240225 (paper) | ISBN 9780764243158 (casebound) | ISBN 9781493446551 (ebook)
Subjects: LCGFT: Christian fiction. | Romance fiction. | Novels.
Classification: LCC PS3620.U7455 M44 2024 | DDC 813/.6—dc23/eng/20231025
LC record available at https://lccn.loc.gov/2023049988

Scripture quotations are from the King James Version of the Bible.

Author is represented by Sarah Younger, Nancy Yost Literary Agency.

Cover by Kelly Howard
Cover image from Lee Avison/Trevillion Images

Baker Publishing Group publications use paper produced from sustainable forestry practices and postconsumer waste whenever possible.

24 25 26 27 28 29 30 7 6 5 4 3 2 1

In Memory of Susan Gibson Snodgrass

An avid reader who was with me from my very first published book and who became not simply a woman who went out of her way to support my work but a dear friend.

You are truly missed.

Godspeed, my friend.

Love,

Jen

This book is also dedicated to my Ohio Valley friends who didn't hesitate to step up and share their memories of the Valley with me, as well as give me quite the lesson regarding things like . . . ramps. I had no idea. Your suggestions, as well as your willingness to help me with the local vernacular, definitely allowed me to take this story to a different level, and for that, you have my heartfelt thanks. It was fabulous getting the opportunity to reconnect with so many of you, and to remember why, to this day, the Ohio Valley still feels like home.

Love you!

Jen

One

HUDSON RIVER VALLEY
SPRING 1889

Being chased by highwaymen was certainly cause for concern, as was the idea she was in imminent danger of losing her seat because riding sidesaddle, and while dressed in the most fashionable of riding habits, was not exactly conducive to escaping from a most dire situation.

Leaning over the neck of her horse, Fiona, an unpredictable mare at the best of times, and this certainly wasn't the best of times, Miss Camilla Pierpont cemented her grip on the saddle pommel, wondering how she was going to escape her pursuers with her life intact and how she'd even landed in such a predicament in the first place.

She was not a lady prone to unfortunate predicaments, having acquired the reputation of being one of the most consummate ladies to ever grace the Four Hundred some eight years before when she'd made her debut.

Consummate ladies did not find themselves fearing for their lives often, if ever, but that certainly seemed to be what she was facing now.

Why the men had singled her out was bewildering to say the least because, being not quite nine in the morning, it wasn't as if she were sporting any Pierpont jewels. She also didn't have a single coin on her because she didn't have a reason to carry funds during her morning jaunts. The objective of her early gallops was to gather her thoughts for the day before she was obligated to attend the many society functions that were expected of a lady who held such a renowned societal position.

Gathering any thoughts at all at this particular moment was next to impossible, and the few thoughts that were whizzing through her mind were random at best, such as why she'd had the brilliant idea to secure a single-shot derringer she'd recently learned to operate to her leg by means of a garter, something that had seemed quite risqué when she'd slipped on the derringer that morning, but now seemed downright ridiculous. It wasn't as if she could access the derringer, what with the many layers of undergarments she was wearing, as well as the heavy fabric that made up her oh-so-fashionable but rather cumbersome riding habit.

"This is hardly the moment for such a disclosure, but I've decided I'm a complete ninny, because stowing my pistol in a saddlebag was an utterly ludicrous decision," Lottie McBriar, Camilla's recently hired paid companion, who'd once been in the employ of Frank Fitzsimmons, an underworld criminal boss, suddenly exclaimed, drawing Camilla's attention. "It's not as if I can retrieve the pistol when I'm having a difficult time simply maintaining my seat."

Camilla winced when Serenity, the horse she'd personally chosen for Lottie since she normally gave a smooth and steady ride, took that moment to lurch to the right as she galloped unevenly down the lane, almost unseating poor Lottie in the process.

"You're doing a marvelous job, Lottie, especially when you take into consideration you never rode a horse before you started working for me," Camilla said. "As for the pistol business, stowing one in a saddlebag is definitely a better choice over where I decided to stow mine today."

Lottie's eyes widened. "Please tell me you haven't stashed your derringer in your bodice because . . . one wrong bump and you could be missing one of your, ah, charms."

"Stuffing a pistol down my bodice would be almost as impractical as where I actually stashed it, which is on my leg, but since neither of us seem to have embraced an attitude of practicality this morning, I'm afraid we're both soon going to be dead," Camilla said as they took a turn in the road, Fiona tossing her head when Serenity came a little too close. She chanced a glance over her shoulder and frowned when she realized the men were no longer in sight. "Think they might have given up?"

"It's more likely they've taken a shortcut through the forest in the hopes of intercepting us."

"You think they're intending on an ambush?"

"That would be my best guess, which means we should take this opportunity to change direction and head for the river. It might be a rough ride, but it would give us a better chance of escaping them instead of riding into a trap."

Camilla reined Fiona to a stop, wincing again when Serenity, evidently taking that as a sign she could discontinue galloping, something she rarely did, preferring to plod instead, stopped moving with no warning, sending Lottie lurching forward and grabbing hold of the horse's mane to keep from flying over Serenity's head.

"Are you alright?" Camilla asked as Lottie pushed herself upright.

"I'll be fine once we get out of harm's way and I can get off this horse, but for now . . ." Lottie nodded to a thick grove of trees. "You go first."

"Absolutely not," Camilla argued. "You're the fledgling equestrian. You go first so I can come to your assistance if you find yourself in trouble."

"Me losing my seat is the least of our worries since you're obviously the target this morning."

"I would think we're both targets of those highwaymen."

"And I beg to differ because I'm acquainted with men who spend their time robbing travelers, and no self-respecting highwayman would waste their time on two women out for a morning ride." Lottie glanced over her shoulder. "Those men chasing us are kidnappers, if I'm not mistaken, and you, being a grand heiress, are certainly in their sights."

"Kidnappers?" Camilla repeated. "But that doesn't make sense because surely they wouldn't think I'd go along peacefully if they were able to catch us, and I certainly wouldn't willingly ride along on the back of one of their horses."

Lottie's mouth suddenly went slack. "Good heavens, I truly am a ninny because they weren't trying to *catch* us—they were *herding* us, and . . . we need to get out of here." With that, Lottie sent Camilla a pointed look, but before Camilla could do more than steer Fiona toward the trees, the sound of carriage wheels reverberating down the road captured her attention.

A second later, a black coach, flanked by five men, sped into view.

Fear left her immobile for the briefest of seconds until a blast that sounded like a cannon rang out, and that was all it took for Fiona to rear into the air right before she turned and bolted down the road the way they'd just come. Camilla held on for dear life as they rounded a turn in the road, right as a second resounding boom split the air.

A mere heartbeat later, Fiona was rearing once again, but this time Camilla was unable to retain her seat and found herself tumbling head over heels through the air as Fiona thundered away.

An "oomph" escaped her when she hit the ground, but knowing she was now a sitting target, she forced herself to her feet, then stilled when the sound of pounding hooves drawing closer left her with the distinct impression that someone was almost upon her, which meant . . . she needed to bring out the derringer.

Hefting up the skirt of her riding habit, she fumbled her way through layers of fabric and wrenched the derringer free from her garter, but before she could do more than get a firm grip on it with one hand and yank her skirt down with the other, a beast of a stallion came to a stop a few feet away from her right before a hulking brute of a man swung from the saddle.

For a moment, she found herself rooted to the spot because the man now setting his sights on her was the largest man she'd ever seen and radiated a sense of power that was impossible to ignore. With him being well over six feet tall, it was understandable why he was riding such an enormous horse, especially when he wasn't simply tall but also broad, the seams of the ill-fitting jacket he was wearing straining against what she could only assume were impressive muscles—ones probably amassed by doing some manner of physical labor.

Or absconding with people on a regular basis.

That thought had her lifting her gaze from his shoulders, discovering in the process that he was missing his hat and that his hair, an unusual shade of brown mixed with a hint of mahogany, was distinctly windswept, that circumstance a direct result, no doubt, of him having been chasing her only seconds before.

Calling herself every sort of ridiculous for being distracted by a perusal of the man when, clearly, he was a distinct threat to her, Camilla lifted the derringer with an unsteady hand and aimed it his way.

The man's hands were raised above his head a second later. "Whoa there, little lady, let's not be hasty now. What say you stow away that pistol before your feminine sensibilities get the better of you and you end up harming yourself."

For the briefest of seconds, Camilla found herself incapable of mustering up a retort to that nonsense, probably because no one had ever called her "little lady" before in a tone that suggested the man thought she was some witless female, nor had anyone ever had the audacity to suggest she was prone to feminine sensibilities.

She opened her mouth to disabuse him of his absurd notions, but snapped it shut when he began lowering his hands, undoubtedly to gain access to the monstrosity of a pistol she noticed was sticking out of a holster slung low on his hip.

"Don't move," she demanded.

He immediately raised his hands again. "I have no intention of harming you, so tuck that derringer away nice and easy so you don't unintentionally shoot yourself with it."

"I won't be the one I shoot."

"I wouldn't be so certain about that," the man argued. "You've just suffered a tumble from your horse, and you were about to be waylaid by a gang of men with malice on their minds. You certainly can't be expected to be clearheaded right now, and no one should handle a weapon in that state." He nodded to the derringer. "It might be best if you just set that on the ground."

"Would you like me to kick it your way, as well?"

"That's not a bad idea."

She quirked a brow. "Except that, contrary to what you evidently believe, I'm not a complete and utter simpleton."

"I don't recall suggesting you were a simpleton."

"It was implied, given that you think I'm not only going to set my weapon on the ground but also send it your way."

"You're the one who suggested kicking it to me. Nevertheless, my suggestion that you distance yourself from your derringer was simply for your own good, as you're clearly in a highly agitated state and that's when most accidents with guns occur."

"I'm not in a highly agitated state."

"The fact that your voice just raised an octave suggests otherwise," he said before he drew in a deep breath, slowly released it, then drew in another.

"What are you doing?" she asked.

"Hoping you'll follow my example and begin taking a few deep breaths as well, which will do wonders to calm the state of your nerves."

She felt the most distinct desire to pull the trigger and had to refuse the inclination to draw in a deep breath, as that would certainly leave the man believing she was heeding his ridiculous advice. "If you were truly concerned about my nerves," she settled for saying instead, "the last thing you would tell me is to calm down."

"I didn't tell you to calm down," he countered. "I was merely suggesting a remedy that might have benefited your agitated state, a state you seemed to embrace from the moment I got off my horse."

"Because you addressed me as 'little lady.'"

His brows drew together. "You found that aggravation-worthy?"

"It was insulting."

"Huh," the man said before he took a step toward her, something that recalled Camilla back to the troubling situation at hand.

"Don't move," she demanded again as she tightened her grip on the pistol.

He froze on the spot. "I'm really not going to harm you."

"You truly must believe I'm witless if you think for a second that I don't know you're one of the men who was chasing me."

"I wasn't chasing you. I was racing to your rescue."

"A likely story."

The man opened his mouth but snapped it shut when Lottie came rushing down the road, on foot no less, and brandishing a tree limb, which suggested she'd finally lost her seat and Serenity had gotten away from her and taken Lottie's pistol in the process.

In the span of a split second, the man spun around, his concerningly large weapon already drawn from his holster and pointed Lottie's way.

Convinced Lottie was soon going to find herself a victim of a bullet, Camilla did the only thing that sprang to mind—she aimed the derringer above the man's head and pulled the trigger.

Thankfully, the moment after she'd discharged her weapon, the man abandoned his interest in Lottie and swung to face her, his blue eyes already narrowed in what could most assuredly be described as a most menacing fashion.

"You missed," he said.

"I didn't. I was shooting to distract you from my paid companion."

The man's eyes narrowed another fraction. "An interesting decision since you've lent me the impression you think I'm a threat to you."

"You *are* a threat to me."

He re-holstered his pistol, a surprising move considering the circumstances. "If you're convinced I'm a danger to you, why, since you're using a single-shot derringer, would you waste your only bullet on a distraction tactic instead of rendering me incapable of being a continued threat?"

It was beyond irritating when Camilla realized he'd just made an excellent point, but before she could think of a suitable retort, Lottie stole up behind him and slipped the man's pistol straight out of his holster. She then raised the gun into the air and pulled the trigger.

Camilla's ears immediately began ringing as a blast echoed around her, her eyes widening when Lottie went flying backward, the result of a recoil that had literally knocked her off her feet.

Her gaze darted to the man, who, unfortunately, was still standing and seemingly unscathed. Interestingly enough, though, instead of looking outraged, a reaction she'd been expecting, he was squinting up into the tree he was standing under.

Her gaze shifted to what he was looking at, which seemed to be leaves that were rustling in a somewhat unusual manner, the peculiarity immediately explained when a large bundle of gray-and-black fur suddenly hurtled through the leaves, landing on the ground a few feet away from her.

It quickly became evident that the raccoon now hissing in a most concerning fashion had not appreciated its abrupt departure from the tree.

Camilla took a hesitant step backward, stilling when an entire nursery of raccoons began scrambling down the trunk, all of which were making noises that had the hair on the nape of her neck standing at attention.

"Run!" the man yelled.

It was the only piece of advice he'd given her thus far that she was going to heed.

Pivoting on her heel, she yanked up the hem of her riding habit and broke into a run, something she couldn't remember doing since she was in short dresses.

To her relief, Lottie was soon sprinting beside her, and together, they dashed into the trees. Air quickly became difficult to come by, but unwilling to allow the man an opportunity to catch up with them, although given that Lottie still had possession of his gun, they were better prepared to protect themselves, Camilla pressed on, scrambled over a fallen tree, broke into a run again, and . . .

A yelp escaped her as her feet suddenly slid out from under her and she found herself sliding down an embankment she'd failed to notice. By the time she reached the bottom, she was covered in mud, but didn't have a second to contemplate that unusual circumstance because a mere second after she managed to clamber to her feet, Lottie barreled into her, the force of the barreling sending them both tumbling to the ground again and rolling straight into the Hudson River.

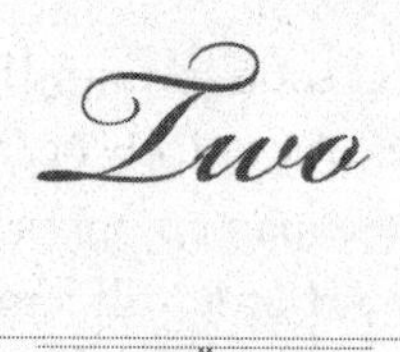

Two

Mr. Owen Chesterfield readily admitted he didn't understand women and had been informed over the years by members of the feminine set that they found him vastly annoying.

Given what had happened a mere thirty minutes before certainly lent credence to the whole annoying business because the prickly woman, whom he'd taken to thinking of as Goldie as they'd never gotten around to exchanging names, had evidently taken great issue with him for calling her a little lady, and then got downright testy when he'd brought the word *calm* into the conversation.

In his defense, he'd merely been trying to defuse the situation before someone got hurt, but instead of Owen accomplishing that, Goldie had surprised him by discharging her tiny derringer, and then he'd had one of his Colt Dragoon revolvers snatched straight out of his holster by a woman he'd heard Goldie mention was her paid companion.

The only paid companion he'd ever met was employed by his great-aunt Elma, who'd had to resort to paying someone to spend time with her due to her querulous nature. That companion, Miss Hester Baker, was a very meek woman who spent her days reading to Aunt Elma or penning letters for his aunt because she refused to wear spectacles and was blind as a bat, which made writing, as well as reading, next to impossible. Hester would never contemplate snatching a man's weapon, let alone firing it, but that's exactly what Goldie's companion had done.

She was obviously an unusual companion and possessed a great aptitude for stealth since she'd appropriated his weapon without him even realizing she was up to something.

All he could conclude about that unlikely circumstance was that he'd been far too distracted arguing with Goldie, which was quite unlike him because even though he aggravated women with some regularity, he'd never become so distracted with their aggravation that he'd fallen victim to larceny.

It was evidently a day for firsts, and he'd not even gotten around to contemplating the onslaught of airborne raccoons or the ensuing altercation he'd had with the pack's leader, an aggressive beast with teeth as sharp as razors.

Luckily, the raccoon hadn't gotten an opportunity to sink its teeth into his skin, but it had managed to rip the sleeve of his jacket, leaving it hanging by a few threads, which meant it was now highly unlikely he was going to make much of a favorable impression during what he'd hoped would be a productive business meeting that morning.

A nicker from George, his stallion, drew Owen from his thoughts. After giving George a scratch behind the ears, he blew out a breath. "I know, it's been a most unusual morning, but there's an extra bucket of oats coming your way since you rose magnificently to a most unexpected situation."

George tossed his head, earning a smile from Owen.

"Of course I didn't doubt for a second you'd be willing to abandon our leisurely pace to chase after those men, although I'm hoping the remainder of the day isn't fraught with additional obstacles." He steered George around a large hole in the road. "I'm wondering, though, if I should take our encounter with those women as a sign I should abandon my plan to present a proposal to that matchmaker. Clearly, members of the feminine set are taking issue with me today, and the matchmaker is a woman, after all, and a society matron at that. I'm relatively sure after Walter Townsend told me she's known to be a stickler for the proprieties, that she'll take issue with the derelict state of my jacket and might also take issue with the idea I'm showing up at her home unannounced."

Owen picked off a loose thread from what remained of his sleeve. "In hindsight, I should have taken Walter's suggestion and sent a letter requesting an audience, but I didn't want to delay our return trip home to Wheeling, what with the Luella situation there, nor did I want to give the matchmaker an opportunity to refuse to meet with me, a decision I may now come to regret."

George gave another toss of his head, which Owen took as a sign of sympathy for his plight and earned his horse a pat.

"Who would have thought this unscheduled visit to the Hudson would get off to such a rocky start?" he asked. "I mean, there I was, after enjoying a delicious breakfast at that inn Walter recommended, minding my own business as we rode along, when I spotted that carriage parked in the middle of the road. My first thought, of course, was that it had suffered a broken axle, but then those riders came racing up to it. Instead of holding it up, which is what I assumed they were about to do, they yelled something to the driver, and everyone took off down the road. It was a suspicious circumstance to be sure and meant we had no choice but to follow them. Good thing we did, though, after those women rode into view and it was clear they were in danger. One would have thought they'd have appreciated me dispersing their would-be attackers, but I evidently got off on the wrong foot with Goldie and never got an opportunity to convince her I was there to save her."

He gave his chin a scratch. "I'm still wondering if I should have gone after them once I managed to extricate myself from the raccoon onslaught. The reason I didn't, though, if you were wondering, and before you judge me for not rushing to the aid of two members of the fairer sex, was because Goldie's paid companion dashed away with one of my Colt Dragoons. While I'm relatively certain that she, quite like Goldie, aimed over my head on purpose before she pulled the trigger, if I'd been able to catch up with them, she might've decided that I really was a threat, which could have resulted in her deciding to aim a second shot to dispatch me instead of warn me off."

George tossed his head again, paired with a nicker.

"Glad you agree with that, and . . ." Owen's voice trailed off as he took note of a lane to his right, one that was flanked by large maple trees and had two majestic stone lions standing on opposite pedestals underneath those trees. He reined George to a stop. "Looks like this might be the place. Walter told me to look for lions."

He checked his pocket watch, frowned when he realized it was almost ten, then nudged George into motion again.

"We're behind schedule, but hopefully this meeting won't take long and then we can return to the station and get my Pullman car hooked up to the train going back to Wheeling."

After a full five minutes of cantering down the lane, the trees finally gave way and Owen found himself looking across acres of well-maintained lawn, complete with well-trimmed hedges and numerous flower gardens that were even now being tended to by a legion of gardeners.

The gravel lane soon gave way to paved stones that led to a magnificent four-story house, one that was crafted from hand-hewn blocks of limestone. Stately stairs led to the front vestibule, where an unusually large black cat was sunning itself on the very top of those stairs. It immediately lifted its head and settled its attention on Owen as he reined George to a stop and swung from the saddle.

After handing George's reins to a young groom who'd appeared the moment he'd reached the house, Owen thanked the lad and told him he wouldn't be long before he headed up the steps, taking a second to give the black cat a belly rub, pausing when the front door began opening.

Abandoning the cat, who sent him a look of annoyance, as if it felt Owen hadn't given him enough in the way of belly-scratching affection, Owen moved toward the door, where an older gentleman dressed formally in a black suit was already in the process of looking him up and down, his face completely expressionless as he finally caught Owen's eye.

"May I help you, sir?" the man asked.

Owen held out his hand. "I'm Mr. Owen Chesterfield, here to speak with Mrs. Pierpont."

After pausing for the briefest of seconds, the man stepped forward and shook Owen's hand. "I'm Mr. Timken, the Pierpont butler." His gaze traveled over Owen yet again, lingering on his dangling sleeve. "If you're here to sell Mrs. Pierpont something, know that salesmen are expected to use the back door."

It wasn't the first time Owen had been asked to use a back door, nor did he expect it would be his last.

He knew he didn't look the part of a man of fortune, and truth be told, he *was* a salesman of sorts, but one who sold vast quantities of nails, iron ore, copper, and bauxite to the titans of industry, of which he was considered an esteemed member.

He cleared his throat. "I don't believe Mrs. Pierpont would have an interest in any of the products I sell, Mr. Timken. However, I'm not here to sell her anything, except maybe on the idea that I would certainly make it worth her while if she were to agree to take on a project for me."

Mr. Timken's brow furrowed. "I'm afraid you have me at a disadvantage, sir, because I cannot imagine what type of *project* you'd want to propose to Mrs. Pierpont."

Owen cocked his head to the side. "Ah, right. I should have been more discreet since I'm sure deniability is a must in this household whenever someone arrives out of the blue, looking to secure Mrs. Pierpont's services, which are probably considered a sensitive topic with Mr. Pierpont."

"Mrs. Pierpont's services?" Mr. Timken repeated.

"Indeed, but know that I don't think those services are common knowledge except amongst ladies involved with the Four Hundred. I only learned about them through Mr. Walter Townsend, a business associate of mine who was kind enough to pen me a letter of introduction to present to Mrs. Pierpont, proving I'm a legitimate man of business and have earned the respect of men like Astor, Vanderbilt, Rutherford, and of course, Walter Townsend himself."

Owen began searching through his pockets. "Ah, here it is." He pulled out a crumpled piece of paper and held it out to Mr. Timken, who took the paper with one hand, slipping his other hand into his breast pocket and pulling out a pair of spectacles.

After settling them into place, Mr. Timken uncrumpled the paper, looking over the rim of his glasses to meet Owen's gaze after he scanned the page. "It states that Walter Townsend is well-acquainted with you and finds you to be an upstanding individual with whom he often does business." Mr. Timken handed the paper back to Owen. "It does not mention why you want to seek out an audience with Mrs. Pierpont."

"I think that's best left discussed between Mrs. Pierpont and myself."

The man inclined his head. "Perhaps, but I'm afraid you won't be able to discuss anything with Mrs. Pierpont today because she's not at home."

Owen frowned. "Do you know when she's expected back?"

"The beginning of June."

"Surely not."

"Surely so because she's currently in Paris."

"Paris?" Owen shook his head. "No, I'm afraid you must be mistaken because Walter specifically mentioned that Mrs. Pierpont was currently in residence here on the Hudson, and that I needed to present myself at a proper hour because she doesn't care to receive guests at the crack of dawn."

"It's barely past the crack of dawn."

"It's almost ten. Half the day is considered gone where I'm from."

"And while I'm waiting with bated breath to learn what far-off land that may be, know that if Mrs. Pierpont were in residence, which again, she's not, you wouldn't be able to speak with her right now anyway because she never leaves her chambers until noon."

Owen gave his nose a scratch. "This is a very curious state of affairs because Walter never mentioned a thing about Mrs. Pierpont enjoying a long lie-in every day, or anything about Paris." He frowned. "Could it be that Mrs. Pierpont hied herself off to Paris on a spur-of-the-moment trip to secure a match for someone?"

Mr. Timken blinked. "Good heavens, Mr. Chesterfield, I believe I'm finally beginning to understand this rather unusual conversation. You've evidently suffered a misunderstanding with Mr. Townsend because you seem to be under the misimpression that Mrs. Pierpont is the matchmaker in this family. She's not. You're looking for her daughter, Miss Camilla Pierpont."

"I suppose I could have confused a Miss for a Mrs., but correct me if I'm wrong—aren't matchmakers usually married women and of an, ah, advanced age?"

"Miss Pierpont is an exception to the matchmaker rule, and frankly, her success over the years has far surpassed the more seasoned matchmakers out there."

Owen frowned. "How could she have possibly achieved that success when it seems peculiar that an unmarried lady could effectively orchestrate societal matches when she hasn't been successful securing a match of her own?"

For some reason, Mr. Timken's eyes began to twinkle. "When Miss Pierpont returns, and if she's agreeable to meeting with you, you're going to have to make sure to ask her that."

"Because . . . ?"

"It might be amusing."

"And amusing her might encourage her to consider the business proposal I'm here to present?"

"I didn't say she'd be the one amused."

"Huh." Owen let that settle for a second. "Perhaps I'll keep my matchmaking assumptions to myself."

"Probably a prudent move," Mr. Timken said before he gestured toward the door. "With that out of the way, if you'll follow me?"

"You're not going to relegate me to the servants' entrance?" Owen asked.

"Since Walter Townsend vouched for you, I believe the front door is a more appropriate choice."

"And if he hadn't provided me with that letter of introduction?"

"Given the questionable state of your attire, I would have sent you on your way without a second's hesitation." Mr. Timken gestured toward the house again. "Miss Pierpont is currently not at home, but I expect her to return momentarily. You may await her arrival in the back parlor, which has a lovely view of the Hudson. I'm sure you'll enjoy it, as well as the refreshments I'll arrange for you after I get you settled."

"And you believe Miss Pierpont will be receptive to meeting with me?"

"She's a proper lady, Mr. Chesterfield, which means, if nothing else, she'll at least grant you a few minutes, although I can't say whether or not she'll lend you more time than that to present your proposal."

Taking that as rather promising because he'd been known to close business deals in less than three minutes, Owen fell into step behind Mr. Timken, greeted by the sight of an ornate heart-shaped staircase as he made his way into the grand entranceway, one that split in two when it reached the second floor and was carpeted in a deep shade of burgundy. A chandelier hung from the very center of the second-floor landing, its many crystals catching the morning light and sending prisms of color glittering down walls that were papered in green silk.

After they passed the staircase, Mr. Timken led him down a long hallway where numerous oil paintings and watercolors lined the walls, then past a dining room where china plates, crystal goblets, and silverware that gleamed against linen napkins sat on a very long table, looking quite as if the Pierponts were expecting guests to join them at any moment.

His table at home was never formally set and, in fact, could usually be found with a variety of mismatched dishes sitting on it, ready to grab whenever he found a spare moment to eat. Fishing lures could also sometimes be found scattered about, and occasionally one of his hounds, either Cleo or Calamity, climbed up on the table because in the morning, it was, at least in his dogs' opinions, a great place to catch the first rays of sun.

If the Pierponts owned a dog, he had a feeling it would never be permitted on top of any table.

"Here we are—the pink parlor, as Miss Pierpont fondly refers to it," Mr. Timken said, gesturing Owen into a room that certainly did seem to boast a lot of pink. There were pink chairs, pink settees, and even a pink lampshade, one that had little tassels hanging from it.

"Please make yourself comfortable," Mr. Timken said. "I'll be back directly with some refreshments."

As the butler bowed himself out of the room, Owen set his sights on a pink chaise, sitting tentatively down on the very edge of it and earning a rather worrisome creak from the chaise in return.

Knowing he was hardly going to make a good impression on Miss Pierpont with his tattered sleeve, and not wanting to worsen that impression by breaking her pink chaise, he set his sights on a hardback chair, a sigh of relief escaping him when he sat down and didn't earn a single groan from the chair, suggesting it was more than capable of supporting his weight.

He settled back, crossed his ankles, decided that was too casual of a pose and might lend Miss Pierpont the impression he wasn't there on a serious matter of business, so sat forward again, debating whether to cross his arms over his chest or not when the door that led to the backyard suddenly opened.

His mouth went slightly agape when a woman staggered in, followed by a second woman, both of whom were streaked with mud and soaking wet.

"The first order of business is to ring for a bath," one of the women said, "and then . . ."

Her voice trailed to nothing when she caught sight of him and froze on the spot. "What are *you* doing here?" she demanded.

Recognition was swift because standing in front of him was none other than Goldie, the same prickly woman he'd tried to save earlier, the storm clouds gathered in her eyes a sure sign she'd only gotten pricklier as she'd made her way home.

Before he could do more than rise to his feet, the other woman, the paid companion, whipped out *his* Colt Dragoon and aimed it his way.

His hands were in the air a second later.

"While I understand your shock, or perhaps it's disbelief, over seeing me again," he began, "may I suggest that the two of you—"

"If he tells us we need to calm down, just shoot him, Lottie."

It was not encouraging when the paid companion, apparently Lottie, cocked the hammer and arched a brow his way. "*Were* you about to tell us to calm down?"

"Not exactly."

"Then exactly what were you about to tell us?" Goldie demanded.

"I was simply going to suggest that the two of you get your overly excited nerves in check before someone gets shot."

Goldie's eyes flashed. "The only one going to get shot around here is you."

"There's no reason to shoot me, Goldie. As I've said numerous times, I'm not a threat to you."

Flames began practically shooting out of Goldie's eyes. "Did you just call me Goldie?"

"Since we never got around to exchanging names and you didn't like me calling you 'little lady,' I did."

"And you think Goldie is better than 'little lady'?"

"Indeed, since I chose it due to the brightness of your hair and because I once had a dog by the name of Goldie whose coat was almost the same color as your hair, although . . ." He shot a glance to the hair in question. "It's definitely not golden right now, more along the lines of dirty blond, and has me wondering what happened to you after we parted company."

"First off, we didn't part company. Lottie and I fled from you. Secondly, we obviously suffered a mishap, and thirdly, am I to understand you're calling me Goldie, not simply because I usually have golden hair, but because I remind you of a *dog*?"

He winced. "Your voice seems to have risen another octave again, but there's really no reason for you to have taken offense because my dog Goldie was an adorable mutt that everyone loved."

"I remind you of a *mutt*?"

It truly was amazing how much animosity Goldie could extend his way with a few short words.

"Perhaps I phrased that poorly."

"And perhaps Lottie really should just shoot you and put all of us out of our misery."

Before Owen could think of a response to that nonsense, Mr. Timken entered the room, pushing a cart, but stopped in his tracks the moment his gaze settled on Goldie.

"Miss Pierpont," Mr. Timken exclaimed. "What happened to you and . . ." His gaze darted to Lottie. "Why is Lottie pointing a gun at Mr. Chesterfield?"

It was difficult to resist a groan as it became glaringly obvious his day was not destined to improve since the woman he'd come to present a business proposition to was none other than Goldie.

Given the glare she was directing his way, there was little hope she'd be receptive to his proposal. In fact, it was far more likely she'd soon encourage her paid companion to take a shot at him yet again, and with his own revolver to boot.

Camilla drew in a deep breath, then another, then another after that, but finally abandoned the whole deep breathing process when she realized it wasn't doing a thing to help her regain control of a temper she rarely lost.

"I believe a more pressing question over why Lottie is holding that man at pistol-point, Mr. Timken," Camilla began, directing her attention to her butler, "is how he gained access to our house when he's nothing more than a common criminal."

"Criminal?" Mr. Timken repeated, his eyes widening.

"Quite right, and one Lottie and I believe has nefarious plans to abduct me."

Mr. Timken sent the man he'd called Mr. Chesterfield a look of great disdain before he nodded to Lottie. "Keep that trained on him while I send a groom to fetch the police. It won't take me but a few minutes."

"You might want to fetch a weapon of your own on your way back, Mr. Timken," Lottie said, her hand shaking the slightest bit. "I'm not certain how much longer I can keep this beast of a gun aloft. It's far heavier than I was anticipating, and it was a miracle

I was able to retain my hold on it when Miss Pierpont and I took an unexpected dousing in the Hudson."

"You ended up in the Hudson?" Mr. Timken asked, returning his gaze to Camilla.

"It was purely unintentional, a result of a tumble we took down an embankment as we were fleeing the man you called Mr. Chesterfield, as well as a pack of aggravated raccoons." Camilla dashed a sopping strand of hair out of her eyes. "We then almost drowned because Lottie refused to let go of the weapon she's currently wielding, which turned into nothing short of an anchor after she got pulled into the current. She was then swept underneath the water, but thankfully, I managed to haul her back to shore, a daunting feat because Lottie wouldn't relinquish the gun, which made it impossible for her to assist with swimming since she had a choke hold around my neck with her other hand."

"It's too fine a weapon to condemn to a watery grave," Lottie argued. "As I mentioned, after we finally got to shore and you gave me that look you use when you're annoyed, I told you that I'm familiar with a gun dealer down in Five Points who'll give me top dollar for it."

"Considering your past history, and the fact there are still members of the criminal underworld, specifically one Victor Malvado, who would love nothing more than to find you and force you back into shady dealings, the last thing you should be doing is seeking out a gun dealer in Five Points, no matter how much he'll give you for that revolver."

A loud clearing of a throat drew Camilla's attention to Mr. Chesterfield.

"You have something you'd like to say?" she asked.

"Quite a few things," Mr. Chesterfield began. "The first is, of course, my concern that your companion is intending to sell one of my Colt Dragoons. They were a present from my grandfather, and as such, they hold a great deal of sentimental value for me."

"Then perhaps you should have left them at home and brought less sentimental weapons to use during your abduction attempt."

Mr. Chesterfield gave his nose a rub. "Forgive me, Miss Pierpont, but even though I know I'm at risk to incur more of that formidable temper of yours, I feel compelled to point out yet again that I wasn't trying to abduct you."

"I don't possess a formidable temper, and am, in fact, considered a lady of admirable composure, which I never lose."

"I wouldn't say you were admirably composed when you took that shot at me earlier," Mr. Chesterfield muttered.

Mr. Timken took a single step toward Camilla. "You tried to shoot Mr. Chesterfield?"

"Only because he was about to shoot poor Lottie," Camilla said. "I had no other option to distract him from that dastardly intention *except* to use my derringer."

"I wasn't going to shoot your companion," Mr. Chesterfield argued. "I was merely of the misimpression that she was one of the men I'd chased away. If you'd not shot at me and redrawn my attention, I assure you I would have lowered my weapon as soon as I realized Lottie was no threat."

"She was wielding a tree limb," Camilla pointed out.

Amusement flickered through Mr. Chesterfield's eyes. "True, but Lottie is a wee-bitty thing and I'm fairly confident I wouldn't have suffered much damage if she'd gone on the attack."

"She's far more lethal than she looks."

"Duly noted," Mr. Chesterfield said, catching her eye before he winced. "However, since you're continuing to display what I can only describe as an annoyed look, something Lottie suggested you do often, lending credence to my observation that you possess quite the temper, allow me to return to the second item I wanted to broach—my reason for traveling to the Hudson Valley today. I assure you that abduction was never on my mind as I'm here on a legitimate matter of business."

Camilla lifted her chin. "If I'm currently looking slightly annoyed, which is not a usual happenstance for me, know that it's a direct result of you seemingly being under the impression I'm completely gullible."

"I don't recall suggesting that."

"It was certainly implied, as you seem to think I'm going to believe you're here on legitimate business, when you and I both know you're here because your abduction plan was foiled and you've now been forced to modify that plan."

His brow furrowed before he smiled. "Ah, I see where you're going with your train of thought, but I'm afraid you've read the situation wrong, Miss Pierpont. And before you try to explain why you're not wrong, allow me to explain why you are."

He nodded to the revolver Lottie was still holding aloft, although her arm had begun shaking more than slightly. "From what's been said, my Colt Dragoon went into the Hudson River with you, and it wasn't simply in the river but was fully submerged. That means the gunpowder residing in its cylinder is now wet, as are the percussions caps, which means there's no need for her to continue pointing my own revolver at me because it's been rendered inoperable."

"How could that possibly prove I'm wrong about your intentions?" Camilla asked.

"Because you're a, ah, diminutive lady, which I hope doesn't offend you as much as calling you 'little lady' did, and as such, and given the differences in our sizes, if I *were* here to abduct you, and because I know the revolver Lottie is holding is useless, you would already be slung over the back of my horse, riding down the road."

Camilla stripped off a soggy glove and used it to dash aside a glob of mud that was trailing down her cheek, needing a few seconds to digest everything Mr. Chesterfield had said.

Frankly, he'd made some excellent points because he was, indeed, almost twice her size and could have certainly made off with her, as well as rendered Lottie and Mr. Timken incapacitated, with very little effort.

"May I dare hope, since you've had a moment to consider what I've said," Mr. Chesterfield began, "that you're now ready to admit we've merely suffered from an unfortunate series of misunderstandings and agree to a fresh start between us?"

The doubt that had been worming its way through Camilla intensified, but after the harrowing events of the morning, she wasn't quite ready to abandon caution just yet. She turned to Lottie. "There's little point in keeping that weapon aloft, although I suggest you keep hold of it because if we're mistaken and Mr. Chesterfield does have nefarious plans in mind, you could always drub him over the head with it."

"I don't need a drubbing," Mr. Chesterfield muttered.

"Perhaps not, but until I'm absolutely certain of that . . ." She turned toward the door and whistled, which resulted in the sound of nails clattering down the marble hallway a blink of an eye later. A second after that, Gladys, a poodle that was a disgrace to the breed since she refused to wear bows and loathed any attempt at grooming, bounded into the room, followed by El Cid, a cat who'd been all but foisted on her by her very dear friend Adelaide Duveen, or rather, Mrs. Gideon Abbott these days.

"Gladys, El Cid," she began, sending a nod Mr. Chesterfield's way, "guard him."

It took a great deal of effort to keep her mouth from going slack when Gladys immediately sidled up next to Mr. Chesterfield, where she promptly began, not snarling at him, but nuzzling him, while El Cid moseyed up to Mr. Chesterfield's other side and promptly rolled on his back, demanding homage in the form of a brisk belly rub.

"Traitors," she muttered, earning a grin from Mr. Chesterfield before he scooped El Cid from the ground and settled him against his shoulder as Gladys plopped down on his feet, something that didn't seem to bother the man in the least.

"Don't take their acceptance of me as a betrayal of their loyalty," Mr. Chesterfield began. "I simply have a way with animals, as well as with children, the elderly, and the majority of men. It's mostly members of the feminine persuasion who seem to take issue with me, although . . ." He shook his head. "I suppose I should revise the statement about animals since I definitely failed to bond with those raccoons earlier and was fortunate to escape with only a tattered sleeve."

"May I assume you won the battle because you resorted to shooting that leader?" Camilla asked.

"I couldn't have in good conscience shot any of them since it was hardly their fault their morning nap was disrupted when bullets began flying," he said, scratching El Cid behind the ears. "This handsome boy was also enjoying a nap when I first arrived, but did I hear you call him El Cid, and if so, may I presume he's named after Rodrigo Díaz de Vivar?"

"You know El Cid was the nickname of Rodrigo Díaz de Vivar—a Castilian nobleman from medieval Spain?" Camilla asked slowly.

Mr. Chesterfield gave El Cid another scratch. "I should probably be insulted that you apparently take me for an uneducated man, although I understand I haven't lent you the most favorable of impressions. With that said, though, I minored in history in college, majored in engineering, so yes, I know who El Cid is, and I'm impressed you named your cat after such a fascinating man."

"I can't take credit for the name," Camilla admitted. "My friend, the former Adelaide Duveen, a great lover of cats, is responsible for naming him. She's an avid reader and chose the name because there's a poem written about Rodrigo Díaz de Vivar that she particularly enjoys."

As El Cid began purring rather loudly, the purrs increasing when Mr. Chesterfield gave him a bit of a snuggle, Camilla took to considering the man, the thought springing to mind that there was something to be said about not judging a book by its cover because, clearly, her first impression of Mr. Chesterfield might have been a little off the mark.

Instead of the criminal she'd assumed he was, it appeared he was an educated man, and one who seemed to have a particular way with animals, given the way El Cid, who held the greatest disdain for most humans, was now purring more earnestly than ever.

"If we could return to this Adelaide Duveen," Mr. Chesterfield said, snapping Camilla from her thoughts. "Walter Townsend mentioned her yesterday, as well as mentioned that you were responsible for convincing the Four Hundred they needed to abandon their quest to give her the cut direct."

"You're acquainted with Walter Townsend?" Camilla asked.

"I am, but perhaps I should back up and approach this as if we're just becoming introduced." He presented her with a bow, something El Cid apparently took issue with because he gave him a bat of a large paw, although since his claws weren't extended, it evidently wasn't meant to harm the man, merely show a touch of displeasure.

Mr. Chesterfield didn't miss a beat, merely took to cradling El Cid in his large arms before he sent Camilla a smile. "I'm Mr. Owen Chesterfield, of Wheeling, West Virginia, and Walter and I are business associates. To prove that . . ." He shot a look at Lottie. "I'm going to retrieve something from my pocket, and no, it's not my lone remaining weapon. That means there's no reason for you to consider giving me a drubbing with an inoperable weapon that happens to be my property."

Lottie didn't lower the revolver she was still brandishing like a baton, although she did settle a faint smile on Owen. "I'll be more than happy to return this to you, but only after I'm completely convinced you're not a threat to Miss Pierpont."

"If I were a danger to either of you, you'd already be disarmed and Miss Pierpont would be on her way to wherever abductors take their victims," he returned before he juggled El Cid around, then stuck his hand into his pocket, pulling out a crumpled piece of paper. He then apparently decided to err on the side of caution because he handed the paper to Mr. Timken instead of trying to move closer to Camilla.

"If that's not enough proof for you, I can also provide you with one of my business cards."

"I wouldn't be opposed to seeing your card," Camilla said.

A second later, Owen handed a card to Mr. Timken, who glanced over it before he walked over to Camilla and handed her both items.

"As you can see," Owen began as Camilla read through a referral Walter Townsend had, indeed, provided Owen with, "my name is embossed on my business card. That's certainly further proof I didn't set out to kidnap you because I doubt any self-respecting criminal would carry around a card that reveals their identity when they're in the midst of perpetrating a crime."

Camilla looked over Owen's card before she lifted her head. "It says you're the owner of Chesterfield Nail Manufacturing."

"I am," he admitted. "And not to brag, as I'm only telling you this as further proof I never had any intention to abduct you, but my company provides almost the entire country with nails. I also own iron ore, copper, and bauxite mines, and have factories that manufacture iron, along with steel, which is how I've been able to corner the market on the nail industry."

"It sounds as if you operate a lucrative endeavor."

"And is exactly why I have no reason to abscond with you—or anyone, for that matter," Owen said.

"A valid argument."

"Indeed," Owen agreed. "And now, with that out of the way, shall we proceed to why I'm here?"

Manners drummed into Camilla since childhood had her shaking her head. "Before we get into that, Mr. Chesterfield, I believe that I need to extend to you my most heartfelt appreciation, as well as an apology. You, and at great risk to yourself, came to my rescue, and instead of thanking you for your assistance, I behaved quite badly."

"No need to apologize, Miss Pierpont," he didn't hesitate to say. "You were being chased by hoodlums, and being a woman and all, well, it's no wonder you were a little frazzled."

Any charitable feelings she'd begun holding toward the man disappeared in a flash, but since she'd just remembered her manners, she ignored the irritation that was now thrumming through her and summoned up a smile. "How gracious of you, Mr. Chesterfield, but frazzled-ness aside, perhaps it *would* be best if we turn the conversation to why you're here."

Owen set El Cid on the ground and straightened. "I'm in need of procuring your special services."

She blinked. "Are you suggesting you're here because you want me to sponsor you on the marriage mart?"

"The last thing I need is a wife. My life is complicated enough as it is."

"I'm afraid you have me at a disadvantage then, because I have no idea what else I could possibly do for you."

Owen bent over again, this time to give Gladys, who was now directing pitiful whines his way, a pat. "I need to make use of the talents you employed when you took Miss Adelaide Duveen from a wallflower to one of the most sought-after ladies of the New York Season."

"You want me to turn you fashionable?"

He straightened again before his eyes took to crinkling at the corners. "No offense, Miss Pierpont, but I think that would be beyond those impressive skills Walter mentioned you possess. I'm well aware I'm socially inept, and, frankly, I don't have time, what with how my businesses have been booming over the past decade, to improve my manners or concern myself with spending hours with a tailor just so I can stroll around Wheeling looking like a dandy."

"I'm not sure, even if you were dressed in the first state of gentlemanly fashion, that a man like you could ever look like a dandy. You're a little on the . . . large size."

"Dandies aren't large?"

"Not the most successful ones."

"Huh."

Her lips twitched. "Yes, well, dandies aside, if you don't want me to turn you fashionable, and you don't want me to find you a wife, how can I possibly assist you?"

"I want you to take my sister, Luella, in hand," Owen said before he caught her eye. "However, in the spirit of full disclosure, I feel compelled to divulge that, to put it bluntly, she's a bit of a handful."

Four

Even though Camilla normally wouldn't consider sponsoring a lady their own brother called "a bit of a handful," she'd still felt compelled to agree to hear more of the particulars about this Luella because . . . she'd been raised to present herself to the world as a lady possessed of unwavering composure, but that composure had gone missing the moment she'd encountered Mr. Owen Chesterfield.

Granted, it hadn't been completely beyond the pale when she'd leveled her derringer on him because she'd truly believed he was a threat. However, she'd then lost her temper, something she prided herself on always maintaining, when she'd taken him to task over the whole "little lady" business. If there was one thing that had been instilled in her by her many governesses and decorum instructors, it was this: A lady never lost her composure because doing so was considered common—a trait true ladies avoided like the plague.

A lady was also expected to exude a dignified and serene air at all times and was never to lend anyone the impression she was annoyed. That was evidently an area she needed to improve upon since, not only had Mr. Chesterfield remarked on her exasperated state, but Lottie had also mentioned she'd taken note of an irritated expression on Camilla's face, and frequently at that.

Her decorum instructors, if they'd witnessed her blatant deviation from the rules of proper behavior, would have immediately resorted to rummaging around their reticules in search of smelling salts, and she certainly couldn't have blamed them. The blatant deviation from rules that had been her constant companion from practically birth was exactly why she hadn't refused Owen's proposal on the spot, but had, instead, agreed to speak with him further about the matter, but only after she'd had an opportunity to change out of a riding habit that had been dripping water all over the polished marble floor, another serious breach of ladylike behavior.

"Would you like a short jacket to wear over your morning gown, Miss Pierpont?" Bernadette Millersport, a woman who'd recently stepped into the role of Camilla's lady's maid, but only temporarily, asked as she placed one last pin into the chignon she'd been arranging. "You're bound to still be chilled after your immersion in the river, especially when you refused to allow me to draw you a bath."

Given the distinct trace of disgruntlement in Bernadette's tone, it was clear the woman was still put out that Camilla had not taken her advice and climbed immediately into the tub to stave off any possible ill effects that might result from taking a plunge into incredibly frigid water.

Frankly, it was a novel experience having a lady's maid who didn't hold her opinions in check, especially when Camilla was accustomed to being seen after by Miss Donovan, a reserved woman who rarely expressed personal opinions, and who'd been her lady's maid from the time Camilla started wearing long skirts until a scant month before.

Miss Donovan, after accompanying Camilla to Paris for a brief shopping excursion, had barely stepped foot into the Pierpont residence on Fifth Avenue before she'd received an urgent message informing her that while she'd been gone, her mother had suffered an accident and needed round-the-clock care while she convalesced.

There'd been no question that Miss Donovan would be given an extended leave of absence—with pay, of course—and after seeing her off at the train station, Camilla had returned home, intent on contacting an employment agency to fill the lady's maid position until Miss Donovan returned.

She was spared the bother of that, though, after discovering that Bernadette had recently been hired as a kitchen assistant for the Pierpont household. It turned out that Bernadette was more of a hindrance in the kitchen than a help. But, as luck would have it, according to Mrs. Barney, Camilla's longtime housekeeper, Bernadette had mentioned during the hiring process that she'd once spent time at a theater off Broadway. She'd evidently been responsible for dressing actresses before their performances, as well as assisting them with their hair, experience Mrs. Barney felt might make Bernadette the perfect substitute for Miss Donovan. Mrs. Barney also thought turning Bernadette into a temporary lady's maid might go far with soothing the tender sensibilities of the Pierpont chef, who'd been threatening to quit on a daily basis because of Bernadette's ineptitude in his kitchen.

Not wanting to lose a chef who turned out spectacular dishes, Camilla had agreed to Mrs. Barney's suggestion, but only after having Bernadette style her hair to ascertain she had some talent in that area, which, thankfully, the woman certainly possessed.

But while Bernadette was more than competent with arranging hair, as well as getting Camilla dressed, she was also the most forward employee Camilla had ever met, an attitude she wasn't accustomed to, but one she'd decided to tolerate since it wasn't as if Bernadette would be in the position long.

"Have you changed your mind about the bath?" Bernadette asked, drawing Camilla from her thoughts.

"Of course not," Camilla said, rising from the vanity stool and shaking out the folds of her ivory-colored morning gown. "I can hardly leave Mr. Chesterfield lingering about in the parlor for the length of time it would take me to bathe and change again. However, since you're evidently concerned I'm going to come down with a cold if I don't take a bath at some point this morning, know that I'll be happy to climb into the tub after my meeting with him."

Bernadette frowned. "On second thought, I doubt you'll come down with a cold, and not taking a bath until this evening will spare me the bother of undressing and then redressing you again."

Camilla refused a sigh. "It would at that."

Leaving her lady's maid saying something about the bath matter being settled, Camilla made her way to the grand staircase that led to the main floor, stepped into the back parlor a few moments later, and found Mr. Timken and Owen standing by a floor-to-ceiling window, engaged in conversation. She cleared her throat, drawing Owen's attention.

"Ah, Miss Pierpont, there you are," he said.

"Why do I get the distinct impression you wanted to add a *finally* to your sentence?" she asked as she glided across the room and settled into a chair upholstered in a delicate shade of blush pink.

"But I *didn't* add a finally, which suggests I'm valiantly striving to avoid annoying you again," Owen said, which left her lips twitching ever so slightly.

After accepting a cup of coffee from Mr. Timken, Camilla took a sip before she tilted her head. "It only took me a mere twenty-five minutes to change, a monumental feat if there ever was one, but one undertaken because you mentioned you needed to return to Wheeling posthaste."

"You were gone twenty-nine minutes to be exact, and twenty-nine minutes is not what I'd consider returning momentarily, which is how long you told me it would take you to change."

"What *would* you consider momentarily?"

"Less than five minutes."

"I can barely get my gloves off in five minutes, and I would think, since you told me you have a sister, that you're more than familiar with how long it takes a lady to change."

"Luella prides herself on being able to change in five minutes flat."

"She must have one extraordinary lady's maid."

"She doesn't have a maid."

"Why not?"

"She doesn't think they're necessary, although I believe her original decision to refuse the services of a lady's maid was a direct result of my mother hiring Flora when Luella turned fourteen. Flora made it a habit to report to Mother anytime Luella did something questionable, which, unfortunately, was quite often."

Camilla took another sip of coffee. "Ah, so your mother hired Flora to not only dress your sister but keep an eye on her."

"Something I never considered, but I wouldn't put it past Mother to have hired a spy in the form of a maid, given how Luella and Mother shared a somewhat acrimonious relationship back in the day."

"You might want to ask your sister about that, but tell me this—how does Luella manage to get dressed without the services of a maid, and so rapidly at that?"

"She seems to prefer wearing frocks one can simply toss over one's head."

"And she prefers those . . . why?"

"I think it has something to do with her aversion to what she calls 'unmentionables.'" Owen shook his head as he took a seat across from her. "I'm not sure what unmentionables she was specifically speaking about, but she's apparently opposed to most of them. She's vowed to never stuff herself into garments she's convinced are harming her, ah, parts, or attach a birdcage to her behind for the sole purpose of achieving a certain silhouette." He gave his nose a scratch. "I wasn't aware birdcages were an option for ladies to wear, but before I forget, I should also mention that Luella has an extreme aversion to bows."

Camilla fought a grin. "I believe Luella was referring to bustles, which can occasionally be similar to birdcages, and seeing as how I get the impression your sister is around eighteen, she *should* have an aversion to bows."

"Luella's nineteen, almost twenty, but why should she be opposed to bows?"

"Bows should be reserved for young girls, not ladies who've come of age."

"Huh . . ." Owen said before he frowned. "Sally Murchendorfer wears bows all the time, and she and Luella are of the same age."

"Is your sister friends with this Sally Murchendorfer?"

"Luella currently loathes the entire Murchendorfer family, except perhaps Sally's father, Mr. Russell Murchendorfer, who isn't around much."

"Which might explain the extreme bow aversion." Camilla set aside her cup. "Tell me more about this loathing for the Murchendorfer family."

Before Owen could do exactly that, Mr. Timken walked over to her and handed her a small plate of cheese. "This should hold you over until lunch, Miss Camilla, but if you'll excuse me? Mr. Chesterfield and I were making arrangements for your safety while you were changing. I need to see if the footman I sent to summon the authorities has returned." After presenting Camilla with a bow, Mr. Timken turned and headed out the door.

"I almost forgot about the attempted abduction," Camilla admitted.

"I'm not surprised since ladies normally don't care to dwell on unpleasantness."

Camilla paused with a piece of cheese halfway to her mouth. "I don't believe anyone, ladies or gentlemen, care to dwell on that."

"Perhaps, but gentlemen are far more likely to respond to unpleasant business, whereas ladies, well, that's why you have gentlemen around, and why you don't need to worry your pretty little heads with such matters."

After sticking the piece of cheese into her mouth in an effort to avoid the dressing-down she longed to give the insufferable man, Camilla made a point of chewing for an incredibly long time as she strove to get her renewed irritation in check.

"Got a hard piece of cheese, did you?" he asked.

She swallowed and summoned up a smile. "Not at all."

"Why are you smiling at me?"

"I normally make it a practice to smile at guests."

"But the smile you're currently wearing isn't what I'd consider a pleasant one, and almost suggests you're . . ." His voice trailed off as he frowned, considered her for a moment, and sat forward. "You're not put out with me again, are you?"

She kept her smile firmly in place. "I suppose that depends on if you were deliberately trying to annoy me when you said I didn't need to worry 'my pretty little head' about unpleasant matters, or if you're merely oblivious regarding why I'd take issue with your current choice of phrase. If it's the second reason, I can now fully understand why, as you mentioned, you have trouble with the ladies."

He blinked. "I hear other men saying 'don't worry your pretty little head' all the time, and if you ask me, there's no reason for a lady to take offense at that, particularly when the phrase has the word *pretty* in it."

"And while ladies don't take offense at the word *pretty*, the whole 'little heads' business is what's wrong with the phrase, since it suggests we ladies don't have much in the way of intellect."

"Huh, well that certainly explains why Miss Doreen Morrison abandoned a fishing excursion I took her on after I told her she didn't need to worry her pretty little head over taking her fish off the hook because I'd do it for her."

"Glad I could clear that up for you."

He nodded. "You did, and thank you for that because I never have been able to puzzle out what I did wrong that day. I'll now refrain from using that phrase again, but returning to ladies not knowing how to handle a difficult situation—I feel compelled to remind you that you're the one who said you'd forgotten about the abduction event, whereas I'm the one who remembered and took steps with Mr. Timken to assure your safety."

"Are you now expecting me to present you with a medal for that?"

To her surprise, his lips quirked. "For a lady who claims to be the picture of serenity, you're very prickly."

"I've never been prickly in my life."

"And before I'm tempted to argue with that, no doubt incurring more prickliness from you, allow me to move the conversation to safer territory and simply tell you about the safety precautions Mr. Timken and I have arranged for you."

Camilla opened her mouth to argue with that nonsense, realized she might actually be a little prickly at the moment, so closed her mouth and settled for sending him a nod, something that left him grinning.

She opted to not address the grin, stuffing not one but two pieces of cheese into her mouth instead, which was yet another serious breach of proper etiquette, but definitely left her incapable of voicing a prickly remark since her mouth was so full.

"Where was I?" he asked.

It was more than annoying when she couldn't immediately answer, what with all the cheese in her mouth. Finally, and after a great deal of rapid chewing, she inclined her head. "I believe you were about to explain the safety precautions you and Mr. Timken have put in place."

"Quite right, and I'm sure you'll be relieved to learn that besides summoning the authorities, we've organized your staff, sending footmen out to patrol the perimeters of your estate until the authorities arrive."

Camilla frowned. "You think those would-be abductors might try again?"

"You're an heiress, Miss Pierpont, and holding heiresses for ransom is lucrative business." He leaned forward. "I'm curious, since you must be aware there are threats to you out there, why you were riding without the benefit of a guard."

"The Hudson Valley is the one place I've always felt safe, unlike the city, where I have guards who shadow me anytime I step foot out of the house."

"I'm afraid the Hudson isn't safe for you any longer."

"I'm afraid you're right, which means I can now expect the small bit of freedom I've enjoyed here to disappear as soon as my father learns about the particulars of what happened today."

"He should hear about those particulars soon, as Mr. Timken instructed the footman who was sent after the authorities to also send your father a telegram."

Camilla's shoulders slumped the slightest bit. "Then I expect Father will board his yacht the second he gets that telegram, just as I expect I'll soon find myself imprisoned in this gilded cage I call home minutes after he lands in the Hudson Valley."

Owen glanced around the room. "I can think of worse places to be imprisoned."

"True, but since the mere thought of having my activities severely curtailed is rather unsettling, why don't you tell me more about your sister and why you want me to take her in hand."

"What would you like me to tell you about her?"

"How it came to be that she turned into a bit of a handful."

He drummed his fingers against the arm of the chair. "I suppose that all started when she turned sixteen and my mother began making plans for her debut."

"Luella didn't want a debut?"

"I don't think she was opposed to that at first—until Mother learned that Ada Mae Murchendorfer was intending on holding a debut ball for her daughter, Sally."

"The lady who has a fondness for bows?"

"Indeed." Owen shook his head. "Mother and Ada Mae always seemed to be in competition with each other, and Mother evidently decided Luella's debut ball couldn't be overshadowed by Sally's ball. That's when things turned a little concerning, and then turned downright alarming when Ada Mae decided to hold her ball on the same night Mother had chosen for Luella's."

"Did Ada Mae decide that on purpose?"

"I would say . . . probably."

"Sounds like there was more than just competition going on between your mother and Ada Mae."

"I never considered that, but you might be right," Owen said. "However, once Luella discovered what Ada Mae was intending, she flatly refused to have a debut, which sent Mother into an agitated state, one that didn't dissipate until my parents made the decision to go on an extended holiday to Paris."

"Did they decide that because of Luella's refusal to make her debut?"

"I believe it had more to do with my father's weak heart. Mother, you see, was concerned Father's heart might suffer an acute attack after she decided that the manor house they were building in the country needed a few modifications to the original design."

"Why would he have an acute attack over that?"

"Because our second home was supposed to be a simple farmhouse until Mother learned the Murchendorfers were building a grand manor house a few miles away. Father, wanting to appease Mother's agitated state, agreed to allow the architect to modify the plans, but Mother had a hard time deciding exactly how the house should be modified, which was causing Father some agitation as well." He shrugged. "Mother apparently realized at some point that she might be bringing on Father's imminent demise, and decided the only option to protect his heart was to leave the country. She then left me in charge of completing the house, and then, after Luella flatly refused to leave our beloved grandmother and threatened to jump overboard if our parents insisted she travel on holiday with them, left me in charge of Luella."

Camilla frowned. "How long have they been on this holiday?"

"About two years," Owen said. "Mother adores Paris and has taken to painting along the Siene, and somehow convinced Father he loves to paint as well. From their letters, they spend their days with their easels set up, and then enjoy dining in Parisian restaurants most nights. Since Father hasn't had a single episode with his heart since they arrived in France, Mother's decided they're going to stay there for the foreseeable future."

"Which is lovely for your parents, but have you told them about the difficulties you're experiencing with your sister?"

"And have them board the first ship available and return home? Absolutely not." He blew out a breath. "Frankly, I thought Luella would return to her normal delightful self after Mother wasn't around to badger her, but she now seems convinced that my sole purpose in life is to make her miserable, arriving at that decision after I made the mistake of suggesting we hold a small party for her instead of a ball." He shook his head. "In my defense, though, I was under the misimpression she wanted to make some type of debut because every other young lady of the same age was doing exactly that, and I didn't want her to feel left out."

"Is that why you want me to take her in hand—to convince her to allow you to host that party for her because you're still worried she feels left out?"

"I think the whole launching Luella into Wheeling society is a ship that's firmly sailed." He released a sigh. "However, given what recently happened to my sister, I'd like to bring you on board to help her become more refined, which might help her regain her pride, something Stanley Murchendorfer recently harmed."

"This Murchendorfer name seems to be coming up often, and if I were to hazard a guess, I'd guess this Stanley Murchendorfer is a relation of Ada Mae and Sally Murchendorfer."

Owen nodded. "Your guess would be correct since he's Ada Mae's only son and Sally's brother, but he's a scoundrel of the worst sort, who, regrettably, masqueraded as Luella's good friend for years."

"I'm surprised you didn't intervene when your sister began associating with a scoundrel."

"Stanley wasn't always a scoundrel. That's a recent development," Owen said. "He's three years older than Luella, and because the Murchendorfer home on Wheeling Island is adjacent to our home there, he and my sister used to roam the island together throughout their youth."

"Luella didn't prefer roaming around with Sally?"

"Sally doesn't roam, but Stanley, on the other hand, enjoys the same activities Luella does. That's why they spent hours together in their youth." Owen rose to his feet and moved to look out the window. "I was always aware they were good friends, but what I didn't know until recently was that they had an understanding between them, one that lent Luella the impression they'd always be together."

"As in married?"

"Indeed, and apparently after Stanley finished college."

"Should I assume Stanley recently completed his studies?"

"Their timeline got disrupted after Stanley's father, who owns Murchendorfer Stogies, a prominent cigar factory in Wheeling, insisted his son take a grand tour of Europe after graduation."

"And something unfortunate happened when Stanley finally returned from his tour?"

"Quite right, because Stanley, you see, couldn't even be bothered to send Luella a note informing her of his return. She had to hear it through the staff grapevine because, while we own a house on Wheeling Island, which again, is directly next to the Murchendorfer house, Luella prefers to stay at our grandmother's cabin that's located not far from the country house that's just recently been completed. According to Mrs. O'Connel, our part-time housekeeper, she noticed Stanley walking through the neighborhood. Knowing how much Luella had been looking forward to reuniting with him, Mrs. O'Connel sent a message to her. Luella didn't hesitate to jump on her horse and canter right on down to Wheeling Island, apparently taking a shortcut to get there, which had her arriving at Stanley's house covered in mud and looking, from what Luella admitted to me, somewhat bedraggled. Unfortunately, Stanley's mother had arranged for an afternoon soiree, which was in full swing by the time Luella, who'd not been invited, arrived."

Owen raked a hand through his hair. "Luella was then told by the Murchendorfer butler to wait on the front porch, not even given the courtesy of being allowed into the entranceway. She apparently lingered there for a good twenty minutes before Stanley showed up. From what I understand, Stanley immediately launched into a tirade, telling my poor sister that it was 'beyond the pale' for her to arrive unannounced at a gathering she'd not received an invitation to. He then demanded she leave and return to our grandmother's cabin, telling her he'd call on her in a day or so to discuss the subject of their friendship more thoroughly."

"Did he show up within a day or so?"

"It took him two weeks to pay a call, during which time Luella never said a word to me about what happened. When Stanley finally mustered up his courage, he tracked Luella down at her favorite creek, obviously done so because he's terrified of our grandmother, and informed my sister that he'd matured during his time away and that he'd been fortunate to glean an air of sophistication while traveling throughout Europe. That sophistication evidently had him realizing that he could no longer associate with the likes of Luella because she, according to Stanley, gave new meaning to the term *unrefined*. He then told her that he couldn't afford to be seen in her company anymore because she was an embarrassment and would ruin his chances of cementing his status within Wheeling society."

Owen shook his head. "Luella, evidently still cherishing Stanley's friendship, responded to all that idiocy by informing him that she could easily transform herself into a most refined young lady. After she was done telling him that, though, events took a somewhat disastrous turn because Stanley's reply to Luella's heartfelt declaration was to laugh."

"He didn't," Camilla breathed.

"Oh, I'm very much afraid he did."

"What was Luella's response?" Camilla forced herself to ask.

"She punched him."

Camilla blinked. "Surely you meant to say she slapped him, didn't you?"

"Luella wouldn't waste her time delivering anyone a mere slap, Miss Pierpont," Owen admitted. "And because I may have shown my sister the rudiments of boxing a few years back, she knows her way around a good punch, so . . . she broke Stanley's nose."

Five

Camilla got up from the settee and made her way to the French doors, her gaze traveling over the back lawn and lingering on the river she'd recently been submerged in, needing a moment to contemplate what Owen had just disclosed about his sister.

She'd never met a lady who'd broken anyone's nose, and that Luella had managed to accomplish that, well—it suggested she was far more than "a bit of a handful."

Squaring her shoulders, she turned and caught Owen's eye. "Forgive me, Mr. Chesterfield, but given what you've just told me transpired between your sister and Stanley Murchendorfer, I'm afraid I don't possess the qualifications needed to rectify the whole breaking-a-gentleman's-nose situation."

Owen rose to his feet. "Luella doesn't make a habit of inflicting bodily harm, Miss Pierpont. I fear she was simply overcome with temper after Stanley mocked her, which I'm sure you'll agree was ungentlemanly decorum on his part. In all honesty, Walter Townsend's recommendation alone regarding your incredible success with Adelaide Duveen is enough to assure me you're fully qualified to carry out what I acknowledge is going to be a daunting undertaking."

"Daunting might be an understatement."

"A fair point, but from what Walter disclosed, Adelaide had been facing social ostracization until you stepped in and turned her into one of the most sought-after ladies of the New York Season. Not only did you manage that impressive feat, you were also responsible for matching her up with Gideon Abbott, one of the most eligible bachelors in New York last year."

Camilla refused a sigh as she moved to retake her seat. "While I might have dabbled in a touch of matchmaking between Adelaide and Gideon, I hope you're not about to suggest that I not only take Luella in hand, but also smooth matters over between her and this Stanley character. If Walter neglected to mention this, I'm officially retired from the matchmaking business."

"You're not completely retired," Mr. Timken contradicted as he walked into the room.

Camilla frowned. "Of course I am."

"Then explain why I have it on good authority that you've been considering taking on Charles Wetzel and Leopold Pendleton to sponsor, at least unofficially."

"What *good authority* told you that?"

"A proper butler never reveals his sources."

She settled back on the chair. "A proper butler also never contradicts his employer in front of a guest."

Mr. Timken sent her a wink. "Touché."

She bit back a smile. "May I assume there was a reason you abandoned your normally strict adherence to what you always refer to as the rules of butler brotherhood?"

"I might have been hoping that by reminding you that you're not actually retired, you might consider Mr. Chesterfield's proposal."

"Because?"

"Disclosing that reason would once again leave me abandoning my normal adherence to the butler brotherhood."

"But since you've come this far, you might as well disclose away."

Mr. Timken inclined his head. "Very well. I'd like you to consider taking on Luella Chesterfield because you've been suffering from ennui often of late. Assisting that young lady would fill up your days, and given that Mr. Chesterfield admitted she's a handful, your ennui would no longer be a problem."

"A somewhat valid point," Camilla admitted.

"It's an excellent point, and you know it."

"There you go again, abandoning your butler brotherhood rules of proper behavior."

"But only because I have your very best interests at heart."

Since there was no arguing with that as Mr. Timken had made a point of looking after her from almost the moment she'd been born, Camilla settled for sending him a smile, which he responded to with a wink before she returned her attention to Owen. "If we may return to your sister, I asked if you wanted me to smooth matters over with Luella and Stanley."

"That's the last thing I want, as does Luella, since she's decided she's never going to contemplate marriage again. With that said, though, she's also decided to prove Stanley wrong and turn herself into a refined young lady." Owen leaned forward. "Given your success with Adelaide, I'm convinced you're the one person who can help her achieve that goal."

"My success with Adelaide was completely different," Camilla argued. "For one, she's from a Knickerbocker family, whose position within the Four Hundred is firmly cemented."

"Not firmly enough if society was going to ostracize her."

Drawing in a deep breath in the hopes of dispelling the irritation that was once again plaguing her, she arched a brow his way. "Do you make it a habit to contradict everything everyone says, or is that simply something you reserve for me?"

"I wasn't contradicting you. Merely pointing out the obvious."

It was difficult to keep her jaw from clenching. "Be that as it may, I think you're missing the point."

"And I think you're missing that Adelaide was in the same situation Luella now finds herself in and that you were able to step in and fix everything."

"Adelaide didn't break anyone's nose."

"True, but she was responsible, according to Walter, for pressed duck going airborne during a dinner party, which I don't imagine many ladies—or any ladies—have ever managed to accomplish. Since you were still capable, even with pressed duck raining down on members of the upper crust, to get Adelaide reestablished within the Four Hundred, it stands to reason that you're more than capable of doing the same with Luella."

"Pressed duck that unexpectedly takes flight isn't the same as inflicting bodily harm on a man."

"Perhaps not, but I have to imagine if that flying duck smacked someone in the face, it inflicted a bit of damage as well."

It was rather telling when a distinct urge to throttle the man hit from out of nowhere, an urge she firmly shoved aside. "It's not the same scenario at all. Adelaide didn't purposely make the duck fly, whereas Luella deliberately punched Stanley in the nose. However, since we're clearly not going to agree with this, nor agree over the fact I know I'm unqualified to assist your sister, allow me to lend you some useful advice. Your best option to help your sister acquire an air of polish would be to enroll her in a ladies' finishing school because teaching young ladies how to become refined is what they do."

Owen shook his head. "I already sent her off to the Wellington Academy for Young Ladies, but unfortunately, Wellington didn't agree with Luella."

"Because . . . ?" Camilla forced herself to ask.

"She was asked to leave three days after she arrived."

"She got expelled?"

"The headmistress never used that particular word."

"But . . . ?" Camilla pressed when Owen didn't elaborate further.

"I'm not sure there's anything else to say since clearly Luella and finishing school didn't suit."

Camilla pressed a finger to her temple where an ache was beginning to form. "She didn't break someone else's nose, did she?"

"Of course not. As I mentioned, she doesn't go around assaulting people because she's not a violent person. She merely suffers from a rather tumultuous temper at times, something I'm sure you understand."

Camilla lifted her chin. "I have never assaulted anyone."

"Not even in your imagination?"

Unfortunately, that question had her coming up short because she'd just considered throttling the man, which could certainly be considered a form of assault.

Deciding there was no gracious way to address that particular inclination, Camilla settled for changing the subject instead. "If Luella didn't break someone's nose at Wellington Academy, why was she asked to leave?"

"I prefer to look at it as an amicable parting of the ways."

She arched a brow Owen's way.

"That's a very effective use of that brow, Miss Pierpont," he began after he swallowed a piece of cheese from the plate Mr. Timken had just handed him. "But since it's evident you're not going to move the conversation forward until I give you a few additional details, I'll simply say this—Luella was asked to leave because she rose magnificently to the defense of another student, earning the displeasure of the headmistress in the process."

"Exactly what manner of rising did she do?"

He hesitated for a second before he blew out a breath. "She may have challenged another student to a duel."

Camilla's mouth went a little slack, but before she could summon up a single response to a statement she certainly hadn't been expecting, Owen sat forward.

"From what Luella said about 'the incident' as she refers to it, Miss Jane Something-or-Other was all but terrorizing poor Miss Bertha Hamilton, apparently so much so that Bertha was unable to eat—a circumstance Jane declared to the entire student body was a blessing in disguise because Bertha was apparently, at least in Jane's opinion, overly plump. My sister then decided that Miss

Jane needed to experience some terror of her own, so she challenged her to a duel."

"Of course she did," Camilla muttered.

"To give Luella credit," Owen continued, as if Camilla hadn't taken to muttering, an odd circumstance for her to begin with, "she didn't suggest they use pistols for the duel, but rapiers, because Luella is an expert markswoman and she's quite capable of shooting a pistol out of an opponent's hand. She's less proficient with rapiers, although she does have some impressive skill with them, which is why she offered to duel with her left hand instead of her right, and before you ask, yes, she's right-handed."

"Should I assume you taught her how to use rapiers?"

"My grandmother did."

"What an interesting, ah, grandmother you must have" was all Camilla could think to say to that.

"That's one way to describe her, but to return to the duel . . ."

"Do not say Luella and Jane went through with it or, worse yet, that Luella maimed this Jane in the process."

"Luella wouldn't have seen the duel through, even if she'd been given the chance," Owen argued. "She simply wanted Jane to experience what it feels like to be placed in a humiliating situation."

"Was the decision made to stop the duel before these young ladies had the opportunity to meet on some desolate field?"

"Jane evidently went directly to the headmistress after Luella issued her challenge, and the headmistress showed up the next morning on the field where the duel was supposed to take place instead of Jane. Needless to say, Luella was sent packing within the hour."

"Of course she was since challenging someone to a duel isn't exactly the conventional attitude finishing schools are trying to impart to their students."

"I can't argue with that because I doubt embracing an unconventional attitude is mentioned anywhere in a finishing school's syllabus." Owen caught Camilla's eye. "Nevertheless, in case you're concerned Luella wouldn't be agreeable to adopting a conventional attitude, know that there's a specific ball—Mr. Henry Fulton's ball, to be exact—that she's determined to attend at the beginning of June. She's assured me that if I'll escort her there, and if she's able to figure out how to adopt a polished air, she'll not have another go at Stanley, and . . . she'll try her best to behave in a ladylike fashion throughout the entire ball."

Camilla blinked. "Did you just say Luella needs to adopt a polished air by June—of *this* year?"

"I did."

"That's only a month away."

"True, but from what Walter told me, you're a very accomplished lady, so I'm sure you'd be more than able to whip Luella into shape by then."

"I'm not a miracle worker, and . . . did you also say that Stanley's going to be in attendance?"

"I did, but did you miss the part where I said Luella promised to not have another go at him?"

"Given what is obviously a questionable temper, I'm not sure she'd be able to restrain herself if Stanley insults her again."

"But Stanley's mother, Ada Mae, will be there as well, and I know she won't allow Stanley anywhere near Luella because she seems to like her son's face."

As far as conversations went, this was the most unusual one Camilla could ever recall participating in. She took a moment to gather her thoughts before she blew out a breath. "While I truly feel for your sister's plight, Mr. Chesterfield, I'm sorry, but I cannot agree to step in and assist her, nor do I agree with her idea to attend this ball, especially not when the Murchendorfers will be in attendance."

"You're afraid Luella won't be able to contain her temper?"

"I'm more afraid that she'll walk into the ball and find herself immediately ostracized by the prominent families of Wheeling, no matter if she's acquired a refined air or not."

"Because?"

"Well, if I'm not mistaken, Stanley Murchendorfer is probably considered quite the catch in town. Believe me when I say that the ladies who have him in their sights will not be kind to the lady who punched him."

"They might not be openly hostile if you'd walk into the ball beside Luella."

"Which might be true if we were attending a ball in New York, but Wheeling is not New York. No one will have any idea who I am. And before you suggest we simply apprise them of my standing within the Four Hundred, that would be a serious breach of etiquette because it's considered quite beyond the pale to purposely apprise anyone of a particular social status."

"I think everyone would conclude on their own that you're the personification of what a proper lady should be and would certainly curtail any impulses they may want to make toward Luella if she were in your company."

"And while I thank you for that unexpected compliment," Camilla returned, "I'm sorry, Mr. Chesterfield, but no. I cannot in good conscience agree to sponsor Luella because, while I understand you believe having me by her side will shield her from unkind remarks, I'm not convinced that will be enough. I would not want to be responsible for your sister suffering additional slights."

Owen opened his mouth, but before he could get a word out, Bernadette came sauntering into the room, her gaze immediately going to and then lingering on Owen, her lips curving into a smile a second later as she dipped into a curtsy.

"Beggin' your pardon for interrupting," Bernadette began, sending a flutter of lashes in Owen's direction before she turned to Mr. Timken. "The sheriff, along with a few of his deputies, have just arrived. I took the liberty of ushering them through the door since you were nowhere to be found. I'm sure you'll be pleased to learn that I told them to make themselves at home in the blue drawing room."

Mr. Timken frowned. "Why didn't you escort them into the receiving room, where we usually take visitors?"

"I'm a lady's maid, Mr. Timken. How would I know where to take visitors?" Bernadette countered before she shrugged. "Besides, these men aren't your everyday visitors. They're men of the law. I've always found it beneficial to go that extra mile where men of the law are concerned. Tends to make them less likely to cart anyone off to jail."

"They're not here to arrest anyone, Bernadette," Mr. Timken said. "They're here to take statements regarding the attempted abduction of Miss Camilla this morning."

"That may be," Bernadette shot back, "but Ember Starlight, an actress I dressed in the theater district, thought the lawmen who came backstage one night were just there to pay their respects to her. Before she had a chance to accept any flattery, though, she found herself hauled off to jail. Granted, she'd been helping herself to the contents of the cashbox when no one was looking, but still. It was quite the nasty surprise for her."

Mr. Timken frowned. "I'm not sure what your point is."

"My point is that just because you think you know why men of the law have come to call, there's always the chance you're mistaken."

"I'll keep that in mind" was all Mr. Timken said as his lips twitched ever so slightly before he turned and quit the room.

As Camilla watched him disappear, the thought sprang to mind that the composed world she normally resided in was nowhere to be found today—a thought that was reinforced when she returned her attention to Bernadette and found that, while she'd been watching Mr. Timken's retreat, her lady's maid had sidled closer to Owen and was plucking a few threads from Owen's tattered sleeve, which, unfortunately, left that sleeve completely parting from the seam and sliding to the floor.

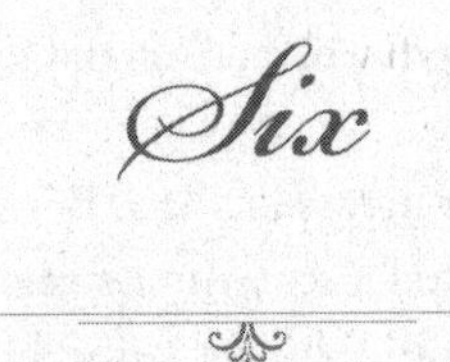

"Would you look at that," Bernadette exclaimed, batting her lashes Owen's way at a downright remarkable speed. "I seem to have unintentionally ruined your sleeve, but no need to fret because I'm a more than proficient seamstress. If you'll excuse me, I'll just nip up to my room and fetch my sewing basket. I'm sure you'll be relieved to learn that I have the skills that will see that fine suit jacket of yours returned to tip-top shape in a jiffy."

Given that Owen was now looking quite like a poor deer caught in the lantern lights, it was obvious that an intervention was in order.

Swallowing the oddest desire to laugh, that urge undoubtedly a direct result of the fact her day was becoming more peculiar by the second, Camilla lifted her chin and marched across the room. She took a second to snatch up Owen's tattered sleeve, which, given its abysmal condition, would never be able to look in tip-top shape again, before she inserted herself between Owen and Bernadette, having to resort to giving her lady's maid a none-too-subtle nudge to get her to step aside.

Bernadette immediately sent Camilla what could only be described as an injured look.

"Was there anything else you needed, Bernadette?" Camilla asked, ignoring the look.

"I wouldn't be opposed to an introduction to this delightful gentleman."

Having never had a maid ask for an introduction to anyone before, Camilla frowned, but before she could summon up any type of response, although what she could possibly say was beyond her, Owen presented Bernadette with a bow.

"I'm Mr. Owen Chesterfield."

Bernadette dimpled and dipped into a curtsy. "And I'm Miss Bernadette Millersport, Miss Pierpont's lady's maid, but know that I have every intention of becoming a famous actress, which is far more impressive than being a maid."

"My grandmother once had ambitions to tread the boards, but she came to her senses and married my grandfather instead."

Bernadette went from smiling to scowling in the span of a heartbeat. "There's nothing wrong with becoming an actress."

Owen blinked. "I don't recall saying there was."

"You implied that your grandmother would have taken leave of her senses if she'd chosen acting over marrying your grandfather."

Knowing the conversation was only going to go downhill from there, Camilla cleared her throat, drawing Bernadette's attention. "I'm sure what Mr. Chesterfield intended to say was that he's certain you'll make a wonderful actress, but your future aspirations aside, weren't you telling me earlier that there are only so many hours in a day and that you don't think you have enough time to get everything ready for our departure to Newport?"

Bernadette frowned. "Is that your way of telling me you'd like me to get back to work?"

"You're the one who said you're having difficulty getting my clothing in order for the summer Season."

"Anyone would have difficulty with that since ladies are apparently expected to change seven to ten times a day, which, over an eight-week span of time, translates to hundreds of pieces."

"I can always ask Lottie to assist you."

"And leave her concluding I'm not up for doing my job? Absolutely not." Bernadette released a sniff. "I'm perfectly capable of getting everything ready, but before I get back to the grind of packing up your many, many outfits . . ." She stuck her hand in her apron and pulled out an envelope. "I almost forgot to give this to you. When I went above and beyond my job requirements by opening the front door when the lawmen arrived, there was a telegram boy standing with them. He gave me this to give you." Bernadette thrust the envelope at Camilla. "You'll notice I didn't open it."

"I would hope not, since it's addressed to me," Camilla said before turning to Owen. "This is probably a response from my father regarding this morning's events. I'm sure the contents will revolve around his insistence that I don't leave this house until he's made proper arrangements for my safety, but there's no need for you to wait around while I read through it and then write out a response to send back to him."

"Will those arrangements include having the Pinkertons brought on to investigate matters?" Owen asked.

Camilla shook her head. "We have connections with a private investigative company known as the Accounting Firm in the city. They'll most assuredly be hired by Father to provide me with twenty-four-hour surveillance until the matter is resolved, something I willingly admit I'm not looking forward to."

Owen's lips suddenly began to curve. "You wouldn't have to contend with round-the-clock protection if you agree to my proposal, because I doubt anyone would expect you to take off for West Virginia. It's not exactly known as a state that members of the Four Hundred clamor to visit."

"An interesting point," Camilla conceded.

"I believe what you meant to say was it was an intriguing concept," Owen countered. "But to make it even more intriguing, know that there would be no need for you to worry about your safety. I would personally handle all the details surrounding that, and I'm more than capable of standing between you and any danger that may arise."

Before Camilla could muster up a response to that, Bernadette was back to fluttering her lashes, paired this time with a bright smile that was, of course, directed at Owen, her annoyance over his acting comment evidently a thing of the past.

"Not that I know much about what this proposal of yours might entail, Mr. Chesterfield, although I did overhear a little when I was, ah, lingering outside the door, but I think having Miss Pierpont travel to . . . I believe you said West Virginia, would be the perfect solution to keep her safe." Bernadette's smile turned brighter than ever. "I know, as Miss Pierpont's lady's maid, that she'll surely descend into a state of moroseness if she's forced to remain sequestered because of threats against her. However, since you've offered to protect her—and make no mistake, I have a feeling you know your way around how best to protect a lady—I think it's a plan Miss Pierpont will definitely want to accept. And, just to be clear, if you can convince her to do exactly that, know that I'll be traveling with her."

It wasn't much of a surprise when Owen began looking like a deer in the lantern lights again, and Camilla couldn't blame him, not when her lady's maid was behaving completely beyond the pale.

"I believe it's time for you to return to your duties, Bernadette," she began, "and no, you won't need to start packing us up to travel to West Virginia because, while Mr. Chesterfield's idea has merit, I won't be accepting his proposal."

She ignored the frown Bernadette was now leveling on her and turned to Owen. "Thank you again for rescuing me today, but now I believe it's time for us to part ways, although know that I do wish you well with your sister."

He considered her for a long moment before he presented her with a bow. "You're welcome for the rescue, but I won't claim I'm not disappointed by your decision, although . . . would you reconsider if I offered to pay above and beyond your usual fee for sponsoring young ladies?"

"I don't charge a fee."

"Huh."

She smiled. "You weren't expecting that, were you?"

"Can't say I was, but . . ." He tilted his head. "Do you not charge a fee because you look at sponsoring young ladies as a remedy for that ennui you apparently suffer from?"

Her smile faded just a touch. "You're very astute, aren't you, Mr. Chesterfield?"

"I tend to notice things, and then I tend to think about those things, which is why I'm now wondering if that ennui might start plaguing you more than ever once your normal activities are curtailed and you're placed under twenty-four-hour surveillance."

"Besides being astute, you're also evidently tenacious, and while that's a solid argument to advance your desire to get me to West Virginia, I'm sorry, but no. I really do need to decline."

He blew out a breath. "Then I suppose there's no need to keep badgering you. But if you happen to change your mind, I'm off to give a statement to the sheriff about my take on this morning's event, although I doubt that'll take me long."

"I won't change my mind since I don't believe I can successfully help your sister, nor do I want to give her false hope by even attempting to take her in hand."

"And I think you're selling yourself short, but it's not my place to continue arguing with you since I certainly don't want us parting on prickly terms."

"I'm not prickly."

Owen's lips twitched. "Of course you're not."

He presented her with another bow, did the same to Bernadette, who responded with another onslaught of fluttering lashes, then quit the room.

"You've clearly taken leave of your senses," Bernadette said a mere second after Owen disappeared from sight.

"And you've clearly forgotten, or you're unaware, that it's a serious breach of expected behavior to flirt outrageously with guests."

Bernadette blinked. "I wasn't flirting. I was merely being friendly."

"You kept fluttering your lashes."

"That's what lashes are for, but . . ." Bernadette frowned. "If you thought I was being flirty, why didn't you say something?"

"I wouldn't have wanted to embarrass either you or Mr. Chesterfield. Besides, conversations such as the one we're currently holding are best held privately."

Bernadette's brow furrowed. "None of my other employers ever hesitated to take me to task, or flat-out fire me, if they thought I was doing something wrong, so allow me to thank you for not embarrassing me."

"You're welcome, and may I dare hope that you'll now keep your flirting with guests in check?"

"Mr. Chesterfield didn't seem like he was a guest."

"True. Perhaps I should have hoped you'd agree to keep flirting in general in check."

"That might be expecting too much, but before I give you time to think up something else to hope for that I won't be capable of accomplishing, I should take my leave."

As Bernadette headed for the door, Camilla turned her attention to the telegram in her hand. After opening the envelope, she glanced over the message, having to read it a second time for the contents of that message to actually sink in.

Unfortunately, it was not from her father, as she'd expected, but from Gideon Abbott, her dear friend and also a partner at the Accounting Firm.

A dull throb settled at the base of her neck as she read the telegram through yet again, this time out loud.

LORD SHREWSBURY EN ROUTE TO NEW YORK STOP

DIVORCED HIS WIFE STOP

SUSPICIOUS CIRCUMSTANCES STOP
HE'S A THREAT TO YOU STOP
LEAVE NEW YORK STOP
ADDITIONAL EXPLANATIONS SOON STOP
I'LL BE HOME IN THREE WEEKS STOP
GIDEON STOP

"Are you alright?"

Camilla lifted her head and found Lottie standing a few feet away, watching her closely.

In all truthfulness, she didn't know how to respond because George Sherrington, or Lord Shrewsbury if one wanted to properly address a man who was an earl, was the gentleman Camilla had fallen madly in love with when she'd made her debut eight years before.

He was also the gentleman who'd shattered her heart and left her vowing she'd never marry.

There she'd been, all of seventeen, and surrounded by gentlemen who'd flocked to her side the moment she'd stepped foot into the Patriarch Ball, her mother brimming with satisfaction when one gentleman after another declared that Camilla was certainly going to be deemed the Incomparable of the Season.

Introductions had commenced with far too many gentlemen to count, all begging to add their names to her dance card, but any interest in those gentlemen disappeared the moment she clapped eyes on George.

He'd been standing across the room beside Mrs. Martin Barsdull, an esteemed society matron, but he'd not been directing his gaze at that lady—he'd been gazing at Camilla.

Her very breath had mired in her throat, and the entire room faded away except for George because he was the most handsome gentleman she'd ever seen.

Before she could prepare herself, he was walking across the room with Mrs. Barsdull, who immediately performed an introduction, and then . . . George presented her with a bow, kissed her gloved hand, and claimed her first dance of the night.

It was the first of many dances over the next three weeks.

Society, of course, immediately took note of Lord Shrewsbury's interest in her, and what a delightful interest it had been.

He'd been charming and lavished outrageous compliments on her, and because she'd been fresh out of the schoolroom, she'd completely lost her head. When he'd whispered in her ear at the Belmont Ball that he was utterly in love with her, she'd known he was the man she was going to spend the rest of her life with and had been thrilled when he told her he was going to ask her father for her hand in marriage.

Her father, Hubert Pierpont, had been anything but thrilled.

Hubert had spent a mere five minutes speaking with George before he'd seen him for exactly what he was—a fortune hunter, one of the many aristocrats who'd come to New York in search of an heiress to plump up their coffers and rebuild their crumbling country estates.

Her father had refused George's request for Camilla's hand and explained to the earl in no uncertain terms that if George tried to convince Camilla to marry him without Hubert's permission, he wouldn't receive so much as a cent from the dowry Hubert had settled on his one and only daughter.

George had then been escorted out of the house by Mr. Timken and four burly footmen, a circumstance that sent Camilla, who'd been blatantly eavesdropping through an adjoining door, stomping into the room to confront her father.

It was the first time Camilla had ever displayed even an inkling of temper to anyone in her family, as well as the first time she'd ever openly rebelled against her father. She'd told him in no uncertain terms that she and George didn't need a dowry and that she was going to marry the earl with or without his blessing.

Regrettably, when she'd met up with George later at another ball, he'd not been exactly keen to run off with her. Instead, he'd taken hold of her hand, kissed it, then explained how his mother—without his knowledge, of course—had arranged for him to marry another lady and, being an honorable gentleman, he had no recourse but to see the marriage through, especially when notices had already been sent to all the papers.

If that hadn't been bad enough, George then told her that she was the absolute love of his life, would always be the love of his life, and he would be forever bereft without her . . . right before he wandered away to take to the floor with Miss Eleanor Deerhurst, the lady he was now going to marry.

At the time, Camilla, being young and incredibly naïve, believed George truly did love her, and because of that, and because she was heartbroken and furious with her parents, she'd made a vow to never marry, no matter that she was her parents' only child and the Pierpont bloodline would end with her.

With time, she'd come to realize exactly what her father had been trying to save her from. George truly was a fortune hunter, as well as a coward, because he'd been unable to tell her the truth—that her fortune had been her greatest appeal and he'd never loved her.

Even realizing she'd been duped, she'd never changed her mind about marrying again as she'd never been able to forget the pain George had put her through.

That was why it was more than troubling to learn that George was heading back to New York—as a divorced man, no less—especially when it seemed, from what she could conclude about Gideon's telegram, that George was coming back to New York for . . . her.

Frankly, there was a part of her—the strong, self-assured part—that wanted to confront George, tell him exactly how much she despised him and what a cad he was, but the other part of her, the part that had suffered unwarranted humiliation after he'd cast her aside, wanted to never encounter the man again, especially not when there was a possibility, however slight, that she might decide to try her hand at that throttling business she'd been contemplating with Owen.

Ladies were not supposed to physically throttle anyone, no matter if she would have gleaned a great deal of satisfaction from trying her hand at that with George.

"What's wrong?" Lottie asked again, pulling Camilla from thoughts that were leaving her somewhat queasy.

She gave herself a bit of a shake and summoned up a smile. "Nothing."

Lottie rolled her eyes. "Please. You're white as a ghost." She nodded to the telegram. "Is your father intending on hiding you away, something I know you're probably dreading?"

"It's not from my father. It's from Gideon."

"He's back from Europe?"

"He'll be back in about three weeks."

Lottie took a step closer to Camilla. "May I assume he sent you troubling news, maybe something to do with the men who tried to abduct you today?"

"It's highly unlikely Gideon's been apprised of that circumstance yet since he's in England, although . . ." Camilla stilled when a thought sprang to mind. "It might be, given the cryptic nature of his message, that he's uncovered some dastardly plan Lord Shrewsbury has in mind for me, perhaps one that revolves around my attempted abduction."

"Who is Lord Shrewsbury?"

"He's a fortune hunter who broke my heart when I was seventeen when he married another woman. According to Gideon, Lord Shrewsbury has now divorced."

"And Gideon wanted you to know those details because . . . ?"

"Lord Shrewsbury is on his way to New York, and Gideon, for some reason, believes he's a threat to me and has told me to leave the city."

"Ah, Gideon thinks this Lord Shrewsbury is coming back for you—or, more likely, your fortune."

"How did you arrive at that?"

Lottie shrugged. "When you're involved with the criminal underworld for years, you begin to think like criminals. From what you've said, it stands to reason that Lord Shrewsbury would only seek out a divorce, something that's not exactly common, if he'd gone through his wife's fortune and needs another one. However, since he previously chose another woman over you, it's likely he's afraid you won't be keen to welcome him with open arms, so he's probably plotting out ways to secure your cooperation—abduction possibly being one of those ways, which means the idea I've arrived at regarding this morning's events is off the mark."

"What idea?"

"The one where you weren't the target—I was. And the man behind the attempt being Victor Malvado, who we both know was interested in bringing me into his criminal enterprise after Frank got carted off to jail."

"I didn't even consider Victor Malvado."

"I didn't either until I was taking a bath. But Victor's more feared in the city than Frank was, and we did hear those rumors before we repaired to Paris that he wanted to acquire me since I know how to read and Frank found that useful with his underhanded business deals."

Camilla took a second to gather her thoughts. "It appears to me," she finally said, "as if we have no choice, since we both could be in danger, except to heed Gideon's suggestion and get out of New York." Her lips quirked ever so slightly. "As luck would have it, we have the perfect place to hide."

"West Virginia?"

"Indeed, which means we need to gather our things posthaste because Mr. Chesterfield mentioned he wants to depart from New York as soon as possible, and I now have every intention of being with him on that train bound for Wheeling."

Seven

"I find it rather telling, Mr. Chesterfield, that during the many hours we've spent together in your Pullman car—those hours increasing after we encountered mechanical problems—you've been unable to provide me with much information regarding your sister that will actually assist me with forming a strategy to help her turn refined, which suggests you might not know your sister very well at all."

Owen pulled his attention away from the scenery passing outside the window and settled it on Camilla, who was currently in the process of tapping her pencil against the notepad she'd been perusing, a faint hint of what seemed to be exasperation in her eyes.

The exasperation left him smiling, which was odd since he usually didn't find exasperating women in general to be amusing.

"Luella and I share a close relationship, and I've told you a lot about her," he argued.

"Telling me that Luella enjoys fishing is hardly helpful since I doubt the prominent ladies of Wheeling spend their time engaged in fishing expeditions instead of sitting down to tea."

"Luella enjoys tea and something to prove I know her well is this—dandelion tea is her favorite."

A small crease formed between Camilla's brows as she scribbled something into her notepad. "I've never heard of dandelion tea."

"Never?"

"I'm afraid not."

"It's a staple in West Virginia, but it might be one of those acquired-taste things I hear bandied about, such as when associates of mine encourage me to eat caviar, which I haven't found to my liking, nor do I think continuing to eat it will change my mind about that. It's rather . . . fishy."

"Considering caviar is fish eggs, it's supposed to be fishy, but caviar aside, tell me this, does your sister put cream or milk in her dandelion tea?"

"Why would anyone do that, or, better yet, why do you want to know?"

"Many ladies add cream or milk to their tea to make it more substantial, and I need to know because if Luella adds one of those to her tea, I have to make certain she knows the proper way to stir it."

Owen frowned. "There's a proper way to stir?"

"When sitting down with other ladies to a proper tea, certainly."

"And when you're by yourself?"

"It's been my experience that if proper manners are adhered to at all times, they become second nature. That's why ladies should be accustomed to only using a teaspoon when stirring milk, cream, or sugar into their tea, then stir twice, and only twice, before tapping the spoon gently once against the rim of the cup before placing it on the saucer, and never on the table."

"It's a good thing Luella takes her dandelion tea plain then, because I don't think she'd be agreeable to learning that type of nonsense."

The exasperation in Camilla's eyes turned to downright annoyance. "Learning proper table manners is never nonsense because little things like stirring tea properly is something others take note of. If Luella doesn't bother to learn some basic rules when it comes to sitting down to tea, she won't achieve her goal of becoming refined."

"But what happens if you haven't given your tea a good enough stir and everything isn't blended well together?"

"Then you simply have to suffer through a cup of tea that isn't to your liking."

"What's the point of having tea, then?"

"Sitting down to tea with ladies is never about drinking tea. It's all about the art of how you drink it."

"Huh." Owen gave his jaw a rub. "Seems a little ridiculous that so much time needs to be devoted to stirring tea, but as Luella drinks her dandelion tea plain, we won't have to worry about her balking at a stirring lesson."

"But will she balk over dance instructions, time spent assessing her proficiency with musical instruments, and styling her to look the part of a lady of refinement?"

"I already told you that I don't think Luella's proficient with any musical instruments because I distinctly remember, when Mother insisted she take piano lessons, that her lessons didn't last long because Luella's playing always sent Goldie, the dog that reminds me of you, howling."

"It might be for the best if you would refrain from telling me that I apparently resemble your dog."

"Goldie's no longer with us, bless her heart, but I didn't say you resembled her. I just said your hair is the same color her fur was, and to be clear, she had quite the glorious coat of fur."

Camilla began tapping her pencil against her notepad again. "Why do I get the distinct impression, given your smile, that you think you just complimented me?"

"Because I did, and before you explain why I didn't, I would think a lady would find it flattering anytime a gentleman directed the word *glorious* her way."

"Unless it's paired with the word *fur*, and not the kind you wear," Camilla said before she returned to her notepad, wrote something down on it, then lifted her head. "I've made a note that it's not an option to ever suggest Luella sit down in front of an audience to play the piano since we certainly don't want to set any dogs to howling. With musical instruments probably out of the picture, can you think of any talents she possesses that I could use to our advantage?"

"She's really good with a pistol."

"And I'll be sure to keep that in mind if we happen to get invitations to a shooting party delivered to us once we get to Wheeling, although I'm not going to hold my breath waiting for one of those." She squared her shoulders. "What about needlepoint?"

"What about it?"

He wasn't certain, but he thought Camilla might have released a bit of a snort before she settled a somewhat narrowed eye on him. "Have you ever seen any embroidered pillows lying about your house?"

"My mother has them all over our house on Wheeling Island."

"And was your sister responsible for embroidering them?"

"I'm going to say . . . probably not?"

"Wonderful," Camilla muttered before she bent over her notepad again and wrote something else down. "Moving on to dancing."

He smiled. "I know for a fact Luella's had dancing instructors over the years, although . . . she's never been to a ball, but she does enjoy doing reels at family gatherings, and I believe she also enjoys square dancing."

"What about waltzing?"

Owen thought about that for a moment before he smiled. "I think she might know how to waltz because after the ballroom was completed a few months back in our country house, she said something about it being a wonderful space to waltz across."

"You have a ballroom at your country house?"

"Mother wanted to build a home where she could entertain on a grand scale."

Camilla frowned. "Your mother must have been incredibly concerned over your father's health to have abandoned a house she evidently would have adored but didn't have time to enjoy before it was completed."

"I suppose she was, but I imagine she'll return at some point, although I hope she doesn't return too soon because I've yet to hire anyone to decorate or furnish the house."

Camilla set aside her notepad. "Didn't you say you were going to have me stay at your country house—one that's apparently unfurnished?"

"I did, and the reason behind having you stay there is because the Murchendorfers live directly next to our house on the island. Since Luella has refused to go back there after her encounter with Stanley, there's no choice but to have you stay at the country house."

"Does Luella stay there by herself?"

"She stays at our grandmother's cabin, where I didn't consider having you stay because my grandmother lives there."

"Does she not like to entertain guests?"

"She's more partial to family, and besides that, she might be a little . . . difficult."

"So, if I'm understanding you correctly, I'll be staying at the country house with Mr. Timken, Lottie, and Bernadette, and Luella will join me there for lessons?"

Owen shook his head. "That would give Luella far too many opportunities to avoid scheduled lessons, so I'm going to entice her to stay at the country house by telling her I need her to guard you when I, or the men I've already had my manager, Edward Stevens, hire to guard you, aren't available." He smiled. "Luella won't balk at that because she adores situations where weapons might come into play."

"She does sound delightful," Camilla murmured.

"She's actually more delightful than she sounds, but if you're worried about living in an unfurnished home, no need to fret.

When I sent that telegram to Edward, I also asked him to pick up a few basics for the house, such as beds and perhaps a few chairs."

"A table probably wouldn't be remiss."

Owen winced. "I didn't think about a table."

"And dishes."

"Dishes might be a good idea as well."

"Eating is something I must insist upon doing every now and again during my stay, and besides that, it'll be imperative that I have Luella sit down with a formal setting and teach her how to negotiate her way through a twelve-course meal."

Owen frowned. "Do you often sit down to twelve-course meals, because you certainly don't possess the type of figure one would expect a woman who eats that much to possess."

"Do you always say whatever pops to mind?"

"Should I take that to mean I've just said something you disapprove of yet again?"

"Gentlemen should never remark on a lady's figure."

"Not even to compliment it, which I just did to yours if you missed that?"

"Telling me you're surprised I'm not larger than I am is not what I would consider a compliment. And yes, I do sit down to twelve-course meals often, although ladies only sample the courses, never eat all of the food that's set before them."

"Duly noted, as was the fact you need a table and some dishes."

"Along with silverware."

"Because eating with your fingers is probably frowned upon?"

Camilla began rubbing her temple. "Do not tell me you make it a habit to eat with your fingers, or that your sister does that as well."

He grinned. "We're not barbarians, Miss Pierpont. In fact, we know the basics when it comes to table etiquette because my mother made certain of that. I just wanted to see how you'd react if I suggested we might not use silverware often."

"Why would you want to see that?"

"Because you keep claiming you're not prickly, and I seem to derive a great deal of satisfaction from proving you are."

"Anyone would get prickly when faced with the idea that silverware is optional."

"I've added silverware to the mental list of the additional necessities you're going to need."

"Wonderful, but know that if I think of additional items your country house needs, I can always take Luella with me to the shops. We could also begin looking at some furnishings for your home because decorating a home is something that all ladies of refinement are expected to know how to do."

"Luella's never lent me the impression she's interested in decorating."

"From what I've been able to gather, she hasn't lent you much information at all over the past few years, but tell me this—you said Luella will be staying with me at the country house, but will you be staying there as well?"

"Since it would be impossible to provide you with that protection I promised if I were on Wheeling Island and you weren't, I will, although I'll have to travel to my factory on a daily basis, but I'll be home before dark." He smiled. "Luella, who again, is an expert with a pistol, will be in charge of keeping you safe, as will those men Edward hired."

"You'll have to tell me how much you're paying those men so I can reimburse you for their wages."

Owen stretched out his legs, earning a growl from El Cid, who'd been napping on his lap. After giving the cat a scratch, Owen shook his head. "I don't think I have to do any such thing."

"Why not?"

He took a second to consider the question before he caught Camilla's eye. "Do you remember how offended you got after I told you that you reminded me of Goldie?"

"That would be difficult to forget, but I thought we'd agreed to never discuss Goldie again."

"We did, and I won't mention her again after this, but it seems relevant because you, Miss Pierpont, have just offended me quite like I offended you."

"I don't recall comparing you to my dog."

Owen shot a glance at Gladys, who was snoozing on the floor beside Camilla. "I would hope not, since Gladys and I don't resemble each other in the least."

Her lips twitched ever so slightly. "I suppose she is rather fluffier than you, but I'm afraid I have no idea where this conversation is going."

"It's going in the offended direction because I'm rather put out that you would even think I'd consider taking money from you to keep you safe."

"I have a lot of money."

"So do I, but even if I didn't, as a man, it would be, as I think you would say, quite beyond the pale for me to take money from a lady. It's just not something a real man should ever do."

For the briefest of seconds, Camilla merely gazed back at him, something interesting flickering through her eyes, until she smiled, and not just any smile, but a genuine one.

All the air seemed to get sucked out of the Pullman car because, while he hadn't neglected to notice that Miss Camilla Pierpont was a beautiful woman, since he was a man, after all, when she smiled like the way she currently was, she was beyond beautiful and was also the most captivating lady he'd ever met, but one who, unfortunately, was far above the reach of a man like him.

Eight

"I beg your pardon, Mr. Chesterfield, but are you alright?"

Owen gave himself a bit of a shake, which resulted in air returning to his lungs, and after drawing in a deep breath, he discovered that Camilla was no longer smiling at him, but watching him rather warily.

"I'm quite alright, Miss Pierpont. Why do you ask?" he finally managed to get out of his mouth.

"You were looking somewhat . . . odd."

He settled back against the seat. "I suppose that was on account of you smiling at me."

"You found it odd that I would smile at you?"

"Well, after telling you I was offended, sure."

She blew out a breath. "Then I must beg your pardon yet again because I certainly wasn't amused over offending you. I was more along the lines of surprised by how I offended you, as well as taken aback by a realization that struck me from out of the blue."

"A realization?"

"Quite right, and one that has to do with you calling yourself a man."

He frowned. "I didn't realize that was in question."

Her lips immediately curved. "It's not, and I'm making a muddle of this, so before I make everything completely muddled, allow me to simply say this. You called yourself a man, but you're mistaken, because what I've just realized is that you're a gentleman in every sense of the word, and you should refer to yourself as that from this point forward."

"I've never claimed to be a gentleman because I'm lacking some basic gentlemanly manners."

"Just because you might be a little rough around the edges doesn't prevent you from being a gentleman, Mr. Chesterfield. The very idea that you refuse to accept money from a lady speaks volumes about your character, and know that I truly did not mean to offend you. That I apparently did so, whether unintentional or not, demands that I beg your pardon yet again."

Warmth began traveling up his neck to settle on his face, and unable to remember a time when anyone had made him blush, something that didn't seem very gentlemanly at all, Owen ducked his head and took to giving El Cid another scratch. "There's no need to apologize again, Miss Pierpont, although I can't help but wonder now if you actually know any gentlemen who'd take money from you?"

She opened her mouth, but before she could get more than an "Ah" out, Mr. Timken walked through the door of the Pullman car, the butler having made it a habit never to leave Camilla alone in Owen's company for more than ten minutes.

"Were you aware that Bernadette has set herself up with a makeshift business endeavor on this train?" was the first thing to come out of Mr. Timken's mouth as he took a seat, a distinctly disgruntled expression on his face.

"Lottie mentioned something about Bernadette styling a passenger's hair a few hours ago," Camilla returned. "However, I wasn't aware she charged that lady for her services."

"She didn't, but Bernadette apparently did such a good job with the chignon that other passengers began clamoring for her services. Evidently being a woman who can't pass up an opportunity to earn some extra money when it all but lands in her lap, Bernadette started charging fifty cents a style, increasing that amount if a lady wanted something more complicated than a chignon."

"And you're disgruntled because you disapprove of Bernadette's entrepreneurial spirit?" Camilla asked.

"She's being paid a very nice wage to attend to you, not every other lady on this train."

"I don't need any attending to right now," Camilla pointed out.

"It's the principle of the matter," Mr. Timken grumbled. "But enough about Bernadette. She's enough to give me an ulcer." He nodded to Camilla's notepad. "Have you developed a plan for Luella yet?"

"Unfortunately no, because Mr. Chesterfield has been somewhat sketchy with details regarding what Luella can do pertaining to feminine arts. He has, however, told me that his country house has a ballroom, and he believes Luella may know how to waltz. I also think we may have access to a piano, although I'm not sure about that since Luella set a dog to howling when she last used it." She returned her attention to Owen. "Speaking of waltzing, you haven't mentioned if you're capable of competently taking a few turns around a floor."

"And you need to know that because . . . ?"

"Luella will need a partner."

"I thought *you'd* partner her."

"I'll certainly show her some steps, but if we have access to your piano, I'll be the one playing it. I'll also need to observe her from afar to be able to assess her skills. I'm sure you'll agree that the last thing we want is to arrive at that ball she's determined to attend and have her stumble about on the dance floor."

"I know how to waltz, although I've never been light on my feet, probably because of my size. Luella knows this, and I can guarantee that she'll balk at the idea of practicing with me."

"Perhaps we'll need to address that lightness-of-foot issue of yours while we're in the ballroom."

"I don't recall mentioning that I longed to resolve that issue."

"I can spot an unspoken cry for assistance a mile away," she said before she turned to Mr. Timken. "It seems I may need you on this trip for more than assuming the role of my chaperone, especially when you were the best dance instructor I ever had—unofficially, of course."

Mr. Timken settled back against the seat. "And while I would adore stepping into the role of dance instructor, my chaperoning duties must take precedence over everything else."

To Owen's surprise, Camilla rolled her eyes. "Should I assume that ridiculous response is a sign that you're still put out with me?"

"A proper butler never becomes put out with his employer."

Camilla's lips twitched before she turned to Owen. "Contrary to what you must be thinking, Mr. Timken is actually the most proper of butlers. However, because he practically raised me, I tend to share a more familiar relationship with him than most people share with members of their staff, hence the reason he doesn't hesitate to speak his mind with me."

"I was wondering about that," Owen admitted.

"Well, wonder no more, but may I assume your butler doesn't share his opinions with you?"

"I don't employ a butler, but any of the butlers I've encountered over the years when I visit business associates don't seem quite so . . . opinionated."

"A direct result of Mr. Timken, as I said, having a very large hand in raising me."

"I would think your parents were responsible for that."

Camilla shook her head. "Parents within the Four Hundred have relatively little to do with their children, Mr. Chesterfield. They hire nannies and governesses to mind their offspring. However, after Mr. Timken caught one of my governesses reading to me in a monotone voice, he took over that job and read to me every night, even changing his voice for every character. He then took it upon himself to teach me things like how to swim or how to sail my toy boat in the small lake at Central Park. He also decided he would be the one to practice my dance steps with me after my dance instructors left for the day because he's more than light on his feet."

"And it gave us uninterrupted time to talk about each other's day," Mr. Timken added, settling a warm smile on Camilla, which she didn't hesitate to return.

Owen moved El Cid, who was currently in the process of trying to sharpen his claws against Owen's leg, to the seat beside him, garnering a disdainful look in the process, before he returned his attention to Camilla, taking a moment to consider everything she *hadn't* said.

It didn't take a genius to realize that, while she'd grown up in the lap of luxury, her life might have been a lonely one except for the fact that the family butler had stepped in to spend his time with a little girl who most people would have envied, but a little girl who'd obviously relished the attention she'd received, not from her family, but from a member of their staff.

"I've been trying to get Mr. Timken to allow me to call him Uncle Thaddeous, or at least Uncle Timken, for years," Camilla said, pulling Owen from his thoughts. "He, of course, has flatly refused to allow me to address him as anything other than Mr. Timken, but I'll eventually wear him down."

"You won't," Mr. Timken said.

"Of course I will," Camilla replied. "But before you argue with that, allow me to return the conversation to the topic of you assisting with some dance instruction. Will you help me?"

"It depends."

"On what?"

"I would think that's obvious."

"Think again."

Mr. Timken shifted on the seat. "Oh very well, since I'm certain you're soon going to turn tenacious about the matter, to put it plainly, I'll agree to assist you if you'll tell me exactly why you made the rash decision to travel to Wheeling."

"I would think that obvious."

"And as you just told me—think again."

Camilla turned to Owen. "If you haven't realized this, there are occasional drawbacks to sharing such a close relationship with a member of your staff."

"Something you and I can agree upon since Mrs. O'Connel, our part-time housekeeper, once boxed my ears when I was ten after learning I'd snuck out of Sunday services to go fishing with my friends." Owen shook his head. "Because she'd known me since birth, she felt it was her place to make sure I never did that again."

Camilla's lips curved. "And did you?"

"Mrs. O'Connel has hands the size of meat cleavers. Of course I didn't."

Mr. Timken cleared his throat. "While learning your housekeeper has meat cleavers for hands is rather unsettling, if we may return to the topic at hand—that being why we're trundling ever closer to Wheeling." He arched a brow Camilla's way, to which she responded by lifting her chin.

"I already told you why we're going, because, did I or did I not mention that Lottie broached the matter of Victor Malvado, which left us wondering if perhaps she, not I, was the target of yesterday's abduction?"

"You did mention that," Mr. Timken admitted.

"Well, there you have it," Camilla said. "I thought it best to remove Lottie and myself from New York until the Accounting Firm has time to investigate the matter. And, besides that, Mr. Chesterfield did rescue me, and I might have decided it would be churlish to refuse him his small request."

"There's nothing small about what he's asked you to do, and while those sound like perfectly legitimate reasons for your decision, you should know that Bernadette told me you received a telegram, one you didn't mention a word about to me."

"I really should think about firing that woman because she's a bit loose with information," Camilla grumbled. "However, that telegram was simply from Gideon."

"What did he say?"

"He's returning from England in three weeks."

"Is that all he said?"

"It was a telegram. How much more could he have said?"

Mr. Timken crossed his arms over his chest. "The telegram I received from your father before we left the Hudson said quite a bit—most of it centered around the notion that he wanted you to remain in the house on the Hudson and await his arrival." He sent Camilla a knowing look. "Clearly that's not what you did, and since I'm now a collaborator in your flight from New York, I'm sure I'll soon find my position terminated and my elderly self cast out on the streets."

Camilla smiled. "Perhaps you, quite like Bernadette, have missed your calling on the stage, because that was drama at its finest. But you know Father isn't going to send you packing since he's well aware that I've occasionally disregarded his requests when I feel he's being unreasonable."

"The only time you've ever felt your father was being unreasonable was when you got yourself involved with Lord Shrewsbury."

"I prefer not to speak about that dreadful man."

"I'm sure you don't, but . . ." Mr. Timken's brow furrowed. "Didn't you just say Gideon's in England?"

"Ah . . ."

Mr. Timken sat forward. "I think I now understand exactly why we've made a mad dash from New York. Gideon sent you something about that scourge of a man who presents himself to the world as a noble aristocrat, didn't he?"

"Perhaps," Camilla murmured.

It was a one-word response that spoke volumes.

Before Owen could ask who the scourge was, or ask if this scourge was the real reason behind Camilla's decision to travel to Wheeling, the train began to slow and then squealed to a stop.

Ten minutes later, and after he'd gone about the tricky business of getting El Cid into his traveling basket, something the cat clearly didn't like since he'd immediately begun to hiss, Owen told Camilla, who was standing on the train platform, holding fast to Gladys's leash, to wait for him there until he could ascertain that their transportation was ready.

Stepping from the platform, with El Cid now yowling somewhat forlornly from the safe confines of his basket, Owen grinned when he caught sight of Edward Stevens, a manager at Chesterfield Nail Manufacturing, but more importantly, his best friend since primary school.

"I knew you'd be here," Owen said, covering the distance that separated them before shaking Edward's hand.

Edward gave him a clap on the back. "How could I not be here after you sent that telegram asking me to make arrangements for guests of yours?" He leaned closer. "You never have guests, nor have you ever asked me to arrange for security. Care to explain what's going on?"

Owen shifted El Cid's basket to his other hand and tried to ignore that the cat was now yowling in earnest. "I suppose *guests* isn't the proper way to describe them because they're more along the lines of a solution to Luella's situation, or at least one of them is—Miss Camilla Pierpont. The other people in her party are what one might consider her entourage." He glanced back to the platform, where Camilla was standing beside Mr. Timken. "That's Miss Pierpont over there."

Edward's gaze shifted to the platform, his eyes widening a second later. "That's some solution to Luella's situation, but where did you find her, and exactly how could a lady like that be a solution to Luella's current dilemma?"

"Miss Pierpont enjoys the reputation of being capable of rehabilitating young ladies with unfortunate reputations."

"She's a teacher?"

"Not exactly. She's a member of what the fancy folks in New

York City call the Four Hundred, as well as considered one of the most fashionable upper-crust ladies to ever grace the social scene there."

Edward's brows drew together. "And she agreed to travel to Wheeling to help out a girl she's never met before?"

"She apparently suffers from boredom on a frequent basis."

"Helping Luella will certainly put an end to that, but . . ." Edward caught Owen's eye. "Dare I hope that Miss Pierpont isn't simply here to help with Luella, but, perhaps, has agreed to take on such a daunting task because the two of you have formed an . . . attachment?"

Owen brushed that aside. "Please. A lady like Miss Pierpont would never be content with a man like me. She's practically royalty where she's from, and I'm merely a man who doesn't have a way with the ladies, as was proven recently by the trouble I encountered with Curtistine Longerbeam and Pauline Zavolta, two ladies who haven't been shy about telling everyone what an idiot I am."

"They're only telling everyone that because they were hoping to become Mrs. Owen Chesterfield and you weren't as keen as they were to see that come to fruition."

"I wasn't keen because I had no idea marriage was even on the table with either of them."

"An experience I'm sure won't happen again because it's happened to you twice now."

"I'm thinking it might be for the best if I simply avoid ladies for the foreseeable future," Owen admitted as Gladys suddenly began yipping, drawing his attention. She surged into motion a second later, her long, spindly legs eating up the ground as she headed his way, dragging Camilla behind her.

Owen thrust El Cid's basket into Edward's hand and strode to intercept Gladys, snagging hold of her collar and pulling her to a stop, which earned him an injured look from the poodle and a smile of relief from Camilla.

"I've never seen her move so fast," Camilla said as Edward

walked up to join them, setting El Cid's basket down, which Gladys immediately began to nuzzle, causing El Cid to cease with the howling.

"And here I thought Gladys merely tolerated El Cid, but I may have been wrong about that," Camilla said before she turned her attention to Edward, smiled, then arched a brow Owen's way.

He fought a smile of his own. "It's amazing how proficient I'm becoming with deciphering your wiggling brows."

"My brows do not wiggle. They arch."

"It looks like wiggling to me, but since I doubt you want to engage in an argument right now, allow me to present Mr. Edward Stevens." He nodded to Edward, who was watching him with one of his brows quirked, although what that brow business was about was beyond him at the moment. "Edward, this is Miss Camilla Pierpont. Camilla, this is Mr. Edward Stevens, who manages Chesterfield Nails but has been a friend of mine for years."

Edward took hold of Camilla's gloved hand and pressed a kiss on it. "It's a pleasure to meet you, Miss Pierpont," Edward began. "Owen tells me you're here to assist Luella."

Camilla inclined her head. "It's delightful to meet you as well, Mr. Stevens, and yes, I am here on Luella's behalf, and hopefully, we'll enjoy some success with . . ." Her voice trailed off as if she wasn't certain how to phrase what she was hoping to enjoy success with.

"Transforming her from a ragamuffin into a polished, sophisticated young lady?" Edward finished for her.

Camilla arched another brow in Owen's direction. "I know you said your sister didn't embrace a fashionable attitude, but you didn't mention anything about a ragamuffin state, something that's completely different than being unfashionable."

"I would think ragamuffin and unfashionable are two peas in a pod."

"They're not, and given the wariness flickering through your eyes, you know they're not." She tilted her head. "Did you purposefully withhold the ragamuffin business because you were concerned I wouldn't agree to take your sister in hand?"

Owen rubbed a hand over his chin. "That thought may have crossed my mind, although I figured, after you were actually on the train bound for Wheeling, that you probably wouldn't throw yourself out of the train if I got around to admitting that Luella may have recently begun abandoning expected grooming, er, protocols."

"And yet, even though you thought I wouldn't throw myself off the train, you never said a word about any of this, so explain what grooming practices she may have abandoned."

It really was amazing how downright sparky Camilla's eyes could get.

He refused a wince. "Well, she seems to have an aversion to combs at times, and . . . perhaps an aversion to washing her face."

It was not an encouraging sign when an entire storm began brewing in Camilla's blue eyes, eyes he hadn't neglected to notice were rather compelling, but were now no longer sparky but flashing in a manner that suggested that the tempest currently brewing in them was just about to break.

Knowing any further delving into Luella's disregard for grooming habits in general was not going to endear him to Camilla—not that she seemed overly endeared by him in the first place, although she had sent him that lovely smile on the train—Owen was spared an attempt at changing the topic, which probably wouldn't have been successful anyways, when Bernadette strolled up to join them.

It came as no surprise when Camilla's lady's maid immediately settled her attention on Edward right before a commencing of lash fluttering began.

"You didn't mention a thing about a gentleman meeting us at the station," Bernadette murmured as she smiled at Edward, which earned her a bit of a sigh from Camilla.

Before Camilla could get anything but a sigh past her lips, though, Gladys suddenly bounded forward, yanking Camilla into motion, the poodle's attention focused on something across the train yard.

"I'll be back," she called over her shoulder, Owen moving to pursue her but stopping when he caught sight of Mr. Timken dashing across the train yard, dodging passengers left and right and finally catching up with Camilla when Gladys abruptly plopped to the ground, her tongue already lolling out. A second later, Camilla was handing poor Mr. Timken a handkerchief, which he promptly put to use to dab his forehead as Camilla did the same with a second handkerchief she pulled from her sleeve.

He couldn't help but wonder if that was normal, keeping so many handkerchiefs at the ready, and if it was, he also wondered if handkerchiefs might turn into a bit of an issue with Luella because she usually never had one available when she needed it, let alone several. Truth be told, he'd seen her wipe her forehead, and occasionally, her nose, with her sleeve, something he had a feeling Camilla was going to have a problem with.

"Seems like Gladys tuckered herself out," Bernadette said before she glanced Owen's way. "Gladys aside, though, I imagine you were probably getting ready to introduce me to your friend before we were interrupted with the peculiarities of Miss Pierpont's neurotic poodle."

It came as no surprise when Bernadette shifted her attention to Edward and the batting of lashes immediately commenced again. Knowing the only way to get past all the batting was to introduce Edward to a very unusual lady's maid, Owen turned to his friend. "Edward, allow me to present Miss Bernadette Millersport. Bernadette, this is a good friend of mine, Mr. Edward Stevens."

"Charmed, I'm sure," Bernadette said, extending her hand to Edward, a tinkle of laughter escaping her when he pressed a kiss to her fingers.

"Of course I'm charmed, Miss Millersport, and—" Edward suddenly stopped talking as his gaze drifted past Bernadette and settled on Lottie, who'd moseyed up to stand behind Bernadette. "Who's that?" Edward all but whispered, which was a rather unusual thing for him to do since he wasn't really a whispering type of gentleman.

The smile on Bernadette's face disappeared in a trice as she shot a look at Lottie, but it was back in place a second later when she returned her attention to Edward. "This is Lottie McBriar," she said. "She's Miss Pierpont's companion. Lottie, this is Mr. Edward Stevens."

Edward released Bernadette's hand and stepped toward Lottie, who was in the process of dipping into a curtsy.

Oddly enough, instead of acknowledging Lottie's curtsy with the obligatory bow, Edward merely stared at her, his mouth slightly agape, not saying a single word as what could only be described as a dazed expression settled on his face.

Before Owen had an opportunity to figure out how to snap Edward out of what appeared to be some type of stupor, Camilla glided up beside him, no longer tethered to Gladys, who'd apparently been remanded to Mr. Timken's care. Camilla's gaze drifted from Edward to Lottie, back to Edward, then to Bernadette, who now had her arms crossed over her chest, an honest-to-goodness scowl on her face.

Why Bernadette was scowling at his best friend was curious to say the least, but before he could contemplate that curiosity further, Camilla stepped closer to Edward and gave him, much to Owen's surprise, a soothing pat of her gloved hand.

"Mr. Stevens," Camilla began with a lovely smile, something that left Owen feeling somewhat dazed as well, although Edward didn't notice the smile since his attention was still riveted on Lottie, "now that you've made the acquaintance of everyone in our traveling party, except for Mr. Timken, my butler and stand-in chaperone, would you be so kind as to show us to the carriages we're to use, as well as perhaps assist us with moving our portmanteaus from the Pullman car to a wagon?"

Edward gave himself a bit of a shake, tore his gaze from Lottie, and turned to Camilla. "There's no need for you to concern yourself with your trunks, Miss Pierpont. I've already arranged a wagon for them, as well as brought men to help load and then unload everything once we reach Owen's home on Wheeling Island, then reload everything when you travel to his country home tomorrow."

"How wonderfully efficient of you, Mr. Stevens, but wouldn't it have been even more efficient if we went directly to the country house?"

"Owen wasn't certain what time you'd arrive in Wheeling, given the mechanical difficulties you experienced with the train. He sent me a telegram telling me everyone would spend tonight on the island because, while the country house is only about four miles out of Wheeling, the roads are somewhat questionable to traverse after dark."

"Perfectly understandable," Camilla said before she took hold of Edward's arm, another surprising move, and tugged him into motion, saying something to the effect that she'd be more than happy to assist him with arranging the logistics of the ride as she strolled away, but not before Owen could have sworn she sent him just a hint of a wink.

He was still pondering the wink ten minutes later as he found himself, not astride his stallion, George, who'd been unloaded five minutes before from the livestock car, but sitting on the seat of a carriage opposite Camilla, George having been tethered to the wagon that was now packed with trunks. Following that wagon was a carriage holding Bernadette, Lottie, Mr. Timken, and Edward, who seemed just as surprised as Owen had been that he was apparently going to escort them home.

Owen braced himself when Camilla sat forward and felt more than confused when he took note of a very unusual twinkle in her eyes.

"Tell me everything you know about Edward," she surprised him by saying.

"What?"

"Edward," she repeated. "What can you tell me about him?"

"You arranged for us to be in a carriage alone together so that you could ask me about Edward?"

Camilla frowned. "Why else would I have arranged our present circumstances?"

"I thought you wanted to press me further about Luella's questionable grooming practices."

"I think her aversion to combs told me all I needed to know about that." Her brows drew together. "You didn't realize I'd want to discuss Edward?"

"How could I have realized that?"

"I made a point of winking at you before I went off with Edward to assist with logistical arrangements."

"And I was supposed to know that wink meant . . . what exactly?"

She released a sigh. "That Edward's obviously smitten with Lottie, and that I was going to arrange matters so that he'd have an opportunity to spend additional time with her."

"You thought I'd glean all that from a wink?"

"It was an obvious wink."

"Not to me. But . . . you think Edward's smitten with Lottie?"

"I don't *think*, I *know*. But you didn't pick up on that?"

Owen raked a hand through his hair. "I might have thought he was acting somewhat peculiar, considering he stopped talking when he was introduced to Lottie, but I didn't take that as a sign he was besotted with her."

"Of course he's besotted with her. In fact, I think we just witnessed that whimsical love-at-first-sight scenario."

"That's only in fairy tales," Owen argued before he frowned. "However, your interest in Edward, Lottie, and a belief you just witnessed them falling in love suggests you now have matchmaking on your mind. To remind you, you've been quite vocal regarding your hanging up of your matchmaking hat, except for those two men you mentioned you were unofficially sponsoring."

"If you'll recall, I didn't mention that. Mr. Timken did." She smiled. "He finally revealed who his good authority was regarding that matter—Petunia Wetzel, Charles's mother." Camilla shook her head. "Petunia's been quite persistent with her desire to see her son married, interrogating me at every turn to see if I've made any progress finding Charles a suitable match."

"I don't imagine you appreciate being interrogated."

Camilla waved that aside. "It comes with the territory of being a matchmaker, but returning to Edward and Lottie." She leaned forward. "Surely after seeing the sparks fly between those two, you can't believe that I, a former—and need I add, very successful—matchmaker could ever ignore such a delightful opportunity, can you?"

"When you put it like that, probably not. Nevertheless, while I'll admit Edward was not himself during his introduction to Lottie, I didn't detect anything curious about Lottie's reaction to him, something that suggests you're mistaken about the love-at-first-sight scenario."

"I'm never wrong about affairs of the heart, and while Lottie's reaction could have been easily missed because it was very subtle, she blushed. Lottie isn't a lady prone to blushing."

"I definitely missed any blushing going on, but have you considered that her face was merely flushed due to all the steam that was filling the train yard?"

"She wasn't flushing, but blushing, and before you argue with that, know that I wasn't overheated in the least. If you've forgotten, I'd been standing out in the train yard longer than Lottie and had also taken a bit of a gallop around the yard with Gladys."

"I'm sure you had to have been a little overheated after your gallop."

She wrinkled her nose at him. "Must you argue with everything I say?"

He wrinkled his nose right back at her. "I wasn't arguing, merely pointing out the obvious. I noticed you were blotting your forehead after Gladys plopped to the ground."

She blinked. "Are you suggesting I was perspiring earlier because . . . I wasn't."

Owen opened his mouth, realized he was about to argue yet another point, and settled for sending her a quirk of a brow.

"I wasn't," she reiterated again.

"It's not a crime to perspire."

"It's considered a serious breach of etiquette for ladies, which is why I've taken steps to avoid perspiring in general, such as limiting myself to two dances in any given evening and always having numerous handkerchiefs at the ready." She lifted her chin. "With that settled—and no, I won't discuss perspiration further with you—allow me to return to Edward and Lottie, a match just waiting to happen if there ever was one."

"Not that I want to argue with you again . . ."

"But you're going to," she muttered.

"Well, quite, because I think you're conjuring up a romance where none exists. Edward and Lottie don't even know each other, nor do I imagine they have anything in common. Edward is a respectable man of business, as well as a man with a philanthropic heart, devoting his spare time to building schools for the underprivileged of Wheeling and the surrounding area. He also volunteers his services teaching in those schools. Lottie, on the other hand, is a former criminal."

"It's hardly gentlemanly of you to point that out."

"And if you'll recall, I told you I've never claimed to be a gentleman, but I don't see how pointing out the truth is wrong."

"You could have stated it differently instead of speaking so baldly."

"How could I have stated that Lottie's a criminal any differently?"

"You could have said that she suffered from an unfortunate past."

"That would have made it sound like she was beset by misfortune, not that she chose to become involved with members of the criminal persuasion."

"Lottie was never a true criminal because she didn't voluntarily work for Frank Fitzsimmons, and even if that hadn't been the case, can you claim to have never made a mistake?"

"Of course I can't, especially when it seems I've just made a grave mistake by stating that Lottie was a criminal."

He wasn't certain, but it seemed as if Camilla's lips twitched before she inclined her head. "It's nice to discover you're willing to admit that, just as I'm sure you're going to admit you're wrong about Lottie and Edward having nothing in common after I tell you that Lottie's father was a tutor and that she's always aspired to become a teacher."

"Are you going to get all prickly with me again if I don't admit I was wrong?"

"Are you going to realize that accusing me of being prickly probably isn't the best way to avoid me descending into that condition?"

"Ah, so you admit you can be prickly."

"I didn't admit anything of the sort."

"Your tone right now speaks volumes for you."

She drew in a breath, released it, then drew in another before she finally settled what looked to be a remarkably forced smile on him. "Why don't we simply agree to allow their romance to unfold without any interference from us, at least for now, and leave it at that?"

He was hard-pressed not to laugh. "If your 'for now' is equivalent to your you'll 'be back momentarily,' we probably have a different perception of how long 'for now' will end up being."

She smoothed a wrinkle from her skirt. "I suppose we could agree on an actual timeline, although, considering Edward didn't balk when I suggested he ride beside Lottie in their carriage, I may not need to interfere at all."

"Edward didn't balk because, for one, you told him Lottie's life might be at risk, which meant she needed a big, strong gentleman to keep her safe. You then made a point of telling him that Lottie is deathly afraid of heights and would surely be terrified to travel over the Suspension Bridge without someone familiar with that bridge sitting beside her, who could convince her that the cables wouldn't break and hence, she wouldn't plunge to a watery grave."

"I thought it spoke highly of Edward's character when he was more than willing to sit beside her in the carriage, even knowing she could very well take a death grip on his arm while traveling over the bridge. Those types of grips are notorious for leaving bruises, and yet he willingly offered to take the seat right next to her. He also assured her that even though he didn't fully comprehend why her life might be at risk, he was more than capable of protecting her."

"Edward's been shooting since he could walk, so he knows his way around a weapon, but . . ." Owen frowned. "It seemed to me that Lottie was rather surprised to learn she was terrified of heights."

"Was she?" Camilla asked before she turned her attention out the window. "Would you look at that? It's a department store."

"A less-than-subtle attempt to change the subject, but . . ." Owen looked out the window. "That's Stone and Thomas."

"I wasn't expecting Wheeling to have a department store."

"And while I understand my small city enjoys the reputation of being along the lines of a cow pasture, Wheeling is home to many successful industrialists who enjoy having convenient places to shop."

Camilla pulled her attention from the window and caught his eye. "Forgive me. I fear my words came out rather condescending, but I truly didn't mean to insult you or your town. I'm simply ignorant when it comes to West Virginia in general. From anything I've ever heard about your state—and yes, cow pastures have been mentioned—I never got the impression it was an up-and-coming city of any sophistication."

"There's no need to apologize, but to disabuse you of your misimpression of my city, allow me to point out some businesses on Market Street that will hopefully show why Wheeling is a city now worthy of the word *sophisticated*."

For the next few minutes, Owen directed Camilla's attention to theaters that housed operas, plays, and balls; Hancher Diamond store; Murchendorfer Stogie Factory; as well as a bakery that sold the most delectable pastries.

He then launched into a brief history of the Wheeling Suspension Bridge when the carriage turned onto it, smiling when Camilla pressed her nose against the glass to get a better look at what had been called a modern marvel of engineering.

"Is it my imagination or is the carriage swaying?" she asked right as El Cid started yowling, the yowls having Gladys, who'd been sleeping on the seat beside Camilla, opening one eye before she closed it again and went straight back to sleep.

Owen pulled El Cid's basket onto his lap, which earned him a hiss in return, suggesting the cat wasn't in the mood to be consoled. "The bridge sways because of how it's constructed, the cables moving whenever traffic is heavy, but there's no need to fear it's unsafe."

"Reassuring to know," Camilla said, returning her attention to the scene outside the window, silence settling over them except for the sound of the wheels clanking against the steel grates of the bridge.

Less than five minutes later, they were turning onto Zane Street, and a moment after that, the carriage pulled to a stop in front of his house.

Glancing out the window, his gaze traveled over his three-storied home. Built in a classical revival style, it was crafted from red brick and sported a full porch that spanned the entire length of the house that had clusters of fluted wooden columns set into the brick, a design feature that was a common sight on many of the houses on Wheeling Island.

He set El Cid's basket aside and stepped out of the carriage, extending his hand to Camilla. After helping her to the sidewalk, he called for Gladys, who refused to budge and tucked her head underneath her paw instead—until Camilla mentioned something about a treat, which had the poodle leaping out of the carriage, her pom tail wagging furiously as she turned hopeful poodle eyes on Camilla, who was now rummaging through her reticule, pulling out what seemed to be a piece of a biscuit.

"I'm not above bribery to get her moving," Camilla said, tossing the biscuit to Gladys, who snapped it out of the air.

Owen grinned. "Bribery appears to work."

"Of course it does, but it's rather embarrassing to have to resort to such tactics, as well as keep biscuits stuffed in my reticules, which can make a bit of a mess, something Bernadette complains about often." Camilla looped Gladys's leash around her hand before she directed her attention to his home. "This is yours?"

"It is."

"It's quite lovely, but . . ." She gestured to the front steps. "Why are those so steep?"

"Practicality," he said. "The foundations on most of the houses on the island are raised a half story before you reach the first floor because of potential flooding." He nodded to the house next to his, and then to one across the street. "When the river rises, our furnished floors don't get ruined, and we have drainage systems in place that allow us to get rid of the water that seeps into our basements just as soon as the river retreats."

"How clever," Camilla said as her gaze traveled over Zane Street, her brow furrowing a second later. "Forgive me, but I have to ask—is it an usual circumstance for people to walk pigs down this street?"

A sense of foreboding began crawling through him the second he directed his gaze to where Camilla was peering and caught sight of his sister, Luella, who was in the process of trying to haul a pig up Zane Street—and not just any pig but one that went by the name of Esmerelda, a menace to the world if there ever was one.

The foreboding turned to downright alarm when he noticed that the beautiful spring flowers that usually flanked the brick sidewalk leading up to his house were nowhere in sight. All that was left of them were a few stalks, and the ground where they'd once been planted looked as if something had been rooting around in it, searching out the bulbs.

His gaze darted to the Murchendorfers' house next door, his

alarm increasing when he noticed Mrs. Murchendorfer's flowers were mutilated as well.

His attention swung back to Esmerelda, although what she was doing on the island was a question in and of itself, but given the destruction he'd just noted, it was a foregone conclusion that the pig, one that was surly during its every waking hour and weighed almost three hundred pounds, had been on a bit of a rampage.

He moved closer to Camilla, wanting to get her into the house before Esmerelda got too close because the pig was questionable around people and downright nasty when it came to other animals, especially dogs.

Before he could take Camilla's arm, though, Gladys's fur stood on end, the dog having taken note of Esmerelda, who was now squealing in what could only be considered a menacing fashion. A mere heartbeat later, Esmerelda bolted forward and headed directly for Gladys, straining against the rope Luella was trying to hang on to.

Gladys didn't hesitate to turn and dash in the opposite direction, dragging Camilla behind her as she raced through the Murchendorfers' front yard, right as Esmerelda slipped from the rope restraining her.

As if sensing the approach of a now unrestrained pig, Gladys changed directions and dashed toward Owen's front porch, her abrupt about-face causing Camilla to launch forward, looking for the briefest of seconds as if she were flying through the air, quite like a kite, but one that was tethered to a frantic dog.

Unfortunately, the flying state wasn't meant to last, and in the span of a split second, Camilla plummeted to the ground, landing in what had once been a lovely garden of tulips but could now be considered more along the lines of a pigsty.

Ten

Considering she once again found herself in the most perplexing of predicaments, Camilla could no longer deny that her once-predictable life had taken a decidedly unexpected turn.

Not only had she been chased by would-be abductors, had raccoons rain down on her, took an unintentional dip in a river, agreed to assist a young lady who was apparently known as a ragamuffin secure a bit of polish, and been informed that Lord Shrewsbury was returning to the States, she now found herself face-down in what she was afraid might be manure.

It wasn't much of a stretch to realize that most of these events were a direct result of her becoming acquainted with Owen.

One would have thought, given the concerning direction her life was taking these days, that she'd want to put as much distance as she possibly could between herself and a man who'd introduced sheer chaos into her life, but oddly enough, that wasn't exactly the case.

For some reason, she found herself drawn to the man, which was curious to say the least, because unlike every other gentleman of her acquaintance, except for Gideon, Owen seemed to spend a lot of his time disagreeing with her. He also didn't fawn over her, and certainly didn't attempt to impress her by lavishing compliments on her like most members of society did. Truth be told, the compliments he *thought* he was extending her were usually more like insults.

However, even though he frequently insulted her, the very idea that he had absolutely no interest in her fortune was remarkably refreshing, considering that the majority of gentlemen who'd tried to court her—Lord Shrewsbury included, of course—might have found her company pleasant but her fortune downright enticing.

Granted, there were occasions when Owen spoke his mind without a second thought, and left her itching to throttle the man, but even though he had the ability to aggravate her, there was something about him that she found ever so slightly . . . appealing.

It was an odd circumstance to be sure, and even curiouser was that she was contemplating his appeal while Gladys continued to strain against the leash because there seemed to be a mad pig on the loose.

The reminder of the pig sent Camilla flipping over on her back just as Gladys jerked the leash straight from her wrist, dashing away before Camilla could stop her.

"I'll get her," Camilla heard Lottie yell before she went rushing by, Edward following in her wake as Camilla pushed herself to a sitting position. Her hands immediately sunk into inch-deep muck, but any thoughts of muck disappeared straightaway when she realized that the pig was only five feet away from her and was releasing deep, guttural-sounding snorts.

"Is it rabid?" she managed to get out of a throat that was now somewhat constricted, due no doubt to the imminent threat of being attacked by a mad pig.

"She's not," Owen said, moving in front of her to shield her from the pig in question.

"She sounds like she is."

"Esmerelda always sounds like that because she's a menace with a questionable disposition."

"Don't your neighbors have an issue living on the same street as a menacing pig?"

"I'm sure they would if Esmerelda lived on the island. She doesn't, which is why I'm a little confused what she's doing here now."

He turned his attention to a young lady plastered in mud, who was currently struggling to tie a rope around Esmerelda, who evidently didn't want the rope tied around her since she'd grabbed hold of it with her mouth and was shaking it back and forth, causing the lady to wobble about. "Care to explain why Esmerelda's here, Luella?"

It really came as no surprise that the mud-encrusted lady was Owen's sister, one who lifted her head and settled narrowed eyes on her brother. "You'll need to take that up with Meemaw."

"Meemaw's here?"

"She's inside. Making pies." Luella yanked the rope from the pig's mouth, looped it underneath an enormous stomach, took a second to knot the rope, then straightened. "We were expecting you back earlier."

"My train got delayed, but what are you doing here?"

"You'll have to ask Meemaw. It was her idea to come to the island, and no, I don't know why, nor do I know why she insisted we bring Esmerelda."

"There's no need to get testy. It was just a question."

Luella tossed one of her pigtails over her shoulder. "I've just spent the past hour running around the island, chasing a pig whose sole purpose in life is to create as much destruction as possible. Of course I'm testy. You know everyone on the island already thinks I'm some country bumpkin who is the very definition of unrefined. Scrambling down one street after another, trying to lasso a squealing pig, certainly didn't do anything to change that impression."

"I'm afraid you're probably right," Owen admitted. "Which is why I'm sure you're going to be relieved to learn that I've brought a solution home that should rectify everyone's less-than-favorable impression of you." He turned, winced when his gaze settled on Camilla, and blew out a breath. "I do beg your pardon, Miss Pierpont. I'm afraid I forgot for a moment that you're lingering about in all that mud."

He immediately offered her his hand, and she found herself pulled from the wreckage of someone's former garden a second later.

"I'm sure your forgetfulness was simply a result of an unexpected pig attack," she said, wiping her hands down the front of a traveling gown that was definitely not going to be salvageable.

"Is *she* the solution to my problem?" Luella asked, stepping closer as her gaze traveled over Camilla.

"She is, but before we get into any details regarding that—Luella, this is Miss Camilla Pierpont. Camilla, my sister, Miss Luella Chesterfield."

Even though, given the circumstances, it felt rather ridiculous to dip into a curtsy, that's exactly what Camilla decided to do, since she was, after all, there to take Luella in hand and teach her a few manners. "It's delightful to meet you, Miss Chesterfield. Your brother's told me a lot about you."

Instead of dipping into a curtsy of her own, Luella thrust her hand Camilla's way. Not wanting to be rude, Camilla soon found her hand clasped in a firm grip, then shaken exactly twice, which was, surprisingly, the proper way to shake a hand—well, at least amongst gentlemen. Luella then took a step back, wiped her muddy hand, some of the mud having been transferred to her from Camilla's mud-drenched glove, down the front of a dress that resembled a potato sack, and smiled, something that lit up her face and had Camilla realizing that Luella Chesterfield, underneath all the mud, was an incredibly beautiful young lady, a tidbit Owen had neglected to mention.

A sense of anticipation began swirling through her as she mentally redressed Luella in a fashionable gown, removed her hair from pigtails and into an elaborate chignon, and cleaned the mud from a face that was downright arresting, complete with blue eyes that were rimmed with extremely long lashes.

"How much did you have to pay her to be the solution to my problem?" Luella asked, settling a scowl on her brother.

Owen scowled right back at her. "Just because you're in a testy frame of mind doesn't give you an excuse for rudeness, brat."

"Calling me a brat is hardly likely to cause my testiness to abate, and it's not rude, but a legitimate question because you had to fork out a small fortune to get me enrolled in that fancy finishing school, and we both know how well that didn't turn out. I'd hate for you to have yet another dismal return on an investment, something that's a distinct possibility with this latest solution of yours."

"I'm not paying Miss Pierpont anything."

Luella's gaze suddenly shot to the wagon piled high with portmanteaus before she returned her attention to her brother. "There's an awful lot of trunks over there, which suggests Miss Pierpont is here for an extended, or perhaps even permanent, stay."

"She's a lady who merely enjoys numerous wardrobe changes a day."

"A ready response if there ever was one, and one that seems rather practiced, so . . . what are you hiding from me?"

"I'm not hiding anything."

Luella tapped a finger against her chin, then stilled as her eyes widened. "Oh my word, you've evidently taken Mother's last letter to heart and decided to fix my problem, as well as appease her greatest desire, by getting yourself one of those mail-order brides, which then means—you've clearly lost your mind."

"My mind is fine, and I don't recall Mother even mentioning a mail-order bride in her last letter."

"She didn't," Luella returned. "But she did strongly suggest you procure a bride in the near future because she knows the house on the hill will never get properly furnished until you get married. She obviously thinks it needs a lady's touch, and clearly doesn't believe I'm qualified to pick out a few couches and chairs."

"I'm hardly likely to make the monumental decision to get married simply because Mother is concerned the house she insisted on building before she left for Paris lacks furnishings," Owen muttered.

"But you *would* contemplate marriage if you thought that state would have Mother returning home, and"—Luella held up a muddy hand when Owen opened his mouth—"before you argue with that, having Mother return to the States would allow you to relinquish your guardianship of me, and bringing home a bride would also serve the purpose of having all the talk surrounding me fading into the background because everyone would become all but rabid in their quest to ferret out the juicy details regarding why you decided to marry a lady who isn't local."

"As you very well know, local ladies seem to find me vastly unpleasant, but that unfortunate state certainly wouldn't cause me to look into securing a wife through the mail." Owen shot a look at Camilla. "And, just as an aside, I wouldn't even know how to go about procuring one of those."

"I didn't know you could order a bride through the mail," Camilla admitted right as the thought struck that her day, instead of returning to any semblance of normalcy, was becoming downright peculiar. "Nevertheless, before we find ourselves engaged in a conversation revolving around what a person can actually purchase through the mail, perhaps I should explain what I'm doing here to Luella since that might expediate the matter, as well as discourage any other outlandish ideas she may soon form about me."

Luella gave her nose another scratch. "Since you're not a mail-order bride, I was thinking you might have arranged one of those marriages of convenience with Owen."

"You clearly have quite the imagination, Miss Chesterfield, but no, and to be clear, I don't have any intentions of marrying your brother. I'm merely here at your brother's request to aid you with your Stanley situation."

Luella took to fiddling with one of her braids before she smiled.

"Ah, I see. You must owe him a favor, since it's not exactly common for an instructor to not get paid, especially when you must be aware of the fact that the Chesterfield family is loaded."

"I am aware that your family is wealthy—*loaded* being a word that a lady would never use—and while we're on the topic of acceptable things to say to people, it's never permissible for a lady to state how much money her family possesses."

Luella crossed her arms over her chest. "We Chesterfields believe in speaking bluntly."

"You also, at least in your case, believe in breaking gentlemen's noses, but that doesn't mean it's acceptable behavior. Curtailing your tongue, as well as your fists, is going to be a must if you expect anyone to believe you're capable of becoming a lady of refinement."

"Then I guess it's a good thing I've changed my mind about that."

Camilla stole a glance at Owen, who was now rubbing his temple, quite as if he were developing a headache.

"You no longer want to become proper so that you can attend that ball come June?" he asked.

"Why bother?" Luella shot back. "It's not like anyone will believe I've changed, especially after Martha Wellington and Clarice Colleens, two of my dearest friends until two days ago, asked Stanley, along with three of his friends, to accompany them on a picnic up to McGovern Pond—where my former friends knew I was going to be swimming."

"And they're your former friends because they should have known you wouldn't want to see Stanley again?" Owen asked.

"They're no longer my friends because I think Martha might have her eye on Stanley now that I'm no longer in the picture. And before you ask if that bothers me, no, but what does bother me is that they knew I'd be swimming in the pond because I'd asked them to join me, but they told me they had other plans—plans that I now know revolved around mortifying me."

"Should I ask what happened?"

"Since talk is rampant regarding yet another Luella incident, you're certain to hear about it, so I might as well 'fess up." Luella drew in a breath. "Since I was alone—well, except for Esmerelda, who always seems to know when I'm off to swim and followed me—I saw no reason to swim in a bathing costume because, again, I was alone. Imagine my dismay when a mere ten minutes after I shucked off my clothing, Martha, Clarice, Stanley, and his friends showed up."

Camilla raised a hand to her throat. "You were . . . naked?"

"Close enough," Luella admitted. "Not that anyone saw anything because I stayed underneath the water, and then Esmerelda did me the very large favor of running everyone off about five minutes after I was discovered because she prefers lounging in the pond in silence, something all the laughter coming from everyone disrupted."

Camilla drew herself up. "Are you telling me that Stanley and his friends didn't immediately beg your pardon and take their leave the second they realized you were inappropriately attired in the pond?"

"That's exactly what I'm saying, and not only didn't they leave until Esmerelda chased them off, but they also then spread the story around Wheeling. That right there is why I won't be attending any balls in the near or distant future since I have no intention of setting myself up as a source of continuous amusement amongst the local set. It's also why I didn't want to accompany Meemaw to the island this morning, and you can bet your last dollar that I'll never come here again, not when I'm sure everyone will be all aflutter to spread the tale about me running down Zane Street trying to lasso a crazy pig. I think it'll be best all around if I just retreat to Meemaw's cabin forever."

"You can't spend the rest of your life hiding out with Meemaw," Owen pointed out.

"I don't see why not. I adore Meemaw."

Camilla cleared her throat. "Forgive me for interrupting, but I find I'm having a difficult time following the conversation as I don't know who this Meemaw is."

Luella and Owen exchanged a look before Luella frowned. "She's our grandmother."

"Your grandmother's name is Meemaw?" Camilla asked.

"Of course not. It's Beulah."

"Then why do you call her Meemaw?"

It was rather telling when Luella took to looking at her as if she were some unknown creature from another land before she shrugged. "Since you've evidently never heard the name *meemaw* before, know that everyone in these parts calls their grandmother that—well, except for the Murchendorfers, who've turned all hoity-toity and are now calling their meemaw *Grandmother*, although I have heard Sally slip a few times and call her Granny." Her lips curved. "Sally would be appalled to learn that Meemaw has always refused to allow any of her grandchildren to address her as Granny because she says Granny evokes images of old ladies wearing square spectacles and smoking pipes."

Owen leaned closer to Camilla. "Just so you know, Meemaw doesn't smoke a pipe, but our great-aunt Elma has been known to do so upon occasion."

Camilla blinked. "Great-Aunt Elma sounds, ah, well, delightful."

"Not a word anyone ever uses to describe her."

Before Camilla could do more than blink again, Gladys gamboled into view, dragging Edward behind her as Lottie jogged by his side.

A split second later, Esmerelda stopped chewing what seemed to be a tulip stalk and released a squeal that left the hair on the back of Camilla's neck standing at attention.

"Esmerelda, no!" Luella yelled as the pig surged into motion, tearing the rope from Luella's grasp as she charged straight for Gladys, who was now frozen in place, evidently too terrified to move.

Time seemed to slow down until a blur of black fur whizzed past Camilla, El Cid having apparently managed to escape the confines of his traveling basket.

In the span of a heartbeat, the cat was in front of Esmerelda, back arched and fur standing on end, hissing up a storm right before he raised a paw and swatted the pig right across the snout, earning a squeal of outrage in return.

Eleven

For the briefest of seconds, Camilla braced herself for the worst, until she realized that Esmerelda was not preparing for an imminent battle.

Instead, the pig was simply standing still as a statue in the middle of the road, her little piggy eyes fixated on El Cid, who was now spitting as well as hissing as he held his ground in front of Gladys, clearly having appointed himself her protector. A bit of a snuffle escaped the pig before she dropped her head and lumbered her way over to the Murchendorfers' destroyed flower garden, plopping onto her stomach and dropping her pink head in between her front hooves.

"What in the world has that beast of a cat done to my darling Esmerelda?"

Glancing over her shoulder, Camilla discovered an older lady striding from Owen's house, her gray hair pulled into a messy bun, wearing an apron over a faded blue dress that ended above her ankles, revealing sturdy black boots that were similar to ones Camilla had seen her gardeners wearing.

"I think a more important question, Meemaw, would be how Esmerelda was able to wreak havoc on the entire neighborhood," Owen countered.

Meemaw shot a glance at Esmerelda, who was still lying in the Murchendorfers' decimated flower bed, then took a moment to look up and down the street, wincing a second later.

"Looks like my darling must have gotten through the back fence somehow, although I know I didn't leave the gate open, what with how Esmerelda's been known to wander."

"Knowing your pig, she probably gnawed her way through the fence," Owen said before he walked over to his grandmother and placed a kiss on her cheek. "The question of the hour, though, is why she's here in the first place, or for that matter, why you're here. You haven't come to the island since Mother and Father left town."

"I needed to make a statement."

"And that statement involved bringing your pig?"

"'Course it did." Meemaw nodded to the Murchendorfer house. "Ada Mae was rude to Luella and had me realizing she needed to be reminded of her roots. She seems to have forgotten she was raised on a farm, played in the mud with your father when they were children, and used to take great enjoyment minding the pigs her father kept." Meemaw began wiping her hands on her apron. "These days, Ada Mae's turned far too pretentious for my tastes. After she didn't invite Luella to Stanley's homecoming tea, and then didn't reprimand him for having the audacity to tell his once-dear friend that she wasn't good enough for the likes of him, my tolerance for idiocy came to a rapid end."

"You never have tolerance for idiocy," Owen pointed out.

"Too right I don't." Meemaw drew herself up. "I hesitated to get involved in the matter, though, knowing how these matters can escalate and turn troublesome. However, after Luella told me about the pond debacle, and that Stanley, with all his talk about refined airs, didn't have the decency to remove himself and his friends from her vicinity once he realized Luella was practically naked, I had no choice but to insert myself into what could very well turn into a repeat of the Hatfield–McCoy fracas."

"We are not going to get into that type of feud with the Murchendorfers, even if they have insulted the family," Owen argued.

"I don't know how else we can resolve the matter because it's doubtful Stanley or Ada Mae will apologize."

"We'll resolve it peacefully with the assistance of Miss Camilla Pierpont," Owen said, sending a nod Camilla's way.

Camilla immediately found herself under the unwavering stare of Meemaw, fighting the peculiar urge to fidget as the lady gave her a thorough perusal.

"Good heavens, dear, you look like you've literally been dragged through the mud."

"Truer words have never been spoken," Camilla said, glancing down at a gown that certainly no longer resembled the Parisian masterpiece she'd donned earlier. "And while I'm unaccustomed to meeting anyone's grandmother while drenched in substances that may not only be mud, I'm Miss Camilla Pierpont, as Owen mentioned, and you're apparently, ah . . . Meemaw?"

"Might be more comfortable for you to be calling me Mrs. Chesterfield, or Beulah would be fine, unless . . ." Beulah's gaze sharpened on Camilla. "If you're fixin' to marry my grandson, you might as well call me Meemaw from the start since that'll save you the bother of switchin' names after vows have been exchanged."

"Oh, I'm not planning on marrying your grandson," Camilla said. "I'm simply here to—"

The rest of her explanation got lost when a carriage came trundling down Zane Street, pulling to a stop in front of the Murchendorfer house. A second later, the door flung open, and a lady dressed in an afternoon gown of palest blue all but leapt to the ground.

It was quite telling that the lady hadn't waited for the groomsman to open the door for her, just as it was telling that the lady's face began to mottle the second she caught sight of Esmerelda lying in the midst of what Camilla assumed had once been a delightful flower garden.

The lady's nose shot into the air before she began advancing

Beulah's way. "I presume you have something to do with that pig in my yard, Mrs. Chesterfield?" the lady demanded.

Beulah didn't so much as bat an eye. "Don't be ridiculous, Ada Mae. I certainly couldn't have anticipated Esmerelda making her great escape from the backyard. Rest assured, your garden will be replanted by tomorrow evening, as will everyone else's in the neighborhood, so there's no need to take that snotty tone with me."

"I don't go by Ada Mae these days. It's simply Ada, although I prefer Mrs. Murchendorfer."

"You'll always be Ada Mae to me since I've known you since you were knee-high to a grasshopper," Beulah countered. "Why, I can remember clear as day how you used to steal into my kitchen with my Hiram after I put my pies up to cool, snitchin' pieces of it and gobblin' it down without botherin' to use a fork." Beulah took a step closer to Ada Mae. "Truth is, I have three of those pies in the oven as we speak, but unless you're plannin' on giving my Luella a proper apology for your unacceptable southern manners, because don't think word hasn't reached my ears about all the gossiping you've been doing of late, I won't be bringin' a pie to you ever again."

"Apology?" Ada Mae all but shrieked. "I have nothing to apologize for. Your granddaughter broke Stanley's nose, which proves I wasn't wrong in my assessment regarding her lack of refinement. Ladies, as even you know, do not physically assault anyone . . . ever."

"Stanley deserved that punch in the nose, and he knows it," Beulah didn't hesitate to say. "Frankly, he should be ashamed of himself for whining about it to his mama. A man should take a punch like he's a man, 'specially when he was due one, and 'specially when it was delivered by a girl."

"Due one?" Ada Mae scoffed. "Don't be ridiculous. All Stanley did was decide he no longer cared to continue any type of association with your unquestionably unrefined, and need I add violent, granddaughter. Besides that, it's not as if they were ever anything but the most casual of friends, which is exactly why I didn't invite her to the tea I hosted to celebrate Stanley's return from his grand tour."

"Stanley stood on the porch of my cabin a few years back and promised Luella that even though he was off for college, he would always return to her," Beulah countered.

"As a *friend*."

Beulah shrugged. "Sounded like he wanted more than friendship from where I was lurkin' behind the door, but even if he only meant he wanted to maintain a friendship with her, one doesn't treat a friend as shabbily as he's treated Luella." She narrowed an eye on Ada Mae. "Do you know that boy of yours had the audacity to come upon Luella whilst she was swimming in McGovern Pond? Instead of doing the proper thing, though, and leaving her alone, he, along with his insufferable friends, lingered about until Esmerelda went after him."

Ade Mae's nostrils flared. "Is that why you brought your pig to the island—to let it have another go at my son?"

"Wish I would have thought of that, but . . ." Beulah glanced at Esmerelda and tilted her head. "When *is* Stanley expected home?"

It wasn't exactly a surprise when Ade Mae began swelling on the spot.

"You will *not* set your pig on Stanley because it's hardly his fault your granddaughter made the poor decision to abandon all sense of decency when she decided to take a dip in the pond while being practically in the, ah, buff. Her apparent preference for swimming in that state is exactly why she's always forced to swim alone."

Camilla's temper, something that had begun to simmer the second Ada Mae had stomped over to join them, ratcheted up a notch. "It seems to me," she began, drawing Ada Mae's attention, "as if a few of Luella's lady friends frequently enjoyed swimming with her until you and your son took it upon yourselves to publicly humiliate her, which then resulted with the residents of Wheeling seeing Luella as fair game for their cruel remarks."

Ada Mae drew herself up. "Luella's unbecoming behavior is what caused her to become unpopular with the most prominent families in Wheeling. And not to be rude, but I have no idea who you are or why you're inserting yourself into this conversation."

Camilla drew herself up as well. "I get the distinct impression you might make a habit of accidental rudeness, Mrs. Murchendorfer, but before you attempt to argue with that, which might come across as intentional rudeness, I'm Miss Camilla Pierpont. And while it was certainly somewhat rude of me to insert myself into your conversation, I did so because I've been made privy to what transpired between you, your son, and dear Luella. I'm certainly not the type of lady who'll stand silently by and allow you to attempt to further besmirch Luella's character."

"I've never heard of any Pierponts before, which suggests you're not from a family of any standing around here," Ada Mae said before she looked her up and down, settling what was certainly a condescending smile on Camilla a moment later. "If I were to hazard a guess, I'd say, given your somewhat cultured tone of voice, that you're a decorum instructor, probably a former governess, brought here by Owen in a desperate attempt to teach his sister a few pointers in the etiquette department before she completely ruins what small amount of influence her family still retains in town."

Camilla squared her shoulders, but before she could get a single word of rebuke out of her mouth, Bernadette came stomping up to stand beside her, shaking her finger in Ada Mae's direction.

"Miss Pierpont is certainly no decorum instructor," Bernadette snapped. "She's the daughter of Hubert Pierpont, one of the wealthiest gentlemen in the country."

Ada Mae's nostrils flared. "And who are you to think I'm simply going to take what sounds like a completely ridiculous story as truth?"

Bernadette's nostrils flared right back at her. "I'm Bernadette Millersport, Miss Pierpont's lady's maid, which means I'm in the know about everything regarding the Pierpont family. If that's not enough to convince you, then I would hope that you, a lady who seems determined to put on some fancy airs, know that decorum instructors don't have the means to hire maids, nor do they belong to the New York Four Hundred, which Miss Pierpont most certainly does. Truth be told, she's a leader amongst the upper crust in New York, a very exclusive group of the wealthiest and most proper families in the country." Bernadette drew in a breath of apparently much-needed air. "Besides all that, know that the traveling gown she's wearing is from Worth—as in the Parisian Charles Worth—and that single gown costs more than any decorum instructor would make in a year."

Ada Mae's mouth dropped open for the briefest of seconds before she sent Bernadette a scowl and then arched a delicate brow Camilla's way. "What's a member of the New York Four Hundred doing associating with a family of ne'er-do-wells?"

Camilla's temper intensified to boiling, which made thinking a little tricky as she took a step toward Ada Mae, who immediately took a step backward. "You forget yourself, Mrs. Murchendorfer, because the Chesterfields are a family I'm proud to be associated with and most certainly aren't ne'er-do-wells. As for what I'm doing here, Mr. Owen Chesterfield invited me to travel to Wheeling to become better acquainted with his beloved grandmother, as is only proper."

"Why on earth would that be proper?"

Camilla arched a brow. "I would think that's obvious, but since it's apparently not, the rules of etiquette demand that introductions be made to the matriarch of a given family before any formal announcement is made."

"Formal announcement?" Ada Mae repeated.

"Indeed, and one of the matrimonial variety, if that's in question."

Ada Mae blinked. "Surely you're not saying you're intending to marry Owen Chesterfield, are you?"

"That, my dear Mrs. Murchendorfer, is *exactly* what I'm saying."

Twelve

During the hour and a half that had passed since Camilla dropped the unexpected revelation that she was apparently almost engaged to him, Owen had found himself chuckling more than a few times, earning concerned looks from Meemaw and Luella in the process, as if they'd never taken note of him chuckling before.

Even his gardener, whom he'd been helping repair the back fence that Esmerelda had chewed her way through, had been looking at him oddly, and had moved to another section of the fence at one point, quite as if he'd wanted to put some distance between them because he was seemingly of the belief that Owen had lost his mind.

Frankly, Owen couldn't pinpoint exactly what he found so amusing, other than the fact that Camilla, as she'd risen to his family's defense in a most magnificent fashion, had obviously been just as astonished by her pronouncement as everyone else had been, given the way her eyes had widened ever so slightly.

Other than that, though, she'd not given Ada Mae a single reason to question what had obviously been a spur-of-the-moment declaration, instead merely lifting her chin and sending his neighbor a glacial glare before she'd turned on her heel and glided into his house.

It had been a most impressive departure if he'd ever seen one, even with Camilla covered in mud and trailed by El Cid, Gladys, and Esmerelda, who seemed, oddly enough, enamored with El Cid. Meemaw's pig was even now waiting outside the back door, snuffling through the screen and releasing forlorn-sounding snorts, probably because El Cid was nowhere to be found, having followed Camilla as she'd repaired to the second-floor bedroom Meemaw had assigned her, telling Owen she'd be back directly after she freshened up.

Being back directly, at least in Camilla's case, evidently took over an hour and a half, but as she'd certainly had a trying day and was probably now aghast about the whole imminent announcement she'd told Ada Mae was in the works, Owen couldn't blame her for taking all the time she needed to think through the intricate details pertaining to their impending betrothal.

He was beyond curious how she was going to handle a situation she'd created, and all because she'd obviously allowed her temper, something she continuously denied she possessed, get the better of her.

From his perspective, she had two options—she could race back to New York and pretend she'd never met him, or . . . she could continue with what was a rather unprecedented charade, which, if that was her choice, suggested that the Lord Something-or-Other she'd briefly mentioned, but hadn't expanded on, might really be the main reason she'd changed her mind about helping Luella in the first place.

"I apologize for my lengthy absence," the object of his thoughts said as she breezed into the room, looking resplendent in a gown of palest green, her blond hair swept up on top of her head and sporting not a single smidgen of dirt anywhere, the pinkness of her cheeks suggesting she'd lingered in the tub for quite some time.

"There's no need to apologize because I just got back from fixing the fence," Owen said as Camilla settled herself on a chaise done up in a floral chintz, one his mother had purchased when her Wheeling friends had decided flowers were all the rage some five years before.

He'd always found the floral motif a little fussy, but since his mother was no longer in town to redecorate and his grandmother had no interest in furnishing trends, that idea reinforced by the fact she'd had the same furniture in her cabin for the past forty years, and Luella had always seemed indifferent to what the interior of the house looked like, he'd not bothered to change the décor.

Camilla stopped rearranging the folds of her skirt and lifted her head. "You fixed the fence?"

"Esmerelda did quite a bit of damage, and we only keep one gardener on the island, Mr. Bannock. I wanted to lend him some assistance before Esmerelda had an opportunity to make another great escape."

"You know that's not the only reason you helped," Luella said, strolling into the room, her wet hair trailing down her back and wearing a dress Owen was relatively sure had been Meemaw's at some point. "Mr. Bannock only has one good hand, which would have made it tricky for him to fix a fence whether there was a time challenge or not."

"You have a one-handed gardener?" Camilla asked.

"Most of our help have physical limitations in one form or another," Luella said, sitting down on a chair sprinkled with bright pink flowers woven into the fabric. "Owen makes a point to hire men who've been hurt in mining and factory accidents, which, unfortunately, this area sees far too often." She reached down and gave El Cid, who'd followed Camilla into the room and was now rubbing against Luella's skirt, a pat. "Mr. Bannock's left hand was crushed in some machinery when he worked in a glassworks factory. He didn't lose the hand, but he's not capable of holding much with it."

"Owen also hired Johnny Nemeti, known as simply Nems, who lost a leg when there was an explosion at a coal mine up near

St. Clairsville, to drive our carriages," Meemaw said as she pushed a cart stacked with plates, cups, a coffee urn, and an apple pie into the room, Mr. Timken hovering directly behind her, as if he were itching to take over and assume his usual role of butler. "Nems was thrilled with the offer, although he grumbles a lot because we don't use our carriages often. He feels guilty about drawing a salary when he's not called upon to do much work."

"His services will undoubtedly be required more frequently now that Miss Pierpont's come to visit," Luella said before she quirked a brow at Camilla. "You are going to stay, aren't you, even after engaging in that contentious exchange, which I enjoyed tremendously, with Mrs. Murchendorfer?"

Camilla winced and turned to Owen. "I suppose there's really no choice *but* for me to stay, since I've complicated an already precarious situation. I've taken some time to consider the matter, Mr. Chesterfield, and we might be able to use what I can only call a lapse in sanity on my part to our advantage."

He smiled. "Don't you think, since we're evidently practically engaged, that you might want to start calling me Owen?"

Camilla's shoulders drooped just the slightest bit. "I suppose that's a practical suggestion, as I'm sure people would remark upon it if we maintained an air of formality between us. Nevertheless, before I say another word about a situation that's entirely my fault and how I'm going to go about resolving matters, allow me to apologize for placing you in what is certainly an unenviable position. I simply don't know what came over me that caused me to blurt out a forthcoming announcement."

"Why would you think finding myself almost engaged to you would be an unenviable position?"

"Because when we don't get married, people like Ada Mae will start spouting more nonsense about your family being ne'er-do-wells again, which will certainly be why they conclude I didn't go through with marrying you." She lifted her chin. "However, I've already figured out how to save your reputation."

"Shouldn't we be more concerned with your reputation?" Owen asked.

"Given my advanced age and the fact I'm from an esteemed family, I don't face as much censure as most ladies do. Besides that, there's little chance anyone in New York will hear even a whisper of what I've been up to in Wheeling."

"I can surely attest to the advantages of the advanced-age business," Meemaw said as she took hold of the coffeepot but paused instead of pouring out a cup. "After I reached seventy, I didn't bother to censor anything I wanted to say, and I have yet to have anyone reprimand me about any frank opinions I might voice."

"You've *never* censored your speech, even before you turned seventy," Owen argued. "And the reason no one reprimands you is because you're slightly terrifying."

"Only slightly?" Meemaw asked before she settled a quizzical eye on Camilla. "But returning to something you just said, how is it you're so certain we're not ne'er-do-wells? It's not as if you're overly familiar with the Chesterfield family."

"I don't need to be overly familiar with any of you to conclude that, especially after your grandson didn't hesitate to rush to my rescue when I was under attack by armed men who probably wanted to abduct me. A ne'er-do-well would have never bothered becoming involved, and . . ." She turned her attention to Luella. "You challenged a fellow academy student to a duel because she was being cruel to another girl. A ne'er-do-well wouldn't have lifted a finger to help her, and . . ." She glanced at Meemaw. "You hauled a pig to Wheeling Island to make a point to a woman who's responsible for your granddaughter now finding herself ostracized from her long-time friends." She smiled. "It seems to me, and forgive me if I'm wrong, but if you were a ne'er-do-well, you would have hauled that shotgun that I'm almost positive you own to the island and threatened Ada Mae with that instead of a surly pig."

"I do own a shotgun," Meemaw admitted. "Five, in fact."

"And yet you didn't threaten Ada Mae with a single one of

those, proving she's completely off the mark about you and your family, something I'm already well aware of."

Meemaw set down the coffeepot, then all but thrust the cup she'd just poured into Mr. Timken's hand and gestured toward an empty chair, which Mr. Timken immediately lowered himself into, undeniably done so because Meemaw was wearing her *I-mean-business* look, before she poured two additional cups of coffee and strode over to the settee Camilla was sitting on.

She gave Camilla one of the cups, then took a seat beside her and swigged a hefty gulp of coffee, her eyes immediately taking to watering, probably because the coffee was hot, not that Meemaw admitted that. Instead, she settled her now-watery gaze on Camilla.

"I believe, before you continue with how you're going to use your upcoming pretend nuptials to my grandson to everyone's advantage," Meemaw began, "you should explain exactly how it came to be that you agreed to travel to Wheeling with my grandson in the first place."

Camilla took a dainty sip of coffee and set the cup on a small table directly beside her, after she scooted aside a porcelain figure of a cherub holding flowers in its hand, then drew in a breath before she launched into the particulars of what she admitted had been a very unsettling week.

As she spoke, Owen walked to the coffee cart and poured his sister a cup, then one for himself, Meemaw having apparently been far too anxious to hear Camilla's story to get her grandchildren settled with a beverage.

He stifled a grin when Mr. Timken sent him an apologetic grimace, the butler evidently a bit too terrified of Meemaw to get out of his seat and perform duties that had undoubtedly been instilled in him for decades.

Twenty minutes later, Camilla finished with "and even though, as I mentioned, I was skeptical I'd be of much use salvaging Luella's tarnished reputation, since she did break Stanley's nose, although I'm sure it was warranted, even if a lady should never lose her temper, I've now devised a plan that will most assuredly see Luella soon finding herself in high demand."

Meemaw sat forward. "And while I'm curious to hear this plan of yours, I feel compelled to point out that you, my dear Camilla, certainly lost your temper with Ada Mae, the result of which probably has a good portion of Wheeling already aflutter regarding your impending engagement to my grandson."

"I'm afraid you're right about that," Camilla agreed, "just as I'm sure my loss of temper would severely disappoint the decorum instructors I've had over the years, as well as send the headmistress of the ladies' academy I attended into a fit of the vapors." The corners of her lips curved. "I'll have you know that I was given an award from that headmistress for being considered the most poised and proper lady who'd ever attended that school, but I may need to consider returning that award after what just transpired with Ada Mae."

"At least you didn't assault her like I did with Stanley," Luella pointed out.

"I'd have to remove myself from the Four Hundred altogether if I ever did that."

Meemaw settled back against the settee. "I'm curious about this Four Hundred you've mentioned a time or two. What is that?"

"It's merely a name Mr. Ward McAllister, who's considered the social arbiter of New York high society, came up with to describe the most influential people who travel within the upper crust." Camilla smiled. "Rumor has it that the reason Ward settled on four hundred was because that's how many people can comfortably fit into Caroline Astor's ballroom in her brownstone on Fifth Avenue. Mrs. Astor, if you're unaware, has been considered the queen of high society for years."

"And where do you fit in with this Four Hundred?" Meemaw asked. "From what your lady's maid said, you're considered one of society's leaders."

"I won't deny that I hold considerable influence within society, but that's mainly because my parents are Knickerbockers, the name given to families who first settled in New Amsterdam, what New York City used to be called. However, before you ask, no, I won't ever be in the running to take Caroline Astor's place as *the* leader of the Four Hundred because I'm not married, nor do I ever intend to embrace that state."

"Why not?" Meemaw asked.

"It's a very long, very dramatic story, and right now we'd be better served discussing the plan I've come up with to salvage our current situation."

Meemaw snorted. "That was an impressive attempt to avoid telling me about the broken heart you're obviously suffering from."

"I don't have a broken heart."

"How encouraging to hear you've recovered from that unfortunate state, but you and I both know that at some point in time, a gentleman treated you shabbily, hence your decision to avoid marriage."

Camilla opened her mouth, then closed it again before she reached for her coffee, took an honest-to-goodness gulp of it, then smiled, although it seemed rather forced. "The state of my former love life isn't something I care to discuss—now or ever—and besides, it has nothing to do with the important matter we need to address, that being how we're going to handle my unintended proclamation of marital intentions." She settled her gaze on Owen. "I can't very well return to New York knowing people like Ada Mae are going to use our supposed broken engagement as further ammunition against you."

"I don't care what people say about me," Owen said.

"But you care about your family," Camilla countered. "That's why, after Luella becomes in high demand, we're going to make an announcement that Beulah has made the decision to *not* grant us her blessing."

Meemaw paused with her coffee cup halfway to her lips. "Why would I do that?"

"Because it'll put a rapid end to the farce I unintentionally put into motion when my temper may have gotten the better of me." Camilla smiled. "You admitted that you're not shy about voicing your opinion, so you'll proclaim that you cannot in good conscience support a union between your beloved grandson and a lady who is completely unsuited for him."

It was not a good sign when Meemaw's lips pursed, she narrowed her eyes on Camilla, and then she shook her head.

"I have no idea why you'd be opposed to withholding your blessing on what is merely a clever bit of fiction I conjured up after Ada Mae annoyed me," Camilla said, returning the whole narrowing-of-the-eye business Meemaw was still sending her way.

"I'm opposed because I'm not one for telling fibs," Meemaw shot back. "I'd have to spend a week on my knees, asking the Lord's forgiveness, if I were to proclaim I found you unsuitable for Owen, and my knees aren't what they used to be."

"It wouldn't be a fib because Owen and I *aren't* well-suited for each other."

"And to that I say hogwash," Meemaw countered. "You two are very well matched indeed."

"How could you have arrived at that conclusion when you just met me?"

Meemaw lifted her chin. "You didn't hesitate to rush to defend the honor of the Chesterfield family. That told me everything I need to know about you."

"No, it didn't."

"What else do you think I should know?"

Camilla crossed her arms over her chest. "Well, since you seem keen to embrace this nonsensical notion that Owen and I would make a wonderful match, allow me to simply say that, as a former matchmaker, I've spent years becoming adept at reading signs that lead to successful matches. Believe me when I tell you that I haven't met my match in Owen, and he certainly hasn't met his match in me."

"Why not?"

"I can't speak for your grandson, but I have, and frequently at that, not that this speaks highly of my character, felt an almost irresistible urge to throttle the man."

Meemaw's eyes began to gleam. "But that's wonderful."

"You find it wonderful that I want to inflict bodily harm on your grandson?" Camilla asked.

"It suggests the two of you could very well be experiencing that enemies-to-something-delightful scenario that authors often write into their romance stories."

"*You* read romance novels?"

"I read everything, dear, which has opened up my world and lent me invaluable insight into this troublesome condition we call being human."

"Owen and I aren't intertwined in a plot from a romance novel."

Meemaw turned to Mr. Timken, who was watching the exchange with lips that were definitely twitching. "You obviously know Camilla far better than I do. Care to express your opinion about her suitability for my Owen?"

"As Miss Pierpont's butler," Mr. Timken began, "I seldom, if ever, voice personal opinions, at least to anyone outside the family. That tends to tarnish the established formalities butlers are expected to adhere to."

"Ah, so you agree with me but are choosing to keep your thoughts close to your chest. A prudent move." Meemaw nodded to Owen. "I believe this is the point in the conversation where you convey to Camilla how wise I am, and that she should simply accept that I've decided the two of you will see your engagement through to a wedding. That will then allow both of you to experience those happily-ever-after moments that are also written about often in those books I enjoy."

Owen couldn't help himself—he laughed, sobering up when Meemaw leveled a glare on him. He cleared his throat. "Since Camilla just disclosed that she's dreamed about throttling me, and often at that, I think I'll adopt Mr. Timken's stance and keep my opinions to myself."

Evidently undaunted, Meemaw quirked a brow Luella's way. "What do you think about a match between Owen and Camilla?"

"I think it's somewhat thought-provoking that Camilla owned up to her desire to harm Owen, given that she's been raised to be a proper lady." With that, Luella rose to her feet, moved to the coffee cart, and began slicing up pieces of Meemaw's famous apple pie.

"I wouldn't say there's anything thought-provoking about my desire to occasionally throttle Owen," Camilla argued. "Especially not when he doesn't seem to have to put much effort into frequently exasperating me."

Luella slid a slice of pie onto a glass plate that had been crafted in one of the local glass factories before she nodded. "Owen does make it a habit of garnering irritation from the feminine set, that most recently seen when he procured the ire of Miss Curtistine Longerbeam."

"There's no need to revisit the Miss Longerbeam situation," Owen muttered.

Camilla leaned forward. "I disagree, since I'm now brimming with curiosity to hear all the gory details, but before we get to those—her name isn't truly Curtistine Longerbeam, is it?"

Owen pressed his fingers to a temple that was beginning to throb. "You only want to hear about Curtistine—and yes, that is her name—because you're trying to distract Meemaw from focusing on a relationship she's convinced is genuine and not a figment of your imagination. However, since I don't relish revisiting unpleasant circumstances from my past, I don't feel compelled to appease that curiosity of yours, no matter if that decision leaves you with another urge to throttle me or not."

"This Miss Longerbeam didn't actually *try* to throttle you, did she?" Camilla asked.

"I believe I'm simply going to adhere to my statement about not enjoying revisiting unpleasant circumstances from my past and leave it at that."

After sending him a look that suggested he'd managed to irritate her yet again, Camilla turned to Luella. "It seems it's going to be up to you to explain all about Miss Longerbeam, so . . . did she resort to throttling your brother?"

"I'm sure she at least contemplated throttling after she somehow concluded that, because Owen asked if she, along with her parents, wanted to accompany him to view his new project underway up by our country house, that he was intending on showing her the initial plans for another house he was beginning to build, one she assumed he was building for her."

"Why would she assume that?" Camilla asked, catching Owen's eye.

"Hard to say," he admitted.

"Had you been spending a great deal of time with Curtistine?"

"Define 'a great deal.'"

"More than a few outings."

He shook his head. "I'm going to say no because I only went to dinner with her twice, but her parents were included as well, and before you ask, no, I didn't specifically ask her to dine with me. Her father had recently put in a lucrative order for nails, and I thought treating the whole Longerbeam family to dinner would be seen as a gesture of appreciation."

Camilla frowned. "Did you specifically tell Mr. Longerbeam that you wanted Curtistine included?"

"I think I said something when I extended the first invitation about how nice it would be if Mrs. Longerbeam and their daughter could join us."

"And the second invitation?"

"Well, Mr. Longerbeam had returned to the nail factory, you see, telling me he was there to place another order, and then . . ." Owen tilted his head. "He mentioned how much Mrs. Longerbeam and Curtistine enjoyed our previous dinner, so I offered to host dinner again."

"And it never occurred to you that Mr. Longerbeam may have put in another nail order, and then broached the dinner idea, because he and Mrs. Longerbeam were hearing wedding bells on behalf of their daughter?" Camilla asked.

"It was just dinner."

"It's never just dinner when a young lady with marital prospects on her mind is involved."

"Considering Curtistine is friends with Miss Pauline Zavolta, a lady who literally crosses the street if she sees me coming, it never occurred to me that Curtistine would ever turn her eye on me as a potential suitor."

Camilla frowned. "Why not?"

"Because it's not a secret that Pauline has mentioned to all her friends that I'm a cad."

"Because . . . ?"

"I think the answer to that falls under the whole I-don't-care-to-revisit-unpleasant-situations."

It was hardly surprising when Camilla began tapping out a rapid tattoo with the tip of her dainty shoe, but when she took to narrowing her blue eyes on him as the toe-tapping increased, he set aside his coffee and blew out a breath.

"Fine. If you must know, Pauline Zavolta believes I'm a cad because of an unfortunate riding incident we didn't enjoy together."

Camilla blinked. "I've never heard of a man being accused of caddish behavior during a riding excursion."

"There's always a first time for everything," Owen muttered. "But I had the best of intentions when I offered to take Pauline Zavolta riding. She'd suffered a mishap on her horse a few months prior to our conversation, and because of that, she was nervous about riding again. I offered to help get her back in the saddle, but my good intentions turned into a complete fiasco after Pauline met me in my stables." He shook his head. "The second I got Pauline situated on top of Clementine, the gentlest horse I own, she started sobbing, although I got the distinct impression her sobs were somewhat rehearsed."

"You thought she was feigning her distress?" Camilla asked.

"Pauline is known to be overly dramatic," Luella interjected. "She thrives on attention and uses tears to persuade people, especially gentlemen, to get what she wants."

"Ah, I see," Camilla said before she sent a nod Owen's way. "As a matchmaker, I've seen all sorts of convoluted situations set up by young ladies hoping to achieve a certain result from a gentleman they've set their sights on. If I'm not mistaken, in your particular case, this Pauline wanted to set the stage so that she could enjoy a hero moment, one where she probably imagined you sweeping her from the saddle a second after she started sobbing, enfolding her in your strong arms, and giving her consoling pats on the back. However, I get the distinct feeling that's not what happened, so what did you do instead?"

It was oddly satisfying to learn Camilla had taken note of his arms, and apparently thought they were strong, and . . .

A loud clearing of a throat from Luella had him blinking out of his wandering thoughts, then blinking again when he realized he'd completely lost track of the conversation. "What was the question again?"

"I asked what you did when Pauline started sobbing," Camilla said as Luella began watching him a little too closely.

His collar suddenly took to feeling a tad too tight. "Ah, well I clearly didn't give her one of those hero moments, because instead of sweeping her into my *strong* arms, I told her that equestrians had no business weeping when they were in the saddle because a rider should always keep their wits about them for obvious safety reasons."

Camilla's eyes twinkled. "Definitely not a hero moment, but may I assume her tears immediately dried up after you told her she had no business weeping?"

"Too right they did, which suggests she really wasn't in distress in the first place, but before I could comment on that, Pauline hopped to the ground, called me a monster, and stalked off. I was then paid a visit by her father, Albert, who informed me that, although I was one of the wealthiest men in the state, I wasn't to even consider courting his daughter from that point forward because Albert would never want his little precious to be involved with a brute like me." Owen sat forward. "And that is exactly why I wouldn't have thought Curtistine, who, again, is friends with Pauline, would have ever turned a romantic eye in my direction."

"But you sat with Curtistine's family during a church service not long after taking the Longerbeams out to dinner," Luella pointed out after she handed Meemaw a slice of pie.

"Only because Curtistine was lingering by the entranceway of the church and invited me to sit with her family since I arrived late to the service and there was limited seating available."

Camilla eyed him over the rim of her coffee cup. "You do know that sitting with a specific young lady at church lends the impression a gentleman has courting on his mind, don't you?"

Owen blinked. "Does it really?"

"You didn't know that?"

"How could I know that?" Owen asked. "It's not as if there's a manual out there that states all these little everyday occurrences that women apparently take to mean they're being courted."

Camilla set aside her cup. "Perhaps I should consider penning such a manual because I never realized gentlemen could be so naïve about such matters."

"And maybe I should write a manual as well because calling a gentleman naïve isn't exactly what I'd consider proper manners, especially coming from a lady who once won a prim-and-proper award."

A widening of the eyes was Camilla's first response to that. "I must beg your pardon, Owen, because you're exactly right. That was a most improper thing for me to say, and I truly have no idea what's wrong with me lately since I don't normally make a point to insult people."

"There's nothing wrong with you, dear," Meemaw said before Owen could do more than blink at what had certainly been an unexpected admission. "You're obviously already more than comfortable with my grandson, which has allowed you to unbutton that cloak of propriety you've clearly been keeping buttoned up for far too long—something that's incredibly telling, if you ask me."

"The only thing that's telling is that I've clearly taken leave of my senses," Camilla argued before she turned to Owen. "But to return to the Longerbeam situation, if you didn't have courting on your mind, why did you invite the entire Longerbeam family to accompany you to view whatever it is you're in the process of building, which I'm going to assume isn't a second house?"

Owen gave his jaw a rub. "My invitation was merely a result of Mr. Longerbeam having mentioned over that second dinner how much he enjoys fishing. Since I'm in the process of damming up a stream to make a fishing pond, I thought he'd find the damming process interesting. I also thought, since the dam is located quite a distance up National Road, that he might like to make it a family event so he'd have company during the trip up and back."

He rose to his feet and took the plate of pie Luella was holding out to him. "Unfortunately, Curtistine completely misread the situation once she and her family arrived at the dam. She somehow came to the conclusion that I possess a romantic nature simply because I'd set up a picnic luncheon for everyone to enjoy."

"What happened next?" Camilla asked.

Owen handed Camilla the slice of pie before he retook his seat. "I think we should just leave it at she misread the situation because the rest of the story is somewhat embarrassing."

Camilla arched a brow toward Luella. "What happened?"

Luella didn't hesitate to grin. "Curtistine took one look at the charming picnic scene, raced up to poor Owen, wrapped her arms around his neck, told him that of course a house would be perfect by the pond, and then asked if he was agreeable to holding a late-summer wedding."

Camilla was suddenly directing her arched brow his way. "I hope you're about to tell me that Luella is mistaken."

"She's not," Owen admitted. "And after I untangled myself from Curtistine, I'm sure you won't be surprised to learn that what should have been a pleasant afternoon spent by my pond turned anything but pleasant, especially after Mr. and Mrs. Longerbeam began extending me their heartiest congratulations, and I . . . well, I think I may have stammered something about an enormous misunderstanding, and then . . . the conversation went downhill from there." He blew out a breath. "The Longerbeams haven't spoken to me since, and Curtistine has added her name to the very long list of ladies who evidently believe I'm some type of fiend."

Camilla frowned. "I imagine there *were* hard feelings when you apparently rejected what almost seems like a proposal from Curtistine, but I'm not certain I understand why she thought you were building her a house. From what you've said, you already have a house in the country, so why would you build another one?"

"I think she assumed we'd want to have our own house once my parents returned from France."

"I thought you mentioned your parents weren't intending on returning to the States anytime soon."

"Oh, they're not, especially since, according to Mother's letters, they're relishing their lives in Paris and don't miss Wheeling in the least."

"That's not true," Meemaw said. "Your parents will abandon Paris in a heartbeat once they learn about your upcoming engagement, and to a New York socialite at that." She settled a knowing eye on him. "You know your mother, dear. Betty Lou won't be able to resist the opportunity to crow about her son managing to get himself engaged to a proper lady, one whose social status will certainly be the envy of every lady of ambition throughout Wheeling."

"You do recall that I'm not actually engaged to your grandson, don't you?" Camilla asked.

Meemaw waved that straight away. "Betty Lou won't need to learn that until after she returns home, but I have no qualms about using your supposed engagement as a way to finally get my son and daughter-in-law back to the States."

Owen paused with a piece of pie halfway to his mouth. "You can't send them a telegram telling them Camilla and I are engaged because, qualms or not, that would be a fib, and you told Camilla you never lie. Think of the state of your knees if you send a telegram like that."

"It's not a lie, simply a craftily disguised small untruth."

Owen opened his mouth, an argument on the tip of his tongue, but he swallowed that argument when Luella sat down beside Meemaw and took to fiddling with a strand of her wet hair before she blew out a sigh.

"I think, if you're going to send any telegram at all, it should be one that explains what's been happening with Stanley," Luella began. "It wouldn't be fair to Mother to not know that her daughter has disappointed her yet again, or fair for Mother to hie herself back to West Virginia when we're all but in the midst of a feud with the Murchendorfers, a family Mother's been in competition with for years."

Meemaw frowned. "You've never been a disappointment to Betty Lou."

"Of course I have," Luella argued. "Mother wanted a princess for a daughter—a little girl who loved ribbons in her hair and fancy dresses with bows on them—but instead she got me. I loathe ribbons and bows. I also loathe spending my time indoors, working needlepoint samplers, something Sally Murchendorfer spends hours doing every week. Sally also enjoys going for tea and shopping, whereas I much prefer spending my time outside, doing things more suitable for a boy than a girl."

"Surely you don't believe your mother makes it a point to compare you to Sally and then finds you lacking, do you?" Meemaw asked.

"Mother spent three days in her bedroom after Mrs. Murchendorfer decided she was going to hold Sally's debut on the same night Mother had chosen to hold mine." Luella gave a sad shake of her head. "It doesn't take a genius to understand why Mother locked herself away, because Sally has always been more sought-after than me, which meant that everyone would attend Sally's debut, and mine would be a complete failure."

"People would have shown up for your debut," Meemaw argued.

"Well, yes, our entire family would have been there, but you know that's not who Mother wanted to impress." Luella began fidgeting with her wet hair again. "I've been holding off writing her about Stanley because that'll just be another disappointment for her, as will be the idea I've decided to embrace life as a spinster."

"There's no need for you to become a spinster," Meemaw countered. "Camilla's here now, and I believe she mentioned she has a plan."

"It's been so long since I broached that plan, I almost can't recall what it is," Camilla admitted as she took a sip of her coffee.

Luella's brow furrowed. "This plan of yours doesn't have anything to do with you using those matchmaking skills you apparently possess, does it, because I really am fine proceeding with life from this point forward as a confirmed spinster."

"Whether you choose to marry or not is completely up to you," Camilla said. "I'm not here to meddle with that part of your life but merely to get you accepted within Wheeling society, or at least reclaim your confidence to where you won't decide to hide yourself away in your grandmother's cabin."

"I like Meemaw's cabin."

"You can't spend the rest of your life there."

"I can if I decide I don't like this plan of yours."

Camilla smiled. "It's not a complicated plan, and, in fact, it's one I've already used to great success." She finally took a bite of the pie Owen had given her a few minutes before, her eyes widening a second later. "Goodness. This is a most excellent apple pie."

"It's a secret family recipe," Meemaw said right before her eyes began gleaming in a somewhat concerning fashion. "I'll be more than happy to present you with the list of ingredients at my earliest convenience."

Camilla paused with another forkful of pie halfway to her mouth. "Why would you give me a secret *family* recipe?"

"Because you said you find the pie to be most excellent."

"I'm sure everyone finds this pie to be excellent, but again, you said it's a secret family recipe, which suggests you don't share it with just anybody."

Meemaw smiled. "But you're not just anybody, are you, dear?"

"If you were going to add that I'm your almost-granddaughter-in-law, you can just nip that comment right in the bud. So, to direct the conversation back to what we should be discussing, on to my plan."

"I'd rather put talk of that on hold while I just nip into the kitchen and get you that recipe before I forget."

"And I'm going to say that can wait since I'm beginning to grow more than suspicious about this recipe and why you're so determined to get it into my hands."

Owen bit back a grin when Meemaw began muttering something about suspicious natures, mutters that Camilla blatantly ignored as she set aside her pie.

"The basics of my plan are quite simple," she began. "From what I've been able to gather thus far, there seems to be quite the competition amongst Wheeling ladies to reach the pinnacle of the local societal ladder. All we have to do now is use my unexpected declaration about being almost engaged to Owen to our advantage."

Luella frowned. "How do you intend to do that?"

"Since Bernadette told Ada Mae that I'm a leader within New York society, it stands to reason that every lady possessed of social ambition is going to want to become my new best friend." She smiled. "And given that Ada Mae is certain to tell a few ladies, who will then tell a few additional ladies, that I'm all but engaged to Owen, I can guarantee that everyone will be clamoring to invite the Chesterfield family to all their events."

"I doubt my name will be on any of those invitations," Luella argued.

"And you would be wrong about that. You mark my words, within the next few weeks, those friends of yours who've been only too eager to join in with making you persona non grata will most assuredly reach out to make amends. That means by the time that ball rolls around in June, you'll already be firmly established as a lady in high demand and my task here will have been accomplished."

Luella tilted her head. "You think I'll become in high demand simply because of my association with you—my supposed soon-to-be sister-in-law?"

"I do."

Satisfaction flickered through Luella's eyes. "Excellent, since that means I won't need to concern myself with wasting my time becoming refined, something I wasn't looking forward to doing anyways, as I have other more important and pressing matters to attend to."

"I'm afraid those pressing matters will need to take a back seat for a while, since there's no question you'll still need to put a great deal of effort into learning how to become refined," Camilla said.

The smile slid from Luella's face. "Why?"

"Because everyone is going to expect me, your soon-to-be sister-in-law and a member of the New York Four Hundred, to take you in hand."

"Why?"

"Because they'll assume I have certain expectations when it comes to presenting myself, and, by association, soon-to-be family members, to the world. That means a Luella transformation is definitely in order."

"I'm not sure I like the sound of that," Luella muttered.

"Which is unfortunate since my plan is nonnegotiable, but if it makes you feel any better . . ." Camilla turned to Owen. "As I just mentioned, everyone will expect me to take your entire family in hand, although I'm not ridiculous enough to even suggest that to Beulah. You, on the other hand, are a different story, which means you'll need to prepare yourself for a bit of a transformation as well—and no, that's not negotiable either."

Fourteen

Camilla shifted on the hard seat of Beulah's wagon, drawing her attention. "Since we now find ourselves quite alone as Lottie, Mr. Timken, and Bernadette are off with Edward to Stone and Thomas to pick up a few essentials, and Owen was called into the factory to deal with an unexpected machinery issue, now would be the perfect time to delve into the events of last evening."

"Except we're not truly alone since Luella's following directly behind us and that girl has ears like an elephant," Beulah argued.

"I don't think Luella would appreciate having you compare her ears to elephant ears."

"I wasn't saying she has large ears, only that she has remarkable hearing."

"Maybe you should stick to simply saying in the future that Luella has remarkable hearing because the image of Luella sporting elephant ears is exactly what sprang to my mind the second you mentioned elephants," Camilla suggested. "However, even if Luella hears extraordinarily well, since she's assumed the role of my guard today, she's much too busy at the moment keeping an eye out for possible threats to eavesdrop on our conversation."

"Luella's capable of doing multiple things at once," Beulah said, turning the wagon off National Road and onto a gravel drive that meandered up a steep hill as far as the eye could see, the two draft horses pulling the wagon not slowing their pace in the least, even though Esmerelda was snoozing in the back of the wagon bed—all three hundred pounds of her.

"If that's your way of avoiding talking about last night, it was a fairly halfhearted attempt."

Beulah grinned. "I suppose it was, so fine, let's discuss last night. I'll start off by saying that it was a most delightful evening. I particularly enjoyed that parlor game you taught us—the Key of the King's Garden."

"You didn't seem to be enjoying it when you lost."

"I must admit I'm not fond of losing, and I do think the next time we play that game, that some allowances should be made for me, the poor, elderly woman whose memory isn't what it used to be. That right there was directly responsible for me having to forfeit my spot in the game after I got all those sentences turned around when it was my turn."

"You know there's nothing wrong with your memory, just as I know you're deliberately avoiding the event I want to discuss."

"My memory is obviously faulty because I have no idea what event you're talking about."

Camilla refused a snort. "You don't recall stealing into my room after everyone said good night with the express purpose of sneaking that apple pie recipe under my pillow?"

"Oh . . . *that* event." Beulah cocked her head to the side. "I suppose I do recall it, but only because my ears are still suffering from all that shrieking you did. Why, my poor old heart will probably never recover after I found myself on the wrong end of your derringer, and then on the wrong end of Owen's Colt Dragoons after he raced to your rescue, which, you must know, was some mighty fine chivalrous behavior on his part."

It hadn't escaped Camilla's notice that Owen had shown up in her room, weapons at the ready, mere seconds after she'd begun shrieking.

Unwilling to dwell on his obvious chivalrous nature while sitting beside a woman who'd decided it was now her sole mission in life to convince Camilla that she and Owen were well-suited, Camilla lifted her chin.

"It's your own fault your ears and heart suffered because you're the one who chose to creep into my room, even though I'd told you there's a chance that a known criminal boss, one Victor Malvado to be exact, may be after me or Lottie—we're not exactly certain who his target is. However, because of that threat hanging over me, Owen and I are on high alert. You're lucky one of us didn't shoot you."

"And you're lucky I didn't expire on the spot because of heart palpitations. As I already said, I'm elderly and need to be treated with the utmost care."

"If that's your way of suggesting I stop pressing you about why you're so determined to get that apple pie recipe to me by one underhanded means or another, I'm not buying it. So . . . what's the significance of the recipe, and don't tell me it's just a list of ingredients to make a pie."

"You're a bright girl. I'm sure you can figure that out on your own."

"Perhaps I'm not that bright, unless . . ." Camilla took a second to watch a bird fly by before she frowned. "The recipe isn't some type of love charm or something of that nature, is it, where the recipient finds themselves an involuntary member of the Chesterfield family after taking possession of it?"

"See? You are bright after all."

"Bright enough to know that even if you manage to get that recipe into my possession, I won't soon find myself married to your grandson."

"We here in West Virginia believe in the power of what I'm sure you'd consider superstitions, but our traditions shouldn't be taken lightly. I'll have you know that anyone who's earned the privilege of obtaining the list of ingredients for the Chesterfield apple pie has, indeed, become a Chesterfield."

"May I assume you gave the recipe to your husband?"

"Thoney, my late husband, being the Chesterfield in that particular case, slipped it into my pocket a few days after I saw him standing in town, covered in coal dust from a mine he'd just begun to build. He took one look at me, I took one look at him, and it was love at first sight."

"Thoney's not a name I've heard before," Camilla said.

"He ended up with that name because his mama didn't know how to read or write much," Beulah said. "The story has it that she was aiming to name him Thomas but had written Thoney in the family Bible. After someone pointed that out, Thoney's mama decided the name had a nice ring to it and everyone called him Thoney from that point forward."

"And did Thoney's mama approve of him slipping that recipe to you?"

"'Course she did. Round these parts, love at first sight isn't taken lightly either, but in all honesty, I didn't even need to gain access to the recipe, given how much I adored Thoney. Nevertheless, I was thankful to have it in my possession all the same as I decided it was best not to take any chances with the Chesterfield tradition."

"Your grandson doesn't seem to believe in love at first sight since he's still arguing with me about my belief that Lottie and Edward have succumbed to that delightful happenstance."

"Owen believes in love at first sight. He just enjoys annoying you."

"Because . . . ?"

"I'm not completely sure, but it might be his unusual way of earning your affections."

"Or a death wish," Camilla muttered.

Beulah released a cackle. "I do appreciate your fondness for frequently wanting to inflict bodily harm on Owen, which I'm sure, being a matchmaker and all, you already realize is a direct result of your emotions becoming engaged, and—" She suddenly leaned forward. "Duck!"

Thinking it was an odd time for Beulah to point out a duck since she'd been in the midst of getting ready to dispense what she'd undoubtedly consider sage advice, Camilla glanced upward right before leaves suddenly obscured her vision as the wagon barreled underneath a low-hanging limb—one that was responsible for knocking her straight out of the wagon.

Landing on the ground, an "oomph" escaping her a second later, a noise that had, oddly enough, escaped her often of late, Camilla pushed herself up on her elbows right as Nems, Owen's one-legged carriage driver, steered his carriage to the side of the road. Before it came to a complete stop, Luella leapt from it, landed on the ground without a hint of a stumble, then set her sights on Camilla and broke into a run.

"Good heavens, Camilla, are you alright?" she demanded, kneeling down beside her.

"I think I'm fine, but where did you learn how to do that?"

Luella frowned. "Do what?"

"Leap from a moving carriage and land on your feet."

"Luella's always been graceful," Beulah said, hurrying up to join them. "People just never notice because of her unconventional attitude."

Camilla smiled. "I can work with graceful."

"I'd rather you work with the fact you're a member of the Four Hundred and get everyone in Wheeling to simply accept me because of that rather than going through the bother of refining me," Luella grumbled.

"Nice try, but no, and also know that you'll be accepted much more easily if you don't take to grumbling when you're conversing with anyone at the ball."

"That might be asking far too much, but grumbling aside . . ."

Luella turned to Beulah. "It's not like you to drive underneath such a low-hanging branch."

"I tried to tell Camilla that I'm getting senile, but she didn't want to believe me."

Camilla wrinkled her nose. "You haven't mentioned a thing about senility, merely said your memory isn't what it used to be."

"See? I've forgotten that already, although I do distinctly recall telling you to duck when I realized running under that limb was inevitable, although I have no idea why you didn't listen to me."

"I thought you were directing my attention to a duck flying by."

Dead silence greeted that admission until Beulah started cackling again and Luella started grinning.

It was a novel experience, being the source of amusement, but curiously enough, there was something lovely about it, as well as lovely about being around people who didn't bother to stifle their amusement simply because she was a grand heiress who'd apparently come to the wrong perception of the word *duck*, something that, now that she thought about it, was definitely cackle-worthy.

Her lips began to curve. "I think I should state, for the record, that the next time I'm riding with Beulah and she yells 'duck' that I won't take to looking to the sky."

"Owen will probably insist you never ride with Meemaw again after he hears about this latest fiasco," Luella said. "I'm sure he'll also launch into a lecture with me since he tasked me with the job of protecting you on the ride to the country house."

"Protecting me against *would-be-abductors*, not your *grandmother*," Camilla pointed out.

Beulah's nose immediately shot into the air. "You certainly don't need protection from me. With that settled, I say we get back on our way, especially since my senility may have let me forget that there could be a real threat to you out here on the road, and yet, here we all are, lollygagging about. We'll be easy pickings if that Victor Malvado's discovered where you've gone and is currently lurking about, waiting for an opportunity to snatch you."

Luella immediately held out a hand, helped Camilla to her feet, then headed for the carriage. "Don't worry that you're not well protected, Camilla," she said over her shoulder. "I've been shooting since I was six, and since Owen taught me, well, I don't think I really need to say anything else."

"Why are you still lollygagging, Camilla?" Beulah called from where she'd already resumed her seat on the wagon. "Like I said, we're sitting ducks out here, and I, for one, have had enough of ducks for today."

Biting back a grin, Camilla hoisted herself into the wagon, taking a firm grip on the seat when Beulah snapped the reins and the draft horses took off at a fast clip.

After checking to make sure there weren't any low-hanging tree limbs in the near vicinity, Camilla turned on the seat. "Luella said she learned how to shoot when she was six, but isn't that a little young to be handling a weapon?"

"Depends, and in Luella's case, Owen didn't have a choice *but* to teach her after Luella snuck into her daddy's gun cabinet, helped herself to a pistol, and headed out into the forest to try it out."

"How did Owen know she'd headed out to the forest?"

"Owen kept a close eye on his little sister back then because she was always finding trouble. He saw her sneaking from the house and followed her, finding her in the apple orchard, gun loaded and ready to go. Knowing how obstinate Luella can be, he had no choice but to teach her properly. She was an expert markswoman a mere three years later. She then decided to learn how to shoot while on a moving horse, which is when I really noticed how graceful she was."

"Do you think that gracefulness can be conveyed to a dance floor?"

"Luella can do just about anything if she's got the mind to, except for musical instruments." Beulah gave a bit of a shudder. "She's tone deaf. Takes after me in that regard."

"Which I'll take as a reason not to ask you to play the piano for me while I teach Luella, as well as Owen, a few of the more popular dance steps the Four Hundred is embracing these days." She smiled. "I thought that might go far to impress the guests at Mr. Fulton's ball."

"I am capable of humming, which I will gladly do if it means you'll get to practice some steps with Owen instead of having him learn them with Luella while you play the piano, although . . . I'm not sure where Betty Lou stored the piano she bought for Luella. Might be back on the island."

"We'll worry about that later, but don't think I don't realize that your less-than-subtle offer to hum was your peculiar way to get me spending more one-on-one time with your grandson."

It was quite telling when Beulah began cackling. "You do seem to have the uncanny ability to see right through me, which suggests I should simply proceed with you in a straightforward manner, so returning to the subject of Owen, allow me to take a few minutes to tell you more about him and *his* many stellar attributes since I already touched on a few of Luella's."

Camilla felt the unusual impulse to try her hand at cackling as well but settled for sending Beulah a slight narrowing of her eyes, which resulted in Beulah cackling louder than ever.

As Beulah pulled a handkerchief that had chickens embroidered on it from the bodice of her dress and took to dabbing at now-watering eyes, Camilla settled back against the seat, knowing she was in for a bit of grandmotherly bragging about Owen.

In all honesty, she wasn't opposed to hearing more about him because what she'd begun to realize was this—he was a kind man at heart, and even though he had the ability to annoy her, she looked forward to their verbal skirmishes and enjoyed the fact that he didn't guard his every word with her as everyone had always done.

It was refreshing, having someone speak plainly to her for a change, and what was somewhat curious was the fact that she spoke plainly to him in return. She normally considered every word before allowing one out of her mouth, but with Owen, that simply wasn't the case, which . . .

"Contrary to popular feminine belief," Beulah said, stuffing the handkerchief back into her bodice and interrupting Camilla's thoughts, "Owen is not a lout. Yes, he's somewhat awkward when it comes to speaking with women, but I believe that's simply a result of him spending most of his time around men."

"An interesting theory, and one that might explain why Owen called me 'little lady' when we first met, and then suggested I calm down a moment later."

"What did you do when he suggested you calm down?"

"I had to resist the urge to shoot him with the derringer I was already pointing his way."

Beulah released a bark of laughter. "And that right there, my girl, is exactly why you're perfect for him."

"Because I refrained from shooting him?"

"Well, that was considerate of you, but no. You're well-suited for him because you're not intimidated by him. I don't know of any other lady who would have dared such a thing, given that ladies in general are unsettled by the sheer size of Owen, as well as his brusque nature."

"What makes you think Owen doesn't unsettle me?"

Beulah turned the horses onto yet another drive before she frowned. "An interesting question, and one I'll need to consider further, but not right now since we're almost to the house."

"Why does my question need further consideration?"

"Because I've gotten the impression you pride yourself on always being composed, but since you've all but admitted my Owen unsettles you, well, there could be a myriad of reasons to explain that. I simply need to figure out which reason is the right one, although I'm relatively sure it's the one where you, a matchmaker, realizes that you've met your match in Owen, but because you're so immersed in the business end of romance with other people, you're simply too blind to see what's clearly in front of your face."

Camilla opened her mouth to argue but closed it when Beulah drove around a bend in the road and a beautiful mansion came into view, one that captured Camilla's attention and erased all thoughts of arguing.

Gazing at the building located between large, leafy maple trees, Camilla lingered on a portico at the very center of the house, one that had six white Ionic pillars forming a semicircle leading to the front door, the white of the pillars providing a lovely contrast against the saffron yellow the house had been painted. Situated back from the pillared entrance was the front door, painted a deep burgundy. Seven leaded-glass windows inlaid across the middle section of the house sparkled in the sunlight and drew attention to what was the centerpiece of the house, even though there were indented wings on either side of the main building, which was a somewhat atypical architectural design for a house that was mostly built in the Greek Revival style.

"It's beautiful," she said as Beulah drew the wagon to a stop in front of a short flight of steps that led to the impressive portico.

"I preferred the house Betty Lou and Hiram originally began building," Beulah countered. "It was a charming eight-room farmhouse."

"This is certainly no farmhouse."

"Too right it isn't." Beulah released a sigh. "The farmhouse plan changed once Betty Lou discovered that the Murchendorfers were intending on building a thirty-room mansion about half a mile from here. Betty Lou immediately decided the farmhouse wasn't going to impress anyone, and off she went to speak with the architect, who was more than happy to take the bones of the farmhouse that had already been erected and transform it into what is standing before us."

"It's charming."

"*Charming* isn't exactly a word I'd use to describe a house that has thirty-seven rooms, one of which is a ballroom that takes up the majority of the second floor."

"And is a room I'm apparently going to be spending a lot of time in now that I'm being taken in hand," Luella said as she strode up to join them, tucking a pistol into the holster she was wearing low on her hip, but whipping it out again a second later when a shout came from the side of the house right before a handful of men came rushing into view, all of them heavily armed.

"Riders comin' up fast," someone yelled.

A blink of an eye later, Beulah had what could only be described as a sailor's grip on Camilla's arm as she propelled Camilla up the steps and through the front door.

"Stay here, and for heaven's sake, stay out of sight. Your enemies have evidently come to call," Beulah barked before she spun on her heel and headed out the door, saying something about fetching her rifle.

Not particularly caring for being shoved out of the way and told to stay out of sight, Camilla unsnapped her reticule, pulled out her derringer, then moved to the nearest window and twitched the drapery just the slightest bit to catch a glimpse of what was transpiring outside.

A frisson of alarm stole through her when she caught sight of two riders approaching, reining to a stop when Beulah stepped forward and aimed her rifle at them.

"That's close enough," Beulah yelled.

"No cause for alarm," one of the men shouted. "We're just here to see Camilla Pierpont."

"We know why you're here," Beulah countered. "But you won't get to Camilla unless it's over my dead body, and I have no intention of dying today."

"Is that a Kentucky long rifle?" one of the men called next, which was a rather unusual thing to concern himself with, given the circumstances.

"Too right it is," Beulah yelled back.

"I heard that rifle is capable of shooting a fly off a fence."

Camilla stilled when she realized the voice sounded familiar.

"It surely is capable of that," Beulah yelled next.

"Are *you* capable of that?" the man called back.

Recognition finally set in and had Camilla pushing the drapery aside, but before she could yell to Beulah to stand down, Beulah shifted her stance, took aim, and fired.

A second later, a blast resounded through the air right before the hat one of the gentlemen was wearing went skittering off his head—a gentleman who just happened to be Mr. Leopold Pendleton, a dear friend of hers. He was in the company of Mr. Charles Wetzel, another friend, and obviously neither man was a threat to her, but both men were now facing imminent danger because every person in possession of a weapon, save herself, was now pointing those weapons Leopold and Charles's way.

The first inkling Owen had that something might be amiss was the sight of four of the men he'd hired to guard Camilla milling about the front lawn of his country house, all of them toting rifles.

He urged George into a gallop, then swung from the saddle as he reached the closest man, Andy Sklenicka, who'd worked for Chesterfield Nails for over ten years, but more importantly, knew his way around a weapon.

"What happened?" Owen demanded, earning a shake of the head from Andy in return.

"There was a titch of a situation."

Trepidation was immediate. "A . . . titch?"

"It was the darndest thing."

As far as responses went, that was hardly informative.

"What was?" Owen asked.

Andy gave a jaw that sported at least a week's worth of stubble a scratch. "Well, you see, there was these two riders comin' upon the house real quick-like. But they must've not seen all of us streamin' out of the woods and roundin' 'bout the house to confront them, cuz they just kept a-comin'—until your meemaw started hollerin'."

"Meemaw didn't have the good sense to stay out of sight and let all of you who've been hired to protect the house do your job?"

"I ain't touchin' the subject of whether your meemaw has good sense or not, Owen. You know she terrifies everyone half to death. Don't reckon I wanna get on her bad side."

"A fair point, but what happened after Meemaw started hollering?"

"The men pulled up their horses, one of them asked something about the rifle your meemaw was aimin' at him, and then . . ." Andy gave his chin another scratch. "Your meemaw went'n shot the hat clean off that man's head."

"I knew I never should've stopped at the factory instead of escorting Camilla here."

Andy waved that aside. "Now, no need to start all that frettin'. You 'bout have an army hired to see after that little lady, and she's well-protected. Ain't no one would've gotten near her, not with Nems, Miss Luella, and your meemaw keepin' watch over her. Everyone done knows that Nems is a better shot than even Luella, and that's sayin' something. And 'fore you forget, your little lady was ridin' in a wagon with that surly pig. Ain't no one with any sense a'tall gets close to that beast, although . . ." Andy frowned. "Seein' as how your meemaw keeps company with the sow, well, it might be sayin' somethin' about her sense after all."

Owen stifled a sigh because, as was often the case when trying to get to the crux of a story being told by a man who preferred meandering his way around a tale instead of spitting out the most pertinent details, he still had no idea what had actually transpired.

"Can I assume the men who came after Camilla have now been secured?"

"Secured? Why'd we want to do somethin' like that? Turns out them men are personally acquainted with your little lady. The situation was just a hellacious misunderstandin', and your meemaw is feelin' somethin' awful 'bout ruinin' that man's fine hat." Andy smiled, revealing a few missing teeth. "I think that's why she's cookin' up a storm, makin' chicken and apple dumplings." He tilted his head. "There was some bone of contention between your meemaw and the little lady about an apple pie. Not sure what all the ruckus was about, but from what me and the boys could figure, the little lady didn't want to get nowhere near that there recipe. She did, at one point—odd as I was thinkin' this was—suggest your meemaw give it to Mr. Leopold Pender-Something-or-Other, and that left your meemaw mutterin' about matchmakers being bona fide menaces."

Owen didn't know whether to laugh or get back on his horse and ride to saner pastures.

"I think it's past time I get my hands on that particular recipe and hide it before it causes a full-out war between Meemaw and Camilla," he said.

"A man's got ta do what a man's got ta do," Andy said as he shifted his rifle to his other shoulder. "I'm off to patrol the perimeter again, but don't you be worryin' none that if any real trouble shows up that me and the boys ain't up for taking care of it. That little lady is in fine hands with us around."

"I'm sure she is," Owen said before he strode into motion, slowing to look over his shoulder a second later. "Would you see George settled in the stable before you head out on patrol, and . . . a word of advice. You might want to stop calling Miss Pierpont a 'little lady.' Turns out that particular phrase is considered an insult to the feminine set."

"Huh, and here I thought I was makin' progress understandin' ladies in general, seeing as how I recently started callin' on Miss Annabelle Stuckley, and she done tuckin' told me that I was a real ladies' man."

Owen frowned. "Are you sure she meant that as a compliment?"

"Hard to say since Miss Annabelle seems ta have a full-up schedule and hasn't been able to find any spare time for me to get down to the business of any courtin'."

"I'll have to ask Miss Pierpont if being called a ladies' man is a positive thing."

"Don't know why it'd be considered anything else, but you let me know if your little . . . ah, er, not lady, but Miss Pierpont believes differently." Andy took hold of George's reins and began leading him away.

Striding into motion again, Owen settled for merely nodding to Constantine Daroma, George Bringmann, and Frank Dopkiss, knowing full well that if he slowed his pace, the three men he'd also brought on to protect Camilla would launch into their renditions of Meemaw shooting at a stranger. Since all the men believed, as Andy did, in meandering about with any tale they told, it would take at least thirty minutes to hear them out—thirty minutes he wasn't willing to lose, not when he needed to learn exactly what the situation was with the two men who'd apparently come to call.

Setting his sights on the house, he moved up the front steps, across the portico, then through the door.

The sound of laughter coming from the back of the house drew Owen down the marble hallway, but he stopped in his tracks just outside the receiving parlor at the sight that met his eyes.

What had been a cavernous and empty room that echoed because of lack of furniture the last time he'd been in the house, which had only been a little over a week before, was now filled with a variety of pieces, some of which were still wrapped in brown paper, a stack of what seemed to be paintings propped up against the wall where Luella was standing.

His sister wasn't alone, but with an older gentleman whose hair was standing on end, which suggested he might be the man who'd had his hat blown off by Meemaw. The man didn't seem overly concerned about that, though, since he was currently in the process of attempting to level a painting on the wall, inching along as he kept the painting hoisted in the air, his inching continuing when Luella took to shaking her head.

Owen turned his attention to the opposite side of the room and discovered Lottie and Bernadette tossing suggestions at Edward, who was maneuvering an attractive, yellowish-colored couch in front of a fireplace bricked in river stone.

Frankly, he wouldn't have thought to purchase such a couch on his own, given the feminine color, which, even to his untrained eye, suited the yellow walls of the receiving parlor. That there were two wingback chairs in the same yellow pushed to the right of the French doors suggested all the pieces might be part of a set, but not being proficient with furniture trends in general, he couldn't say for sure.

Before he could question where all the furniture had come from, or even who the gentleman was helping Luella, a glimpse of a lady's ivory skirt swishing around outside the French doors captured his attention.

His feet were in motion a second later, but he came to an abrupt stop when he caught sight of Camilla standing on the brick terrace. She was looking quite unlike her usual self, given that her hair was covered with one of Meemaw's kerchiefs, there was a streak of dirt running across her cheek, and she had an apron wrapped over her gown, something Owen thought looked incredibly charming.

All thoughts of how charming Camilla looked disappeared in a trice, though, when he realized there was a man standing beside her—a man who was bending his head close to Camilla and whispering something into her ear, something that was causing her to smile.

Owen's stomach took that moment to begin doing some odd topsy-turvy business, which was curious to say the least because his stomach never gave him issues. Nor did he usually feel a spontaneous urge to escort a man who was evidently a guest in his home straight out the door and on his way, which was probably better for the man than the other urge Owen was feeling, one that involved his Colt Dragoons and . . .

"Mr. Wetzel," Luella called out, pulling Owen from what were curious ponderings indeed. "Could we borrow you for a moment?

Mr. Pendleton thinks he needs another set of eyes to get this dratted painting straight."

Owen backed away from the door and stepped behind a large potted plant he'd never seen before, not particularly caring to have to exchange the expected introductions and pleasantries just yet with a man he was considering doing some manner of bodily harm to, something that might very well annoy Camilla since she'd certainly appeared to be enjoying the man's company—and enjoying it a bit too much, in his humble opinion.

Thankfully, Mr. Wetzel didn't see him as he strode over to join Luella, where he immediately said something about a little more to the left, earning a dramatic sigh from Mr. Pendleton.

"Owen, what are you doing lurking behind that plant?" Camilla suddenly asked, sticking her head around the plant in question and leveling a frown on him.

It was rather annoying, earning a frown from her when Mr. Wetzel had earned a smile, and a far too delightful smile at that.

He pushed aside his annoyance and summoned up a smile of his own, hoping that might result in Camilla smiling back at him.

Unfortunately, she merely took to looking at him in concern. "Is something the matter?"

Since he couldn't very well admit he'd taken to lurking about in order to avoid giving in to a very great temptation to pummel one Mr. Wetzel for being the recipient of Camilla's smile, Owen forced himself to keep his smile firmly in place. "I can't think of a thing that's the matter."

"Then, again, why are you lurking behind that plant?"

"Ah, well, I'm, ah . . ." His smile widened when the perfect answer sprang to mind. "I'm doing some bug inspection. I once had a plant that was infested with critters, and they invaded the house and caused all sorts of havoc before I was finally able to get the situation under control."

She cocked her head to the side. "One bug-infested plant caused havoc throughout an entire house?"

"It was a surprise to me as well."

"I'm sure it was, but there's no need to worry about that plant. It came directly from the greenhouse Luella has out in the woods somewhere. Since she's an amateur horticulturist, I imagine she's pretty diligent when it comes to garden pests in general."

"Luella's an amateur horticulturist?"

"You didn't know that?"

"Are you going to lecture me again about how well I don't know my sister if I admit I didn't?"

"That depends."

"On what?"

"On whether you know where all the furniture came from that's now in this room."

Owen blinked. "I figured you were responsible for it."

She blinked right back at him. "While I'm certainly an efficient sort, I'm not that efficient."

Owen stepped from behind the plant, his gaze traveling around the room again, lingering on Mr. Wetzel, who was now browsing through a stack of paintings. Owen gestured toward the man. "Can I assume that gentleman is responsible, which may explain why you were smiling at him earlier?"

Camilla frowned. "You say that as if I don't smile often."

"You don't smile that *warmly* often," he corrected.

"I'm sure you're mistaken about that, but no, Charles Wetzel isn't responsible for the furniture or all the paintings in the room, which means you should definitely brace yourself for a lecture regarding your sister."

Owen rubbed his jaw. "Luella acquired all these items?"

"She, besides being an amateur horticulturist, has developed an interest in interior decorating."

"Since when?"

"There hasn't been time to get all the details from her, but I know for a fact that she's amassed quite the collection of furnishings over the past few months, and she made a point to mention that if she'd had more notice about guests arriving, she'd have had everything already in place by now."

"If I'd known about the furnishings, I'd have sent her a telegram so you wouldn't have had to worry you were going to be living in a country house with nothing more than a few chairs and beds."

"But you being unaware of Luella's acquisitions suggests you really don't know your sister well these days, but luckily for you, you're going to be spared an immediate lecture because I have something of greater importance to discuss with you, which is why I'm delighted to discover you've returned from the factory."

"You didn't seem delighted when you were frowning at me just a few moments ago."

"Because I couldn't figure out what you were doing behind that plant, but now that we've settled that, I'm no longer frowning, which means . . ." Her eyes began to sparkle. "I can finally tell you about an unexpected circumstance that's arisen that I've been dying to share with you."

"Does it have anything to do with the two gentlemen who've come to call?"

"In a manner of speaking," she said before she took hold of his arm and began, not drawing him over to be introduced to the two men who were evidently responsible for the unexpected circumstance, but hustling him straight across and then out of the room.

"Where are we going, or better yet, why did you just avoid introducing me to the gentlemen I was told had come to call on you?" he asked as she tugged him down the hallway.

"Leopold Pendleton and Charles Wetzel, two very dear friends of mine who've been sent by the Accounting Firm to provide me with extra protection, are intending on staying here as long as I'm here. That means they'll be available for introductions *after* we've had a chance to speak privately."

The knot that had been in his stomach ever since he'd seen Camilla smiling at Charles Wetzel began to unravel.

"They're only here to protect you?" he asked.

"That was their original intention, although . . ." She tugged him into an empty room painted in a robin's-egg blue, not that he'd known what the color was called until Luella corrected him when he'd said it was merely blue a month before. "Protection may not be their only mission now since there's been an intriguing development."

"There's a development?" was all he could think to ask as the knot began reforming in his stomach, undoubtedly due to the idea he was relatively certain this development centered around one Charles Wetzel—a far-too-smiley gentleman if there ever was one.

"I think Beulah may have just found herself a . . . beau."

Owen's mouth dropped open. "What?"

"You heard me, a beau—and not just any beau, but Leopold Pendleton, an upstanding gentleman who is already more than smitten with your grandmother."

"I was only gone three hours," Owen pointed out as the knot in his stomach loosened yet again, although he couldn't quite ignore the touch of queasiness that was beginning to take the knot's place.

"The smitten-ness happened within seconds, a direct result of Beulah impressing Leopold with her shooting abilities."

"One would think this Leopold would want to put as much distance between himself and Meemaw as possible, not set his sights on, ah, courting her."

"Love works in mysterious ways, but your grandmother is crafty, which is why I need your help to get Beulah to accept the idea that Leopold is perfect for her."

Owen blinked. "You want *me* to help *you* arrange a match between Meemaw and some gentleman I've never met before?"

"Did you miss the part where I told you that Leopold's an upstanding gentleman?"

"I don't care how upstanding he is. He has no business courting my grandmother."

Camilla waved that aside. "Don't be a child."

"I'm not a child, merely a concerned grandson."

"I would think my validation of Leopold would be enough to alleviate any concerns you have. But since that doesn't seem to be the case, know that he's a widower, possesses a very large fortune, and is a member of the Four Hundred."

"That tells me next to nothing about the man."

"It tells you that he's respectable."

"No, it doesn't. It merely tells me that he's from the world you inhabit, which isn't a world Meemaw would ever be interested in."

"Leopold isn't like most men involved with the Four Hundred because he led quite an adventurous life before he settled down to become an established member of society. He's no stick in the mud and would keep your grandmother highly entertained, as well as assure she's never lonely."

"Meemaw has never complained about being lonely."

"That's simply because she's one of those suffer-in-silence types."

"She's rarely silent."

"True, but I doubt she'd want to burden her grandchildren with the notion her life hasn't been all sunshine and lima beans, something she apparently finds absolutely delicious."

"You don't know what lima beans are?"

"I will after supper, as Beulah calls it, instead of dinner, because, as I just said, she's whipping them up for me right now."

"You don't actually whip up lima beans. You just boil them."

"I'll keep that in mind if I ever find myself in a kitchen, in front of a stove, boiling water no less, which I readily admit I've never done before. However, none of that has anything to do with Beulah and Leopold. You need to believe me when I say they're perfect for each other. And before you think the smitten state is one-sided, know that Beulah turned decidedly flustered after Leopold kissed her hand. Beulah doesn't strike me as the type who gets flustered often."

Owen's mouth dropped open again. "Leopold kissed my grandmother's hand?"

"Twice."

He spun on his heel. "I believe it's past time I had a word with this man."

"Absolutely not," Camilla argued, snagging hold of his hand and pulling him to a stop. "The last thing their burgeoning romance needs is for you to turn all blustery over the expected behavior from a gentleman when he makes the acquaintance of a lovely lady."

"There isn't any burgeoning romance transpiring right now, nor, if I have a say, will there be any burgeoning in the future."

"That's just wishful grandson thinking on your part. And while I understand that it's uncomfortable to think about your meemaw as a woman a man might want to court, you need to pull yourself together and do what's best for her. She's not ancient, you know, and I imagine she'd love spending her days with a dashing gentleman to keep her company."

"I saw Leopold in the receiving parlor just a moment ago and I'm not certain *dashing* is the word that springs to mind to describe him."

"Of course he's dashing, although I suppose he's looking a little windswept still, what with how Beulah did shoot his hat off his head, leaving his hair rather untidy—not that Leopold has noticed that state." She smiled. "He's much too interested in pulling information out of Luella regarding your grandmother to concern himself with shot-up hair."

"What kind of information could my sister possibly lend Leopold that would aid his romantic intentions toward Meemaw?"

"I'm sure Leopold is interested in the basics—such as what Beulah enjoys doing throughout the day, what types of books she reads, what type of chocolate she prefers, and what her favorite flowers are."

"He will not be plying my grandmother with chocolate and daisies."

"How delightful to learn your grandmother and I share the same proclivity for daisies."

"Which is surprising, but do not tell Leopold I told you what Meemaw's favorite flowers are. The last thing I want to see is this house blanketed in daisies."

Camilla crossed her arms over her chest and took to looking grumpy. "Why is it surprising to learn I enjoy daisies?"

"Because Curtistine and Pauline told me that proper ladies prefer roses."

"And they would be mistaken about that, but returning to your grandmother, as you may suspect by now, it's difficult for me to resist becoming involved with matchmaking pursuits when I know the match in question is worthy of my attention."

"Hence the reason Lottie and Edward went traipsing off to Stone and Thomas together earlier," Owen muttered.

"I had nothing to do with that. Edward merely mentioned he wasn't certain what essentials he should be picking up and Lottie volunteered to accompany him. The only input I had with that situation was to suggest Bernadette travel with them as chaperone, and then Mr. Timken, after telling me that nothing screams inappropriate chaperone quite like Bernadette does, insisted on accompanying them." She smiled. "If I'd actually been dabbling in matchmaking with those two, I'd have gone as their chaperone because I'm very good with gently steering conversations in a way that allows a couple to become better acquainted in a seamless fashion."

"There will be no gently steering any conversations between Meemaw and Leopold."

"Gentle isn't what I had in mind, not when Beulah seems to be slightly reluctant to accept the idea that a handsome gentleman might be interested in courting her. She's already turned slightly contrary about the matter and tried to distract me from extolling all of Leopold's many stellar attributes when I tracked her down to the kitchen."

"Meemaw's very good with distractions."

"Truer words have never been spoken. Do you know that she

sent me the sweetest smile as I was telling her about Leopold's proficiency with a variety of weapons right before she asked me to fetch her apple dumpling recipe?"

"That doesn't sound like much of a distraction."

"It is when she had an ulterior motive in mind—that being the apple pie recipe sticking up in the *A* section of her recipe box, just waiting for me to grab hold of it." Camilla released a bit of a huff. "Thankfully, I noticed before it was too late and suggested she ask Leopold to procure the dumpling recipe instead of me."

"I'm beginning to get a better understanding why some of the men outside said there was a bone of contention between you and Meemaw, especially when it seems you've uncovered the secret of the family recipe."

"Too right I have, and know that the bone of contention revolved around the fact that, after I mentioned Leopold and the recipe, your grandmother called me a matchmaking menace, snatched her recipe box straight out of my hands, then marched out of the room, probably to hide the box so I couldn't get the recipe to Leopold."

Owen frowned. "You don't seem overly concerned that Meemaw called you a menace."

"I'm more complimented than concerned because Beulah is a formidable woman, and that she considers me a menace suggests she realizes I'm formidable as well. All that's left to do now, and with your cooperation of course, is to wear her down and have her come around to the notion that a Chesterfield wedding will certainly be transpiring in the future, but just not one that has me and you as the couple exchanging vows."

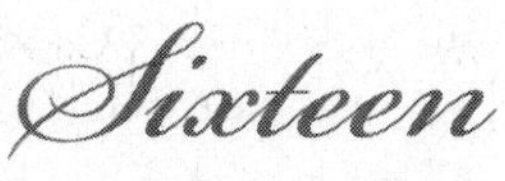

Sixteen

Before Owen could argue the point about an upcoming Chesterfield wedding, or contemplate why Camilla's insistence that this particular wedding wouldn't involve them was slightly depressing, which was odd as their supposed forthcoming engagement was merely what she referred to as a clever bit of fiction, she suddenly moved to the window, peered through the glass, sucked in a sharp breath, then turned on her heel and dashed out of the room.

Having no idea what all the dashing was about, but praying it wasn't because a real threat was knocking on the door, Owen raced after her, almost barreling into Meemaw, who, upon seeing him, thrust what looked to be her recipe box behind her back before she waved him on, saying something about how she wasn't up to anything, so keep moving.

Wondering how it had come to pass that his life was turning downright peculiar these days, even though he suspected that state was a direct result of Camilla accompanying him to West Virginia, Owen raced through the front door and down the steps.

It didn't take long to spot Camilla, who was now halfway down the drive, yelling up a storm and flapping her arms about as she continued running full tilt ahead, an odd circumstance to be sure because he was relatively certain that a lady who'd once won an award for poise probably didn't make it a habit to do much flapping, or running for that matter.

Nevertheless, given that Camilla was a rather sensible sort, he doubted she was waving down men with kidnapping on their minds, but having no idea what all the fuss was about, he set his sights in the direction of the flapping, blinking when Gladys zoomed into view, zigzagging through the trees, the zagging evidently a direct result of the two coonhounds chasing her.

Camilla continued charging in the direction of the hounds, waving her arms more frantically than ever in an obvious attempt to distract their attention, which wasn't the brightest thing for her to do, especially since she apparently thought the hounds posed a threat to Gladys, which meant she should realize they could also pose a threat to her, even though they weren't vicious sorts, not that she knew that.

Realizing he needed to take charge of the situation before Camilla harmed herself with all the dashing and gesturing about she was doing, Owen let out a whistle that had the coonhounds abandoning their pursuit of Gladys and charging his way.

A blink of an eye after that, Gladys, rather than fleeing to safer, coonhound-free pastures, spun around, released a yip, and bounded, not toward Camilla, but directly after the hounds.

"Don't just stand there, Owen, catch her," Camilla yelled as she hitched up the hem of her skirt, changed directions, and began running after a poodle that was clearly in a state of frenzied excitement.

It quickly became evident that Gladys didn't want to be caught, because the second Owen took off after her, she began bounding about on her spindly legs, yapping up a storm, the yapping turning to flat-out barks when the coonhounds, Cleo and Calamity, began baying.

A second later, all three dogs bounded away, frolicking with one another as they bounded, which suggested all three of them were well on their way to becoming fast friends.

"I take it those dogs weren't chasing Gladys because they were in need of a snack?" Camilla asked, stopping three feet away from Owen, where she promptly whipped out a handkerchief from the pocket of the apron she was wearing and began, not daintily dabbing, as he'd been expecting, but completely mopping her face with it.

He reached into his pocket, pulled out his handkerchief, and handed it to her.

"What's this for?" she asked.

"You seem to have an aversion to perspiration. You might need a spare on the off-chance you find yourself chasing Gladys again, although I doubt that'll be necessary since she's simply playing with my dogs."

"I wouldn't say I have an *aversion* to perspiration. It's more along the lines of a commitment to hold it at bay, but thank you for the spare." She tucked his handkerchief into her sleeve. "As for Gladys playing with your dogs, you should know that this is a very peculiar circumstance indeed, because she never exerts herself to do anything as frivolous as playing."

"Perhaps she's playing now because country life agrees with her," Owen said, nodding to where Gladys was now rolling around on the lawn as Cleo did the same beside her, while Calamity licked Gladys's face.

"Perhaps, but Gladys doesn't resort to frolicking about when I take her to the family house on the Hudson, which is out in the country."

"Maybe she's partial to West Virginia country."

Camilla tilted her head as Gladys took that moment to dash into the woods with Cleo and Calamity. "It does appear as if she's coming out of her lackadaisical shell here in West Virginia country, but should I be concerned about her encountering any dangerous wild animals?"

"She'll be fine as long as she sticks with Cleo and Calamity, but you should be aware that we do have a resident bear that goes by the name of Teddy, who's claimed Meemaw's backyard as part of his territory. I found him in a poacher's trap about a year ago when he was just a baby. Meemaw and I nursed him back to heath, but while we returned him to the wild, he still enjoys checking in with Meemaw every once in a while." Owen caught Camilla's eye. "He's relatively harmless, but you shouldn't let your guard down if he shows up, and whatever you do, if you encounter him, don't run. But you can do more of that flapping you were doing earlier."

Camilla lifted her chin. "I certainly wasn't flapping, but perhaps it'll be best if I simply avoid Beulah's cabin."

"Avoidance might be tricky since Meemaw will undoubtedly start badgering you to help her with her garden." Owen grinned. "Excessive nagging doesn't begin to describe the tactics she employs during the spring when she needs to get all her vegetables into the ground. She's notorious for sending out invitations for unpaid labor to the family." He smiled. "I'm sure you won't be surprised to learn that no one refuses her invitations, not when everyone in the family is fairly terrified of her."

"Your entire family is terrified of Beulah?"

"Well, not her siblings, but the younger generations are rather leery of her, all seventy-something of them."

"You have seventy people in your family?"

"There're over a hundred relatives at last count. Meemaw comes from a family of seven siblings, and then my mother, Betty Lou, has quite the extended family as well, which my father began taking responsibility for directly after he married her." Owen shook his head. "We used to gather together every month or so, but I'm sorry to say that hasn't happened much over the two years my parents have been gone."

"Why not?"

"Mother took over organizing those events from Meemaw years ago because my grandmother was getting a little surly about all the time it took to arrange matters. Since Mother's not available anymore, I should be the one in charge, and while I've been meaning to invite everyone to the country house, now that the construction is complete, I simply haven't gotten around to it."

"Then allow me to suggest that I, along with Luella, host an event sometime around the planting that's evidently going to be happening soon. That'll give me an opportunity to show Luella how to organize an event, which refined ladies are expected to know how to do."

A different sort of feeling settled in Owen's stomach, a sort that wasn't a knot or a dose of queasiness, but something that felt rather warm. "You wouldn't mind stepping in and planning a family reunion?"

"Not at all."

"Do you organize family reunions for your family often?"

"I'm afraid my family isn't all that close, nor are we a large family. I'm an only child and my father was an only child, as was my mother, and the only time we get together with my two sets of grandparents is to enjoy Christmas Eve services at Grace Church in the city."

Owen frowned. "You only see your grandparents once a year?"

"No. I see them separately, of course, but only occasionally at a few balls during the Season, or at the Newport Casino if they decide to summer there."

"But you don't share a close relationship with any of your grandparents?"

"Not since I made the decision to avoid marriage after my debut Season, something that left all my grandparents believing I'm a disappointment to the Pierpont and Rhinelander, my mother's family, names."

"I bet their disappointment would abate if you were to abandon your decision and decide to settle down."

"I fear there won't be any abating for my grandparents since it's not as if I've been contemplating abandoning my decision."

"Not even after Charles Wetzel arrived here, apparently determined to protect you?" Owen heard pop out of his mouth before he could stop himself.

"What does Charles have to do with anything?"

It was difficult to know how to explain. After clearing his throat a time or two, he finally shrugged. "You were smiling at him, and in a manner that suggested you were *incredibly* fond of him."

"I am incredibly fond of him, but that doesn't mean it's fondness of the romantic type." Her brows drew together. "You aren't under the misimpression that every warm smile a lady sends a gentleman means she's romantically interested in that gentleman, or vice versa, are you?"

"Not if the smiles are directed at a man, say of Mr. Timken's age, or a relative. However . . ." He caught Camilla's eye. "Curtistine and Pauline made a point of smiling at me a lot, and very warm smiles at that. And after the fiascos I experienced with both those ladies, Luella told me that I should have realized, given the warmth of their smiles, that they were sent my way to engage my affections. She then told me that I shouldn't have smiled so much in return because my smiles obviously lent the misimpression I was romantically interested in both those ladies."

Camilla turned her head, but not before Owen caught sight of her lips curving into a grin. She dabbed at her lips with her handkerchief, then turned back to him, not a hint of a grin left on her face. "I'm starting to get the impression your sister may enjoy ruffling your feathers."

"That definitely might explain why Luella dissolved into a fit of laughter when she caught me standing in front of a mirror, practicing smiles that weren't overly warm," Owen muttered.

A bit of a snort drifted Owen's way before Camilla pressed together lips that were definitely twitching, then took a second to dab those lips with her handkerchief again and settled eyes that seemed to be filled with amusement on him. "While I certainly would have enjoyed seeing that type of practice, tell me this—have you put any of those less-than-warm smiles to good use?"

"I thought, given Luella's amusement, that I wasn't capable of enacting a credible less-than-warm smile, so I've simply abandoned any attempts to smile in general, which hasn't been all that difficult since I seem to be garnering more than my fair share of scowls from ladies these days." He winced. "Curtistine even went so far as to mouth the word *lout* when I saw her a few weeks ago crossing Main Street in Wheeling."

"Oh, for heaven's sake, you're not a lout, merely somewhat naïve when it comes to women in general, which is actually rather charming."

Satisfaction of the male variety began running through him, brought about no doubt by the notion Camilla apparently found him rather charming, which wasn't exactly the same as finding him completely charming, but it was a far cry from her thinking he was a lout.

Before he could enjoy the satisfaction for long, though, another coonhound came loping across the lawn, baying up a storm the moment it took note of Cleo, Calamity, and Gladys, who'd raced out of the trees to greet the new arrival.

"Oh no," he muttered as Gladys bounded toward the new arrival, a dog by the name of Alma.

"Since you're not racing after Gladys, should I assume that's another one of your dogs?" Camilla asked, shading her eyes with her hand as she kept her gaze on Gladys, who'd already reached Alma. A nuzzle was Gladys's first order of business, something Alma apparently enjoyed because a second later, the two dogs dashed across the lawn, joined a moment later by Cleo and Calamity.

"Alma's not mine. She belongs to my great-aunt Elma, but since Alma's here, and Aunt Elma rarely lets Alma out of her sight, we're evidently soon to be honored with a visit from a relative of mine who holds the reputation of being difficult."

"More difficult than Beulah?"

"Beulah looks like a cuddly bunny compared to her sister, who's been likened to a grizzly bear at times."

Camilla blinked. "A grizzly bear?"

"Indeed, you know, one of the grouchiest and meanest bears out there."

"Well, how delightful," Camilla muttered. "But grouchiness aside, isn't it a little odd that your aunt Elma named her dog Alma, which is remarkably similar to her name?"

"Aunt Elma choosing Alma for her dog's name exactly explains my aunt's difficult attitude. She didn't make her choice because she thought Elma and Alma were catchy. She did it to annoy her twin sister, Alma, who is the sweetest woman you'll ever meet. Alma apparently did something to provoke Elma, which is why Elma decided to retaliate, hence the reason for naming her dog Alma."

"That was a whole lot of Elmas and Almas, enough to make your head spin. However . . ." Camilla's eyes twinkled. "Why did your great-grandmother name twin daughters Elma and Alma? One would think twins would be confusing enough without such similar names."

"It's West Virginia. We tend to do things a little differently here" was all Owen could think to say, spared from having to embellish his remark when a wagon rumbled into view, Aunt Elma holding the reins, her ever-present rifle propped up against the seat. Surprisingly, Mr. Timken was sitting on the seat beside her, and Miss Hester Baker, Aunt Elma's long-suffering paid companion, was perched behind the seat in the wagon bed, holding onto what appeared to be chairs, the entire back of the wagon filled with them.

"Where in the world does all this furniture keep coming from?" he asked.

"I told you, Luella's responsible, but I don't know any details surrounding her many furniture acquisitions. All I know is that Beulah and I stumbled on Luella's stash when we were looking for an appropriate place for Esmerelda to sleep at night after I told Beulah her pig wasn't going to be staying in your new house."

"Esmerelda's staying with us?"

"Beulah thinks Esmerelda will be bereft if we take her away from El Cid, and also believes that Esmerelda can double as a guard pig in case any of my would-be abductors show up."

Owen tilted his head. "Esmerelda is a surly sort, but did you actually tell Meemaw that her prized pig couldn't sleep in the house?"

"It's a pig. She belongs outside, and no, Beulah wasn't thrilled about that, but again, she apparently realizes I'm a formidable opponent and didn't put up too much of a fuss about it, although she might have mumbled something about me being a menace again." Camilla grinned. "At the rate I keep incurring the menace statements from her, it won't be long until she abandons the whole we're-perfect-for-each-other notion and declares to Wheeling at large that I'm ill-suited to become part of the Chesterfield family."

Any lingering male satisfaction running through him over Camilla stating she thought he was rather charming disappeared in a flash. "You do realize that it's somewhat insulting when you keep declaring, and vehemently, that we're so ill-suited, don't you?"

She gave his arm a pat. "There's nothing insulting about it. I'm a matchmaker. That means I'm an expert when it comes to matters of romance."

"You don't think I'm capable of romance?"

"I never said that, although given some of those romantic fiascos you recently told me about, you might benefit from having me give you a few pointers."

"They only would have been romantic fiascos if I'd been romantically interested in those ladies."

"A fair point."

Owen released a grunt. "Too right it is, and just so you know, I'm sure I could do romance properly if I set my mind to it."

"Duly noted," Camilla said before she glanced over his shoulder and winced. "Further talk of romance is going to have to wait, though, because your great-aunt is almost upon us. Given that you said she's a difficult woman, I suggest you greet her with a smile and kiss on the cheek, which may result with her turning less difficult."

Owen shook his head. "Aunt Elma will most certainly box my ears if I try to kiss her cheek."

Before Camilla could do more than grin, Aunt Elma pulled the wagon to a stop directly beside him and narrowed her eyes on him, although she might have simply been squinting to make sure it was him, then held out her hand.

"Don't just stand there, boy. I ain't gettin' any younger, and I'm itchin' to meet that girlie standin' beside you." Aunt Elma switched her attention to Camilla, completely ignoring the hand Owen had immediately held out for her the second he stepped close enough to the wagon. "I done heard rumors about Owen havin' found himself a hoity-toity fiancée, or almost fiancée, but you should know right now, li'l missy, that what with his mama still on holiday, it won't just be up to Beulah to decide if you're fittin' enough to join the family. That'll be up to me and the rest of our kinfolk as well, and know that I plan to keep a very, very close eye on you."

Seventeen

Given that she was currently on the receiving end of what could only be described as a glare, and a scorching one at that, it was a curious state of affairs when Camilla felt the most compelling urge to laugh.

That urge only increased when Owen finally got hold of Elma's arm and helped her out of the carriage, shooting Camilla a slightly wary look before he leaned forward, placed a kiss on Elma's wrinkled cheek, then winced as Elma gave his ear a bit of a wallop.

"What in tarnation's the matter with you, boy?" Elma demanded, her indignation somewhat suspect considering her cheeks were now pink. "You jist 'bout gave me heart palpitations since you know darn tootin' I'm not a woman who appreciates no physical sign of affection."

Owen gave his ear a rub. "Honestly, Aunt Elma, you know you're my favorite aunt. Of course I'd want to show you affection by kissing your cheek after not seeing you for almost a month."

"You haven't seen me for nigh on two moons," Elma shot back. "You done been avoidin' me cuz you know I had a roof needin' fixin'."

"I sent men to repair your roof the day after you told me it needed fixing."

"Should've come yourself," Elma muttered. "I pickled eggs just for you."

Owen's lips quirked at the corners. "That was unusually nice of you."

"It won't never happen again, since I heard tell you didn't come to do my roof because Alma needed your help at her place."

"Aunt Alma's stove caught on fire and burned down the wall behind it. If you'll recall, that was during a spring snowstorm. Aunt Alma needed my assistance far more than you did because snow was pouring into her house. You merely needed a few roof tiles replaced."

"Everyone always favors Alma," Elma said with a sniff before she glanced at Camilla. "You responsible for turnin' him affectionate?"

Camilla swallowed yet another unexpected laugh. "I don't believe Owen needed me to assist him with that because I'm sure he's always been an affectionate sort when it comes to family."

"No one mentioned you were daft, girl," Elma said before she turned to Mr. Timken, who was still sitting in the wagon, looking highly amused. "One would think, as her butler—although why anyone totes a butler around like a fancy piece of luggage is puzzlin'—you'd have mentioned somethin' about her lack of sense when you told me you was in her employ."

"Considering I found myself at the wrong end of your rifle, Miss Elma," Mr. Timken began, his eyes crinkling at the corners, "you'll have to forgive me for not divulging Miss Camilla's entire life history or idiosyncrasies to you in explicit detail. Although, I will state here and now that Miss Camilla is in no way daft."

"Why were you holding poor Mr. Timken at rifle-point?" Camilla asked, settling a frown on Elma.

"I stumbled on him rootin' around the spare barn," Elma began. "What else was I to think but that he was robbin' the place? He don't have the look of a local 'bout him, so I figured he'd done heard tell about Luella's treasures and knew she stashed them away from the house."

"*You* knew about Luella's furniture acquisitions?" Owen asked.

Elma arched a gray brow Owen's way. "*You* didn't?"

"Not until today."

A swat to his arm was Elma's first reply to that. "Maybe you and Miss Daftness here are doomed to be together after all since you don't know what your own sister's been up to of late. Talk around the valley has it that our Luella is doin' the Chesterfields proud with her philanthropic work since she's decided to make a difference in the community just like you, your daddy, and your daddy's daddy done did."

"I'm not sure how buying furniture correlates into philanthropy," Owen said.

"She's done been savin' strugglin' businesses," Elma said. "From what Hester"—she sent a nod to the woman still sitting in the back of the wagon—"heard when she was at Daniel's Diner, where everyone done knows gossip flows quicker than the Ohio after a rainstorm, Luella single-handedly saved Stu Wiggley's carpentry business."

Owen blinked. "She did?"

"Darn tootin'," Elma said. "Hester also heard that Luella introduced Stu to the Stiffel family, the textile manufacturers downtown, and they're now cooperatin' together and producin' some furnishin' that's sellin' like the buttermilk pies Beulah and Alma make to donate to the preacher's bake sale. To top it off, Luella's been hikin' into the hills and findin' all sorts of what she says are brilliant artsy types, snapping up the paintings and sculptures them artists are makin' and givin' 'em a fair price as well. Why, she's probably responsible for them artists being able to put meat and potatoes on their tables these days. She's so determined to help them that I heard she's been deliberately smearin' dirt all over herself as them hill people don't trust no one who looks too clean."

"Perhaps your sister's grooming problem isn't as bad as we initially thought," Camilla muttered.

Owen smiled ever so slightly before he returned his attention to Elma. "I'm curious how you knew Luella's been mingling with the hill folks. You haven't been sending Miss Baker up into the hills to keep an eye on her, have you?"

Given that Miss Hester Baker, who Camilla remembered Owen mentioning was Elma's paid companion, turned her head and began taking an interest in Gladys, who was now snoozing beside the coonhounds, it was evident that Elma *had* been sending her to snoop.

Elma shrugged Owen's question aside. "Hester likes when I send her to wander around the valley. Gives her a reason to part company with me for a spell."

"I'm sure she does enjoy an occasional break from your oh-so-pleasant disposition at times, but Hester's a paid companion, Aunt Elma, not a spy," Owen pointed out.

"Companions make excellent spies, my boy," Elma said with a knowing nod. "No one ever takes notice of them, but don't you fret I overtax her. I have other sources to glean interestin' tidbits, one of them sources bein' the ice-wagon driver, Howie Mitchell. He's the one that done told me about you fixin' to get hitched to Miss Peedmont."

Owen ran a hand over his jaw. "It's Miss Camilla *Pierpont*, and I fear I've set aside all semblance of manners because I've just realized I've yet to introduce the two of you properly."

"That's sure 'nough easily fixed." Elma nodded to Camilla. "I'm Elma McColloch, widow of Seth McColloch, a no-good, lying dog if there ever was one, and the reason the whole family gets to say their piece a'fore any vows are exchanged." She leaned closer to Camilla. "Seth done got himself blown up makin' moonshine 'bout thirty years past. You don't have a love of the bottle, do you, Miss Pierpont?"

"I have an occasional glass of wine or champagne," Camilla admitted.

"Long as it's not the whole bottle, that's acceptable," Elma said. "I myself am known to enjoy a titch of dandelion wine every now and again, but only on special occasions, mind you." Elma dusted her hands together. "Now that all them manners have been taken care of, I say let's get back to business." She took hold of Owen's arm. "Help me into the house because there ain't no sense in jabberin' away out here in the sun. Since you haven't seen fit to get me one of them fancy wheeled chairs I heard tell you got for Nems, my bad hip is painin' me more than usual and walkin' any distance is a chore."

"I got Nems a wheeled chair because he's missing a leg and his crutches chafe his underarms if he uses them too often," Owen said.

"It's a sad day when you cater more to a man in his prime over your old auntie" was all Elma said to that before she tugged him into motion, moving remarkably fast for a lady who claimed to suffer from a bad hip.

"I feel as if we've landed in an alien world," Mr. Timken muttered as he climbed off the wagon seat, then assisted Hester Baker over the side of the wagon. He then introduced Hester to Camilla before offering each of them an arm.

"May I assume you suffered no ill effects from Elma brandishing that rifle in your direction?" Camilla asked as they headed for the house.

"I can't claim I wasn't taken aback," Mr. Timken began. "However, Miss Baker, who possesses a very sensible nature, realized straightaway that I wasn't a thief. After I explained who I was, she then used my position as your butler to get Elma to lower her weapon."

Camilla's gaze shifted to Hester. "How did you do that?"

"I simply mentioned that butlers were known, at least from what I've read in books, to be in possession of titillating tidbits about their employers." Hester smiled. "Elma forgot all about shooting Mr. Timken because, after Howie told her about the gossip swirling around over you and Owen, Elma decided we needed to have a chat with Beulah lickety-split. Beulah, of course, wasn't at her cabin, but then we heard a rifle shot, which left Elma thinking her sister had gone over to the big house to do some target practice. Elma loves nothing more than shooting things, so off we went."

"It was rather disconcerting the way Elma can switch from rifle-threatening woman to a sweet grandmotherly type," Mr. Timken admitted as they walked across the portico and through a door that had been left open, Mr. Timken making a point to close it after they entered the house, shaking his head and muttering something about his nerves.

Camilla gave his arm a pat. "Since Charles and Leopold are now here to protect me after Father informed the Accounting Firm that I'd taken off for the wilds of West Virginia, you're more than welcome to return to New York, which may spare the state of your nerves for the foreseeable future."

"I'm not leaving you here with a bunch of rifle-toting women. Besides, I'm also your chaperone. I intend on continuing to act in that capacity until you return to New York."

"You and Owen aren't going to live here after you get married?" Hester asked.

Camilla was spared a response to that rather tricky question when she caught sight of Owen, who was in the process of having his hand pumped by a beaming Leopold, something that was leaving poor Owen looking yet again like a deer caught in the lantern lights.

"I think Owen might need some assistance," she said before she excused herself and headed down the marble hallway.

"Ah, Camilla, there you are," Leopold boomed as he released Owen's hand and settled his smile on her. "Charles and I were just about to come looking for you. It certainly doesn't speak highly of our guarding abilities that we've been sent to protect you and yet somehow misplaced you for a few minutes."

She returned his smile. "I wasn't misplaced, merely with Owen, which means I was perfectly fine. Frankly, I'm sure you'll misplace me a few more times while we're here since your attention seems to be focused on someone other than myself."

"I was just remarking to Owen about how delightful I find his grandmother," Leopold said, his smile turning brighter than ever.

Owen shuddered ever so slightly. "He told me Meemaw's a fine figure of a woman and hopes I'll put in a good word for him, and . . . You were right about the whole cozying up to my relatives you suggested he might be doing because when I introduced him to Aunt Elma, he kissed her hand."

"Did she box his ears?"

"No. She turned red as a tomato, muttered 'go on with you,' and dashed off to speak with Meemaw, bad hip and all."

Camilla laughed. "I have a feeling it's going to be an interesting afternoon."

"Let's just hope no one else in the family shows up," Owen murmured.

"And wouldn't that simply be a shame since I find myself downright enamored with all the Chesterfields I've met so far, at least as pertains to the ladies," Leopold countered. "But speaking of ladies"—he took hold of Camilla's arm—"what say we repair to the parlor? I imagine Luella still has numerous decorating tasks to be completed, although I readily admit she's not been overly impressed with my picture-hanging skills."

"I doubt you're eager to return to the parlor because of decorating tasks," Camilla said, walking with Leopold down the hallway as Owen fell into step beside her.

"You've found me out," Leopold said cheerfully.

"It wasn't difficult," Camilla said. "You've been less than subtle regarding your interest in Beulah."

"When you reach my age, there's no time for subtlety, just as, according to Beulah, there's no time like this evening for me to sample a local delicacy she's specifically making for me that goes by the name of corn pone." Leopold smiled. "I think her willingness to share the local fare with me suggests she may find me almost as intriguing as I find her."

It wasn't exactly a surprise when Owen took to scowling, but before Camilla could do more than grin, they were walking into the parlor, Charles excusing himself from where he was helping Luella and Bernadette position an abstract sculpture on one side of a fireplace that dominated the room.

"You must be Owen," Charles said, holding out his hand for Owen to shake. "Camilla told me a little about you earlier. I hope you'll forgive us for arriving on your doorstep without prior notice. Hubert Pierpont, Camilla's father, was on the verge of personally coming here to fetch his 'wayward daughter,' as he's taken to referring to her, but decided against that after Gideon Abbott, who's a partner at the Accounting Firm, sent him a telegram, explaining the Lord Shrewsbury situation. Hubert then decided it would be best for him to stay in New York to monitor Lord Shrewsbury once he shows up there."

"Wasn't Lord Shrewsbury the man you told me was dreadful?" Owen asked, settling a frown on Camilla.

"Indeed."

"And he's evidently traveling to New York?" Owen pressed.

Charles's brow furrowed as he turned to Camilla. "Why am I getting the distinct impression you haven't disclosed much to Owen about George?"

It was difficult to refuse a sigh. "I did mention George to Owen, although I might have also simply said he was a scourge of a man and left it at that."

Owen's lips twitched. "Has it escaped your notice that this scourge of a man shares the same name as my horse?"

"I noted that straightaway," Camilla said. "However, know that George, as in your horse, is far more amiable than George, the scourge, could ever be."

Charles cleared his throat. "And while this is a fascinating turn in the conversation, and I'm sure George the horse is a delightful creature . . ." He caught Camilla's eye. "Lord Shrewsbury could be a key figure in the mess you've landed yourself in."

"I know that, and before you say it was irresponsible for me to not come clean to Owen about George, I know that as well. The only excuse I have for withholding that information is that I don't particularly care to talk about the man who's responsible for the most humiliating event in my life."

"What's this about some man and humiliation?" Elma demanded, barreling up to join them. "You ain't using my great-nephew to make this man who humiliated you jealous, are you, cuz round about these parts, we don't take kindly to nonsense like that."

"Perhaps we should all take a seat so we can discuss everything rationally, without anyone threatening to fetch any rifles" was all she could think to suggest, earning a grunt from Elma in return, although Elma did march over to the nearest chair, plopping down on it a second later.

"I'm listenin'," she said.

Realizing she had no choice but to disclose all, Camilla took a seat on a delightful yellow settee, taking the next several minutes to fill everyone in on exactly who George Sherrington was, information that Owen took in stride, waving off her apology of not being completely upfront with him, and saying that since he didn't care to revisit unpleasant encounters from his past, he certainly wasn't going to hold it against her that she'd withheld unpleasant information from hers.

His willingness to simply accept her explanation without any judgment or resentment had her losing her train of thought for the briefest of seconds, until Elma cleared her throat and sent her a pointed look paired with a knowing smile, which snapped Camilla straight back to the situation at hand.

She immediately launched into a brief explanation about the abduction attempt, then finished up with how it had come to be that she and Owen were feigning their engagement.

Elma squinted in Camilla's direction. "If I'm understandin' what you jist said, Gideon Abbott's investigatin' that scourge, Lord Something-or-Other, cuz he might be fixin' to harm you. And that accountin' firm, which is a mighty funny name for an investigatin' agency, is lookin' into Victor Malvado, who may want to snatch you or maybe that companion of yours, who, if you didn't notice, ain't around right now."

Camilla's gaze shot around the room. "Where is Lottie?"

"She done went off to fetch more furniture with that interestin' lady's maid of yours." Elma shook her head. "'Fore you get to thinkin' your maid is bein' overly helpful, know that she only decided to go with Lottie after Edward insisted on accompanyin' your companion, sayin' something about makin' sure Lottie was kept all safe-like."

Camilla sent a smile Owen's way. "I told you I was right about Edward and Lottie."

"Just because Edward volunteered himself as Lottie's personal guard doesn't mean he's smitten."

"Oh, he's smitten all right," Elma said before Camilla had a chance to argue. "I done know the signs of a besotted man, and Edward's a marked man for sure." She brushed a wispy strand of gray hair out of her face. "I would've gone with them to make it all proper-like, but that maid, while bein' an unlikely chaperone, will done make sure there's nothin' untoward happenin' on account that she's one of them women who likes men to be keepin' their attention on her. She won't cotton to any funny business, at least not when a man might be thinkin' about kissin' someone other than her."

"I wouldn't think Edward, having just met Lottie, would be contemplating any kissing just yet," Camilla said.

"And you found success as a matchmaker?" Elma asked before she let out a bit of a snort and lifted her chin. "Anyhoo, back to what I was sayin'. You, Miss Pierpont, from what I kin gather, have agreed to gussie Luella up within a few short weeks, but I ain't thinkin', given how she started to scowlin' when you mentioned that, she's all that receptive to cooperatin'."

Luella sat forward on the settee she was sharing with Leopold. "Too right I'm not, since I think it would be easier all around if we'd just use Camilla's status within the Four Hundred to get everyone to accept me without going through the bother of making me all refined."

"But that there would deprive me," Elma began, "your favorite auntie, of the opportunity of watchin' you deliver Ada Mae Murchendorfer the comeuppance she rightly deserves after what she done did to you, and likewise what she done to your mama a couple years back."

Luella's brows drew together as she rose to her feet. "What did Mrs. Murchendorfer do to Mother?"

"You ain't heard?" Elma asked before she shot a glance at Beulah.

Beulah winced ever so slightly as she moved to stand beside Luella, taking hold of her hand. "I hope you won't get angry with me for not telling you this before, but you supposedly had an understanding with Stanley. If I would have blurted out what Ada Mae did to your mother, you would have been left feeling less than charitable toward a woman you thought was going to be your mother-in-law someday."

"'Specially when it's Ada Mae's fault your mama hied herself off to Paris," Elma added.

"It's *my* fault Mother went to Paris, even though Meemaw's been trying to convince me otherwise," Luella argued.

"That's nonsense there, child," Elma said, bustling up to Luella and giving her shoulder a slightly awkward pat. "You had nothin' to do with Betty Lou's decision. She up and left for Paris on account of that whist saloon Ada Mae purposefully didn't invite your mama to join but done invited every other woman of standin' in this here valley."

Luella wrinkled her nose. "I can't picture Mother getting bothered about not being able to go to a saloon."

"I think your aunt meant salon," Camilla clarified, blinking when Elma, instead of scowling at her, began to cackle.

"I think you're right, girl, jist as I think you might not be so daft after all, which is why I suppose I have no choice but to help you with fixin' Luella up."

"Oh . . . I don't believe that'll be necessary."

"It sure 'nough is, and besides helpin' you with Luella, I'll help you save poor Owen's reputation by doin' my best to show everyone real personal-like that you really aren't suited to country life." Elma nodded to her sister. "That'll make it more believable when you git around to tellin' everyone you're withholdin' your blessin' from their union."

"Except that I have no intention of withholding my blessing," Beulah argued.

"Why not?"

"Camilla's worthy of the recipe."

Elma blinked. "Don't reckon I was expectin' that, and just when I'd come up with a way to . . ." Elma stopped talking and began moseying around the room, muttering under her breath until she stopped and, concerningly enough, settled a smile on Camilla. "You keen on Beulah not cooperatin'?"

Camilla frowned. "I've already tried to disabuse her of the notion that Owen and I are well-suited for each other, but she doesn't seem to want to listen to me."

"Beulah's stubborn as the day is long, but I can help show her, jist like I said I can show the people of Wheelin', you're not suited to country life, and hence, not suited for Owen."

Wariness immediately settled over Camilla. "What do you have in mind?"

It was less than encouraging when Elma took to grinning, a look that on anyone else might have been pleasant, but on Elma was a look that probably terrified small children.

"Well, see, what with how gossip works around here, everyone's already heard that Owen brought you here to get his meemaw's blessing. Cuz of that, they're gonna expect you to be tryin' to impress, or maybe cater to is a better way to put it, to the family, specifically, his meemaw and . . . me."

"Define *cater to the family*," Camilla said.

"Oh, you know, jist doin' a few chores here and there."

Camilla tilted her head. "That's an interesting way to get yourself some unpaid labor, quite like Beulah apparently does when she sends out invitations to the family to plant her garden."

"Me and Beulah believe in bein' practical when it comes to gettin' tasks done that we don't care to do ourselves, but since you're gonna need my help convincin' my sister to withhold that blessin' in the end, I think it'll behoove you to accept the terms I jist laid out."

"I'm not really sure this is a sound plan because it's not as if anyone but you and Beulah would be around when I'm doing these chores."

Elma waved that aside. "Now don't you fret about that. I'll provide you with an audience to witness your ineptitude. And with that settled, I'll be expectin' you tomorrow at my cabin come sunrise. Don't dress fancy."

"Why not?" Camilla forced herself to ask.

Elma sent her another rather frightening grin. "Cuz I got a white-picket fence that needs whitewarshed, and that fence done got your name written all over it."

"Are you certain Elma won't come after me because I didn't present myself at her house bright and early to do something called 'whitewarshin' a fence'?" Camilla asked, holding on to Owen's arm as they strolled down Market Street, garnering more than their fair share of attention.

"There's no need for you to worry about Aunt Elma," Luella began, stopping to turn on the sidewalk before settling her attention on Camilla. "I rode over to her cabin early this morning and told her you wouldn't be doing her fence today."

"That was awfully brave of you," Camilla pointed out.

"Aunt Elma doesn't scare me, but you'll be pleased to learn I handled the situation somewhat graciously, even after I was forced to take Aunt Elma's rifle away from her after I told her you weren't coming and she grabbed it and tried to head out the door."

"I'm not sure grabbing is ever considered gracious."

"It was in this instance because I gave Aunt Elma's rifle back to her after I explained that your decision to not see to her fence this morning was all my fault."

"Another act of bravery."

"Not when I had control of the rifle at the time." Luella grinned. "Aunt Elma looked fit to be tied for a few seconds until I reminded her that she's been itching to see Ada Mae taken down a few pegs. I then reminded her that the only way that's going to happen is if you're able to turn me into one of those Diamonds of the First Water you mentioned were all the rage in New York."

"You do realize that obtaining Diamond status will require an extreme undertaking on your part, don't you?" Camilla asked.

Luella waved that aside. "Doesn't matter. All that matters is the end result, which, if we're successful, will show Ada Mae Murchendorfer and her cad of a son once and for all that I'm perfectly capable of turning refined."

"You won't balk at fittings, dance instruction, and etiquette lessons that will most assuredly eat up several hours of your days?"

"I'll be exactly like that Miss Adelaide Duveen you took in hand a few months back, the picture-perfect student."

Camilla's lips twitched. "Here's hoping you'll be nothing like Adelaide because she gave new meaning to the word *challenging*. She loathed fittings and had a difficult time sitting still whenever I brought in someone to arrange her hair."

"Since I didn't fidget at all while Bernadette did my hair this morning, nor did a single whisper of complaint escape my lips while your lady's maid altered a few of my older dresses that you deemed salvageable, I think I've already shown that I'm not going to be a problem." Luella smoothed a hand down the sleeve of an afternoon gown of palest yellow that complemented hair that turned out to be auburn once it had been given a good scrubbing. "Mother would be appalled that you had Bernadette de-bow this particular gown."

"I doubt she'd be appalled if she saw you in it since the tailored and frill-free style agrees with you. However . . ." Camilla frowned. "If we may return to Elma, are you quite certain she's reconciled herself to the fact I won't have time to tend to her fence, or any of the many other menial tasks I think she may have her heart set on me completing?"

"Elma's not reconciled herself to that at all," Luella countered. "She expects you at her house tomorrow morning before daybreak to attend to her fence and told me to tell you that in order to fit everything into your schedule, you'll probably need to rise from your bed a few hours earlier than you normally do."

"Ah, I see," Camilla began, tapping a finger against her chin. "Elma's obviously throwing down a gauntlet, one I'm sure she's going to be surprised to learn I won't hesitate to pick up."

"Why would you do that?" Owen asked.

"Because Elma's evidently of the belief I'll be incapable of successfully completing the tasks, and I don't think I should give her the satisfaction of watching me fail, although . . ." She wrinkled her nose. "What exactly is involved with whitewarshing a fence, or better yet, what does *warshing* mean in the first place?"

"It's just a West Virginian way of saying *wash*," Owen began. "And whitewashing a fence isn't complicated. It's just sloshing diluted paint on the pickets."

"I can probably handle that."

"I'm sure you can, but I should warn you that Aunt Elma will undoubtedly take to heckling you as she sits on her front porch, critiquing your technique."

"I've never been heckled before," Camilla admitted. "Should make for a more-than-amusing experience, but dare I hope Elma will expect me to heckle her in return?"

"That might have her whipping out her rifle."

Camilla grinned, the sight of her grin leaving Owen's collar feeling uncomfortably snug and his cheeks a little warm.

Truth be told, he'd found himself becoming warm often over the past day and a half, a direct result of catching Camilla grinning time and again as she went about interacting with his family.

There was something downright enticing about her when she grinned, as if she'd let down her prim-and-proper guard and was allowing herself to simply be Camilla, a lady who seemed to enjoy finding herself thrust into a world she hadn't known existed.

Her interest the evening before in sampling all the local dishes

Meemaw had made for supper had been obvious, and he'd found himself riveted by her different reactions.

Lima beans, morel mushrooms, river trout, and puffers—or rather, potato pancakes—had been her favorites because she'd eaten every bite of the helpings on her plate, whereas corn pone and rabbit stew had obviously not been to her liking. She'd merely taken one bite of each before she'd ever so casually pushed them to the side of her plate.

He readily admitted he'd been completely taken aback when, after everyone finished dinner by enjoying a piece of rhubarb pie, Camilla insisted on helping clear the table, even though Mr. Timken had assured her that her assistance wasn't needed. Camilla hadn't hesitated to argue with that, stating that since Elma and Beulah had fed all the men hired to guard her, as well as Lottie and Bernadette, there were more than a few dishes, along with all the pots and pans, that needed attending to. Camilla had then refused to let Meemaw or Elma lift a finger to clean, stating quite emphatically that they'd cooked the food, so it was only fair that they took it easy while everyone else pitched in to clean up.

It hadn't escaped his notice that after that pronouncement, Meemaw, with Elma in tow, had disappeared, returning a few minutes later with Meemaw's recipe box in hand.

All in all, it had been a more-than-enjoyable day, one of the most enjoyable parts being when he'd joined Camilla in the kitchen, drying the dishes after she washed them, although she'd gotten more water on herself than on the dishes, suggesting she'd never washed a dish in her life, not that she seemed overly concerned about the drenched state of her gown when they finally finished.

She hadn't even repaired to her room to have Bernadette help her change when everyone moseyed out to the back terrace to have a few glasses of dandelion wine. Nems and Andy Sklenicka even pulled out a fiddle and a banjo, which they put to good use entertaining everyone until the mosquitoes started biting.

"If you really want to fit in around here," Luella said, pulling Owen from his thoughts, "you should start saying *you'uns*."

"Younz?" Camilla repeated.

"You . . . uns," Luella corrected. "As in 'are you'uns goin' to be doing the warsh today, or can you meet us at the crick to do some fishin'?'"

"And crick would mean creek?" Camilla asked.

"Indeed."

"I've taken the liberty of writing down some of the local dialect and phrases in a journal," Charles said, strolling up from behind them and stopping beside Luella, Leopold trailing in his wake.

It was a little concerning when Luella's eyes took to flashing. "Why would you write those down?"

Charles blinked. "Shouldn't I?"

"Not if you're intending on going back to New York and using that journal as a source of amusement with your friends to highlight what you evidently see as our backwoods ways."

Charles's eyes widened. "I do most humbly beg your pardon, Miss Chesterfield. I certainly haven't been documenting my observations to make sport of you or the fine people living in this region. I simply wanted to chronicle things I've heard so I can peruse them when I'm at my leisure."

"Why?" Luella asked.

"Because I found myself being the source of Nems and Andy's amusement last night when I asked them to clarify what *dem dare* meant as they were telling a story." Charles shook his head. "It took them a good five minutes to explain in a way I could understand that it meant *them there*, or something to that effect, although in my defense, those gentlemen do know how to meander their way around an explanation."

Luella tilted her head. "You're trying to decipher our local dialect so that you're not made fun of again?"

"Since I've experienced my fair share of derision over the years, Miss Chesterfield, I try to avoid setting myself up for more of that if at all possible. In this particular case, having a grasp of the local jargon may at least leave Nems and Andy with the impression I'm not a complete idiot."

"You're worried about what Nems and Andy think of you?" Luella asked slowly.

"Of course I am. They're very nice men and even invited me to go fishing. I'd at least like to have a handle on some of the local vernacular so that we can enjoy conversations instead of me having to ask them to interpret every other word they say."

"Huh," Luella said before she stepped closer to Charles. "I must say that it speaks highly of your character that you're determined to learn our special language down here, but I find it difficult to believe that you've experienced derision over the years, given you're a member of that fancy Four Hundred Camilla told me about."

"A scornful attitude isn't held at bay simply because one possesses wealth and their family holds a status within a specific social setting, Miss Chesterfield," Charles said. "I've never 'taken' within society, probably because I'm considered somewhat dull, and people who are uninspiring often find themselves bearing the brunt of unpleasant remarks."

"I haven't gotten the impression you're dull in the least," Luella countered. "And, if you haven't noticed, you've been attracting more than your fair share of attention as we've wandered up Market Street." She smiled. "I expect some of the ladies who've been discreetly observing you will muster up the nerve to approach us at some point during our excursion today. I can guarantee once they discover you're a member of New York high society, they won't conclude that a single word that escapes your mouth is humdrum."

Charles's gaze darted to three ladies who were walking toward them, blinking when all of them cast what could only be considered flirtatious smiles his way before they strolled on by. He returned his attention to Luella. "They may be initially impressed, but once they get to know me, they'll decide, quite like all the ladies of the Four Hundred have, that I'm a less-than-riveting conversationalist."

"I'm less than riveting in that regard, as well," Luella admitted with a grin. "In fact, I've been known to bore people to tears when I get on the subject of my favorite plants, especially flowers. To prove that point, know that I could speak for hours about a project I'm in the midst of, one where I'm currently attempting to make a new lily hybrid—not that I've found much success with that yet."

Charles took a step closer to her. "You must tell me all about this hybrid process, Miss Chesterfield, because I wouldn't find that less than riveting in the least since I'm an amateur horticulturist."

Luella raised a hand to her throat. "You are?"

"Indeed, and I'm now waiting with bated breath to learn more about this lily of yours."

Owen felt his mouth drop open when Luella suddenly entwined her arm with Charles's.

"Your breath will not need to be bated for long because I'm more than happy to discuss my lily with you, but before I begin talking your ear off, know that any woman who has ever found you dull must not have been in possession of their senses, as I find you utterly fascinating." With that, Luella tugged Charles into motion and together they continued down Market Street, their heads bent closely together.

It really came as no surprise when Camilla's eyes began to gleam in a far-too-telling fashion.

"Don't even consider it," Owen grumbled, pulling her after his sister and earning an innocent batting of the lashes from Camilla in return.

"Consider what?"

"Matchmaking, or more specifically, matchmaking with Luella in your sights."

She sent him an overly sweet smile. "You know what they say—once a matchmaker, always a matchmaker."

"No."

"Why not?" She nodded to Luella and Charles. "It's been my experience that when a couple shares a common interest, a spark is soon to follow."

"There will be no sparking between Luella and Charles."

"I think there already is."

"There's not, nor will you attempt to get anything between them igniting into something remotely resembling a spark."

"I think that ship has already sailed because—what are the odds that Luella just happens to become introduced to Charles, who just happens to have an interest in horticulture? That's one of those unusual life happenstances that someone like me, a former matchmaker, simply cannot ignore."

"You're going to have to try, although . . ." Owen stopped in his tracks as a thought struck. "Isn't Charles one of the two men you mentioned you were thinking about unofficially sponsoring?"

Leopold was suddenly right beside him, beaming a smile Camilla's way. "Forgive me for eavesdropping," he began, "but am I to understand that you, Camilla, have been discreetly resuming your matchmaking endeavors and that you have two specific gentlemen in mind already, one of whom may happen to be Charles?"

"Having Charles in my sights shouldn't come as much of a surprise since you know his mother, Petunia, has been relentless in her quest to convince me to help her one and only son find a suitable match," Camilla said.

"Petunia does know her way around an unrelenting campaign," Leopold agreed. "And since that was clearly a yes from you about sponsoring Charles, I now find myself curious about that second gentleman you're considering. Dare I hope, since you know I've been rather forlorn of late, given that Vernon, my very best friend, went off to explore Europe with his new wife, that being your aunt Edna of course, that I'm that second gentleman?"

"I hate seeing you forlorn."

Leopold's smile turned brighter than ever. "I'll take that as a yes as well, and if you're unaware, I already have the perfect lady in mind for me."

"It would be next to impossible for me to be unaware of that since your interest in Beulah has been less than subtle."

"She is a most extraordinary lady," Leopold proclaimed.

"I don't think I'm enjoying the direction this conversation is taking," Owen muttered.

"Nonsense," Leopold argued. "I would think you'd be pleased to learn that a gentleman who's well-suited for your grandmother is now determined to win her over."

"I'm relatively convinced that I'd prefer if you'd simply appreciate how extraordinary she is from afar."

Leopold laughed. "That's some wishful thinking there, son, but know that I have only the most honorable of intentions toward Beulah."

"I'm not sure my meemaw will be so receptive to those intentions."

"She's a complicated sort, there's no question about that," Leopold agreed. "Nevertheless, now that I know I can count on Camilla's assistance, I'm convinced it'll only be a matter of time until I procure Beulah's affections."

"While it does appear as if Camilla is very proficient with this whole matchmaking business," Owen began, "I feel it's only fair to warn you that Meemaw would never consider leaving this valley, especially not for a place like New York."

"I wouldn't dream of taking her away from her home, although I'm sure she wouldn't be opposed to doing a touch of traveling." Leopold leveled another smile on Camilla. "I could take her to Europe and meet up with your aunt and Vernon."

Camilla gave Leopold's arm a pat. "I think you're getting a little ahead of yourself. Why don't we simply work on ascertaining that the two of you truly do share a spark and see where that spark leads?"

"I definitely don't want to hear any more about sparks when it pertains to my grandmother—or my sister, for that matter," Owen said.

Camilla turned and patted *his* arm. "Of course you don't, which is why we'll now shelve this conversation for later since I've just spotted Thomas Hughes and Company across the street." She nodded to the storefront. "Edward told me that's the best place to purchase quality clothing for gentlemen."

"Says on the door *gents furnishing goods*," Leopold said, squinting in the direction of the store.

"Then that's where we'll start with Owen's new wardrobe," Camilla said. "You'll, of course, accompany him, Leopold."

Owen frowned. "I thought we were focusing on Luella today."

"Your sister hardly needs you tagging along to the department stores to help her shop for new gowns," Camilla argued. "And since your time is limited as you do run the largest nail-producing company in the country, I thought we'd split up to optimize our shopping expedition."

"I'm not going to leave you unprotected just so I can find a new suit."

"You'll be ordering more than *a* suit, all of them custom-made, unless Thomas Hughes and Company happens to have a suit or two on hand that would fit you properly."

"Custom-made?" Owen repeated.

"That's the only way you'll get a satisfactory fit," Camilla said. "And, before you argue that you don't need a new wardrobe, know that as a titan of industry, you'll garner more respect from others if you look the part of a successful man of business. You're currently taking meetings while wearing ill-fitting suits, and not because you can't afford the best, but because you don't want to take the time needed to have them custom-made."

"Not one industry titan has ever remarked on the fit of my jacket."

Camilla shrugged. "Perhaps not, but they've definitely taken notice, even if they've never said anything, and perception is important in business. My father taught me that, so off you trot to the haberdashery, and no, it's not up for debate."

Owen glanced to where Luella and Charles stood in front of Stone and Thomas department store, their heads still bent closely together—too closely together in his humble opinion.

"I'm really not comfortable leaving you without proper protection for any length of time," he finally said, returning his attention to Camilla. "I can always return to the gentlemen's store tomorrow to place an order."

"Absolutely not," Camilla didn't hesitate to argue. "I'm not going to have time tomorrow to return to town, not since Elma wants me to whitewash her fence, and I'll also be immersing myself in etiquette lessons with Luella. That means I won't have a moment to spare to come with you, and not to offend you, but I don't trust your judgment when it comes to picking out new clothing."

She glanced over her shoulder and nodded to Lottie and Mr. Timken, who were taking in the sights as Andy, who was pushing Nems in his wheeled chair, acted as tour guide. "And, before you mention inadequate protection again as a reason to avoid shopping for yourself, I'm quite well-guarded, so off you go. I'm sure you and Leopold will have a lovely time choosing jacket styles and patterns."

Owen glanced at Charles again, who was now whispering in Luella's ear. "Perhaps Charles should come with me instead of Leopold."

"Charles, while an utter darling, isn't what I'd call fashion motivated, whereas Leopold"—she gave a wave in Leopold's direction—"is always dressed in the most sophisticated of styles. He'll make certain you don't come out of Thomas Hughes and Company dressed like an undertaker, a dismal look Charles adopts on a rather frequent basis."

"There's nothing wrong with looking like an undertaker," Owen muttered.

Camilla grinned. "Will you be more receptive to the idea if I make Leopold promise to avoid waxing on about how extraordinary your grandmother is, or trying to convince you to speak to her on his behalf?"

"I doubt he'll be capable of that, seeing how enthralled he seems to be with Meemaw."

"Indeed I am," Leopold said cheerfully. "But I'll tell you what, I'll try to curtail my enthusiasm for your grandmother, at least until after we see you sporting an entirely new wardrobe."

Owen frowned. "What exactly comprises a new wardrobe? Three suits . . . five, perhaps?"

"We're looking, at a minimum, at ten suits, plus overcoats, cravats, and shirts. A few walking canes wouldn't be remiss either."

"Absolutely not."

"Think of it this way," Camilla said, her eyes twinkling once again. "Your sister is now determined to get herself accepted by the Wheeling elite, done mostly to avenge your mother. What kind of example would you be for her if you refuse to do what it takes to firmly cement your standing—and in essence, your entire family's standing—in Wheeling society, especially when you must know your mother would appreciate any effort you make? Why, your mother might even decide to return home if she knows Ada Mae hasn't won the battle of ostracizing your family, something you know Luella wants your mother to do."

When put that way, there was no arguing the point, which was exactly why Owen found himself a scant ten minutes later shucking out of his ill-fitting jacket, a salesman almost rubbing his hands in glee as Leopold explained exactly what they needed to accomplish that day.

Unfortunately, as soon as Leopold finished his explanation, he immediately returned to the subject of Meemaw, apparently having forgotten his promise to keep all talk away from how lovely he found her, which resulted in Owen having no choice but to turn his full attention to a fashion catalog that had drawings of the latest styles for gentlemen, something his attention would have never settled on before he'd made the acquaintance of Miss Camilla Pierpont.

Oddly enough, the notion that she was clearly disrupting his life wasn't nearly as bothersome as he once might have imagined it would be.

Nineteen

"It's amazing how many salesgirls have been sent to assist us," Luella whispered as Camilla browsed through a rack that held ready-made afternoon gowns. "Do you always receive such stellar service?"

After eyeing an attractive ivory gown with traces of lavender embroidered around a square neckline, Camilla pulled it off the rack, handed it to a salesgirl who'd said her name was Dorothy, then returned her attention to Luella.

"I imagine, after I told the manager of ladies' furnishings what I hoped to accomplish today, he sent out an 'all hands on deck' call, hence the reason we now appear to have half the employees in the store at our disposal."

"It also didn't hurt that the manager had already been told you, an esteemed member of the Four Hundred, were in town," Lottie said, moving up to join them before she held up a riding habit of emerald green. "I thought this would go well with Luella's hair."

Camilla glanced at Luella, whose hair was drawn up on top of her head, Bernadette having teased little curls out of the upsweep. "Green is certainly a complementary color for her, and I'm also thinking we should find something in blue to bring out the color of her eyes."

"I'll see what I can find," Lottie said before she moved across the room and began browsing through another rack of clothing, just as the manager of the ladies' furnishings department, Mr. Kline, hurried up to Camilla, an older woman by his side.

"Miss Pierpont," Mr. Kline began, "allow me to introduce Mrs. Magruder to you. She's our lead associate in our intimate apparel department and will be ascertaining whether Miss Chesterfield has all the proper, ah, unmentionables needed to truly accentuate the many lovely gowns we hope she chooses today." Sending Camilla an inclination of his head, Mr. Kline turned and hurried across the room, stopping to whisper what were probably additional instructions to the salesgirls who were sorting through a rack of garments someone had fetched from a back storeroom.

"I've been informed, Miss Chesterfield, that you're here to add some essential pieces to your wardrobe," Mrs. Magruder said, moving close to Luella and settling a lovely smile on her. "I have missed your mother over the past few years because she was always such a valued customer, spending hours perusing the latest fashions and always returning home with numerous acquisitions for you." Mrs. Magruder's smile dimmed as she gave Luella a once-over. "You don't seem to have any lace or bows on your outfit today, although I distinctly remember that the gown you're wearing, one your mother purchased here before she left on her adventure to France, was originally emblazoned with charming bows and an abundance of lace attached to the bodice."

Luella immediately shot Camilla a look that clearly suggested she had no idea how to respond since Mrs. Magruder was evidently a fan of bows and lace.

"I fear I'm to blame for the lack of Luella's frills," Camilla said, drawing Mrs. Magruder's attention. "Luella, at least in my humble opinion, shows to advantage in more tailored, less embellished ensembles, which is why I had my lady's maid remove the bows and lace on the gown Luella's currently wearing, as well as alter the back so that she has no need of a bustle."

Mrs. Magruder blinked. "Why would you encourage Miss Luella to abstain from bustles when those are imperative in accentuating a woman's figure?"

"Because silhouettes have been changing in New York of late, undoubtedly because we ladies were beginning to grow weary of all the perching we were forced to do, given the large bustles that once-fashionable silhouettes demanded."

"*Once*-fashionable?" Mrs. Magruder asked rather weakly.

Camilla refused a sigh. "Forgive me, Mrs. Magruder, as I truly don't want to upset you, but I'm afraid bustles are no longer quite as in vogue in New York City." She presented Mrs. Magruder with her back. "If you'll notice, I'm not wearing a bustle, merely horsehair padding, which still allows a lovely silhouette but also allows me to sit with ease."

"I believe I need to have a word with our buyers," Mrs. Magruder mumbled before she dipped into a curtsy, then barreled across the store, stopping to whisper something to Mr. Kline, who shot a glance at Camilla before he strode through the department, Mrs. Magruder dogging his heels as they disappeared through an archway.

"I have a feeling Stone and Thomas might soon be displaying gowns cut in quite different silhouettes," Luella said, folding an afternoon gown of lavender over her arm. "It's too bad they didn't learn of New York's abandonment of bustles earlier, though, because all the gowns I'll be buying today require that ridiculous appendage. Poor Bernadette is going to have her hands full altering them."

"She won't be responsible for all the alterations," Camilla returned, eyeing another gown on the rack, but discarding it because pink wasn't a shade that would favor Luella's coloring. "Your grandmother knew, since we're on a time constraint, that it wouldn't be advisable to expect the alterations department here to handle it all, just as she realized Bernadette wouldn't be able to finish everything needed in a timely fashion. That's why she sent notes off to all the members of her sewing bee early this morning with the expectation those ladies will be more than happy to step in."

"Bernadette's going to be relieved to have that assistance."

"I'm sure she will, although I have to admit I was unaware she possessed any real seamstress skills to begin with."

"Bernadette told me, as she was ripping bows off the dress I'm currently wearing, that she was often called upon to fix costumes at the theater," Luella said. "That's where she also learned to arrange hair, because the hairdressers employed by the theater were always showing up late. According to Bernadette, she made a point to excel at alterations and dressing hair because she thought that would eventually lead to the manager of the theater company offering her a spot in one of his productions. From what I gathered, Bernadette longs to take to the stage."

"She's mentioned that to me as well, but since she's found herself in my employ, I assume that offer from the theater manager never materialized. That was obviously a setback for Bernadette, but one that's clearly worked out well for me." Camilla shook her head. "I fear I must admit that my first impression of my lady's maid was completely off the mark."

"Because?"

"She didn't appear to relish the role of lady's maid and complained almost incessantly about how often she needed to assist me with the wardrobe changes that are expected of someone with my social calendar," Camilla said. "Lately, though, she's barely complained at all and certainly surprised me when she insisted on staying behind today to work on the gowns I felt were salvageable from your closet. I would've thought she'd want to come shopping with us."

"Considering Meemaw's sewing bee has probably already gathered back at the house, undoubtedly all aflutter to learn why their help was needed, Bernadette is most assuredly finding herself in high demand, which I imagine has outweighed any regret she may have experienced over not accompanying us since she strikes me as a woman who enjoys being the center of attention."

"I'm almost afraid to ask this, but why would she be in high demand?"

"She's your lady's maid. She knows things about you, and the ladies will want to ferret out that knowledge, especially information pertinent to when Bernadette thinks you're planning on marrying my brother."

"They're in for a disappointment then, since Bernadette can't disclose that information as there aren't any real plans for Owen and me to marry."

"That's why you should prepare yourself for an interrogation from the ladies once we return to the country house."

"And while the idea of an interrogation sounds downright delightful, I overheard you and Charles making plans to go riding later this afternoon. I'm sure the ladies will be more than understanding when I tell them I can't linger around for any interrogating since I'll be assuming the role of chaperone."

"I don't need a chaperone."

"Given the way you and Charles were thick as thieves earlier, chatting about horticulture of all things, and then gazing intently at each other until we were ushered into ladies' furnishings, leaving Charles and Mr. Timken waiting for us on those comfy settees I assume were strategically placed to stash waiting husbands and the like, you, my dear Luella, are definitely in need of a chaperone."

"I've gone riding numerous times in my youth with boys I know and have never bothered to take a chaperone with me."

"But you're no longer in your youth. You're also determined to become a proper lady, and proper ladies, when in the company of a gentleman, require a chaperone to assure that expected proprieties are maintained."

"I doubt Charles would even consider abandoning proprieties

with someone like me. We'll most likely spend our time riding speaking of horticulture. You'll then end up being bored to tears, which means there's no need for you to accompany us."

"Except that a shared interest often leads to other interests, and those interests are exactly why you need a chaperone." Camilla smiled. "However, if you're opposed to me taking on that role, I'll be more than happy to ask Elma to step in. She has, after all, promised to assist me with, as she says, 'gussying you up.'"

Luella blinked. "Oh, I don't think there's any need to involve Aunt Elma."

"Does that mean you're agreeable to me chaperoning you?"

"I'd be absolutely thrilled to have you accompany us on our ride."

"Sarcasm, just so you know, should be used sparingly, but with the chaperoning business settled, off you go to the dressing room."

As Luella made her way across the room, Camilla moved to rejoin Lottie, who was holding up a hat, one she discarded a second later.

"It had a bow" was all Lottie said once Camilla stopped by her side.

"Luella does seem to have an aversion to bows."

"For good reason, since her mother and Ada Mae Murchendorfer apparently engaged in rivalry bow competitions over the years."

"An excellent point, but bows aside, and before I forget, I was wondering if you'd be opposed to stopping by Chesterfield Nails after we complete our shopping today. I've been longing to see how nails are manufactured."

Lottie abandoned another hat. "Please. The only thing you're longing for is an opportunity to create a supposedly random encounter between me and Edward because you've got matchmaking on your mind."

"I have no idea what you're talking about."

Lottie caught Camilla's eye. "Then explain, if you please, why you were all smiles when Edward and I returned with another load of furniture last night, even though he only offered to go with me because he's aware that Victor Malvado might be a threat."

"Since Leopold received another telegram early this morning from the Accounting Firm, who now has Victor under surveillance and hasn't noticed any unusual activity coming from him or his criminal associates, I think the threat level to both of us is relatively low right now."

"But we didn't know that yesterday, hence the reasoning behind Edward's gallant offer to protect me."

"Ah, so you find him gallant, do you?" Camilla smiled. "I'm sure that notion only increased after he chose to sit beside you last night at dinner and made a point of explaining all the local dishes to you before you tasted any of them."

"He sat next to me because you told him to."

"Did I?"

Lottie crossed her arms over her chest. "For a woman who keeps claiming to have retired from matchmaking, you certainly seem to be jumping back into it with gusto—and not only with me."

"Is it my fault that as a former matchmaker I'm finding it difficult to ignore what could certainly be spectacular matches that have all but landed in my lap?"

"Yes, that would be your fault, and while I agree that there's something interesting between Beulah and Leopold, and that learning Luella and Charles share a fondness for horticulture, which I can't believe too many people do, does suggest they might be more than compatible, Edward Stevens and I are not well matched."

"He's clearly besotted with you and spent yesterday practically glued to your side."

Lottie rolled her eyes. "And while his attention was certainly flattering, I'm not the woman for him. Edward, I'll have you know, teaches Sunday school, volunteers teaching English classes at a grammar school three times a week during his lunch hour, and escorts his mother to church two times a week."

"You attend church with me every Sunday, so I know you're not opposed to going to church."

"I never said I was, but besides all that, his mother belongs to that sewing bee of Beulah's and would certainly expect any woman her son might have an interest in courting to join her during her sewing days."

"You don't enjoy sewing?"

"It's not a favorite pastime, but you're missing the point. I, if you've forgotten, was only recently in the employ of Frank Fitzsimmons—a known criminal boss of the New York underworld. I'm not respectable enough for an upstanding gentleman such as Edward."

"You were only in Frank's employ because he threatened to harm your mother if you refused to work for him. And, in case *you've* forgotten, you're the daughter of an educated man who worked as a tutor—a completely reputable occupation."

"I'm a former criminal."

"With aspirations to become a teacher, which means you and Edward are more than compatible."

"We might be compatible, but I'm not marriage material for him, although . . ." Lottie caught Camilla's eye. "Edward did mention, after I told him about my interest in becoming a teacher, that there's a real need for educators in this area. Even without a formal degree, he thinks there are numerous schools that would hire me for the start of school come fall."

"See? That's wonderful."

"No, it's not, because I'm certainly not going to leave you in the lurch without a paid companion after everything you've done for me."

Camilla picked up a hat and began inspecting the brim. "I'm twenty-five years old, Lottie, almost twenty-six. I'm perfectly capable of muddling through life without a companion."

Lottie blinked before her brow took to furrowing. "Clearly I've been uncommonly dense of late because—did you offer me a position, not because your aunt Edna up and married Vernon, leaving you without a chaperone, although both of us decided, since I'm younger than you, that a companion would be more appropriate, but because you wanted to ascertain that I didn't get swept back into the criminal world after we learned that Victor Malvado was keen to have me join his motley band of hoodlums?"

"I wasn't very well going to let Victor get his hands on you, not when he's rumored to be a man lacking any and all redeeming qualities."

Lottie's eyes turned suspiciously bright as she settled a rather wobbly smile on Camilla. "You're far kinder than you allow everyone to know, but thank you for giving me a position to keep me from returning to criminal endeavors."

"You're welcome."

"I suppose now, with all that out in the open, and since I may not be in your employ long, which makes me feel as if I don't need to completely adhere to companion rules, I would like to . . ." Lottie stopped speaking and frowned. "Why does it appear as if you're trying to hold back a grin?"

"Because I wasn't aware you were deliberately attempting to adhere to any rules."

"Of course I was, but if you'll recall, I was only recently immersed in a world filled with criminals. Rules weren't exactly something I needed to worry about, which meant I had to put a great deal of effort into learning all the rules a proper companion was supposed to observe. However . . ." Lottie's eyes twinkled. "We're getting completely off the subject, so what I wanted to say was this—I'd like to lend you some advice."

"Advice?"

"Matchmaking advice, to be exact." Lottie stepped closer. "In my opinion, you need to stop concerning yourself with forging all these matches for everyone and concentrate on something that will benefit you for a change—that being arranging a match for yourself."

"Have you forgotten that I've made a vow never to marry?"

Lottie waved that aside. "Vows like that are meant to be broken. Besides, you're not destined for spinsterhood, not with Owen in the picture now."

"Do not say you've been listening to Beulah and have decided she's right about Owen being my match."

"I didn't need to listen to Beulah to realize that."

"But you should listen to me when I tell you Owen and I are not well-suited."

"Why not?" Lottie asked.

"Because, unlike you and Edward, Owen and I have nothing in common."

"Being a matchmaker, I'm sure you're more than familiar with the idea that opposites attract. Besides that, you speak your mind to him."

"That doesn't mean I want to marry him."

"You should at least consider my point, because you don't speak your mind to other gentlemen," Lottie argued. "I was with you almost constantly during our spring in the Hudson, as well as during our time in Paris. Yes, you spoke with many gentlemen, all of whom plied you with flattery, but none of whom sparked the slightest interest on your part. Owen, on the other hand, interests you."

Camilla opened her mouth with a rebuttal on the tip of her tongue, then closed it again because . . . Lottie wasn't exactly off the mark.

Owen *did* interest her.

There were myriad reasons for why she found him interesting, one of the most prominent ones being the fact that he didn't flatter her. Even more interesting was that she knew he didn't flatter her, not because he wasn't adept with pretty words, but because he wasn't trying to impress her, a novel experience if there ever was one and frankly one she couldn't deny was appealing.

The only problem with finding him appealing, though, was that he'd not shown a single sign that he found her appealing in return.

She was accustomed to having gentlemen going to extreme

measures to win her favor, and yet Owen hadn't done anything to suggest he wanted any favor from her. Quite frankly, he seemed almost oblivious to the fact she was even a member of the feminine set, and . . .

"Oh, this is going to be interesting," Lottie suddenly proclaimed, yanking Camilla from her thoughts.

"What should be interesting?" she asked, glancing around.

Lottie nodded to two young ladies who were standing in the middle of the department, their gazes locked on Camilla—until they exchanged a bit of a look between them, lifted their chins in tandem, and began marching determinedly Camilla's way.

Twenty

"You must be Miss Pierpont," one of the ladies sporting a gown awash in bows exclaimed, stopping directly in front of Camilla and dipping into a curtsy. "I know this is quite untoward since I'm well-aware someone else should perform a formal introduction, but"—she glanced around the room—"since I don't see Luella anywhere, and there's no one else present to introduce us . . ." She returned her attention to Camilla. "I'm Miss Sally Murchendorfer."

"I sure was right about this being interesting," Lottie muttered before she glided away, leaving Camilla in the company of Ada Mae's daughter, a young lady who apparently still trusted her mother's judgment regarding bows.

Camilla dipped into a curtsy of her own. "A pleasure to meet you, Miss Murchendorfer."

"Allow me to present my friend," Sally said, nodding to the lady accompanying her. "Miss Pierpont, this is Miss Curtistine Longerbeam. Curtistine, Miss Camilla Pierpont."

It really wasn't much of a surprise when Curtistine, the lady who'd called Owen a lout over their obvious misunderstanding regarding his intentions toward her, glared at her—until Sally gave her a nudge, which resulted in Curtistine dredging up a rather forced smile.

"Delighted to meet you, Miss Pierpont," Curtistine squeaked out. "I understand that congratulations are in order."

"It's delightful to meet you as well, Miss Longerbeam, although congratulations may be a touch premature considering there's been no official announcement made yet."

"Having seconds thoughts already?"

Camilla's eyes immediately took to narrowing. "Why would you assume that?"

"It's not much of an assumption when Owen holds the reputation of being incapable of capturing a lady's affections for long," Curtistine returned. "Personally, I knew it was only a matter of time until you, an esteemed lady with Knickerbocker status if rumor has it correctly, realized he was a complete and utter bore."

Clearly, the lady's silk gloves were rapidly coming off, which meant she was going to have to shuck off hers as well.

"I fear you're allowing your personal disappointment regarding Owen as a reason to set aside any semblance of good manners, Miss Longerbeam," she began. "He certainly can't be blamed for your erroneous conclusions regarding his intentions toward you."

"Since he's solely responsible for me arriving at those conclusions, I don't know who else I could possibly blame."

"If you understood Owen, you'd realize that he never meant to hurt your feelings. He was simply unaware that you held him in affection, and romantic affection at that."

"I never held Owen in affection, romantic or otherwise."

Camilla's brows drew together. "Then why did you want to marry him?"

"I didn't want to marry him, but I would have because he's considered the most eligible bachelor in the valley, even with him being a snob. Landing Owen Chesterfield would've been a feather in any lady's hat—until you came along, that is."

"I've never gotten the impression Owen's a snob."

"Of course he is because he thinks all the ladies in this area aren't good enough for him. And"—Curtistine held up her hand when Camilla opened her mouth—"case in point. When Ada Mae broached the idea of a marriage between Sally and Owen once Sally reached her majority, Betty Lou, Owen's mother, said that such a marriage would only happen over her dead body. That left Ada Mae with the impression Mrs. Chesterfield thought Sally wasn't good enough for her son. Owen then proved he was of that same thought when he never bothered to mention the subject of marriage to Sally, even though they live right next door to each other."

Everything suddenly made a great deal of sense.

Swallowing a sigh, Camilla turned to Sally. "Was Betty Lou's dismissal of your mother's suggestion regarding a marriage between you and Owen the reason behind Ada Mae neglecting to include Betty Lou in the weekly whist parties?"

"I wouldn't want to speak for my mother, but can you blame her if that's what she did?" Sally returned.

"Not at all."

"Then I'm sure you can also understand why my mother wasn't keen to have Stanley associate with Luella after he returned from his grand tour, or why I haven't lifted a single finger to discourage all the young ladies, who consider me their unspoken leader, from shunning Luella, and not simply because she had the audacity to break my brother's nose."

Camilla frowned. "May I assume the reason behind you not lifting a finger is because you wanted to marry Owen, who, I have to say, was probably unaware of what transpired between your mother and Betty Lou?"

Sally returned the frown. "You don't think he knew?"

"Owen is, at heart, a kind man. He wouldn't have avoided addressing the insult his mother directed your way."

"I'm not sure I agree with you in believing Owen is kind, but none of it matters now since I didn't actually *want* to marry him, although I *would* have married him since he's considered so eligible, had he been receptive to the idea. I prefer gentlemen who aren't quite so intimidating."

It was quickly becoming evident that Sally, along with Curtistine, and likely a lot of the young ladies in the valley if she wasn't much mistaken, were victims of their overly ambitious mothers, and could certainly benefit from some sensible advice for a change.

Camilla began absently tapping a finger against her chin as an idea began to form, one that could very well provide a solution to Luella's unfortunate situation.

"Is something amiss, Miss Pierpont?" Sally asked. "You're suddenly looking rather . . . odd."

She stopped tapping her chin and caught Sally's eye. "It's not that anything is truly amiss, Miss Murchendorfer, but, you see, the longer we converse, the clearer it becomes that both you and Miss Longerbeam could definitely benefit from some guidance in the area of matrimonial pursuits."

"Matrimonial guidance?" Curtistine asked.

"Indeed, and it just so happens that I'm qualified to lend you that guidance."

"Not to be rude, Miss Pierpont," Sally began, "but you're a lady of rather advanced age who has only recently decided to marry. Why would we believe you have the knowledge, or the experience needed, to lend us any guidance with matrimony in general?"

"A perfectly legitimate question, Miss Murchendorfer, although you might have left out the bit about me being rather advanced in age."

"That's what made it a legitimate question."

"Well, quite. However, to address your question, know this—I've been a successful matchmaker within the New York Four Hundred for years. I understand what makes a good match and what doesn't, and I'm willing to impart that knowledge to you—but it'll come with strings attached."

Sally frowned. "Strings?"

"Nothing of worth ever comes for free, so if you want to benefit from my counsel, I'm going to have to insist that everyone immediately discontinues with ostracizing Luella. She had nothing to do with what is certainly some type of feud between Betty Lou and Ada Mae, and it's hardly fair that she's been made the brunt of your mockery and cruel jests."

"If you're suggesting I suddenly turn into Luella's best friend," Sally began, "know that my mother will not be in accord with that."

"I'm sure Ada Mae won't be, unless . . ." Camilla began tapping her finger against her chin again, smiling a second later when another thought began taking shape. "I think we need some type of activity that will allow everyone to put aside their differences, and as luck would have it, I've got the perfect one in mind—quadrille lessons."

Curtistine wrinkled her nose. "Quadrille lessons?"

"Indeed, and at Owen's new manor house in the country, which has a spectacular ballroom. I've already promised Luella that I'd teach her some of the quadrilles that are all the rage during any given Season in New York, and I'll be more than happy to include both of you in those lessons on two conditions—you need to make amends with Luella, and you need to tell your mothers about these lessons and get them to agree that Luella is no longer a target for gossip and exclusion."

"I'm not certain quadrille lessons will be enough of an incentive for my mother to put aside her animosity toward the Chesterfields," Sally said.

"You're probably right, but I can guarantee she'll at least consider setting aside her animosity after you tell her that I'm not going to teach you just any quadrille, but the famous Star Quadrille that I performed in during Alva Vanderbilt's famed costume ball a few years back. And to really encourage her to agree to my conditions, you'll then need to tell her that I intend to make arrangements with Mr. Fulton so that this quadrille will be considered the pinnacle of his ball come June."

"We've never had a quadrille performed in Wheeling," breathed Curtistine.

"Then this would be your chance to bring a touch of New York high society to your town, which I can guarantee will be well received." Camilla smiled. "And if that's not enough incentive for the good mothers of Wheeling, know that we'll need to invite, besides the two of you and Luella, five of your lady friends, of whom Luella will need to approve, and seven gentlemen."

"Why only seven gentlemen when, if I'm doing the math correctly, there'll be eight ladies?" Curtistine asked.

It was difficult to resist a smile. "Your math is quite correct, Miss Longerbeam, but I'm sure you'll be pleased to learn that two of my dearest friends, Mr. Charles Wetzel and Mr. Leopold Pendleton, both members of the Four Hundred, have arrived from New York for a visit. Charles will be more than amiable to leading the quadrille, whereas Leopold, given his age, prefers instructing over dancing."

"I thought you'd be teaching us the steps," Sally said.

"And I will, although I'll also need to be the pianist once we get started, leaving Leopold to supervise the floor."

Sally tilted her head. "My mother is accomplished on the piano."

It was an opportunity Camilla couldn't ignore, not when it was now clear that the animosity between the Chesterfields and the Murchendorfers was not one-sided but had been set into motion by two mothers who'd been determined to outdo each other.

"Ada Mae will certainly be welcome to join us, especially if that'll allow me to devote my time to perfecting everyone's dance steps."

Sally exchanged a look with Curtistine before she settled a frown on Camilla. "And while I know my mother would adore becoming acquainted with two esteemed gentlemen from New York high society, I'm now wondering if suggesting she be included was a wise proposition. What's to say that Mrs. Chesterfield, as in Beulah, won't chase after Mother with her rifle or set her pig after her the second she realizes a lady she obviously considers a nemesis has stepped foot on Chesterfield land?"

Unfortunately, that was a legitimate concern because . . . Beulah *might* whip out her rifle if Ada Mae came calling.

Camilla shoved the image of Beulah running Ada Mae off her land aside and lifted her chin. "I'll make certain to speak to Beulah about the matter, but to err on the side of caution, I'll insist that all rifles and pigs be checked at the door, which should minimize the potential for disaster."

As Sally began saying something about Beulah being a woman who would never abide by any rifle-surrendering edicts, Luella came breezing back into the room, looking downright stunning in the green riding habit Lottie had picked out. She skidded to a stop when her gaze landed on Sally, but she didn't remain immobile for long. After squaring her shoulders, she surged into motion, stalking to Camilla's side.

"This is a less-than-pleasant surprise," Luella said, settling a scowl on Sally. "Aren't you supposed to be attending your weekly luncheon at the McLure House right about now?"

Sally winced ever so slightly, something that suggested she'd been responsible for excluding Luella from that. "I am, but Curtistine and I saw you and Miss Pierpont strolling down Market Street and decided it was the perfect time to welcome her to Wheeling."

"Well, since you've evidently made Camilla's acquaintance," Luella began with a nod toward the exit, "you and Curtistine can just trot on back to the McLure House, where I'm sure they'll have their delicious chicken salad waiting for you."

A touch of fire flickered through Sally's eyes. "I've never been a lady who trots, and for your information, I'm lingering because I want to speak to you."

"About what?"

"You know what."

Luella lifted her chin. "If you think I'm going to stand here and suffer through a lecture about Esmerelda eating your mother's flowers, think again."

"Your brother already had your gardener restore Mother's flower beds."

"Then what do you want to discuss with me?"

Sally shot a look to Curtistine, who sent her an encouraging sort of nod, before she returned her attention to Luella. "I'd like to apologize."

"For what?"

"We could be here all day if you need a true accounting of everything I probably think I should apologize for, but how about I sum everything up with this—I've behaved badly where you're concerned, and I'm sorry about that."

It was obvious an intervention was in order when Luella merely set her jaw and narrowed an eye on Sally.

Camilla cleared her throat. "Don't you think it might be helpful, Luella, if you were to say something in response to Sally's heartfelt apology?"

"Sally doesn't have a heart."

"That's not exactly the response I was hoping you'd make."

A huff was Luella's first response to that before she turned to Sally. "Fine. Apology accepted, but don't think this makes us any kind of friends."

"I'm thinking I might need to include a special lesson in graciousness over the next few weeks," Camilla muttered under her breath as Sally took to whispering something to Curtistine before she lifted her head and resettled her gaze on Luella.

"To point out the obvious, Luella," Sally began, "we've never really been friends. You were always closer to Stanley, no matter that he and Mother are denying that. However, we have known each other since birth, and while I admit I've been less than kind to you, don't you think it might be time for the two of us to at least be civil toward each other?"

"Civility is overrated."

Sally's lips curved the slightest bit. "Perhaps, but in the spirt of extending you an olive branch, what would you say to joining us for lunch today at the McLure House?"

To Camilla's surprise, even though Luella shook her head, her lips began curving ever so slightly as well.

"While I wasn't expecting an olive branch," Luella began, "it's very nice of you to invite me to lunch. However, I'm afraid I'm unavailable today as I have plans to go riding this afternoon. And before you extend the same invitation to Camilla, she can't join you either, as she's decided I need a chaperone."

Sally's mouth went a little slack. "You're in need of a . . . chaperone?"

"Apparently," Luella muttered right as Mr. Kline, in the company of two harried-looking gentlemen, hurried into the room and immediately set his sights on Camilla.

After Mr. Kline introduced Mr. Compton Bennings and Mr. Richard Delbridge to her, Mr. Bennings ran a hand through hair that was decidedly rumpled and caught Camilla's eye.

"Mr. Kline told us that bustles are apparently out of style in New York City," he said, seemingly feeling no need to do anything but cut to the crux of what he obviously thought was a matter of great concern.

"I'm afraid they are," Camilla admitted.

"What are they wearing instead?" Mr. Delbridge asked as he took to blotting a perspiring forehead with a handkerchief he'd pulled from his breast pocket.

"Horsehair padding, which suits the more tailored, less back-heavy styles that began showing up in Paris just last year."

"This is a disaster," Mr. Bennings murmured, exchanging a

horrified look with Mr. Delbridge before the men presented Camilla with bows, turned on their heels, and all but bolted from the room, Mr. Kline giving his apologies before scurrying after them.

"Am I to understand," Sally began, raising a hand to her throat, "that bustles are going out of fashion?"

Luella gave a bob of her head. "They are, and I say good riddance as I never intend to don another one of those dreadful contraptions." She suddenly took to peering at something over Camilla's shoulder. "Oh, look. There's Owen, and . . . he seems to be carrying flowers."

Camilla turned, but her gaze didn't linger on the flowers in Owen's hand, instead roaming over the man himself because . . . he was looking quite different from the last time she'd seen him.

Gone was the ill-fitting jacket he'd started off with that morning, replaced with a gray houndstooth blazer that was cut to perfection and showcased his broad shoulders. He'd also apparently stopped by the barbershop she'd noticed next to the haberdashery, because his hair was now freshly cut, although not too short, but the natural curls he had were brushed back from his face, and . . . He looked exactly how one would expect a successful titan of business to look—except for the fact that he was still an unusually large man, and one who definitely emitted a sense of power, although now that power was accentuated with an unexpected air of sophistication.

She suddenly found it slightly difficult to breathe, that circumstance increasing when Owen was standing in front of her a blink of an eye later, taking her completely aback when he all but thrust a bouquet of daisies her way.

It was only sheer luck she managed to grab them instead of letting them drop to the ground.

She grinned. "You remembered."

"I did," he said before he directed his attention to Sally and Curtistine, who were staring at him with wide eyes. "Ladies," he began, earning curtsies in return, which he acknowledged with a bow before he returned his attention to Camilla. "I apologize that the bouquet is on the small side. I had to practically wrestle those daisies from Leopold, who wanted to buy every daisy in the flower shop for Meemaw."

Something warm immediately began flowing through her. "I thought you didn't want Leopold to know your grandmother favors daisies."

"I didn't, but after Leopold told me he was going to present Meemaw with roses, and dozens of them, I couldn't very well *not* tell him since Meemaw loathes roses."

The warmth that was still flowing through her intensified.

"That was very gracious of you," she said, earning a rather grumpy look from Owen in return.

"I'm not feeling very gracious."

"I can tell. Want to explain why not?"

Owen released a bit of a sigh. "Graciousness in general is eluding me because Leopold's far too competent with knowing exactly how to dress a gentleman. I ended up having to defer to him at the tailor's instead of choosing anything myself because . . . who knew that one shouldn't dare mix houndstooth with plaid?"

Camilla's lips twitched. "A reason to be put out with Leopold for sure."

"Indeed, and then that far-too-competent man, after the tailor told me he didn't think he had anything readily available that would fit me, wouldn't take that as a firm no. He somehow convinced the tailor to allow him to peruse any garments customers had failed to return for, and lo and behold . . ." Owen gestured to his blazer.

Camilla refused a grin. "He should be drawn and quartered for having the audacity to secure you such a dashing jacket that doesn't leave you in imminent danger of splitting a seam."

After rubbing a hand over his face, Owen smiled, although it was definitely along the lines of a very faint one. "I'm sounding churlish, aren't I?"

"I would say you're sounding more like a man who still isn't comfortable with the idea that a gentleman might be sweet on your grandmother, but who is now realizing that the gentleman in question isn't quite so bad after all."

"I'm not putting in a good word for him with Meemaw."

"That would certainly be expecting far too much of you . . . at least for now," Camilla said before she lifted the daisies to her nose. "Thank you for these."

"You're welcome." Owen turned to Luella, whose eyes were sparkling in a rather un-Luella-like fashion. "What?"

"Nothing," Luella said.

"Your smile suggests otherwise."

"I suppose it might at that" was all Luella said before she gestured to her riding habit and gave a bit of a twirl, tripping on the overly long hem before finding her balance. "What do you think?"

"It's very nice, although it seems a little long," Owen said. "Might be difficult to execute any dance steps if you're planning on wearing that to the ball come June."

"It's a riding habit, Owen," Luella pointed out.

"Then it'd be difficult for you to retain your seat, as I imagine all that fabric will get in your way, or worse yet, spook your horse."

"That's why Bernadette will be hacking off a good foot or so of fabric for me."

Owen frowned. "Why would Bernadette be in charge of hacking anything for you?"

"Were you not listening to me earlier?"

Owen blinked. "Should I assume that means you've already mentioned something about Bernadette and hacking?"

Luella released a snort. "I'll take that as a you-weren't-listening because, yes, Camilla and I addressed Bernadette earlier, as in we mentioned she was altering a few of my old gowns, and you were standing right beside us." She frowned. "Didn't you notice that the afternoon dress I wore here is vastly different from the dress Mother bought for me a few years back?"

"Are you going to get all huffy if I admit I didn't?"

Luella tilted her head. "I suppose I could be persuaded to keep my huffiness in check if you offer to foot the bill for my new wardrobe."

"Spent all your allowance on furniture, did you?"

"Not all of it, because Daddy increased my allowance substantially last year, no doubt due to the guilt he's been feeling over abandoning me for Paris. However, I am running a little low on funds, and it would save me the bother of petitioning Daddy for more money if you'll cover my purchases today."

"I was already planning on footing your bill."

It did not escape Camilla's notice that Sally and Curtistine were now considering Owen with clear speculation in their eyes, as if they might very well be reassessing their views on a man who clearly wasn't the ogre they'd thought him to be, not when he wasn't hesitating to indulge his sister with a shopping expedition and had presented his not-quite fiancée with a bouquet of her favorite flowers.

"Forgive me for changing the subject," Sally said, drawing everyone's attention, "but I've just realized, Miss Pierpont, that you said we'll need to round up seven gentlemen to learn the quadrille since Mr. Charles Wetzel will be the eighth. May I assume you need seven because you know Owen wouldn't care to learn the steps?"

It wasn't exactly a surprise when Owen and Luella immediately settled somewhat incredulous looks on her.

"What's this about a quadrille?" Luella asked.

"I've invited these ladies to join us at the country house, which really does need a better name, to learn a particular quadrille to perform at the ball come June. It obviously requires gentlemen, as it's a couple's dance."

Luella began looking at Camilla as if she'd taken leave of her senses, but before she could voice any of the arguments she clearly longed to voice, Owen cleared his throat.

"I think quadrille lessons sound delightful," he surprised her by saying. "And know that I'll be more than happy to partner you if you're wanting to join in on the fun."

Camilla refused to allow her mouth to drop open, but before she could decide if Owen had offered to partner her because they were supposed to be an almost-engaged couple or because he might actually want to dance with her, Luella was beaming a smile at something across the room.

The reason for the smile quickly became evident when Camilla spotted Charles strolling across the room, his gaze settled on Luella. A second later, he was stopping directly in front of her before he presented her with a bow and then pulled two small lily plants from behind his back.

"I'm afraid the pickings were slim at the flower shop when it came to lilies," Charles began as he handed the lilies to Luella. "However, I thought it might be interesting if we were to attempt to graft these two together and see what happens, since one of them is yellow and the other purple."

"Interesting indeed," Luella said before she took a moment to introduce Charles to Sally and Curtistine, who took to fluttering their lashes his way.

It was rather telling when Luella put an immediate cessation to all the fluttering by handing the lilies back to Charles and smiling one of the most angelic smiles Camilla had ever seen her smile.

"Would you be a dear and hold on to those, Charles, while I change?" Luella began. "It won't take me long, and then we'll get right on the road, which should leave us enough time to do the grafting before we go on our ride today."

When Charles merely stared back at Luella, evidently struck speechless by the sight of the smile, Camilla cleared her throat.

"Not that I want to be the bearer of disappointing news, Luella, but you still have numerous ensembles to try on."

Luella gave an airy wave of her hand. "All the garments we've selected today are the same size as this riding habit. That means they'll fit me relatively well, and Bernadette will alter them accordingly from there." She turned and nodded to Owen, sending him a smile that dripped sweetness. "You'll settle my account while I change?"

After Owen inclined his head and headed off to speak to the salesgirls who were congregated around the cash register, Luella turned back to Charles. "I won't be but a few minutes," she said.

Charles gave himself a bit of a shake, probably because he still seemed to be in a somewhat stupefied state, and was smiling at Luella a blink of an eye later. "Allow me to escort you to the dressing room. I'll then wait for you in that cozy-looking chair outside the changing area, perhaps using the time it takes you to change to make some notes about grafting, which we can then discuss on the ride home." With that, he thrust the lilies Camilla's way, took hold of Luella's arm, and off they went.

It wasn't much of a surprise that his attentiveness to Luella had not gone unnoticed by Sally or Curtistine, nor was it a surprise when Sally sidled up beside Camilla.

"Odd as this is for me to admit, but I feel as if a great weight has been lifted from my shoulders since Luella and I have now begun mending some fences, something that was long overdue," Sally began. "That has, of course, left me wondering whether Stanley, who, as I'm sure you've heard, was very close to Luella at one time, may benefit from doing some mending of his own. It seems to me that he might have been overly influenced by my mother and the animosity she holds for Betty Lou. I imagine if he were given the opportunity, he would jump at the chance to make amends for the rather grievous disservice he did to Luella."

"Why do I get the feeling you already have something in mind that would allow Stanley to rectify this grievous disservice?"

"How astute of you, Miss Pierpont, and to avoid beating around the bush, I think you should invite Stanley to participate in the quadrille."

Swallowing the urge to ask Sally if her sudden desire to get her brother back into Luella's good graces had more to do with a personal interest in Charles—a member of the Four Hundred—

over any desire to actually see Stanley make amends with a young lady with whom he'd shared a relationship for years, Camilla took a moment to consider her answer.

Frankly, Luella would probably balk if questioned about the matter because she truly seemed to have no interest in pursuing a relationship with a man who'd treated her so shabbily.

However, given the distress Stanley had caused Luella, she was due some resolution regarding her old friend, and if that resolution also came with a side of Stanley receiving a touch of remorse for his abysmal behavior, well, that would definitely be some icing on what could be considered a comeuppance cake.

"I'm relatively certain," Camilla finally began, "considering Luella is a most gracious young lady, at least at heart, that she'll be, not exactly thrilled, but at least receptive to the idea of including your brother. However, I will need to discuss the matter thoroughly with her, but know that I'll send a note around just as soon as a firm decision is made."

"Then I'll be waiting for that note with bated breath, as I know my brother will be as well after I tell him I've decided he's been more than an idiot with his behavior of late." With that, Sally dipped into a curtsy, sent a telling nod to Curtistine, and after Curtistine dipped into a curtsy of her own, the two ladies turned and strolled out of the department.

"Care to share what that was about?" Owen asked as he rejoined her.

"It's called strategy."

"What kind of strategy?"

"I haven't figured out all the particulars just yet, but I'm hoping, at the very least, that Luella will soon be well on her way to becoming accepted into the folds of Wheeling society, just as I'm hoping the Chesterfield family as a whole will finally attain that recognition your mother was so eager to acquire."

Twenty-Two

ONE WEEK LATER

"I'm still thinking wearing a ball gown to a dance lesson might be a tad bit excessive," Luella said, strolling into Camilla's room, where she promptly plopped down on a darling settee upholstered in pale blue, which matched the rest of the décor in a room Luella had finished decorating the day before.

Camilla turned on the vanity stool, earning a grunt from Bernadette, who was trying to arrange her hair. Ignoring the grunt, as Bernadette was always a little testy when she was in the midst of what she now called her *art*, she settled her gaze on Luella and smiled.

"To begin with, you're not wearing a ball gown, but an evening gown that's normally reserved for formal dinners," she began. "You also look completely stunning, which isn't a surprise because I knew that shade of green would look marvelous on you, as well as draw attention to the red in your hair, and bring out the color of your eyes."

Luella rolled the eyes in question. "My hair would draw attention even without the green since Bernadette styled it, which means of course it looks amazing. However, to point out the obvious, we're not about to sit down to a formal dinner. We're about to breeze around the ballroom for our first official quadrille lesson." She crossed her arms over her chest. "It would be much easier for me to do that breezing if you would have let me wear one of those breezy little numbers I've been pilfering from Meemaw's castoffs this week as you, Leopold, and Charles gave me and Owen early instructions pertaining to the Star Quadrille."

"I didn't balk over your questionable garment choices for dance practice over this past week because you don't need to make an impression on your brother, Leopold, or even Charles, who already finds you delightful, ratty old wardrobe and all."

"That's just because Charles appreciates my mind and enjoys discussing horticulture with me as we quadrille our way around the ballroom."

"Your mind isn't the only thing Charles appreciates," Bernadette muttered, which left Luella rather pink in the face before she cleared her throat.

"Yes, well, I have no idea what else he could possibly appreciate, but returning to what I was saying—I still think that getting me all gussied up for a dance lesson today is taking the whole turning-me-refined business a touch too far. Everyone who'll be in attendance already knows who I am, and just because I'm now looking the part of a refined lady doesn't mean I am one. I also don't believe anyone, especially Stanley, who you know I only grudgingly agreed to include after you sent me that expectant look of yours that you know how to use so effectively, will decide otherwise. It's along the same lines as if we stuffed Esmerelda into a dress and proclaimed her to be proper. She'd still just be Esmerelda, a fashionable pig, but a pig nonetheless."

Camilla got up from the stool, ignored that Bernadette was grunting yet again, even though she'd just finished with Camilla's hair, and made her way to sit beside Luella on the settee. "I seriously hope you're not comparing yourself to a pig because you're a delightful, exuberant young lady who already possesses ladylike qualities. You've merely kept them concealed over the years, probably to annoy your mother. However, do I think you'll ever embrace the role of proper lady all the time? Of course not, because that's not who you are. You'd rather be outside fishing, riding your horse, or hunting down art and furnishings over perfecting a watercolor or doing needlepoint, and there's nothing wrong with that. But since you've now taken to frowning, which suggests you don't believe me, why don't you simply tell me what's really brought on all these misgivings today?"

Luella's shoulders slumped the slightest bit. "I can't help but worry that everyone, no matter how diligent you are with shoring up my somewhat questionable manners, will see straight through me."

Camilla tilted her head. "Did you ever consider that having everyone see you dressed properly and not sporting dirt all over your face may result with them finally seeing you for who you truly are, and not the Luella they thought they knew because they've allowed your deviation from expected normalities to cloud their impression of you?"

"They're not going to change their minds about me merely because I'm wearing a pretty dress and know how to dance."

"I doubt anyone even knows how graceful you are on the dance floor because you told me you've never attended a formal ball, and the family gatherings you attend, where you mentioned you learned how to do reels and even to waltz, weren't attended by anyone other than family." Camilla smiled. "I imagine, when you and Charles take to the floor soon, every one of our guests will be amazed at how competent you already are with the steps."

"I'm only competent because you and Leopold thought it would give me a distinct advantage if I knew the steps before everyone else and have been making me practice for hours every day."

Bernadette dragged the vanity stool over and took a seat directly across from Luella. "If you're about to proclaim that dancing for hours on end in the arms of Charles has been a hardship for you, save your breath, because I've been popping in and out of your lessons and you're always smiling."

"I highly doubt I'm smiling when I'm on the floor with Owen instead of Charles, though, because my brother, if you've neglected to notice, has trampled my toes too many times to count, and given his size, it's not a circumstance to smile about."

Bernadette waved that aside. "Your brother is just as competent as you are on the floor. He merely gets distracted."

"By what?" Luella asked.

"It's more of a whom than a what as he likes to watch Miss Camilla play the piano, or . . ." Bernadette smiled rather slyly. "Perhaps he just enjoys watching her, no matter what she's doing."

Camilla felt heat settle on her cheeks when Luella and Bernadette both turned speculative gazes her way, but before she could think of anything to say to that, Luella sat forward.

"I've been wondering why you haven't partnered Owen even once during our lessons, especially when you clearly want Owen and me to have an advantage over the dancers who'll be arriving today for what is supposed to be everyone's first introduction to this particular quadrille. If you ask me, since you and Owen haven't practiced together, you won't be accustomed to dancing with each other and won't be nearly as competent as Charles and I." Luella gave her nose a rub. "I guarantee you if Owen gets distracted by merely watching you play the piano, he'll definitely get distracted and trample your feet once the two of you grace the floor for the first time."

Bernadette also sat forward. "I think the question of the hour is, why *haven't* you danced with him yet?"

In all honesty, it was a question she'd prefer leaving unanswered because . . . she'd avoided taking to the floor with Owen because he made her feel things she'd never truly felt before—fluttery things that left her slightly breathless.

She didn't like feeling all fluttery where Owen was concerned because he wasn't the sort of man she'd ever thought she'd be attracted to, but attracted she most assuredly was.

It was the oddest thing, this fascination—or perhaps it was almost a case of infatuation—she held for Owen, because after the fiasco with George, she'd truly thought she was immune to gentlemen in general, but that didn't seem to be the case with Owen.

Nevertheless, infatuated or not, it wasn't something she was willing to pursue, not when she certainly hadn't had a change of heart about endorsing spinsterhood, and besides that, Owen hadn't given her the slightest indication he was even remotely infatuated with her.

Yes, he'd presented her with daisies, an incredibly sweet gesture, until she'd had a moment alone to think about the matter and had realized that, because it was Owen, who seemed to be a man who took criticism to heart and then strove to correct whatever problem had been pointed out to him, he'd undoubtedly given her the daisies to prove that he could be romantic if the need arose, and what was more romantic than presenting a lady with flowers she'd proclaimed were her favorite?

"I think we've stumped her," Bernadette said, which left Camilla blinking back to the situation at hand, one where Bernadette and Luella were now exchanging knowing looks, as if they'd been able to read her thoughts—a concerning idea, if there ever was one.

She lifted her chin. "I'm not stumped, and there's a perfectly reasonable explanation as to why I haven't danced with Owen yet—that being I was in charge of playing the piano. It's rather difficult to dance effectively when there's no music."

"Leopold volunteered to take over for you on the piano," Luella pointed out.

"True, but if you'd ever heard Leopold play, you'd know he's not proficient when it comes to that particular instrument. I was merely sparing the state of everyone's sense of rhythm by graciously refusing his offer."

"A likely story," Bernadette said, her eyes twinkling. "In my less-than-humble opinion, I think it's more likely that Mr. Chesterfield makes you nervous, and since you're not a lady who's prone to nerves, you've avoided taking to the floor with him for as long as you possibly could." She smiled. "It'll be interesting to watch your performance with him today."

Given that she'd be dancing with Owen while surrounded by a roomful of other dancers, Camilla was relatively convinced she'd be quite capable of dancing with him exactly like she'd danced with hundreds of other gentlemen she'd taken to the floor with over the years.

"I think it's going to be interesting to watch the reactions of all the other dancers when they realize Owen and I have the advantage of already knowing the steps," Luella said, sparing Camilla a response to Bernadette's nonsense. "Frankly, I've been feeling a little guilty for our advanced instructions and have been wondering if that'll cause some ill feelings with everyone who's accepted their invitations for lessons."

Camilla waved that aside. "There's no need to worry since I would bet good money that Ada Mae, after she responded to my invitation and said she'd be delighted to play the piano for us, set about finding a dance instructor who knew at least the rudiments of the quadrille." Camilla smiled. "Mothers like Ada Mae realize the importance of these types of practices and know that they need to prepare accordingly."

Luella's brow furrowed. "Did you ever have to practice steps before going to practice?"

"Of course. I used to attend the Family Circle Dance Class, sponsored by none other than Ward McAllister, the social arbiter of the Four Hundred, but my mother always brought in my personal dance instructor before I attended a single Family Circle Dance Class practice session. Believe me when I tell you that everyone present knew the steps before the cotillion leader ever stepped foot on the dance floor."

"If you ask me," Luella began, "all this extra practice seems counterproductive, but tell me this—were you as surprised as I was that Ada Mae accepted the invitation, as well as everyone else we invited?"

"Not when I knew Sally and Curtistine would rush to the McLure House last week and immediately inform everyone that Charles, an esteemed—and need I add, available—member of the Four Hundred, is currently a guest of the Chesterfield family. Gossip about him must have spread like wildfire, and I'm sure every mother of every young lady we invited took this past week to dither over what gown their daughter should wear today."

"But if the reason these ladies accepted our invitation is because of Charles, I'm a little confused about how I'm going to miraculously become in high demand, especially when there's a very good chance, what with how I'm all gussied up, that I'm going to stick out like a sore thumb once the other ladies arrive dressed in more appropriate clothing for dance practice."

"If anything," Camilla countered, "you're going to be underdressed because, you mark my words, these ladies are going to show up wearing delectable gowns paired with, if I'm not mistaken, their best jewels."

"I am not wearing that tiara I noticed was sitting on my dressing table."

Camilla grinned. "Good, because I left that there for you to try with the gown from Worth I gave you for the ball that Bernadette's still altering. And just as a side note—tiaras should never be worn except to a ball, or to an event where you might be presented to a member of royalty, but only if it's an evening event."

"I'll keep that in mind, although I doubt I'll be entertaining royalty anytime soon, unless that Lord Shrewsbury would happen to show up."

"Lord Shrewsbury isn't considered royalty and is currently gallivanting around New York with Ward McAllister as his trusty companion," Leopold said, stepping into the room and presenting the ladies with a bow before he waved a telegram Camilla's way. "This just arrived from the Accounting Firm. Says your old beau made it to the city. He's obviously cozied up to Ward to get himself invited to all the right events once everyone travels to Newport, but the telegram says the firm has already put a tail on him, and there's no indication he's been making plans to search for you."

"Did the telegram mention anything about progress in regard to the criminals who concocted Camilla's abduction attempt?" Luella asked, rising to her feet and shaking out the folds of her gown.

"They're still working on that, which means Charles and I won't be relaxing our guard anytime soon, and Owen's men will stay on high alert as well." Leopold moved closer to Luella and smiled. "You do look delightful, my dear, but remember, you need to linger upstairs in your room until we send Bernadette to fetch you."

"I'm not really keen on making a grand entrance," Luella muttered.

"I don't blame you," Leopold said. "But Charles will be waiting for you right inside the doorway, so it's not as if you'll be on your own for long." With that, Leopold held out his arm, Luella took it, and after telling Camilla he'd meet her in the ballroom once he'd escorted Luella to her room, they headed out the door.

Knowing she needed to make her way to the first floor because there was every chance guests would arrive early, Camilla pulled on a pair of kid gloves, thanked Bernadette for arranging her hair, then hurried down the hallway and then the steps, her lips twitching when she peeked into the ballroom and found Beulah holding a paintbrush and can of paint, touching up the frame of the French doors that led to the second-story balcony.

"I don't think anyone would have noticed the few scuff marks that were left from wrestling the piano in here since they were obscured by the curtain," she said, stepping into the room and drawing Beulah's attention.

"It was bothering me that the doors got scuffed after Owen had to winch the piano up to the balcony and then had to muscle it in through doors that were barely wide enough," Beulah said, stopping mid-touchup. "Besides, obscuring the scuffs is in everyone's best interest since, even though I agreed to keep my rifle less than accessible, if Ada Mae, who is more nosy than you can imagine, saw the scuff marks and remarked on them, I couldn't be held responsible if my rifle suddenly appeared, or if Esmerelda suddenly gained access to the house—by accident, of course—and then decided, on her own, with no encouraging from me, to have a go at Ada Mae."

"I've taken the liberty of relocating the three rifles you brought with you today, Meemaw," Owen said, stepping into the room and drawing Camilla's attention, as well as a sharp intake of breath because the man was wearing one of his new suits, and to say he did justice to it was an understatement.

Drawing in another breath in the hopes of calming a heart that was turning all fluttery again, Camilla tore her attention away from a man who was definitely distraction-worthy and settled it on Beulah, who was looking rather disgruntled.

"May I assume you also relocated Esmerelda?" Beulah asked.

Owen grinned. "Of course, as one of the purposes of these dance lessons is to bury the hatchet with the Murchendorfers, but speaking of hatchets, I also removed the hatchet from your wagon, since our mission today would be a complete failure if that happened to come out."

"Spoilsport" was all Beulah said to that before she gave the doorframe a last dab of paint and then sailed out of the room, saying she was off to freshen up and would meet them at the front door momentarily.

"She doesn't seem too thrilled with you right now," Camilla said, taking the arm Owen held out to her while ignoring the additional fluttering her heart began doing the second she got a whiff of his cologne.

"Thrilled isn't a state Meemaw embraces on the best of days, but Mr. Timken sent me to fetch you because Nems sent word that carriages are already moving up the drive. That means further talk of Meemaw and her surly disposition will need to wait."

Exchanging a grin with him, Camilla soon found herself standing in the entranceway, Mr. Timken having assumed the role of butler, something he'd been doing for the past week after he'd mentioned to Owen that he was at loose ends because his chaperoning skills weren't in demand anymore, what with how Leopold and Charles were constantly accompanying her.

Owen, being a far more thoughtful and astute gentleman than she'd given him credit for at first, had evidently realized that, not only was Mr. Timken at loose ends, he was also itching to do something productive, especially when the lackadaisical running of the household was straining the state of Mr. Timken's nerves. Owen had then presented a proposition to the butler, one where Mr. Timken would take on the daunting task of whipping his house into shape. Mr. Timken hadn't hesitated to accept the proposal, telling Camilla more than once that resuming his role as butler had gone far to restore the state of his nerves.

"Prepare yourself because Ada Mae and her children are coming up the steps," Mr. Timken said before he opened the door with a flourish, bowing Ada Mae, Sally, and a young gentleman Camilla assumed was Stanley into the room. Camilla stepped forward to greet them, with Owen at her side a second later.

"How lovely," Ada Mae exclaimed, her gaze traveling around the entranceway before she proffered Owen her hand, which he dutifully kissed before he shook Stanley's hand, although given that Stanley immediately took to wincing, it was evident Owen was still put out with the man who'd insulted his sister and might have taken to gripping Stanley's hand a touch too firmly.

"You must be Stanley," Camilla said, abandoning every etiquette rule there was by introducing herself but seeing no other option, given that Owen still had ahold of Stanley's hand and there was every chance Stanley was going to be sporting a few bruises soon.

"You must be Miss Pierpont," Stanley said, tugging his hand from Owen's grasp and settling his attention on Camilla, his eyes widening a second later. "My goodness, but I see the rumors are true. You're quite lovely."

It was not an encouraging sign when Owen immediately released what almost sounded like a growl.

"Thank you, Mr. Murchendorfer," Camilla said with an inclination of her head. "I have to admit that I've heard quite a few rumors about you as well."

"Those weren't rumors," Beulah said, stealing up beside Camilla and narrowing her eyes on Stanley, quite like Owen was currently in the process of doing. "Dare I presume you're intending on addressing those rumors at some point today, as well as making amends?"

Stanley looked to Camilla, then to Owen, then back to Beulah. "I'm certainly not opposed to speaking with your granddaughter to mend some fences, although if anyone needs to do some mending, it's Luella. She did, after all, break my nose."

"Mother's waving for you to join her," Sally said, giving her brother a none-too-gentle nudge in the direction of Ada Mae, who wasn't actually doing any waving since she'd moseyed away from the receiving line and was currently inspecting one of the paintings Luella had recently hung on the wall.

Obviously realizing he'd just been given the perfect excuse to remove himself from what was certainly now a hostile environment, both Owen and Beulah staring at him with fire in their eyes, Stanley muttered his excuses and headed off in Ada Mae's direction.

"You'll have to forgive my brother," Sally began. "He's still incredibly sensitive about his nose, probably because it now has just the tiniest dent in it, but enough about noses." She extended her hand to Owen, dipped into a curtsy after he kissed it, then turned to Camilla but paused mid-dip when her gaze settled on something over Camilla's shoulder.

"I say, is that Mr. Wetzel over there by the staircase?" she asked.

Camilla turned and nodded. "It is."

Sally craned her neck. "I don't see Luella anywhere yet."

"She'll be along directly."

Sally was suddenly all smiles. "I'm so looking forward to seeing her again, but while we wait for her to make an appearance, I think I'll go and keep Mr. Wetzel company."

As Sally strolled away, Camilla turned and found a line of guests waiting to enter the house, their excitement regarding their invitations to a special quadrille lesson almost palpable.

The next fifteen minutes were spent being introduced to everyone Camilla had not yet met, such as Martha Wellington and Clarice Colleens, two young ladies who'd been close friends with Luella before the pond incident, and who both seemed nervous to have been invited to participate today, their inclusion a direct result of Luella insisting their names be added to the guest list.

After Martha and Clarice wandered over to join Charles and Sally, Curtistine made an appearance, as well as Pauline Zavolta, who merely sent Owen a sniff when he presented her with a bow before she stalked off. Next in line were Mr. Jeromy Witman and Mr. Thomas Stanford, two of Stanley's friends who'd been at the pond that dreadful day, both men perspiring ever so slightly as they greeted Owen, acting quite as if they were worried they were going to be called on the carpet then and there for their abysmal behavior.

To Owen's credit, besides giving the two men what had obviously become his signature firm handshake of the day, which left the men grimacing, he'd welcomed them into his home, then encouraged them to have a look around, which they didn't hesitate to do, practically bolting down the hallway in their quest to get away from him.

"Your restraint was rather impressive," Camilla said, a grin tugging her lips.

"You said I wasn't allowed to be anything but gracious today, and you even wrote down a list of appropriate things I was allowed to say while greeting guests. Challenging someone to a duel unfortunately failed to make that list."

"Of course it did, but I might need to revisit that list and be even more specific, or give you a refresher course on graciousness in general, since you did growl at Stanley and almost maimed Mr. Witman and Mr. Stanford's hands, but other than that, good job."

Owen sent her a grin before he turned to the next guest and welcomed the young lady dithering on the threshold into his home.

Once every guest had been greeted, Camilla took Owen's arm, and together they followed everyone up to the ballroom, Camilla taking a few minutes to disclose who everyone was partnering with, ignoring the grumbles of a few ladies when she stated that Luella would be partnered with Charles.

Any lingering grumbles came to a rapid end, though, when Luella swept into the room, apparently forgetting that she was supposed to linger in the doorway to allow everyone an opportunity to see her since she headed straight for Charles, who immediately excused himself from speaking with Sally and Curtistine and strode to join her.

Camilla couldn't resist a smile when Charles took hold of Luella's hand, kissed it, then held it for a few seconds longer than was strictly necessary, her smile widening when Charles withdrew a lily from an inside jacket pocket and tucked it into the elaborate chignon Bernadette had assembled, the ease with which he did so suggesting he might have very well practiced a few times to make sure his gesture went off perfectly.

"I don't remember that being part of the plan," Owen grumbled beside her.

"It wasn't."

"Can't say I appreciate Charles gazing so adoringly at my sister."

"I don't believe that was planned either, but before you go off and relocate those rifles you hid of Beulah's, what say we get the lesson started."

Owen shot a look at Luella. "Maybe I should partner my sister."

"You're supposed to be almost engaged to me, so . . . no."

Owen blinked. "I almost forgot about that."

"I suggest you remember because we'll hardly find success with our plan if anyone notices us not behaving like an almost-engaged couple."

"I'm not actually certain how almost-engaged couples are supposed to behave."

"They normally behave as if they're dying to sneak off and steal a few kisses together," Camilla heard pop out of her mouth before she could stop herself.

The corners of Owen's mouth quirked. "That was not what I was expecting you to say."

"I wasn't expecting me to say that either, but as a former matchmaker, I have plenty of experience with almost-engaged couples, and I cannot tell you how many times I had to intercede with couples who were simply meandering across a room one minute and then . . . they were just gone. I once found a couple gazing longingly into each other's eyes in an ice room, which, if you ask me, wasn't the most romantic of places to hide, what with how chilly it was."

"I better not discover Charles and Luella in any ice rooms, but . . ." Owen frowned. "Do you think we should make plans to sneak off together so no one gets suspicious?"

It was quite telling when Camilla found the mere idea of sneaking off with Owen a little too appealing.

She shoved that nonsensical idea straight to the farthest recesses of her mind and summoned up a smile. "While that would probably be more than amusing since I get the impression you're probably as good as I am in the acting department, which I'm not good in at all, I don't believe sneaking off will be necessary. Even if we were engaged, we're a more, well, mature couple, and no one expects mature couples to be completely enamored with each other."

"It's not as if we're that mature, and certainly aren't at our last prayers."

Camilla blinked. "I hope you weren't under the impression I was saying I thought you wouldn't be capable of being enamored of a lady. I just thought our age gave us a ready excuse not to turn all stealthy and then force poor Mr. Timken to come after us."

"You think he'd come after us?"

"And with Beulah's shotgun."

"Huh" was all Owen said before he surprised her with a wink. "Meemaw might try to intercept Mr. Timken if she noticed us heading for a quiet place since she's convinced we're perfect for each other."

"Then let's agree we won't try to convince everyone we're almost engaged by seeking out one of those quiet places, because I'm not sure Mr. Timken would win in a match against your grandmother."

"He admitted to me just yesterday that Meemaw still scares him half to death, so I suppose that means I'll agree to no meeting up for a feigned rendezvous, whether that would have been amusing or not."

"Then it's officially agreed upon—no feigned rendezvous," Camilla said as all sorts of thoughts went tumbling through her mind—ones that centered around all the things she knew couples got up to when they stole away, one of those things being kissing, something she might have, a time or two, or twenty, been considering of late.

Owen gave his tie a bit of a tug before he stilled, his gaze settled on something across the room. "Would you look at that—Stanley looks like he might be considering doing some of that throttling you've mentioned you'd like to do to me at times."

Camilla directed her attention to where Stanley was standing with a group of his friends, but he wasn't paying attention to any of them. Instead, he was squinting at Charles, his jaw clenched and his color high.

It took a rather herculean effort to resist a laugh. "I think we might find success with Luella far sooner than I was anticipating, although I'm going to have to put you in charge of making sure Stanley doesn't try to go after Charles."

"What a way to put a damper on an evening."

"Please. You know you wouldn't let Stanley have a go at Charles, even if you think he's being far too attentive to your sister."

"I'm sure you're probably right."

"Probably?"

He blew out a breath. "Fine, I wouldn't, however I doubt there'd be a reason for me to get involved if Stanley would be such an idiot to try to engage Charles in an altercation because, even with Charles being an authentically refined gentleman, he's a man who can take care of himself and would dispatch Stanley in about a second, something I wouldn't mind seeing."

"But then Beulah would get involved, and then her rifle would come out, no matter that you hid them from her or not, and then a good old-fashioned feud would definitely come into play."

Owen frowned. "Why do you think Meemaw would whip out her rifle if Stanley tried to have a go at Charles?"

"Beulah adores Charles and will take it as a personal affront if anyone tries anything with him while under a Chesterfield roof."

"My grandmother adores Charles?"

"She's been trying to get him to agree to learn how to bake pies, or more specifically, one particular apple pie."

"That recipe is taking on a life of its own," Owen muttered.

"Indeed, but . . ." Camilla stopped talking when she spotted Ada Mae strolling up to join them.

"Forgive me for interrupting, but I was wondering if I could have a word with you, Miss Pierpont, regarding the song selection. I've practiced all week with the sheet music you were kind enough to send to me, but I have a question about the timing of a particular stanza."

Telling Owen she'd rejoin him momentarily, which Owen responded to by whispering something about seeing her in an hour, which left her grinning and Ada Mae's brow arching, Camilla took the next few minutes to go over the arrangement with Ada Mae, then walked to the center of the ballroom and called for everyone to join her.

As the partners paired up, all of them seeming somewhat familiar with where they were supposed to stand, Camilla decided there was no use showing everyone the steps since she had the sneaking suspicion everyone already knew them. Instead, she nodded to Ada Mae, who placed her fingers over the keys and began to play.

After dipping into a curtsy while Owen presented her with a bow, then glancing over her shoulder to ascertain that Luella and Charles were alright, which they most assuredly were since Charles, instead of merely bowing to Luella, had hold of her hand again and was placing a kiss on it, Camilla turned front and center, pressing her lips together when she noticed Owen was, unsurprisingly, scowling once again.

She leaned closer and lowered her voice. "We might need to plan out a feigned rendezvous after all because as a former matchmaker, I can tell you that it's a rare sight indeed for a gentleman who is almost engaged, and who's supposed to be somewhat smitten with his intended, to scowl in such an intimidating fashion."

Owen's scowl was gone a second later, replaced with a smile, and a second after that, he was whisking her around the other couples in a complicated step, but she didn't linger on the fact that the week of dance practice had obviously paid off, what with how he was more than accomplished on the dance floor. Instead, she found herself lingering on the surprising realization that their steps were perfectly matched even though they'd never danced together.

As Owen led her through a series of twirls, her mind began to spin quite as fast as her feet because the thought sprang to mind that Beulah might not be so wrong after all and that she, Miss Camilla Pierpont, confirmed spinster by choice, may have finally, and quite unexpectedly, met her match.

Twenty-Three

"Is it just me, or do you also find what Camilla's been able to accomplish of late beyond impressive?" Luella asked as she galloped alongside Owen across the lawn of the country house that she and Camilla had decided was to now be called Moonlight Manor.

It was a question that didn't need much consideration. "It would be difficult not to be impressed with her since we haven't even presented you at the ball yet but everyone in Wheeling seems to be clamoring to spend time in your company," Owen said.

"I must admit all the clamoring is a bit disconcerting, but that Camilla was capable of achieving such success with me, and less than three weeks after she arrived in Wheeling . . . well, I don't think anyone would argue the point that she possesses more than her average share of competency."

"She's definitely been competent with taking you in hand, but I don't think anyone would claim she's been all that capable when it comes to the chores Aunt Elma keeps doling out to her."

Luella grinned. "A valid point, but it was hardly Camilla's fault that Esmerelda decided her backside needed a scratch and just happened to rub against the post where Camilla had set her bucket of whitewash." Luella shook her head. "I mean, poor Camilla. There she was, halfway down a line of pickets, completely oblivious that Esmerelda's wiggling was going to send the post wobbling to such an extent that it would knock the bucket of paint over, drenching her with whitewash in the process."

"I'm sorry to have missed that one, although I did see the results of the paint-dousing once I got home and found Camilla out in the stables, dunking her head in the horse trough, which isn't something I ever thought I'd see."

Luella leaned forward as they rode underneath a low-hanging branch. "She took it in stride, though. Didn't even shriek when that paint went raining over her. Simply took the rag I handed her, told me to mark our place in the etiquette book she was making me read out loud while she whitewashed the fence, then told Aunt Elma, Meemaw, and the sewing bee ladies that she'd be back the next day to finish the job. It was quite impressive how she then lifted her chin and strode off like she wasn't dripping paint everywhere, electing to walk all the way back to the country house because she didn't think it would be fair to get paint all over her horse."

"From what Meemaw told me, the sewing ladies were rather impressed that a fancy lady like Camilla didn't descend into a fit of the vapors once the paint went flying, and that she actually did show up the next day to finish the fence, although she'd evidently wrapped her head in a turban to be on the safe side."

"She also brought El Cid with her," Luella added.

"To keep Esmerelda in check?"

"Indeed, and oddly enough, it worked. As long as El Cid was next to Camilla, Esmerelda contented herself with simply lounging beside the cat, never bothering to give her bottom a scratch on any of the pickets Camilla was painting." Luella shook her head. "I kept trying to convince Camilla to let me help her, since whitewashing usually doesn't take but a few hours, but she was having none of that. Told me my job was to get through the etiquette book while she painted, and then, after I finished the book, she took to quizzing me to see if the chapters had sunk in."

"She's been quizzing me too, after I get home from the factory, mostly to see if I've made any improvements with my conversational skills, which is where she's been concentrating her efforts with me lately in her quest to turn me into a sophisticated titan of industry."

Luella snorted. "I'm not surprised she'd focus on your conversational skills, not after you told Nems last Sunday during church that he needed to stop eating ramps past Thursday since he was proffering a smell that was stinking up the entire chapel—a smell I believe you said smelled like Nems had been run over by a carriage and left to rot in the middle of the road for a week."

"It's not like I said anything that everyone else wasn't thinking," Owen grumbled.

"True, but that doesn't matter, since, according to Camilla—who was gracious enough to not give you a dressing-down in front of everyone, but waited until we were in the carriage riding home—the only socially acceptable response to a smelly person is to ignore the stench and simply continue with your conversation as if nothing is amiss."

"She might have rethought that advice if she'd been sitting directly next to Nems."

"No, she wouldn't."

"Well, okay, probably not, but did you know that she made me apologize to Nems after we got home—and she told me to make it a good apology?" Owen blew out a breath. "Nems certainly didn't know what to make of it at first, but once Camilla was satisfied that I'd extended Nems a sincere apology and she went off to the house, Nems took to looking rather dazed before he told me that if I didn't already have my eye on Camilla, he might try his hand at courting her because, in Nems's words, 'Dem dare woman is as close to an angel as anyone done ever seen.'"

"Ah, so Nems realizes you have your eye on Camilla."

"Of course I have my eye on Camilla since I promised I'd keep her safe. It would be impossible to do that if I wasn't keeping an eye on her."

"You know that's not why you're always watching her, or why you make it a point to come home early from work every day so you'll have enough time to get all spiffy-looking before quadrille practice, which you know you look forward to because it gives you an opportunity to get Camilla in your arms."

Since Owen certainly couldn't argue with that, nor did he feel like getting into a conversation with his sister that centered around his inability to be anything but fascinated with a matchmaker who intrigued him more than any woman he'd ever met, he settled for sending Luella a smile before he kneed George into a run.

It wasn't really a surprise when Luella caught up with him a moment later.

"Nems wouldn't really try his hand at courting Camilla," Luella called to him, because of course she'd want to continue their conversation even while riding their horses at breakneck speed. "He's actually a bit sweet on Bernadette, but don't tell him I told you that because he'll just go complaining to Camilla during what Nems calls his 'gettin' down to turnin' into a proper gent time.'"

Owen slowed George to a trot. "Nems has dedicated special time to spend with Camilla?"

"He, as well as the rest of the men who've been tasked with guarding her, keep showing up one by one while she's doing all those chores for Aunt Elma." Luella smiled. "Apparently, they decided that after Camilla made you apologize to Nems, they might also need to be trained up in the etiquette department since none of them ever considered things like proper manners before. They've been seeking out Camilla's counsel, and she's been giving it to them, although I think they were feeling guilty about interrupting her chores because all of them started trying to help her." Luella shook her head. "Camilla flatly refused their assistance, saying something about that would cause her to lose some kind of challenge she's evidently in with Meemaw and Aunt Elma. That's why you can normally find one of the boys lounging beside Camilla and asking her etiquette questions as she goes about whitewashing fences, hanging Aunt Elma's laundry out to dry, or washing down Beulah's front porch."

"I'm going to have to ask the boys what kind of questions they're asking her."

Luella grinned. "I know none of them will be asking her anything about how frequently a man should bathe after Andy told her he was right proud of himself for taking a plunge in the stream every two weeks, especially when most of his friends only fully submerged themselves once a month."

"Should I assume everyone's bathing more frequently now?"

"There's been a run on tubs at the local hardware store."

Owen laughed. "I'm sure there are a lot of people smelling better these days, not that I'll ever remark on that to anyone except you since Camilla has more than hammered it into me that I shouldn't ever comment on people and smells."

"You're not the only one she likes to reiterate points with, Owen," Luella said, leaning forward to avoid getting smacked in the face by another low-hanging limb. "She's been adamant regarding what I can and can't say to Stanley after what I told him at our first quadrille lesson, when he had the audacity to seek me out and, instead of apologizing, told me how fine I was looking before he asked Charles to switch partners with him, that he was a sorry excuse for a gentleman. I then added that if he didn't want his nose broken again, he'd stay out of my way."

"Since Stanley continues watching you throughout every quadrille lesson, and I did see him say something to you a few days ago when everyone was taking a dancing break, I'm thinking he's determined to change your mind about you wanting him to stay away."

"Stanley can watch me all he wants, but even though he finally mustered up a halfhearted apology a few days ago, saying something about he was sorry we'd suffered a misunderstanding and that he really wanted us to become good friends again, he then demanded I apologize for breaking his nose, which really isn't how I think apologizing is supposed to work."

"Did you apologize?"

"Since I knew I'd suffer a lecture from Camilla if I didn't, yes, but in all honesty, I don't feel sorry for breaking his nose at all, something I've been feeling guilty about. That's why I sought out an audience with Reverend William Braun after church services this past Sunday."

Owen reined to a stop, waited for Luella to do the same, then caught his sister's eye. "What did Reverend Braun say about all that?"

"He told me that because I'm only human, my response toward Stanley was understandable since Stanley had treated me cruelly, and that I probably didn't feel guilty for breaking Stanley's nose because Stanley hadn't lent me the impression he's all that sorry for hurting me. However, Reverend Braun did suggest I truly consider forgiving Stanley whether he was sincere or not because holding on to animosity isn't how one should go about living their life."

Owen frowned. "Does Reverend Braun think you should resume your friendship with Stanley?"

"Not at all. He said that even if I were to forgive Stanley, that it's really my decision whether I want to spend time with him, no matter if Stanley wants to resume our friendship or not." Luella gave her horse a pat. "Reverend Braun believes that there are times we need to accept the consequences of our bad behavior, and in this case, Stanley needs to understand that because he hurt me, that it's solely my decision whether to salvage an old friendship or just deem him a past acquaintance and leave it at that."

"So you don't want to renew your friendship?"

"Perhaps in time I may consider it, but Stanley didn't hesitate to abandon me. And while I understand that Ada Mae encouraged him to do that, done so to get back at Mother because of her refusal to entertain a match between you and Sally—and allow me to say I thought it was very well done of you to apologize to Sally for that nasty business after Camilla told you what Mother had done—it was still Stanley's decision in the end to turn his back on our friendship. After speaking with Reverend Braun, I've come to realize that forgiveness is expected, but it's perfectly acceptable to decide who I want to include in my life and who I don't."

"I've noticed you're spending time with Martha Wellington and Clarice Colleens even though they conspired together to embarrass you at McGovern Pond."

"I decided I *want* those ladies to remain in my life, as they gave me sincere apologies. Martha even cried and told me what an idiot she'd been for setting her sights on Stanley after she learned I was no longer in the picture. Since we were all very good friends at one time, until everyone got swept up into the we-should-be-mean-to-Luella nonsense, I decided to let bygones be bygones." Luella smiled. "Camilla claims she's often seen similar circumstances happen within the Four Hundred and believes it's due to what she calls a group mentality—that people convince themselves their unkind behavior is acceptable because everyone else is doing it. And while that doesn't excuse Martha and Clarice's poor behavior toward me, they've been going out of their way to make amends, and, well, it would be churlish of me to not rekindle those past friendships. Besides, not that I would have admitted this after I found myself ostracized from everyone, but I missed mingling with friends."

A sigh escaped Owen as he kneed George into motion because . . . Camilla had been right all along in that he'd not really known his sister much at all, or at least not the young lady she'd become.

He'd been so focused on the unpleasant disposition she'd displayed from almost the moment their parents left for Paris that he'd never taken the time to contemplate what was behind all that unpleasantness. Camilla hadn't hesitated to point that out to him as they'd traveled from New York to Wheeling, and then had been pointing out all sorts of things about Luella ever since she'd become acquainted with his sister, such as Luella's interest in interior decorating, horticulture, and most surprising of all—fashion.

Luella had evidently never been opposed to fashion, merely opposed to bows and lace, and after having Camilla encourage her to embrace her own sense of style, she'd taken everyone in the family aback when she'd begun looking as if she'd stepped out of a fashion magazine on any given day, something that even Aunt Elma had noticed and, oddly enough, seemed to approve of.

"Why in the world is Meemaw dashing across her front lawn with her rifle in hand?" Luella asked, snapping Owen out of his musings as he glanced around, his gaze settling on Meemaw, who was indeed rushing across the lawn with her rifle.

"Something's wrong," he said before he kneed George into a gallop and took off toward Meemaw.

"Camilla's chasing a bear that's after Gladys. She's heading up the hill into the woods," Meemaw shouted when she caught sight of him.

A second later, Owen had George racing up the hill, urging him faster once they crested it and he saw Camilla standing in a clearing, aiming one of Meemaw's rifles at a bear that was in the process of advancing on Gladys, who was backed up against a tree.

Cleo and Calamity were circling the bear but keeping their distance, as El Cid slunk around the tree, coming to stand in front of Gladys, where the cat immediately took to arching its back and hissing.

"I don't want to shoot you, Teddy, but you're not leaving me many options here," Camilla yelled right as the bear reared up on its hind legs and let out a roar.

A blast resounded a second later, sending a flock of birds zooming out of the tree Gladys was under as Camilla stumbled backward, apparently from the recoil, right before she lost her balance and fell to the ground.

His heart missed a beat when the bear abandoned its interest in Gladys, dropped to all fours, and charged Camilla's way.

His Colt Dragoon was in his hand a second later. He aimed for a spot a foot in front of the bear and pulled the trigger, dirt flying in front of the bear as the blast echoed around the clearing. A roar was the bear's only response before it did an about-face and bounded off into the tree line.

A blink of an eye later, Owen was swinging from George and breaking into a run, reaching Camilla as she pushed herself to her feet. She took one look at him, then took him by complete surprise when she launched herself straight into his arms.

Twenty-Four

The moment Owen felt Camilla trembling, he pulled her closer, holding her until she drew in a shaky breath and stepped away, sending him a wobbly smile.

"Forgive me, Owen," she began. "I certainly wasn't intending on throwing myself at you, but I feel those tender feminine sensibilities you've remarked on a time or two have definitely decided to make an appearance."

He smiled and brushed a strand of hair out of her face. "Since I know better than to remark on feminine sensibilities these days, allow me to simply say that I bet male sensibilities would've come out as well if a man had just been chased by a bear."

"*I* was chasing *it* until it cornered Gladys, and all the arm flapping you told me to use wasn't working, which is why I had to resort to shooting at the tree in the hopes that would scare Teddy, which didn't work, and just as an aside, Teddy's not nearly as friendly as you led me to believe."

He winced. "That, ah, wasn't Teddy."

"What?"

"I find I must now beg your pardon, Camilla, because I should have warned you that Teddy's not the only bear around these parts. There are a lot of mama bears out there right now with cubs. You and Gladys, I'm sorry to say, just tangled with an angry mama bear."

Camilla turned her attention to where Gladys was running into the trees with Cleo and Calamity, El Cid slinking through the tall grass behind them. "It doesn't seem as if Gladys is experiencing any ill effects from her tangle."

"It doesn't, and she's a smart dog, so I don't imagine she'll be trying to befriend additional bears, because I'm sure that's what she was trying to do at first. However, it seems she's heading back to the cabin, so we should probably follow her, just to make sure she doesn't find more trouble on her way down the hill."

After sending Owen a smile, one that left him losing his train of thought for a second, Camilla walked over and retrieved the rifle that had flown out of her hand after she'd fired it, releasing a bit of a huff when Owen held out his hand.

"I'm perfectly capable of carrying this down the hill," she said.

"I'm sure you are, but given how you said your tender feminine sensibilities are currently in play, I think it's best if I carry the rifle for you."

"You said you weren't going to mention anything about feminine sensibilities," she grumbled, handing the rifle to him.

"Which means I'll need to revisit that chapter in the latest etiquette book you told me to read—the one centering around knowing when a lady wants to address a subject with you, and when she doesn't."

"There's nothing in your latest etiquette book about that."

"Then I'm sure you'll find me one that covers that topic," he countered before they began walking across the clearing.

After sending a whistle to George, who immediately headed Owen's way, he waited for Camilla to scoop El Cid out of some tall grass, the meow of protest she immediately garnered suggesting El Cid had been about to pounce on a field mouse and was none too happy to have been interrupted from his pursuit.

Before Owen could do more than give El Cid a scratch under the chin, earning a purr, Gladys gamboled back into view, Cleo and Calamity flanking her. The poodle immediately circled Camilla, gave her a nudge with her nose, then dashed off again, evidently having circled back just to make sure Camilla was okay.

"For a pedigreed dog, Gladys is unusually affectionate. Most of the purebreds I've encountered are more on the distant side," he said.

"She wasn't affectionate with me until we came here," Camilla countered. "In fact, she spent most of her time sleeping and refused to walk with me in Central Park. She'd simply sit down on our way there and refuse to budge until I told her we were going home, and even then seemed less than interested in ever moving faster than an amble."

As Gladys bounded around some trees, Owen smiled. "She's evidently turned over a new and rather rambunctious leaf."

"Beulah thinks that's because Gladys has finally found her true place in the world, meaning West Virginia." Camilla dusted some leaves from the front of the apron she was wearing. "She also believes that even though my poodle has a fancy pedigree, Gladys was never meant to be a pampered pooch, but more along the lines of a mongrel that loves nothing more than rolling in the mud with Esmerelda and letting her fur down as she frolics around with Cleo and Calamity."

"Meemaw's usually right about these matters."

Camilla abandoned her dusting. "She thinks I'm like Gladys."

"She believes you'd enjoy rolling in the mud with Esmeralda?"

"Probably not that," Camilla returned, her eyes beginning to twinkle. "Although now that I think about it, since I've become acquainted with you, *covered in mud* has literally taken on an entirely new meaning for me."

"You do seem to be covered in it quite often, but if not the mud, what do you think Meemaw means about you being like Gladys?"

Camilla shifted El Cid to her other arm. "She seems convinced that even though I was born into the elite world of New York high society, I'm not meant for that world. Beulah evidently has concluded that, quite like Gladys, my place is here, living a life far removed from the frivolities that make up the Four Hundred."

"Don't you miss those frivolities?"

Camilla shrugged. "In all honesty, I haven't had time to think about my time in New York since I've been much too busy whitewashing fences, doling out etiquette advice to Nems and his friends, and attending quadrille practices." She set El Cid, who'd started to squirm, on the ground. "Luella even took me crawdad hunting the other day, which, after I got over my fear of those somewhat terrifying creatures, turned into an amusing few hours. Bernadette, to my surprise, decided to join us as well, forgoing a nap she'd planned to take, although she might have done that because she knew Nems was going to tag along with us."

"Luella told me Nems might be sweet on Bernadette."

"Oh, he is, and has been trying to impress her lately. Frankly, I think she's been enjoying Nems's attention. She's certainly been asking a lot of questions about him to Sally and her friends while she styles their hair, since apparently everyone seems to be related around here, if distantly."

"Meemaw mentioned you've been encouraging Bernadette to take on clients—and paying clients at that."

"Bernadette enjoys having the prominent ladies of Wheeling clamor for her hairdressing skills," Camilla began. "And since I don't need her to dress and style me during the day because, what's the point when I'm doing manual labor for Elma, I thought having her spend her days doing something she loves would keep her out of trouble." She smiled. "Add in the fact that when she's not doing hair, she's altering Luella's clothing, and trouble doesn't seem to be in Bernadette's schedule these days."

Owen took hold of Camilla's arm. "Speaking of trouble," he began as they walked toward the forest, "you're not trying to secure a match between Nems and Bernadette, are you?"

"As if I've had time lately to concentrate on matchmaking."

"You know you always have time for matchmaking."

A rather telling smile was her only reply to that, but before he could do more than appreciate the sight of the smile, Meemaw and Luella rode into view, pulling up their horses the moment they spotted them.

"We heard shots," Meemaw said, swinging from her saddle as Luella did the same.

Owen nodded. "One was from Camilla because a bear—not Teddy—had Gladys cornered. The other was from me after Camilla shot to distract it, but the bear turned on her instead of running away. Thankfully, my shot scared it off."

"Well, thank goodness no one was hurt, including the bear," Meemaw said before she stepped up to Camilla, gave her a hug, then took to giving her a few soothing pats on the back. "What say, since you've suffered such a fright, we forget all about Elma telling you to clean out my chicken coop today?"

Camilla's brow furrowed. "And deprive the ladies of the sewing bee another opportunity to amuse themselves by doling out what they claim is helpful advice? Absolutely not." With that, Camilla began heading down the hill, declining Luella's offer of riding behind her on her horse, saying the walk would be an excellent way to banish any lingering feminine sensibilities she'd been experiencing after a near bear attack.

After exchanging amused looks with Meemaw, and then having no choice but to head after Camilla when Meemaw gave him a none-too-subtle push in Camilla's direction, he caught up with her a moment later, taking her arm when she stumbled over a tree root.

Once Camilla found her balance, he caught her eye. "You know you really don't need to clean out Meemaw's chicken coop, don't you, because if you ask me, Aunt Elma might be taking this whole chore business of hers a little too far with that request."

Camilla waved that aside. "It's a matter of pride at this point. I mean, granted, I know I'm rubbish at most of the tasks—or rather, all the tasks—Elma gives me, but I won't give her the satisfaction of concluding that a city girl doesn't have enough grit to complete everything she throws at me."

"Did she actually tell you that?"

"Right after I had a tussle with the wringer on her washing machine." Camilla's eyes began to twinkle again. "There I was, attempting to figure out the mechanics of that horrible contraption, when I got the hem of Beulah's apron stuck in it. Elma, unfortunately, discovered me stuck to the machine *and* . . . I might have been talking to it. That, of course, had Elma questioning my sanity, as well as suggesting I lacked grit because of my city-girl status, since I wasn't finding much success getting unstuck."

He swallowed a laugh. "What were you saying to the washing machine?"

"Oh, you know, just that it needed to start cooperating, and I might've added something about it not being my fault I was stuck to it when I'd never had an opportunity to wash clothes before."

"I don't imagine you've ever had an opportunity to clean out a chicken coop either."

"Which is why I'm just all aflutter to get back to Meemaw's cabin."

"Where Meemaw's sewing club will apparently be waiting to lend you some more invaluable advice?"

"I would say it's more along the lines of interesting advice over invaluable, although I did finally discover what those ramps are that Nems apparently enjoys."

"They're like onions and can be found along creeks."

"That's what the ladies told me." Camilla grinned. "They also told me there are rules that come with eating ramps, and that you weren't in the wrong for pointing out that Nems smelled that day because everyone is supposed to be aware that you don't eat ramps past Thursday, as ramps can cause a revolting smell to emit from the skin for days after. And, according to Mrs. Johnson, who has a remarkable proficiency with embroidery by the way, no one wants to be 'the stink in the church service'—her words, not mine."

"Truer words have never been spoken."

"Oh, I've been given a lot of true words of late. The ladies are especially keen to throw tidbits at me that are romantic in nature and revolve around things I need to do to keep your attention firmly settled on me. And no, I won't be sharing any specific details with you because that'll just embarrass us both."

"I appreciate your willingness to withhold what were undoubtedly brow-raising disclosures and pieces of advice."

As Camilla took to grinning again, they reached Meemaw's cabin, the front porch filled with ladies from the sewing bee, all of whom immediately sent him knowing looks as he took to greeting each and every one of them, while Camilla took to pretending she didn't notice the looks, saying a moment later that she needed to get down to the business of mucking out the chicken coop.

She'd barely disappeared around the side of the cabin before Aunt Elma pushed herself from a rocking chair and shook a finger his way. "Don't jist stand there, boy. Git movin'. Your little lady is fixin' to clean out the coop, and given her penchant for disasters, I say you should go off and help her."

"She's not going to let me help her after you questioned her grit."

Aunt Elma gave her nose a rub. "She told you 'bout that, did she?"

"She did, which suggests that maybe you would benefit from seeking her counsel regarding proper etiquette like Nems and a few other men are."

"A few other?" Aunt Elma said, releasing a cackle. "Boy, every man 'round these parts is clamorin' to get your little lady's advice." She leaned closer to him. "Some of them, I have to tell you, are interested in more than jist advice cuz she seems to have charmed every male over the age of ten around here, and perhaps even charmed the young'uns as well, since she sure does seem to have a way with children."

"I haven't seen her with any children yet."

"If you play your cards right, you'll have a few of your own with your little lady 'fore you know it."

Not wanting to dwell on the image that had just sprung to mind of Camilla holding a baby that was a mix of her and him, not when he was being watched by ladies who seemed to think it was their mission in life to hand out advice whether their recipients wanted it or not, Owen settled for clearing his throat. "I'll keep that in mind, but . . . why is it that Camilla allows you to get away with calling her 'little lady' when she got annoyed with me for doing it?"

"Don't be daft, boy. That's on account I'm a female, but no sense lingerin' here since me and the ladies are going to hie ourselves off to the chicken coop, seein' as how Camilla's gonna need some suggestions about how best to clean it."

"She shouldn't be cleaning out the coop at all."

"Every country girl knows how to clean out a coop."

Knowing he really had no choice but to traipse along with the ladies who were now moseying off the porch and heading toward the back of the cabin where Meemaw kept her chickens, Owen took Aunt Elma's arm and helped her down the steps, then walked with her around the cabin, coming to a stop when he caught sight of Camilla, who was already in the coop, but wasn't cleaning it. Instead, she was running around, scattering chickens as she ran, a rooster that went by the name of Harvey in hot pursuit.

"Don't just stand there, Owen," Camilla yelled. "I can't stop running to open the door, as that would allow this fiend to catch me."

Owen was in motion a second later, sprinting to the chicken coop and throwing open the door, Camilla dashing through it a second later.

Before he could slam the door shut, though, Harvey charged out and took off after Camilla, who was scrambling up a pile of firewood stacked in Meemaw's yard, Camilla releasing a bit of a shriek when Harvey fluttered his way up to join her.

"I thought roosters couldn't fly," she yelled, edging away from a rooster that was now crowing up a storm.

"They don't really fly—more like propel themselves upward for short distances—but now isn't the time to discuss roosters. Just jump," he called after he reached the firewood and held out his arms. "I'll catch you."

To his surprise, she didn't hesitate to jump, landing in his arms a blink of an eye later, where he promptly pulled her close and took off across the lawn, passing Meemaw on the way, who said something about utter madness before she began running after a rooster that was now chasing Gladys, but a rooster that was also now being chased by El Cid.

"I really hope El Cid doesn't catch Harvey," he said as he came to a stop a safe distance from where all the chasing was still going on and set Camilla on her feet. "He's Meemaw's favorite rooster."

"He's definitely not mine," Camilla muttered, rubbing a hand over an arm that was now sporting a welt.

"He pecked you?"

"He did, and after I saw something stuck to his leg, which I thought he would appreciate me getting unstuck, but, no, he started attacking me the instant I reached for him."

Owen tilted his head. "What was stuck to his leg?"

"It looked like a piece of paper, all rolled up and what you'd expect to find on a carrier pigeon." She frowned. "Now that I think about it, there were other pieces of paper stuck in odd places in the coop as well, most of them in the henhouse where I was supposed to collect the eggs, and . . ." Her eyes took to flashing. "Oh no they didn't" was all she said before she began marching across the lawn, evidently unconcerned that Harvey could still be on the loose.

"Might want to stay back for a minute whilst Beulah gets Harvey settled," Aunt Elma called, moving to block Camilla from where she now seemed determined to return to a chicken coop she'd only recently escaped from.

"I need to see what's tied to Harvey's leg," Camilla said.

Aunt Elma shot a look at Owen. "You best be talkin' some sense into that girl, boy. Harvey done took a dislike to her, so he ain't gonna want her lookin' at his leg, 'specially when what might be attached to it ain't gonna be taken the right way, what with Camilla being in a questionable state after sufferin' a bear tussle and then a rooster one."

"What's attached to Harvey's leg, Aunt Elma?" Owen asked.

"Ain't no cause to git into that, no siree."

Camilla released an honest-to-goodness snort. "There's every reason to get into that, especially if you and Beulah snuck copies of that infernal apple pie recipe into the chicken coop, hoping I'd pick up at least one of the copies as I went about cleaning or collecting eggs, because . . .who in their right mind would expect to find a recipe hidden in a chicken coop?"

Given that Aunt Elma immediately took to wincing, and Meemaw immediately headed into the henhouse with Harvey tucked under her arm, it wasn't a stretch to conclude that Camilla was exactly right and that his grandmother and aunt had been up to some shenanigans again.

And even though he'd never been convinced the apple pie recipe held the power of securing matches, he found himself just a little disappointed that Meemaw and Aunt Elma had been foiled in their latest scheme because—given that he could no longer deny he found Camilla far too fascinating, but knew she was far above his reach—if she'd suddenly found herself in possession of the secret family recipe, perhaps—just perhaps—the odds of him having a small chance of winning her favor might have actually increased.

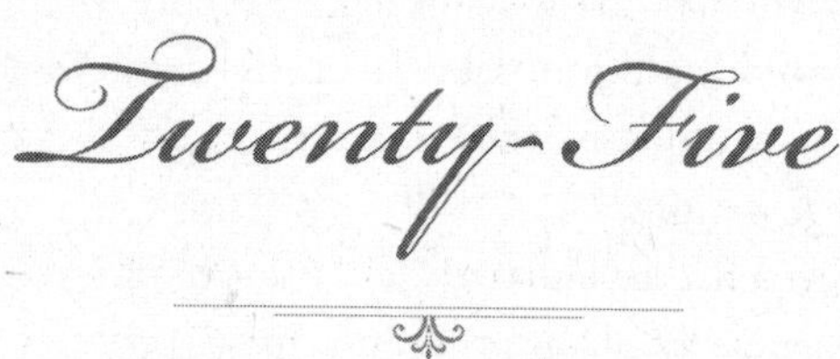

Twenty-Five

"Come across any crumpled-up recipes buried in the dirt as you've been planting those lima beans?"

Camilla straightened after she stuck the last of her lima bean seeds into the ground, finding Charles standing a few feet away from her, holding a hoe and swiping a handkerchief over a forehead that was dotted with perspiration, as well as a great deal of dirt.

Her lips immediately curved. "I'll have you know that I've not run across a single recipe while I've been planting today, although don't think for a minute that Beulah wasn't considering that, at least until I caught her and Elma up to some shenanigans yesterday after you, Luella, and I returned from riding."

Charles folded his hands over the top of the hoe and leaned his chin on it, his eyes twinkling. "Shenanigans? Do tell."

"Well, if you'll recall, you and Luella stayed on Beulah's porch to visit with the sewing ladies while I went in to grab a bowl of water from the kitchen for Gladys and the hounds, since they'd been running after us all afternoon." She grinned. "Guilt does not begin to describe the expressions on Elma and Beulah's faces when I walked in on them in the midst of making more copies of the infamous recipe."

"I'm surprised neither of them thought to just hand you a copy as you walked."

"Oh, Elma tried, but I'm too savvy for that nonsense. And after I safely navigated my way to the cupboard to get the bowl, I then told them in no uncertain terms that if their attempts at skullduggery didn't stop, I was going to have no choice but to delve into some of my own."

Charles's brows drew together. "Do you even know how to delve into skullduggery?"

"Of course not, which Beulah immediately pointed out, but I don't think she was expecting what I said next—that I might not know how to carry out any skullduggery, but that Nems and the boys most certainly would, and that I wouldn't blink an eye over asking them to assist me with coming up with a few ideas that would teach Elma and Beulah a lesson." She smiled. "Needless to say, Beulah and Elma abandoned their pads of paper and pencils and retreated to the porch, Beulah muttering something about Nems being more of a menace than I am."

"I have no doubt Nems would be capable of some interesting skullduggery," Charles said, sending a nod across the garden to where Nems was sitting in his wheeled chair, under the shade of a maple tree. "He's not really a menace, though, even though he's been trailing after me as I've been planting potatoes, observing every move I've made." He gave his jaw a scratch. "I particularly enjoy when he decides I'm not planting properly, like an hour ago when he stopped me with a potato halfway in the ground and told me, and I quote—'Dem dare taters ain't gonna grow right, boy, iffen you plant 'em upside downs.'"

"Nems calls you *boy*?"

"Among other things, none of which are complimentary, but he's taken to slapping me on the back, which Owen told me means Nems likes me."

"You seemed fairly pleased about that."

Charles nodded. "It's nice to fit in for a change, and the men around these parts seem to accept me, especially after we went fishing and I caught the largest catfish of the day." He lowered his voice. "Don't tell anyone, but I had no idea how to get a catfish off the hook, what with their sharp spines, but as luck would have it, the fish I caught did some flopping about as I was carrying my fishing pole off to the side to ponder the matter and ended up hopping off the hook by itself." His eyes crinkled at the corners. "That allowed me to retain my dignity because I wasn't forced to swallow my pride and ask anyone for some much-needed assistance."

"A decidedly fortuitous event, but speaking of people accepting you—Luella certainly seems to enjoy spending the majority of her time in your company."

Charles ducked his head. "It's the oddest thing."

"What is?"

"Luella wanting to spend time with me."

"Why is that odd?"

"Because *I'm* odd, and I wouldn't expect a lady like Luella to give me a second look."

"Oh, she does more than give you a second look, Charles. She adores you, and I know you adore her because why else would you agree to go furniture shopping with her even when you knew I wasn't available to chaperone and Elma was?"

"It was worth Elma's company just to spend an afternoon with Luella."

"A telling statement if there ever was one, just like it was telling when Elma told me that you and Luella talked nonstop during that furniture expedition."

"We never seem to run out of things to say," Charles admitted. "Although we didn't actually talk nonstop since Elma interrupted the conversation quite a few times to dispense what she calls helpful advice pertaining to matters of romance."

Camilla laughed. "I've had my fair share of that type of advice from Elma and the sewing ladies, but tell me, what advice did she impart to you?"

"Well, most of it revolved around kissing."

Before Camilla could do more than emit a bit of a snort, Owen strode up to join them, handing her a glass of sweet tea.

"I hope I'm not interrupting," he began.

"Not at all," she said, taking a sip of tea that soothed a throat she only then realized was downright parched. "Charles and I were just discussing kissing."

Owen's brows shot almost to his hairline as he immediately turned to Charles. "Any specific reason you'd be discussing kissing with Camilla?"

"I suppose we were discussing it because that's what Elma wanted to talk about when she was chaperoning Luella and me the other day."

"Why would Aunt Elma bring kissing into a conversation?" Owen asked.

Charles shrugged. "It's Elma. I have no idea what goes on in that mind of hers. If I were to hazard a guess, though, I'd say she's decided it's her role in life to dispense wisdom to younger generations."

"What kind of wisdom?"

"Most of it revolves around the idea that Elma's not in accord with the idea that couples who find themselves enamored with each other wait until they're married before they get around to doing what Elma said was 'testin' the waters before you jump feet first into the pond.'"

"And that testing centers around kissing?"

"Apparently so."

Owen narrowed his eyes. "And what did Aunt Elma have to say about what's involved with that whole testing-the-water-first business?"

Charles took to blotting his forehead with his handkerchief again. "I'm not exactly sure because Elma does meander her way around a story. But from what I gathered, she's come to some interesting conclusions regarding relationships after being married to Seth McColloch, who was—and in her words—'a no-good, lying, cheat of a man she never done should've married on account of her mama never givin' Seth the recipe cuz her mama done knew he weren't nothin' but a dog.'" Charles smiled. "Elma stopped her tale at that point to say she didn't mean any offense to any dogs out there because all the dogs in the Chesterfield family, as well as Camilla's, were far more upstanding creatures than Seth ever was."

Camilla couldn't resist a grin. "Elma does certainly know how to meander with a tale."

"Indeed," Charles agreed. "But after she said that bit about her late husband, she then went on to say that it's been her experience that if a couple isn't compatible in the kissing department, something she and Seth evidently weren't, they wouldn't be compatible in most areas. That's why she's evidently taken it upon herself to encourage couples to exchange a few kisses before any vows are spoken."

Owen's gaze sharpened on Charles. "Aunt Elma wasn't telling you this because she believes you and Luella should be trying to steal some kisses, was she?"

"I'm not a mind reader, Owen" was all Charles said to that.

"True, but I have the sneaking suspicion you think that's exactly what Aunt Elma was suggesting." Owen pressed his fingers to his temple, as if it was beginning to throb. "I'm going to have to have a chat with Aunt Elma because she will definitely not be chaperoning you and Luella again."

Charles dabbed his forehead again. "Elma's probably not going to like that because I get the distinct impression she relishes her chaperoning duties."

"Relishing or not, there's no possibility she'll be accompanying you and Luella again, and to make sure all the proprieties are going to continue being upheld . . ." Owen took a step closer to Charles. "You're going to promise me here and now that you'll never, as in ever, attempt to steal a kiss from my little sister."

Charles turned the hoe around a few times before he shook his head. "I don't believe I can, in good faith, promise you that."

"Why not?"

"One would think that's obvious."

Owen's face began turning an interesting shade of red. "You've been considering kissing my sister?"

"It might have crossed my mind a time or two."

Owen pressed his fingers to his temple again.

"At least he's honest with you," Camilla couldn't help pointing out.

"And while honesty is an admirable trait," Owen admitted, "that doesn't mean I'm not feeling a distinct urge to, well, it wouldn't be constructive to give Charles advance notice of what I may or may not do to him in the near future if I get the impression he's got kiss thievery on his mind again."

"From what Aunt Elma and the sewing ladies have told me, men have kissing on their minds most of the time," Camilla said.

"Aunt Elma just seems to have a bundle of less-than-helpful tidbits to dispense these days," Owen observed before he nodded to Charles. "However, since Camilla has just pointed out something that may have a lot of merit, you may now expect to have me as your constant shadow from this point forward. And, also know that if I catch you attempting to kiss my sister instead of merely thinking about it, there will be consequences, and not pleasant ones."

"If you're my constant shadow, I don't believe I'll have an opportunity to do more than imagine kissing her," Charles grumbled.

"You're doing absolutely nothing to make me want to set aside the urge to inflict some bodily harm."

Charles's lips curved into a grin, but before he could retort to that nonsense, Nems, who was still on the other side of the garden, released a whistle, waving at Charles a second later.

"Oh, would you look at that," Charles began. "Seems like Nems is ready to supervise me again. This time he'll be watching me plant corn." With that, Charles sent Camilla a wink, sent Owen another grin, then strode away.

"Remember, I'm your shadow from this point forward," Owen called after him.

"You need to stop being ridiculous," Camilla said, tugging him into motion and across the garden, even as Owen kept swiveling his head around to track Charles's progress, probably to ascertain that he wasn't sneaking off to find Luella instead of going to speak with Nems.

Unwilling to slow their pace since that might give Owen an opportunity to change their direction and go after Charles, Camilla settled for merely smiling at the numerous Chesterfield relatives who were calling out greetings to her, all of whom she'd met while attending church services with Owen over the past few Sundays, and all of whom had been more than welcoming after they'd made her acquaintance.

Truth be told, everyone she'd met during her stay in West Virginia had been hospitable, and she'd found herself more than enjoying the time spent amongst Owen's family and friends, delighting in the stories she heard about him as a child, and then learning about all the good he'd done in the community since he'd returned from college and taken his place in the family business.

Not only had Owen financed new schools, he'd also bankrolled the new wing at the local hospital, arranged for a charity pantry to open in town, and spent many an afternoon after work traveling to one relative's home or another to see if they were in need of anything.

As she'd listened to the stories and spent time with Owen's family, she'd found herself longing for the sense of kinship all of them enjoyed, as well as the sense of camaraderie that was always present.

She'd never experienced that before, having been an only child and growing up in a household where she rarely saw her parents or grandparents. On the occasional times everyone was together as a family, though, she'd been expected to behave with utmost decorum, never stepping a toe out of line, or, heaven forbid, getting a speck of dirt on any of her expensive garments.

One of the things she relished the most since leaving New York was the sense of freedom she'd found in West Virginia—a freedom to say what she wanted, dress how she wanted, and never worry that her disheveled hair or the dirt that was often smudged over her face or lingering under her nails would have Owen, or anyone else for that matter, finding fault with her.

"Done with the lima beans?" Beulah asked, materializing beside her and pulling Camilla out of her thoughts as Owen drew her to a stop.

"I am," Camilla returned. "I'm sure you'll be pleased to learn that Elma came by and inspected my work, declaring that for a city girl, I'd done an 'a-okay' job of it."

"High praise coming from my sister."

"I thought so as well, and now that I'm finished doing an a-okay job with the lima beans, I'm heading back to Moonlight Manor to clean up before helping Mr. Timken, along with Luella, who's been more than proficient with organizing an outdoor gathering, with the final preparations for the family reunion."

Beulah took hold of Camilla's arm. "Before I forget, you and Luella might need to reconsider the name you've chosen for the country house."

"Why?"

"Nems and Andy have begun referring to it as Moonshine Manor, thinking that's a hoot, and . . . I'm afraid their version is catching on with the family."

"I'm definitely going to have to include a bit during my next etiquette lesson with those two about it being less than amusing, or chivalrous, for that matter, to rename a manor house after moonshine."

"And that you've taken it upon yourself to disperse etiquette lessons to some of our more colorful characters leaves me longing to slip that recipe right into your pocket."

"Which you'll refrain from doing since those colorful characters, as you very well know, have said they'll assist me if you don't behave yourself."

"You truly are a menace."

Camilla smiled. "You know I adore you, as well."

"Of course you do, dear, but adoring me aside, tell me this. I couldn't help but notice that you seemed to be dragging poor Owen across the garden a few minutes ago. Care to share the reason behind that dragging?"

"Elma shared her kissing insights with Charles and Luella, and Owen, being Owen, isn't taking that very well."

Beulah grinned. "Leopold thought Elma's kissing insights were highly amusing."

Owen blinked. "Aunt Elma talked to Leopold about her views on kissing?"

"She did."

It wasn't exactly a surprise when Owen took to looking grumpy. "You don't think he's taking her wisdom to heart and might be even now contemplating the idea of trying to steal some kisses from you?"

Beulah's eyes began twinkling. "Who's to say he'd need to steal them?"

Owen shuddered ever so slightly. "I'm going to pretend I didn't hear that, but now, if the two of you will excuse me, I'm off to have a little chat with Leopold."

"He's out on the front porch, reading stories to the children," Beulah said before she stepped closer and gave Owen's cheek a pat. "Try not to embarrass yourself, dear, because while it's rather sweet that you're taking issue with all the inescapable romance floating around these days, take some wisdom from your dear old meemaw—sometimes things are simply meant to be, and there's nothing anyone can do to stop them."

"That's the worst piece of wisdom you've ever given me," Owen muttered before he kissed his grandmother's hand, told Camilla he'd be back momentarily, then strode off toward Beulah's cabin, clearly intent on getting to that little chat with Leopold as soon as possible.

"The poor dear," Beulah said, turning to Camilla. "You do realize that he's only concerning himself with everyone else's romantic interests because he's clearly overwhelmed by his own romantic issues, don't you?"

Camilla stilled. "I didn't realize Owen had romantic issues."

Beulah gave Camilla's arm a pat. "You know, I can't help but wonder, because you've spent so much of your time as a professional matchmaker, if, when it pertains to Owen's romantic issues, you're too close to the situation and can't notice what's right in front of you. Unable to see the forest for the trees, so to speak."

"I'm not really seeing anything in what you just said," Camilla admitted.

"Then allow me to explain more precisely—Owen's issues revolve around the idea that you still seem to be intending to return to New York in the not-so-distant future. I'm sure he doesn't want you to go, but he hasn't broached the matter with you because you've been so adamant about avoiding taking possession of the apple pie recipe."

"What does that have to do with anything?"

"It has everything to do with Owen's issues since he, being a man, obviously believes your determination to prevent me and Elma from slipping you that recipe by whatever means necessary equates to you wanting to make certain there's no possibility you'll find yourself married to him."

"But I don't actually believe in the power of the recipe. I've just been determined to thwart you and Elma because I consider avoiding taking possession of the recipe as just another one of the challenges you've sent my way, quite like whitewashing your fence."

Beulah's eyes widened. "Good heavens, child. The recipe isn't a challenge. It's a gift, and one that's only given to people we Chesterfields feel are worthy of becoming a part of our family."

Camilla took hold of Beulah's hand. "Then allow me to beg your pardon, Beulah. I certainly didn't mean to offend you by not truly realizing the importance of the recipe."

"Does that mean you'll accept it the next time I try to get it into your hands?"

Camilla considered the question for a long moment before she shook her head. "I'm afraid, since I'm not convinced Owen holds me in the kind of affection you're suggesting he does, that it wouldn't be fair for me to accept the recipe, not when it could lead to disappointing so many people I've come to care about if or when I return to New York."

"You said *if*," Beulah said, a small smile curving her lips. "That speaks volumes and suggests that you hold my grandson in just as much affection as I know he holds for you."

"I'm not going to argue and say I don't care for Owen, but I'm still not going to accept the recipe from you."

Beulah patted Camilla's arm again. "Which is fine for now, dear. But I am going to expect you to contemplate this matter thoroughly when you're at your leisure. I assure you, if you do that, you'll undoubtedly come to the same conclusion I have."

"Which would be . . . ?"

"That what you've happened upon here in West Virginia is not something you'll ever find back in New York. And, if you're unsure what I'm talking about, know that, to put it simply, what you've found is *Owen*, and he's *your* perfect match in every way."

"Now, son," Leopold began a moment after Owen finished telling the gentleman that he'd appreciate it if there was no more thinking about kissing and Meemaw from that point forward, even if Aunt Elma kept broaching the topic, "while it's understandable why you feel the need to have *the talk* with me, although I'm a little elderly for that type of talk, what I think is this—you're devoting far too much time worrying about everyone else and their kissing when what you really should be devoting your time to is getting around to doing some kissing of your own—and with Camilla, if that's in question."

Owen pressed a finger once again to a temple that was definitely beginning to throb. "That has nothing to do with our current conversation."

"I beg to differ because, in my humble opinion, you're getting yourself all worked up about me and your meemaw, as well as Luella and Charles, and kissing in general, because you don't know how to go about securing a few kisses from Camilla."

"If I'm getting worked up it's because I've been left in charge of the family, and we're talking about my grandmother and sister being the objects of gentlemen wanting to kiss them."

"Kissing is what couples do after they realize they're fond of each other, which brings me back to Camilla—are you not fond of her?"

"I'm not comfortable with the direction this conversation is taking."

Leopold sent him a wink. "Then I won't say another word about you kissing Camilla, but I imagine after you get around to kissing her, you'll be keener to discuss matters of kissing with me. Know that I'm more than willing to lend you advice since your father isn't around and I'm a gentleman of a certain . . . vintage and experience."

"I don't want to hear about this experience of yours."

Leopold laughed. "Fair enough, and with that settled, I think it's time I went off to join your meemaw."

"But not because you want to kiss her."

Leopold got up from the rocking chair and gave Owen a clap on the back. "You just keep telling yourself that, son, if it makes you feel better." With that, and with the echo of chuckles following him, Leopold ambled off the porch, leaving Owen standing by himself until he spotted Camilla walking over to join him.

"How'd the talk go with Leopold?" she asked once she reached his side.

"Not as well as I'd hoped."

"He didn't agree to abandon any and all thoughts of kissing Beulah?"

"I think he might have just wandered off with kissing Meemaw on his mind since I just put that idea into his head."

The corners of her lips quirked. "An unexpected result of your little chat?"

"Too right it was."

"Then allow me to suggest that we get on our way back to the country house so you won't do something ridiculous like shadowing Leopold, just like you threatened to do with Charles."

Owen blinked and glanced around, frowning a second later. "Where is Charles?"

Camilla took hold of his arm. "Relax. He's talking with Nems, who's getting his beard trimmed by Bernadette, and Luella's talking to Lottie and Edward, so none of them have stolen away to take any of Elma's advice."

After giving his arm a bit of a pat, Camilla pulled him into motion and steered him over to where they'd left their horses. Climbing into their respective saddles a moment later, they headed down the path leading to the country house.

Silence settled around them as they rode, which was somewhat unusual since Camilla normally enjoyed chatting away with him.

He couldn't help but wonder if something troubling had been said when she'd been speaking with Meemaw, although other than the fact Camilla was determined to stay as far away from the apple pie recipe as she could, he couldn't think of anything she might have discussed with his grandmother that she'd find disconcerting.

He, on the other hand, was finding it difficult not to dwell on what Leopold had said because now that kissing and Camilla had been introduced in the same sentence, he found himself unable to help *but* think about kissing her, a thought he'd already entertained on numerous occasions due, no doubt, to the topic of kissing dominating so many conversations of late.

The problem with kissing in connection with Camilla, though, was this—she seemed to approach that type of business in a rather no-nonsense fashion, probably because she was a matchmaker and talking about kissing went with the territory. However, she'd never lent him the impression she was personally pondering kissing, which suggested she, unlike him, wasn't spending her time wondering what it would be like to kiss him. Frankly, there was a possibility that if he took Leopold's counsel and broached the matter of wanting to kiss her, she'd take to boxing his ears like Aunt Elma was fond of doing.

Realizing it was less than productive to continue considering kissing in general, especially when such considerations were leaving him rather depressed, Owen cleared his throat, drawing Camilla's attention, which drew *his* attention to her lips, something that wasn't all that surprising given the contemplation he'd just been doing.

"Were you about to say something?" she asked, which had him pulling his gaze from her lips and settling it on her nose, which seemed far safer than her lips were.

"I was, ah, just going to say that I thought it was very considerate of you to tell Bernadette that she didn't need to accompany you back to the house to help you change" was all he could think to say as he forced himself not to allow his gaze to drift to her lips again.

Her brow puckered the slightest bit, and it almost seemed as if her gaze lingered for just a second on *his* lips, but then she shook her head ever so slightly right before she frowned. "I, ah, wasn't, um . . . what were we talking about again?"

His mood suddenly improved by leaps and bounds.

"Bernadette not helping you change."

She gave herself another shake. "Oh, right, well, ah . . . I couldn't very well put an end to Bernadette's impromptu barber shop when she had men waiting in line to get their hair cut and beards trimmed."

"Her services do seem to be in high demand."

"Word has certainly gotten around about her skills with a pair of shears and a razor, although I hope she isn't overcharging the men for her services today."

"She isn't charging them at all. I told her to send the bill to me since she's doing work for my family members or men who work for me."

Camilla's eyes began to sparkle. "It does speak very highly of your character that you're so attentive to your family and employees, but I'm afraid Bernadette will probably inflate her rates by at least twenty-five percent since you're paying."

"I would expect nothing less of Bernadette, especially when I've been coming to the conclusion she possesses quite the head for business."

Camilla halted her mare and turned in the saddle. "That's exactly why I've been considering offering her financial backing so she can set up her own business here."

Owen reined George to a stop, as well. "What makes you think she'd want to stay in Wheeling?"

"She's mentioned more than once that she finds the locals charming, especially Nems, and loves that everyone simply accepts her exactly how she is, flirtatious nature and all. She also seems to really enjoy having so many ladies from prominent families pleading with her to style their hair. Seems to me she'd have a ready-made book of clients."

"I thought Bernadette aspired to become an actress."

"She did, but she's a practical sort. I think she knows her talent with a pair of shears will provide her with a more secure income than dreams of treading the boards ever will."

"But if you help her open her own business, you'll be losing your lady's maid."

"True, but as Reverend Braun said during last Sunday's sermon revolving around verses from Philippians, we should look not only after our own interests, but also the interests of others."

"Seems like you were really listening to the sermon."

She laughed. "That's the point of attending a service—well, that and the fact that Beulah and Elma have taken to quizzing me on the ride home about what Reverend Braun had imparted, which is why I've been listening to every word that comes out of his mouth."

"Why would they do that?"

"They like to keep me on my toes."

"You don't seem bothered by that," Owen said.

She smiled. "I like your grandmother and aunt, even with them being two of the most contrary ladies I've ever been acquainted with, and . . ."

Whatever else Camilla continued to say faded away when he found his attention drawn to her lips again, undoubtedly because they were now curved in a most enticing manner, which made them downright impossible to ignore.

He lost all sense of his surroundings until he realized Camilla had stopped talking, as her lips were no longer moving. Drawing in a breath, he forced his attention from her lips and lifted his gaze, all sense of time completely disappearing when he caught her eye and found himself captured by the fact she was staring at him just as intently as he was staring at her. Before he knew it, he was leaning toward her, his attention returning to lips that were now parted ever so slightly, and . . .

"Ah, Camilla, there you are," a voice suddenly rang out, which left Camilla drawing in a sharp breath as time returned to normal and a slice of disappointment slid over him because, clearly, the moment he'd been highly anticipating for quite some time had just vanished into thin air.

Forcing himself to settle back in the saddle as Camilla took to doing the same, he gave himself a shake to clear his head right as Lottie and Edward rode up to join them, Lottie edging her mare alongside Camilla's.

"I hope we're not interrupting," Lottie said as she looked to Camilla, then to Owen, arched a brow at Edward, who sent her an arch of his brow in return, then turned her attention to Camilla again.

"Not at all," Camilla said in a downright chirpy tone, which left Lottie all but gawking at her. "Owen and I simply stopped for a moment because we were, ah . . ." She glanced around before she gestured to a field off to their right. "Admiring those lovely flowers over there."

"Those are dandelions," Lottie said.

"Aren't they simply spectacular?"

"They're weeds."

Camilla waved that aside. "Perhaps, but they're still lovely, and would look wonderful in those vases Luella found the other day, the yellow ones with the gold rim around them?" She sent a smile

Owen's way, which, unfortunately, had his gaze immediately returning to her lips, until he remembered they had an audience, and a very curious audience at that.

"They would look exceedingly lovely in those vases," he finally mustered up to say when she narrowed an eye on him. "Which is why I'm now going to gather you a nice bunch of them to put in those vases."

A second later, Edward was looking at him as if he'd never seen him before, while Lottie sent him a cheeky grin. Realizing everyone was waiting for him to make a move, he swung from the saddle and took a step toward the dandelion field.

"Perhaps while you do that flower gathering," Lottie began, "Camilla and I will continue on to the house because everyone will be coming over within the hour." She nodded to Camilla. "Beulah thought you might need my help getting ready since you're under a time constraint, but before I forget." She snagged something pink from her lap and held it up. "Beulah asked me to give you this apron, thinking the pink would go well with the afternoon dress you told her you were planning on wearing today."

Camilla, instead of taking the apron, released a snort. "And here I thought she and Elma had decided to abandon their attempts at skullduggery."

"They haven't abandoned anything," Lottie returned. "However, since we share the same suspicions, I've already emptied the pockets of more than a few copies of a particular recipe."

"Did you throw them away?"

"All but one, because that apple pie is delicious, and I'm certainly going to use the infamous pie recipe the next time I make pie."

Edward was suddenly all smiles. "I've heard about that apple pie recipe for as long as I can remember."

Lottie's brow took to furrowing. "Why are you smiling?"

"Because even though you've been reluctant to entertain the thought of me courting you, you're now going to have no choice in the matter since it's all but a given that we're supposed to be together, what with you possessing a copy of that recipe."

"Except that the recipe only works when someone is going to be marrying into the Chesterfield family," Lottie countered.

Edward's smile turned a little smug. "True, but you see, Owen and I are cousins three times removed, which means I *am* a Chesterfield, if a bit distantly related."

For the briefest of seconds, Lottie merely gazed at Edward, disbelief evident in her eyes, until she kneed her mare into motion and took off like a shot, bouncing around in the saddle because of her inexperience with riding, Camilla sending him a grin before she took off after her companion.

The grin left Owen feeling a little discombobulated, but before he could do anything to address that unusual state, Edward swung from his saddle and strode over to join him.

"Is it my imagination or was that a bit of an odd reaction on Lottie's part to discovering we're distant cousins?" Edward asked.

"I suppose it wasn't odd if she actually *has* been reluctant to have you court her and just learned she's in possession of a recipe that usually precedes a couple getting married."

Edward frowned. "I would have thought having possession of that recipe would have convinced her to set aside her reservations since, if you think about it, there's every chance your meemaw deliberately gave that apron to Lottie to give to Camilla, knowing Lottie would riffle through the pockets and find copies of the recipe. That means the matriarch of the Chesterfield family is more than willing to embrace Lottie and has, in fact, bestowed her blessing on an upcoming union between me and Lottie."

"You think Meemaw deliberately set Lottie up?"

"Since she and Elma pulled me aside the other day and asked if I'd gotten around to kissing Lottie—which was, in my humble opinion, a completely unexpected and uncomfortable thing to ask me, since, no, I haven't kissed her, but, yes, I've thought about it—I think they're now determined to make sure Lottie comes to her senses and agrees to become a part of the Chesterfield family, however distant the relationship might be."

"Why won't Lottie agree to you courting her?"

"Her colorful past seems to be the main issue, even though I've told her I don't care that she was once employed by a New York underworld boss."

"She told you about that?"

"She did, the day after she arrived, when we went to Stone and Thomas." Edward shook his head. "Lottie's very ethical, and she thought I needed to know she wasn't a proper lady right from the start because she didn't want me to keep finding myself in her company and developing a friendship with her, only to learn she'd been withholding pertinent information that could have affected whether I wanted to become friends with her or not."

"It clearly didn't affect your interest in her."

Edward smiled. "Of course not. Lottie's the woman of my dreams, and I'll eventually wear her down, especially when it appears Beulah and Elma have now gotten involved."

Owen returned the smile. "I imagine Lottie doesn't stand a chance of refusing your suit since Meemaw and Aunt Elma seem to be in cahoots to change her mind."

"Too right she doesn't, but enough about my romantic problems, let's turn the conversation to you. Anything you care to discuss with me?"

"I suppose we could discuss how many dandelions I should pick to fit into those vases for Camilla," Owen said before he headed for the dandelion field, Edward falling into step beside him.

"I was thinking you'd want to discuss something other than weeds, such as how annoyed you probably are with me after Lottie and I interrupted your rather . . . romantic interlude."

"You noticed that?"

"Would have been hard to miss. However, know that Lottie and I were going to attempt to make a stealthy retreat, but you know she's not good on a horse. When she tried to turn it around, she ended up encouraging it to bolt forward instead, interrupting your moment in the process."

"You might want to consider giving Lottie a few riding lessons," Owen muttered, bending down to begin picking dandelions.

"So she won't be able to interrupt another one of your romantic moments again through inept horseback riding?"

"I'm not certain there'll be another moment because it didn't seem as if Camilla was that disappointed by the interruption."

"Women behave oddly when they're taken by surprise."

"Are you talking about my attempt to kiss her or the interruption?"

"Hard to say."

Owen picked a few more dandelions. "I'm not sure you're the best man to be giving me advice since 'hard to say' isn't exactly helpful, and besides that, you seem to have some unresolved issues of your own."

Edward handed Owen a handful of dandelions and smiled. "You might have a point, which is why I think it might be beneficial if both of us seek out people who can give us some sage advice. In this particular case, I'm going to seek out my father, but I'm going to suggest you seek the advice of a man who knows Camilla—that being Leopold Pendleton, of course."

Thirty minutes later, after Owen got George settled with a bucket of oats in his stall, he headed for the backyard in search of Leopold, who was probably going to be more than amused when Owen set about asking that gentleman for some advice that was, indeed, going to revolve around kissing.

He came to a stop when he rounded the corner of the house, taking a second to allow his gaze to take in the scene in front of him.

Normally, when the family gathered, tables constructed from planks of wood and resting on sawhorses was as fancy as it got, but evidently Mr. Timken, Luella, and Camilla had had other ideas.

Yes, the long tables that were placed over a recently mown lawn were still sitting on sawhorses, but he couldn't tell if the tops were planks of wood because they were draped in white linen and the tables were set with lilac-colored dishes, everything matching, including the lilac flowers someone had placed every few feet as centerpieces.

Chairs, all of them matching as well, marched down both sides of the tables, and resting beside each plate was one knife, one spoon, and two forks, compliments of Mr. Timken, no doubt, who'd obviously realized that some of the Chesterfield relations wouldn't be comfortable sitting down to a formal dining setting.

"Camilla, Luella, and Mr. Timken certainly know their way around organizing a good party," Leopold said, ambling up to join him and sparing Owen the bother of tracking him down. "And your relatives who've taken over the kitchen certainly know how to fashion a fine meal."

"They do indeed, but before everyone arrives for the family reunion, I was wondering if you might have a moment to speak privately with me."

Leopold's eyes began to twinkle. "Have you been thinking up new rules to give me concerning your grandmother?"

"No, but I'm sure a few will come to me over the next day or so." He drew in a breath. "What I really wanted to speak with you about is . . . Camilla."

Before Leopold could do more than smile, and rather smugly at that, Camilla walked into view, dressed in a charming gown of some shade of pink, the apron Meemaw had given her tied around her waist.

As soon as she reached the center of the lawn, where she'd arranged games for the younger set, children streamed out to join her, all of them expecting hugs and a few of them leaving behind evidence on her apron that chocolate ice cream had already been pilfered from the kitchen, which suggested that Meemaw, even with her attempt at additional shenanigans, had evidently known

Camilla would find herself the object of children and their messy hands and had provided her with a barrier for her lovely gown.

Not that Camilla seemed particularly concerned these days about dirt, but . . . still.

"Given the way you're watching Camilla," Leopold began, "perhaps I should be shadowing you as you threatened to do with Charles, although . . ." He leaned closer. "In all honesty, if you're thinking about stealing any kisses, know that I wholeheartedly approve, and even if I were to happen upon you at what you'd consider an inopportune moment, I certainly wouldn't interrupt because if you've yet to figure this out, your meemaw is quite correct in that Camilla is perfect for you in every way."

Owen, especially after almost enjoying a romantic interlude with Camilla earlier, found he couldn't disagree with that.

Before he could contemplate the thought further, though, Leopold gave him a clap on the back. "Now, son, all that's left for you to discern is whether Camilla's figured out how well-suited the two of you are for each other, and if she hasn't, then you're going to need to figure out how to convince her that you're rather perfect for her as well."

Twenty-Seven

During the days that led up to the ball, and after the Chesterfield family reunion, which everyone had deemed a great success, Camilla had found herself barely having a moment to breathe, what with all the last-minute details needing to be addressed before Luella made her grand debut at the ball everyone of social prominence in Wheeling would be attending.

Final fittings were in progress for all the clothing Luella had purchased at Stone and Thomas, along with the ball gown from Worth Camilla had given her, Luella actually standing still for those fittings, but probably only because Charles had insisted on keeping her company. He'd taken to reading out loud from a book on horticulture they both apparently found riveting, although that particular book had put Camilla straight to sleep.

They'd evidently seen that as a prime opportunity because, when she'd woken up, the room had been empty, prompting her to track down Charles and Luella, finding them on the back patio, where they'd definitely been getting somewhat . . . cozy.

Besides tracking Charles and Luella down—and more than a few times—she'd had to schedule extra quadrille practices after Sally Murchendorfer almost had a fit of the vapors when she'd missed a few steps during one session, declaring with tears running down her face that she simply wouldn't be ready in time for the ball. Her tears had instantly dried up, though, after Luella volunteered to give her some one-on-one instruction.

Stanley, who'd been spending his time during their lessons watching Luella far more than Charles would've liked, had then stepped forward, offering himself up as Sally's partner, to which Luella had coolly replied that having him there would defeat the point of Sally getting one-on-one attention from her.

The room had grown silent as Stanley had merely stared at Luella for a long moment before he'd drawn in a deep breath and then told her that he'd been thinking about his past behavior of late, and that he truly was sorry for ever having assumed the role of complete and utter cad.

To give Luella credit, she'd not voiced agreement to that, which suggested the etiquette lessons had sunk in, but instead, had merely inclined her head, although she didn't change her mind about his offer of assistance, something that left Stanley looking rather resigned and Charles rather amused.

"I must say, I do believe the Chesterfields are going to make quite the showing this evening," Elma said, walking with Lottie across the parlor of the Chesterfield house on Wheeling Island, Hester nowhere in sight because Elma had given her companion a week off to visit family.

Her generosity hadn't left Elma willing to completely fend for herself, though, because she'd managed to get Lottie to keep her company and come read to her every day, stating that Camilla could certainly spare her companion for a week since it wasn't as if Camilla needed Lottie to read to her as she didn't suffer from poor eyesight, nor did she need her company because Camilla was always surrounded by people.

When presented with an argument like that, Camilla hadn't felt compelled to argue. Besides, she knew Lottie wouldn't be in her employ long—not when her companion had recently made the decision to pursue a position at one of the Wheeling schools and didn't try to hide the fact that she and Edward had managed to resolve their "issues," as Lottie called them, and were now in the midst of a very charming courtship.

"I see you finally relented and allowed Bernadette to have a go at your hair," Beulah said, nodding to Elma as she strolled into the room, settling a silk wrap overtop an evening gown from Worth, one of three Camilla had brought with her, and one that was a lovely shade of blue and had been altered by Bernadette, who'd been more than busy of late.

"I didn't want the poor girl thinkin' I was doubtin' her abilities by avoidin' her," Elma said, releasing a whistle a second later when Luella glided into the room, looking resplendent in the gown Camilla had given her—a lovely bow-free confection of ivory silk that fit her like a glove and would surely make a splash once they reached Mr. Fulton's paddle steamer.

"And don't you clean up nice," Beulah said, moving to join Luella, where she promptly kissed her on the cheek before she gave her a good squeeze. "Nervous?"

Luella shook her head. "Since Camilla managed the grand feat of getting me reaccepted by old friends weeks ago, as well as accepted by a slew of new ones, I have nothing to be nervous about."

"Except that you'll be performing that fancy dance she taught you in front of all those guests."

"Charles and I have been putting in extra practice time, and that's in addition to the extra time I spent with Sally, so I can do those steps in my sleep."

"When and where were you getting in this practice time with Charles?" Owen demanded, striding into the room and causing Camilla's mouth to drop open just a touch because . . . good heavens. The man did wear formal evening attire exceedingly well.

His jacket, as was always the case these days, accentuated his broad shoulders to perfection, and the pristine white of his shirt, paired with a white cravat, stood out in stark relief against the black fabric of his suit. His hair, arranged by Bernadette, had just a bit of curl to it, although Bernadette had somehow managed to tame the curls that usually had a mind of their own.

The only thing that detracted from his appearance was the scowl he was currently wearing, one that deepened as Charles and Leopold ambled into the room, Charles coming to an abrupt stop as his gaze settled on Luella, while Leopold moseyed directly over to Beulah, taking her hand and placing a kiss on it.

"This is going to be a very, very interesting evening," Lottie said as Edward walked into the room.

"Are you certain the two of you don't want to join us?" Camilla asked after Edward walked over to stand beside Lottie, beaming a warm smile at her as he took her hand and kissed it.

"I'm not one for fancy parties," Edward admitted, keeping hold of Lottie's hand. "Besides, my mother is hosting a dinner for us this evening, and she's been cooking all day, clearly wanting to impress Lottie."

"Your mother doesn't need to go out of her way to impress me," Lottie muttered. "I adored her the moment I met her last week."

"I believe the feeling is mutual," Edward returned.

When Lottie and Edward began gazing into each other's eyes, a feeling of satisfaction swept through Camilla, a direct result of knowing she'd been somewhat responsible for what was clearly going to be a spectacular match. After telling the couple to enjoy their evening, she strolled across the room to where Owen was still scowling, taking hold of his arm.

"There's really no need for you to look so fierce since Charles doesn't find your scowls intimidating these days, considering how often you scowl at him but never do more than that," she said.

"Do you think I should escalate to something a little more threatening?"

"And leave your sister more than morose if you were to happen to scare Charles off, not that I think he'd be easily deterred?"

"I take it that's a firm no to the escalating business?"

"Too right it is, especially when Charles is completely besotted with Luella, and she with him, something Charles's mother, Petunia, is certainly going to be thrilled about." She gave Owen's arm a squeeze. "Did I mention how often Petunia tracked me down in New York to discuss Charles's matrimonial prospects and how I was going to go about helping him end his bachelor state?"

"You did, but I'm not certain that telling me how difficult it was for Charles to find a compatible lady within the confines of the Four Hundred is the best way to convince me he'd be perfect for my sister."

"Learning Charles wasn't compatible with high-society ladies should be reassuring, not concerning because, what I've come to understand about Charles is that he was never meant to marry a lady from the Four Hundred, as he's not the quintessential society gentleman. He loathes discussing current fashions, the weather, or which virtuoso might be performing on any given evening at the Metropolitan Opera House. He prefers honest conversations, which he's been indulging in often of late with Luella."

"But Luella seems to have found a love of fashion, which I'm sure she'll eventually want to discuss with Charles, which suggests he may soon find himself less-than-besotted with her."

"You're reaching and you know it," Camilla countered. "Charles would be happy to discuss fashion with Luella because it interests her, and he, being a man in love, obviously wants to make her happy. And besides all that, another mark in his favor is that Charles accepts Luella exactly as she is."

"Given the stunned expression on his face when he first caught sight of her only moments before, I think he may enjoy the sophisticated and gorgeously gowned Luella over the ragamuffin he first met."

"While Charles is certainly a gentleman who can appreciate Luella's beauty, he's more enamored with her kindred spirit and kind nature, and it doesn't hurt that she can outshoot him on any given day, or that she shares his love of horticulture."

"But Luella was convinced just a few months back that she was meant to marry Stanley, which suggests she could very well be in a rebound state of mind and has simply focused her attention on Charles to vindicate a wounded ego."

"Luella would have never married Stanley because they were ill-matched, something I think Beulah realized since she never tried to get that apple pie recipe into Stanley's hands."

"Huh, she didn't try that, but I haven't seen her give that recipe to Charles, which could mean that Meemaw isn't convinced Charles is right for Luella either."

"I hate to burst your bubble, but I overheard Beulah asking Charles just the other day to fetch her recipe box because she needed to pull out her recipe for anise cookies."

"I don't believe I've ever eaten an anise cookie Meemaw made."

"Which suggests she *is* trying to get that recipe into Charles's hands. She probably had the apple pie recipe sticking out of the *A* section. I don't really think he'd balk if she'd just hand it over to him, but she might like the whole drama of sneaking it to him without his notice."

Owen went to rake a hand through his hair but stopped when Bernadette, who'd been fiddling with Elma's upsweep, sent him a bit of a hiss. He settled for rubbing his jaw instead. "If you ask me, there's been a lot of sneaking around of late. I've been on high alert because I keep catching Luella and Charles just wandering out of rooms—not together, of course—but suspiciously timed wanders that I know are supposed to come across as casual but are obviously nothing of the sort."

It was difficult to resist a smile. "Luella mentioned you've been following her around and springing out at her from behind corners, scaring the poor girl half to death."

"There wouldn't be a need to scare her if she'd try behaving herself, or stop seeking Aunt Elma's counsel, which you know centers mostly on kissing."

"Has Elma been giving you advice about kissing?"

Instead of answering her, Owen merely gave his collar a bit of a tug before he muttered something about needing to have a word with Leopold and strode away, leaving Camilla frowning after him.

In all honesty, his reaction wasn't exactly a surprise because she'd begun to realize that Owen Chesterfield, a man she found completely fascinating, albeit rather annoying again of late, seemed to have an aversion to kissing.

She knew full well that he'd been about to kiss her the day of the family reunion, but he'd not broached the subject of their interruption, nor had he tried to kiss her again, even though she may have—accidentally, of course—arranged for them to run across each other in spots that were far removed from prying eyes.

She'd been considering the matter at length, even during the last few quadrille practices when she'd been swept about the ballroom in Owen's arms, but even though she'd spent hours pondering the reasons behind why Owen hadn't attempted to kiss her again, she'd been unable to come up with a viable explanation except one—he obviously had allowed all the talk about kissing to persuade him to give it a try with her, but after they'd been interrupted, he'd come to his senses and decided that kissing her simply wasn't something he was interested in pursuing.

It was a beyond depressing conclusion because somewhere during her time in Wheeling, she, a matchmaker who'd vowed to never marry, had apparently fallen a bit in love with a man she was convinced would make her happy for the rest of her life, but he didn't appear to feel the same and she didn't know what to do next.

She always knew what to do when arranging matches for other people, but in this particular instance, she had not the faintest inkling of how to proceed because—how could she possibly go about convincing Owen he longed to kiss her, or . . .

"I believe the carriages are waiting on us," Beulah called out. "Shall we get on our way to the wharf?"

Camilla gave herself a mental shake and tried to push all thoughts of kissing aside, which turned somewhat difficult after

Owen returned to her side and took her arm, escorting her to the front door, where Mr. Timken was waiting, holding the door open for them.

After sending Mr. Timken a smile, Camilla walked down the front steps with Owen, who paused at the bottom and caught her eye. "I've been wondering something."

"What would have happened if we'd not been interrupted by Lottie and Edward the other day?" she heard slip out of her mouth before she could stop herself.

Owen blinked. "Is that what you've been wondering lately?"

She blinked right back at him. "Only if that's what you were about to say you've been wondering."

"I was actually wondering if you decided not to return to New York, if Mr. Timken would stay with you."

Disappointment was swift, until what he'd just said began to settle. Camilla tilted her head. "Why would you wonder something like that?"

"I'd rather learn if you really *were* wondering what would have happened if we'd not been interrupted, or better yet, what you actually *thought* would have happened."

"And I'd rather learn if, before you were wondering about Mr. Timken, you'd been wondering the same thing I might have been wondering."

Owen's lips quirked. "We seem to be throwing the words *would* and *wondering* around quite a bit."

"I'm sure that'll stop if you explain everything you've been wondering of late."

Before Owen could do more than consider her for a moment, Nems, who was already sitting in the driver's seat on the carriage, released a whistle, interrupting whatever Owen had been about to say and drawing their attention.

"Woo-eee, you sure is lookin' mighty fine, Miss Camilla," Nems called.

"It would seem we've been interrupted again, but don't think we won't return to this conversation at some point," Owen said, pulling her into motion and stopping beside the carriage where Nems, sporting a neatly trimmed beard, promptly settled a smile on her.

"Why, I ain't seen no one lookin' as purty as you do right now, Miss Camilla," Nems began before he settled his gaze on Owen and grinned. "Best be watchin' over the lady tonight, Owen. Them other gents are gonna be swarmin' around her like flies at the slaughterhouse."

"That's quite the image to now have stuck in my mind," Camilla murmured as Owen laughed. After thanking Nems for what he undoubtedly intended as flattery, she stepped up and into the carriage, Owen joining her a second later.

He immediately focused his now-notorious scowl on Leopold, who was sitting on the opposite seat, all but squished between the carriage wall and Beulah, the reason behind Leopold's squished state being Elma having insisted there was ample room for her, as well, even though she wasn't what anyone would call a slender woman and was currently taking up more than half the seat.

Leopold ignored the scowl as the carriage trundled into motion and sent Owen a smile instead. "Given that rather fierce expression on your face, son, I'm thinking you haven't followed through on that advice I've been giving you."

Owen shifted on the seat. "I'm not looking fierce because of your advice, which, no, there hasn't been time to take, but because Meemaw is practically sitting in your lap."

"I'd be more than willin' to join you on your side, Owen," Aunt Elma said, sending him a wink. "Bet that might make it possible for you to get on with takin' that advice Leopold's been givin' you."

Owen evidently decided his best option was to ignore all that, turning to Camilla instead of responding. "Have I told you about the Zane family yet—or more specifically, Ebenezer Zane, who founded Wheeling in 1769?"

It was difficult to resist a grin when Beulah and Elma began cackling, and Leopold took to chuckling, but knowing the last thing she needed was to have the three somewhat meddling members of the elderly set sitting across from her jump into what they enjoyed doing best, that being meddling, Camilla settled a smile on Owen.

"You have not told me a *thing* about this Ebenezer, and I now find myself more than curious about the man."

As Owen launched into additional history regarding his hometown, Beulah and Elma continued cackling, although they did throw in little tidbits about Wheeling, such as it was built around Fort Henry and that there were currently plans in place to start a new gentlemen's club by that same name that was slated to open within the year.

Ten minutes later, the carriage turned right onto Main Street, slowing to a stop a few minutes after that once they reached the wharf.

By the time they got out of the carriage, the door opened for them by Andy, who'd traveled with them tonight to act, not only as a groomsman, but to provide Camilla with extra protection since, according to the latest telegram from the Accounting Firm, there'd been little progress made uncovering who'd been behind her abduction attempt, a line of guests had already formed on the wharf, the ladies dressed in their best silks, while the gentlemen sported expected evening attire.

Before Camilla could truly appreciate the sight of a paddle steamer that appeared to have at least two levels, if not three, Owen was escorting her up the gangplank that led to the main deck, where Mr. Henry Fulton abandoned the guests he was currently greeting and bustled up for an introduction.

Henry then insisted on ushering Camilla, as well as Luella, who he proclaimed was absolutely delightful, around to introduce them to guests they didn't know, telling Owen he'd return in a trice, which left Owen, as well as Charles, scowling until Beulah elbowed both of them in the ribs.

A trice turned out to be her version of momentarily because

it took Mr. Fulton a good hour to show her and Luella around, Camilla having a difficult time of it refusing an urge to grin when guests thronged to their side and begged, not to be introduced to her, but to Luella, which meant their plan to establish her within Wheeling society had definitely found success.

After all the guests had boarded, the paddle steamer chugged away from the wharf and headed down the river, the breeze drifting off the water making it more than comfortable, even with more than two hundred people milling about.

After making the acquaintance of Mr. Russell Murchendorfer, Ada Mae's husband and a gentleman who turned out to be surprisingly charming, Camilla excused herself from the guests surrounding her after Charles wandered up to stand beside Luella, telling them she needed to return to Owen, which earned her knowing looks all around.

"I was beginning to think Mr. Fulton was planning on monopolizing you for the entirety of the ball," Owen said, handing her a glass of champagne once she'd located him in the crowd, a feat that hadn't been difficult since Owen stood a good head taller than most of the guests.

"He was very amiable," she said.

"I bet he was," Owen grumbled before he took to squinting at something over her shoulder.

"Is something the matter?" she asked.

"There's a boat coming toward us."

"I imagine that's a common occurrence on the river."

"Not when it seems to be on a path to intercept us, and not when it doesn't appear to have any navigational lights on."

Camilla turned and peered in the general direction Owen was staring, detecting an outline of another boat a second later, the only reason she could see it being that the moon had just appeared from behind a cloud. Unfortunately, the boat was almost upon them, and . . .

Shrieks suddenly rang out as numerous grappling hooks hurled over the railing, and then there was a clunk as the other boat pulled directly against the paddle steamer's hull right before men began swarming onto the deck.

"Pirates!" someone yelled as absolute chaos erupted, the ladies trying to flee to the lower level but freezing on the spot as a shot rang out.

"We're not here to harm you," a burly man shouted. "As long as you remain calm, we'll take what we came to retrieve, get on our way, and no one gets hurt."

It didn't take long to discover what they intended to retrieve after one of the men caught sight of Camilla and pointed a finger her way. "That's her."

"Don't worry," Owen said, bending his head close to her. "I think I have a plan."

"A plan?"

"Indeed" was all he said before he hefted her over his shoulder, moved to the railing, and jumped into the swollen waters of the Ohio River.

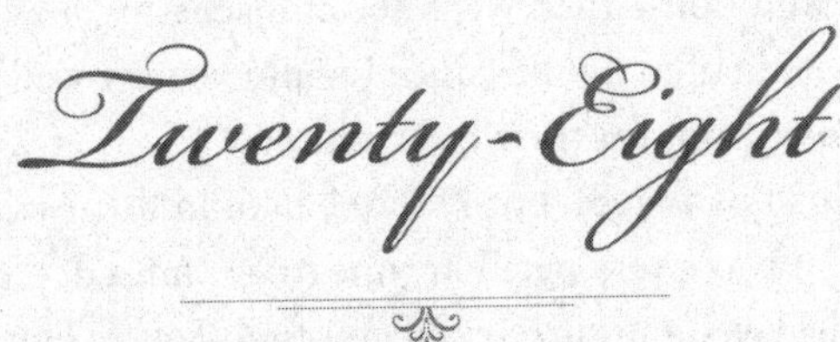

"When you said you thought you had a plan, it never entered my mind you were going to toss me overboard" were the first words that came sputtering out of Camilla's mouth after Owen hauled her to the surface and flipped her onto her back, keeping his arm around her as the current swept them swiftly away from the paddleboat and down a river that was swollen from recent rains.

"What plan entered your mind?" he couldn't help but ask.

"I thought you might have been about to ask me if I had my derringer readily available, and then I'd use my derringer to back you up after you whipped out your Colt Dragoons."

"I didn't have my Colt Dragoons on me."

"Why not?"

"Well, not that this is exactly the moment for this, but I was considering wearing my holster with Colt Dragoons in it until Leopold pointed out that the bulkiness would ruin the lines of my evening attire. That's why I left them in the carriage because who would have thought a paddle steamer would get ambushed?"

"So we're currently being swept down a river because you've decided to embrace a more fashionable approach regarding evening attire?"

"That about sums it up." He pulled her closer to him when she started sinking underneath the water. "Did you actually bring your derringer with you?"

"I tried, but after Bernadette realized I'd stuffed it into my corset since I know better than to attach it to my leg, she made me hand it over. She and Lottie then went about discussing how fortunate I was to have them in my life since I could've very well ended up, er, charm-less if not for their intervention."

He felt his lips twitch, but before he could do anything other than realize it was a very peculiar time to be amused, they reached a bend in the river, the current substantially increasing.

With Owen keeping a firm hold on Camilla, the weight of her gown continuing to drag her under the water, they bobbed their way through rapids that left both of them gasping for breath before they hurtled into calmer waters, where he began swimming for shore.

His breathing became more labored than ever as he fought their way through the current, but finally, and after what seemed like hours instead of just minutes, his feet touched the muddy bottom of the river. Taking a moment to find his balance, he lifted Camilla into his arms and staggered through the increasingly shallow water, making it to dry land a moment later.

After setting Camilla down in the high grass that covered the bank, Owen bent over and took a second to catch his breath, returning his attention to Camilla when she let out a bit of a grunt as she pulled a strand of what seemed to be weeds out of her hair right before she sent him a grin.

"Care to share what's amusing you?" he asked.

"I was just thinking about how, in my almost twenty-six years on this earth, I'd never been in a river before, but after having met you, it seems to be quite a frequent occurrence."

"You don't sound overly upset about that."

"Considering both times I've ended up in a river has allowed me to escape from would-be abductors, I'm not upset in the least, although . . ." She sat up. "I have to wonder how those men found me, and if Victor Malvado is the criminal mastermind who seems determined to snatch me. Clearly, with me being the obvious target tonight, Lottie was probably never in danger."

"From what Lottie has said about Victor, he seems to be an incredibly powerful crime boss who has far-reaching connections. If he is behind this, and maybe he is because he would glean a hefty ransom for your safe return, he's evidently either sent men down here or has found some criminal connection in West Virginia that he used to plan this attack."

"But how could anyone have known where to find me?"

"I'm not sure, although I suppose it wouldn't be a stretch to think that someone from Wheeling traveled to New York and mentioned something about you, because you know people like to mention names of well-known people in order to increase their standing within whatever group they're mingling with. Maybe Victor, or another criminal boss, heard about the conversation."

"It could also be that Lord Shrewsbury might have heard a conversation like that, especially when we know he's back in the city, attending events with Ward McAllister," Camilla said.

"I suppose however someone found out doesn't really matter right now, but what does matter is that we need to get you back to New York posthaste."

"But that's where Lord Shrewsbury is, as well as Victor Malvado."

"True, but it's also where the Accounting Firm is, and I have to believe they have the resources needed to truly keep you safe, unlike me."

"You just saved me from another abduction attempt."

Owen inclined his head. "I did, but you must know they'll try again since they've gone to the bother of tracking you here. Even with the number of men we have watching over you, I'm not sure that'll be enough to keep you safe."

Holding out his hand, Owen helped Camilla to her feet before he took a moment to survey their surroundings, nodding to his right a moment later. "I have a friend, Amos Rook, who has a house not far from here. He'll be happy to give us a ride back to the island."

Entwining his fingers with Camilla's, Owen headed along the riverbank, stopping when Camilla stumbled over the drenched hem of her gown. He eyed her for just a second before he moved closer and hauled her up and into his arms.

Her arms immediately looped around his neck, causing a wave of heat to shoot through him even though he was sopping wet and the wind that was blowing over them held a touch of a chill.

"This really isn't necessary," she muttered as he began striding through the tall grass of a clearing.

"It is when I don't want you to break a limb by tripping over your skirt."

Her arms went a little slack.

He stopped walking and looked down at her face. "What?"

"Nothing."

"That didn't sound like a nothing kind of response. What are you thinking?"

"I'm thinking we should have devoted more time to choosing better responses when engaging in conversations."

"Huh," he said, taking a second to consider the matter before he frowned. "This isn't one of those hero moments, is it? One where I've made a blunder again like I did with Pauline?"

"You already had a hero moment when you tossed me overboard."

The warmth flowing through him intensified. "I see," he said before he caught her eye. "I don't see, though, how I could have chosen a better response to you suggesting that carrying you wasn't necessary because I truly don't want you to break a limb."

She blew out a bit of a sigh. "I'm sure you don't want me to break a limb, but that was an opening you could have used as a, well, attempt to try your hand at being somewhat of a Casanova type."

"You were expecting a Casanovian moment from me?"

"I'm not sure I was expecting that, but I wouldn't have been, ah, opposed to it."

He pulled her a little closer. "Perhaps I should try again."

"I think the moment has passed."

His lips twitched, because she was beginning to sound a little grumpy. "What about if I tell you that carrying you is necessary because it gives me a reason to hold you in my arms?"

Her arms tightened around his neck again. "That's definitely an improvement."

"Then what about if I also add that holding you so close gives me a perfect opportunity to set aside all that wondering I've been doing and learn for myself what would have happened had we not been interrupted the day of the family reunion?"

She drew in a sharp breath but didn't say a single thing to that because . . . her gaze was now settled on his mouth.

Not wanting to spend another second wondering what kissing Camilla would be like, Owen lowered his head until he was only an inch away from her lips, freezing on the spot when he heard a rifle being cocked behind him.

"This here be private property," a man said. "State your business a'fore I decide to shoot."

"This is some seriously bad timing," he grumbled before he lifted his head. "There's no need to shoot, Amos. It's me, Owen."

"What in tarnation are you doin' out here this time of night?" Amos demanded.

Setting Camilla on her feet, Owen turned. "Miss Pierpont and I have run into some trouble, Amos. I was just heading up to your house to see if you could help us."

"You know you don't even need to be askin' that," Amos said, taking a second to look Owen over before he shook his head. "Seems like the first order of business is to git you two into some dry clothes, and then we'll see iffen we can sort out whatever trouble done rained down on you."

Fifteen minutes later, and after he'd explained the basics to Amos and his wife, Cora Beth, Owen was, thankfully, wearing dry clothes, although they were remarkably snug, while Camilla was wearing one of Cora Beth's housedresses that all but swallowed her up.

After Amos called through the front door that he'd gotten Roscoe hitched up to his wagon, Owen took Camilla's arm, and after thanking Cora Beth for the clothes, they walked out of the cabin, joining Amos a moment later.

"I sure appreciate this," Owen said, earning a nod from Amos in return.

"Ain't no problem," Amos said. "You'd do the same for me, but you sure it's wise to have me drive you to the house instead of straight to the police?"

Owen helped Camilla up into the wagon bed. "I'm not sure the police are equipped to deal with the kind of men who are after Camilla, men I would bet are even now scouring the banks of the river for us. I think our safest option is to make a quick stop at my house, grab some necessities, then head out before anyone realizes we were ever there."

"Where you plannin' on headin'?" Amos asked.

"It would probably be best if you don't know in case anyone comes nosing around."

"Sure 'nough you might be right about that" was all Amos said as Owen climbed into the wagon to join Camilla, then covered them with a blanket as Amos got settled on the seat, clicked his tongue, and the wagon lurched into motion.

Owen waited until they reached a gravel road instead of the bumpy dirt drive they'd been on before he turned his head, catching just a hint of Camilla's face under the blanket. "Think now would be an appropriate time to get back to what we were doing before Amos almost shot us?"

Warmth once again flooded over him when Camilla laughed.

"Not to disappoint you, but I don't believe now, while we're hiding out in the back of a wagon, under a blanket that smells like onions, is probably the best time to resume that type of business."

"I suppose the onion smell does put a damper on things."

"As does the idea we're not out of danger yet." She inched a little closer, surprising him when she took hold of his hand. "What's your plan?"

"The only plan I have is to grab a few essentials before we head for the train station."

"You don't want to wait and see if Leopold, Charles, or any of the men who've been guarding me show up?"

"Unless they're already there, no. We don't have the luxury of that kind of time."

"What about Bernadette and Mr. Timken?"

"I don't think they'd be much use to us as guards, what with how Mr. Timken is pushing seventy at least, and Bernadette doesn't strike me as a lady I should hand a gun to since she's a little overly dramatic at the best of times."

"I wasn't thinking they'd be useful as guards but as chaperones."

Owen frowned. "Forgive me, Camilla. I didn't even consider needing a chaperone, but I don't think it's a good idea to bring them with us because we'll be less conspicuous if it's only the two of us."

"Which makes sense. However, you must realize that if anyone spots us traveling alone together, that will mean we'll have to make our feigned engagement official."

His lips began curving on their own accord because it would not bother him in the least if they had no choice but to make that official, especially not after they'd almost shared a kiss again, and . . . she'd seemed completely receptive to the idea of sharing that kiss.

Frankly, he'd been losing sleep ever since Lottie and Edward had interrupted them because Camilla hadn't, up until tonight, given him any indication she wanted him to try kissing her again.

Considering she was a matchmaker—and there was no point thinking of her as a retired matchmaker since she'd certainly returned to her matchmaking endeavors with quite a bit of gusto—Owen knew full well that Camilla knew how to go about this business called romance, and . . .

"Should I take your silence to mean you're currently thinking about how we should revise our plan so we aren't forced to travel alone together?" she asked, pulling him straight out of his thoughts.

Given the slight trace of disgruntlement in her tone, it was clear he'd been allowing his thoughts to wander in the midst of what could be a life-changing conversation—and his life, at that.

"Forgive me yet again, Camilla. I fear I was lost in thought."

"I knew you didn't read that chapter in the last etiquette book that covered how important it was to always keep your thoughts, as well as attention, centered on the person you are engaged in conversation with."

"I read that chapter, but you have to admit, we've been dealing with some extenuating circumstances over the past hour. I'm afraid all that decorum knowledge has gotten shuffled about in my mind."

"I suppose that's a legitimate excuse."

"Indeed, but know that I wasn't considering a way for us not to travel alone together. I was simply thinking that, if we were to be seen, I wouldn't be—"

"We're almost to your house," Amos said, interrupting Owen mid-sentence as he leaned over the wagon seat and lifted the blanket to peer down at them. "I'm just letting Roscoe amble along a bit to make sure the coast is clear." He dropped the blanket back into place as Camilla released a sigh.

"Why is it that when we're getting right down to the good stuff, we're always interrupted?" she whispered.

"Does that mean, when I was carrying you earlier, that you considered that getting down to some good stuff?"

"Perhaps," she admitted as the wagon pulled to a stop and Amos lifted the blanket from them.

"Doesn't seem to be anyone around," Amos said quietly.

After climbing from the wagon, Owen helped Camilla do the same, sent Amos a nod of thanks after he got back on the seat and set the wagon into motion, then took Camilla's arm and led her toward the front steps, the blood in his veins turning to ice when the sound of pounding boots erupted behind them.

"Run!" he yelled to Camilla before he turned and found himself confronted by at least five men.

Planting his fist into the closest man's face, he didn't linger to watch the man crumple to the ground, but cracked his fist into another man's jaw, Owen's head rearing back when a third man managed to land a punch before he grabbed hold of the man's shirt and tossed him aside.

A yell from Camilla had him spinning around and bolting toward the house, rage immediately coursing through him when he saw that a man had her slung over his shoulder and was running down the steps, obviously intent on getting her to the carriage that was now racing down Zane Street.

Owen lowered his head and charged for the man, his progress coming to a rapid end when he felt a sharp pain explode in the back of his head. Everything immediately began turning black as he plummeted to the ground, the shadowy sight of Camilla being hauled away the last thing he saw before darkness claimed him.

Twenty-Nine

As far as abductions went, not that Camilla had ever actually *been* abducted before, this one wasn't exactly horrible, not when the men who'd snatched her had treated her with kid gloves throughout the train ride back to New York.

Granted, they'd not exactly been willing conversationalists. In fact, they'd not spoken to her at all, but after they'd tossed her into a private Pullman car, they'd then taken shifts watching over her while providing her with meals that had clearly been created by a chef, and a talented chef at that.

She was relatively certain that few, if any, abductees warranted travel in Pullman cars, let alone being served meals that any member of the Four Hundred would have deemed impressive.

Truth be told, the only trepidation she currently had centered around what was in store for her once they reached their final destination, which was rapidly approaching now that she'd been transferred from the Pullman car to a carriage, one that had black curtains obscuring the windows.

Frankly, all she could do now was hope a ransom had been delivered to her father, which she knew he'd pay, and then hopefully she'd be set free. Her first order of business after gaining her freedom would be, of course, to immediately set off to find Owen.

She was relatively certain that he hadn't been seriously injured since she hadn't overheard anything from her guards suggesting otherwise, but until she actually saw for herself, she couldn't help but worry.

She also couldn't help but wonder, given that they'd almost kissed again, and she'd gotten the impression he hadn't been opposed to traveling alone together, even though the consequences of that could have led to an immediate marriage, if Owen had come around to the idea that Beulah might have been right after all and they were, indeed, well-matched.

Pushing aside her thoughts about Owen as best she could when the carriage rolled to a stop, she lifted her chin, bracing herself for whatever was in store for her next.

The carriage door opened a moment later, and without saying a word, a man helped her out, keeping a firm grip on her arm as he led her through a courtyard that was surrounded by derelict buildings, the salty scent of the ocean tickling her nose and lending her the impression they might very well be down near the Battery.

Unfortunately, before she had a chance to determine exactly where she was, the man ushered her through a heavy door that looked as if it had been chosen to withstand an attack. A moment later, she found herself in an entranceway that certainly didn't match the exterior of the building she'd entered.

Walls papered in muted-green silk captured her attention before her gaze traveled over a crystal chandelier, marble floors, and a large bronze sculpture of a horse that would have been at home in any house on Fifth Avenue.

Another man, this one dressed in black, a holster slung low on his hips, strode up and presented her with a bow. "If you'll follow me, Miss Pierpont, I'll see you to your accommodations."

Since she certainly didn't have a choice in the matter, Camilla trailed behind the man down the long marble hallway, through a dining room, and then stopped when the man paused in front of a doorway. He removed a key from his pocket, unlocked the door, then pushed it open before he stepped aside and gestured her forward.

Wondering why the door had been locked, which suggested someone else might be locked in the room she was about to enter, which seemed somewhat ominous, Camilla forced herself to step into the room, all but stumbling to a stop when her gaze settled on a man standing beside the fireplace, a man who took that moment to turn around to face her.

She blinked, just once, before she squared her shoulders and marched farther into the room, temper roiling through her because the man now staring at her with narrowed eyes was not Victor Malvado or any other criminal boss, but none other than George Sherrington, Lord of Shrewsbury—and absolutely the last man on earth Camilla had ever wanted to see again.

"What in the world are you doing here, George?" she demanded, stopping a few feet away from him and crossing her arms over her chest.

George set aside the crystal wine goblet he'd been holding and returned his attention to her, his brows drawing together as his gaze swept the length of her, lingering on the housedress Cora Beth had given her. "I think a more pressing question would be . . . what are you wearing?"

Her toe began tapping against the floor. "Is that really the first thing you think you should be asking me right now?"

George gave himself a bit of a shake and was smiling a second later as he closed the short distance separating them and grasped her hand, which he promptly raised to his lips and kissed.

"You're right, of course, my darling," he began, keeping hold of her hand and giving it another kiss, which left her with the distinct urge to jerk her hand away from him, something she was prevented from doing because he had what almost amounted to a death grip on her fingers. "I fear the sight of you had me quite losing my head for a second, although I must add that I'm not sure I like what you've done with the hair on your head. If memory serves me correctly, it used to be a vibrant gold, but now it seems to be a somewhat mousy shade of blond."

"I believe that's because it's long overdue for a wash."

His smile slid from his face. "May I assume you've suffered from some type of mishap that is responsible for you abandoning expected grooming practices?"

"I was abducted, George. I would think the answer to that is obvious."

He gave her hand a pat, a tic appearing on his forehead when she finally pried her hand away from him. "You used to enjoy when I held your hand."

"It's amazing how things change with time."

His lips curved into another smile. "Ah, I understand now. You're still wounded because I was forced to marry another woman. However, I'm sure you'll be delighted to learn that I have every intention of making up for that regrettable circumstance. Believe me when I tell you that I've pined for you for years, dreaming of the day I'd finally be able to see you again."

"You really don't strike me as a pining type of gentleman."

He frowned. "I suppose you're right, as I'm far too manly to succumb to such a feminine emotion. Perhaps I should have said I've been longing for you most fervently over the years."

Reminding herself that contradicting that bit of ridiculousness would only encourage more preposterous statements from a man she'd once thought hung the moon, Camilla stepped back, taking a moment to consider the man.

It quickly became evident that the years had not treated him kindly.

Unlike the George she'd known seven years ago, the man standing before her had acquired a substantial paunch, as well as lost a great deal of his hair, although he was now combing long strands of what hair he had left over his head, which wasn't as attractive as he probably assumed it was.

His face was also on the puffy side, which made his eyes look smaller than she remembered, and he now sported not one but several chins, although . . . She narrowed her eyes on the chins in question, unable to help but wonder if he'd always had a weak chin, and she, being young and apparently incredibly absurd, had simply never noticed.

"May I dare hope you've been longing for me just as much as I have you, and that you're now feeling downright giddy since we've been reunited, although under somewhat questionable circumstances?" George asked.

Camilla tore her attention from his chins. "I'm not certain *giddy* sufficiently describes how I'm feeling at the moment."

"Ecstatic, perhaps?"

"That doesn't describe it either."

George sent her a wink. "You let me know when the appropriate word comes to mind."

"Oh, I already have a word readily available, and that word would be . . . *furious*."

"I think I like *giddy* better, although . . ." George tilted his head. "Could you be furious because your abductors forced you into a dress that I can only describe as an abomination?"

Camilla's jaw took to clenching. "It's a housedress, George, hardly something to become infuriated over, but since I don't care to waste time with you throwing preposterous reasons at me over why I might be beyond infuriated at the moment, allow me to cut to the chase—I'm in this state because, as I mentioned, I've been abducted, and I'm now quite certain you're somehow responsible for my current situation."

"Perhaps we should sit down."

Camilla narrowed an eye on him. "Oh my word, you *are* behind this, aren't you?"

"The settee by the fireplace is remarkably comfortable," George said, completely sidestepping her question. "I've spent the past day and a half lounging on it, reading a dreary book penned by some lady—one Jane Austen, I believe."

Unwilling to argue with that piece of absurdity, Camilla stalked across the room and sat down on a dainty chair upholstered in a paisley-patterned velvet, one that certainly didn't have room for two.

After releasing a sigh, George ambled over to the settee, settled himself on it, crossed one leg over the other, then focused another smile on her again.

Her temper edged up a notch.

"And?" she finally forced herself to ask.

"I've been well of late, thank you for asking. Until, of course, I found myself, ah, well, unexpectedly imprisoned."

"I wasn't inquiring over your welfare, George, although from what I've heard, you haven't been doing well at all, considering you apparently divorced your wife."

"And to that I say, divorce improved my well-being tremendously as Eleanor was mad as a hatter."

"I beg your pardon?"

George gave a sad shake of his head. "You heard me. Eleanor was quite insane, which is why I had no choice but to seek out a divorce. I couldn't very well risk having children with her, not after she began showing signs of insanity shortly after we exchanged vows."

"Eleanor Deerhurst and I attended the same finishing school," Camilla said. "She never once displayed any symptoms of insanity when I knew her."

"Nor did she show any signs of madness before I married her, but that certainly changed not long after the wedding as the silly chit decided she found me repulsive a month after our vows were exchanged." George caught Camilla's eye. "Can you imagine? Me? Repulsive to any woman?"

"Actually, I *can* imagine that."

George waved that aside. "Don't be spiteful. It doesn't become you. However, to return to my story, I can hardly be blamed for being concerned about the downward spiral into insanity Eleanor was clearly traveling at a rapid clip. I mean, I'm an earl. I have obligations to secure the Shrewsbury line of succession, which was impossible to see through to fruition when my wife locked me out of her bedchamber not long after we married and never unlocked her door for me again. Her reluctance to provide me with my required heir, let alone a spare, was when I came to the realization there was something wrong with her mental state—a state that continued to deteriorate throughout the years until I finally had no choice but to have her committed to an asylum."

"You had her committed to an asylum?"

"That's where you send people who've lost their minds."

The notion struck from out of nowhere that her father had been exactly right about George all along.

Yes, she'd realized over the years that George had only been interested in her fortune and couldn't have cared less about her, but her father had also told her that George was a callous and cruel man, something she'd never noticed before, but something she now wholeheartedly believed because . . . what type of man would lock his wife away in an asylum, then divorce her, and . . . why had Eleanor locked herself away directly after marrying him in the first place?

"It's actually a most fortunate circumstance for you, my darling Camilla, that Eleanor lost her mind."

Camilla jerked herself back to what was truly becoming a most concerning conversation. "How could that possibly be fortunate for me?"

He sat forward. "Because I distinctly recall you proclaiming, before I was forced to marry another woman, that I was the love of your life and that you'd go to your grave loving me. Now, since I'm free of the shackle I had to tolerate for years that went by the name of Eleanor, we can be together, and you'll no longer have to be bereft because of your unrequited love for me."

For the briefest of seconds, Camilla found herself speechless, but only for a second.

"You are aware that unrequited means unreciprocated, aren't you?" she asked.

He blinked. "Does it really?"

She pressed a finger against a temple that was beginning to throb because, clearly, she'd been more than an idiot the year of her debut since, not only hadn't she realized George was a complete and utter bounder, he was also not as well-educated as he'd led her to believe.

"Since we don't have a dictionary handy for you to look up the word, yes, unrequited most certainly means unreciprocated, which means, in its simplest form, unreturned," she finally said when George began tapping his finger against his knee, as if he were losing patience waiting for her answer. "That means that the last part of your declaration would have been downright insulting if you'd actually known what you were saying, but to address the first part of your little monologue . . ." She drew herself up. "That you can possibly believe I'd still be yearning for you, especially when I proclaimed my love when I was barely out of the schoolroom and far too sheltered to see you for the cad you truly are, suggests that it might have been prudent for you to have had yourself committed alongside your ex-wife in that asylum because . . . you're clearly just as mad as you claim poor Eleanor is."

George's face began to mottle as he rose to his feet and began advancing toward her.

"How dare you, some mere commoner, suggest that I, Lord Shrewsbury, an esteemed member of British aristocracy, am insane," he spat out before he reached for her arm, stilling when the door suddenly opened and a man strolled in, one nearly as large as Owen.

"Well, well, well," the man drawled, coming to a stop a few feet away from George. "What an interesting conversation I've just been privy to as I was shamelessly eavesdropping through a handy hole in the wall." He shook his head. "It seems to me, Shrewsbury, that you've been concocting some very craftily constructed untruths because contrary to what you claimed to me, Miss Pierpont does not seem as if she's madly in love with you. In fact, I would say she loathes you."

He turned to Camilla and presented her with a bow. "We've not been introduced, Miss Pierpont. I'm Victor Malvado, and I must apologize for the circumstances surrounding our introduction. It's regrettable, of course, although you really brought all this nasty abduction business upon yourself when you offered Lottie McBriar a position. That offer, I'm afraid, disrupted my plans for that cunning girl."

"Ah, so you were behind the attempt on the Hudson, weren't you?" Camilla asked.

"I must admit that I was, and I'm sure you'd like me to put some of the additional speculations you must have to rest. However, allow me to encourage you to get comfortable before we get into all that nasty business." Victor walked to a settee and took a seat, gesturing to a chair beside him. "Please, make yourself at home. I've ordered coffee and tea, not knowing which you prefer, as well as a few treats. As I'm sure you were able to tell by the luxurious accommodations I provided you with on the train, I've wanted to make you as comfortable as possible."

"I'd be far more comfortable if you'd simply release me," Camilla said before she sat down on a chair, not the one he'd indicated, but on the chair she'd been sitting on earlier, earning a hint of a smile from Victor in the process.

"I see you're no shrinking violet, Miss Pierpont, so allow me to get straight to the crux of our situation. When Fitzsimmons got himself arrested, I decided I wanted to add Lottie and her many talents to my organization." He shook his head. "Imagine my disappointment when I discovered she'd left Five Points. I'm not a man who takes disappointment in stride, which is why I decided I wasn't going to let a woman who could read slip out of my grasp, and I sent my spies out to locate her. They returned with news that Miss Camilla Pierpont had hired her as a paid companion, as well as whisked her and her mother away from the city." He caught Camilla's eye. "That's when my curiosity was piqued because it's not every day that a lady hires a woman with a criminal past."

"How unfortunate for me that your curiosity was engaged," Camilla muttered.

"Agreed, especially after I learned you're the sole heiress of Hubert Pierpont's grand fortune. I, of course, immediately abandoned my interest in Lottie because, even though bringing on a girl who can read would have been beneficial to my organization, I decided you would be more beneficial to my bottom line if I were to hold you for ransom."

"Weren't you concerned about the risks you'd be taking by kidnapping a member of the Four Hundred?"

"Life is always so much sweeter when it comes with risks," Victor returned. "Besides, I'm a well-read man, Miss Pierpont, and over the past decade or so, starting when someone made off with A. T. Stewart's body and held it for ransom, I've read numerous accounts of members of the elite being stolen and then returned when a hefty ransom is paid. Frankly, I've been thinking about kidnapping an upper-crust lady for some time because the return on that venture far outweighs any actual risks. I realized it was time for me to enter the ransom business after my search for Lottie led me to you."

"And hence the plan was hatched to abduct me from the Hudson River Valley."

"Indeed," Victor agreed. "I would have preferred making plans to snatch you here in the city because that would have been an easier strategy to execute. Nevertheless, since I had you in my sights and was determined to find myself the recipient of a fat payout, I went through the bother of placing one of my informants in your near vicinity. That informant turned out to be an invaluable asset, sending me word that you weren't intending on returning to the city after your stay on the Hudson, but were going to travel directly to Newport for the summer. Newport would have been a logistical nightmare. However . . ." Victor's lips thinned. "The Hudson attempt turned into a nightmare as well because my men never counted on that oaf Owen Chesterfield rushing in to assume the role of knight in shining armor."

"The role of knight does seem to suit Owen, who certainly isn't an oaf," Camilla countered.

"Ah, how quick you are to defend him." Victor turned to George. "I'm afraid you might be in a little spot of trouble, Shrewsbury, because I'm getting the impression Miss Pierpont truly is not enamored with you since she seems to be smitten with someone else. That means you're not going to come into the windfall you've been expecting after the two of you marry."

George waved that aside. "Camilla could never be smitten with an oaf, not after having met me, but know that I prefer being addressed as Lord Shrewsbury."

"Duly noted, George," Victor said before he returned his attention to Camilla. "Where was I?"

"You were explaining how your first attempt at abducting me failed," Camilla said.

Victor nodded. "Right." He settled back against the settee. "In all honesty, I decided after that fiasco, and after you abruptly left the Hudson River Valley, although I knew where you went because my informant fired off a telegram to me practically the moment your decision was made to leave, that I would abandon my desire to hold you for ransom. The logistics of planning an attack in West Virginia were worse than even Newport, but then . . ." He nodded to George. "He arrived in New York, and lo and behold, he started asking around, looking for someone who could run you down. He said he'd pay handsomely, and wouldn't you know—someone told him to contact me."

Camilla's attention immediately shot to George. "You contacted an underworld crime boss to track me down instead of looking around for a reputable agency such as the Pinkertons, or better yet, a local agency such as the Accounting Firm?"

"I couldn't have used that accounting firm since your *dear* friend, Gideon Abbott, who I've since learned is a silent partner in that firm, sought me out in London, wanting to have a little chat with me." George shook his head. "It wasn't a pleasant chat. He even went so far as to tell me not to contact you again after he learned I was preparing to depart for New York with the sole intention of reconnecting with you. Since I'm not a man to be ordered about, I boarded the first steamship out of London, determined to beat Gideon back to the city."

"Why were you so determined?"

George smiled. "I would think that's obvious, darling. I wanted to have time to convince you, without Gideon's interference, that I'd made a grave error all those years ago and am now determined to spend the rest of my days proving to you that you're the love of my life."

It was incredibly difficult to refuse the urge to bang her head against the nearest wall.

She settled for drawing in a calming breath instead. "If you ask me, I think it's far more likely that you rushed across an entire ocean to beat Gideon here since you're desperate to get your hands on the trust fund I gained access to when I turned twenty-five."

"You have a trust fund?" George asked.

She couldn't help herself, she snorted, earning a widening of the eyes from George in the process.

"You know very well I have a trust fund, as I told you about it directly after I suggested we run off together, since my father wasn't going to settle a dowry on me."

"Ah, *that* trust fund, the one you wouldn't have been able to access for seven or eight years after we would have gotten married."

"That's the one, and because I know you remember it, I'm now convinced that the real reason you want to reconnect with me is because you've exhausted Eleanor's fortune, which is why you divorced her, and are now desperate to convince me you're madly in love with me in order to avoid finding yourself in a paupers' prison."

"I'm not going to dignify that nonsense with a reply," George said before he turned his head and began taking a pointed interest in a vase of flowers resting on the small table beside him.

"All this chatter I'm hearing certainly puts an interesting twist on things," Victor proclaimed right as the door opened and another man dressed in black came into the room, pushing a coffee cart. After asking Camilla which beverage she preferred, he poured her a cup of coffee, added cream and sugar, stirred it exactly twice, which left her lips twitching, and gave it to her. He poured a cup for Victor, then quit the room, leaving George looking more than outraged.

"You should have a word with your servant," George snapped, rising to his feet to pour out his own cup, something he'd probably never done in his life.

"I think it would be more prudent to have a word with you," Victor countered, waiting until George retook his seat before he took a sip of coffee and set aside the cup. "Seems to me you've landed in a bit of a pickle because, to remind you, you owe me a handsome fee for locating Miss Pierpont. You also owe me another substantial amount of money since you suffered heavy losses at one of my gambling dens, being so foolish as to have bet the fee money you were supposed to give me for bringing Miss Pierpont back to the city. If that weren't bad enough, you then convinced the manager of my den to provide you with credit, using your so-called affiliation with Miss Pierpont as collateral, and then losing everything but your shirt when my manager finally curtailed your credit line after you suffered obscene losses."

"The only reason I kept my shirt was because one of your barmaids spilled wine on it and no one would take it to put toward my debt."

"Be that as it may, you told me you'd have my money, after I had you escorted here to assure you didn't try to skip town without paying me, once Miss Pierpont returned to the city." Victor gave a crack of his knuckles. "I'm getting the distinct impression she's not going to lift a finger to address your debt."

Camilla quirked a brow George's way. "Am I to understand that you promised Victor, a man with a formidable reputation, that I'd bail you out?"

"Of course, because, even though you're still sore at me for not marrying you, I know you still love me and certainly won't want to see me, as Victor has threatened, lose a finger or worse—an ear."

"Prepare to be earless."

As George took to gaping at her, Victor laughed. "I do believe I like you, Miss Pierpont."

"Enough to let me go?"

"Not quite that much."

"Pity."

"Well, indeed, but what's more of a pity is what I'm going to have to do to George now that I know he can't honor his debt to me."

It wasn't a surprise when George rose to his feet and began pacing around the room, then stopped in his tracks and smiled. "I think there's an easy solution to this." He nodded to Camilla before he turned to Victor. "Even though it doesn't seem as if she's as enamored with me as she once was, I imagine she wouldn't hesitate to marry me if we were found in a, well, compromising setting. All we need to do is arrange for someone to find us alone together, and then you'll get your fee plus my gambling debts returned to you."

Temper was swift and had Camilla rising from her chair and stalking George's way. "That's the most ridiculous plan I've ever heard, and even if we were discovered alone together, I would never marry you."

"You will if you're about to lose your reputation."

"My reputation isn't so important to me that I'd suffer through life with you." She spun on her heel and nodded to Victor. "As I'm sure you've already sent a ransom demand to my father, and probably a substantial one at that, and since you were so accommodating to me throughout my abduction, will you now arrange for me to stay in a George-free room until the ransom is paid?"

Victor inclined his head. "I see no reason why I can't accommodate that."

"Lovely," Camilla said before she returned to her seat, took a sip of coffee, and frowned. "May I also ask a few questions while we finish our coffee?"

"You don't seem like you're the type of lady who would stop asking even if I said no," Victor muttered.

"You're probably right, so . . ." Camilla set aside her cup. "You introduced yourself to me, which seems odd since I can now identify you."

"I don't plan on remaining in New York after my transaction with your father is completed." Victor steepled his fingers together. "I've already set up plans to take my organization to another city far from here, one I won't disclose to you, of course, but one that will be more than welcoming to the type of business I operate."

"How prudent of you," Camilla said.

"Indeed," Victor agreed. "And with that answered, anything else you'd like to ask me before I take my leave?"

"I suppose the only truly pressing question I have left is . . . who was your informant?"

Victor smiled. "I would've thought you'd have figured that out by now, my dear, seeing as how you seem to be such a clever sort."

"I'm apparently not as clever as you believe."

"Then allow me to assuage your curiosity, although I'm sure you're going to feel quite the idiot to learn that the informant who sold you out in exchange for obtaining her greatest desire in life—that being an opportunity to take to the stage—was Bernadette."

"Am I to understand *you're* the gentleman my daughter traipsed off to the wilds of West Virginia with?" Margaret Pierpont asked as her gaze roamed over Owen.

Given that Owen was currently looking as if he'd taken up bare-knuckle boxing and gone more than a few rounds with a champion pugilist, what with how he was sporting two black eyes and had a large gash running down the side of his face, caused when he'd lost consciousness and plummeted to the ground, he could certainly understand the incredulousness in Mrs. Pierpont's tone.

In all honesty, he'd never imagined meeting Hubert and Margaret Pierpont in their Fifth Avenue mansion under what could only be considered difficult circumstances. It was a forgone conclusion that he probably wasn't making a very good first impression, even though Mr. Timken, who'd traveled to New York with him after he'd regained consciousness, had made a point of telling Camilla's parents that Owen had fought tooth and nail to save Camilla, until he'd been rendered incapacitated.

Owen inclined his head Margaret Pierpont's way. "I am the gentleman Camilla traveled to West Virginia with, but before we get into the particulars of everything that's happened of late, allow me to first apologize for being ill-equipped to prevent Camilla's abduction."

Margaret's lips thinned. "Why were you ill-equipped, Mr. Chesterfield?"

"I underestimated the situation. I had security in place for Camilla, as well as the protection services of Charles and Leopold, but I never considered that anyone would attempt to abduct your daughter from a paddle steamer filled with a few hundred people. I also didn't anticipate that the men behind her abduction would have additional criminals waiting at my residence on Wheeling Island on the chance the abduction plan on the water was unsuccessful."

"I don't believe anyone could have foreseen that," a man said, striding into the receiving parlor and up to Owen, immediately holding out his hand. "I'm Gideon Abbott."

"Owen Chesterfield," Owen said, shaking Gideon's hand. "Camilla told me about you. Dare I hope you have any leads as to where she's being held?"

"We have every agent from my firm out searching for her. So far, we've not been able to find her."

"We do have our suspicions regarding who took her," a lady with black hair and dressed in a deep shade of purple said as she strolled into the room, stopping in front of Owen, where she promptly dipped into a curtsy. "I'm Adelaide Abbott, Gideon's wife as well as an agent with the firm. I'm also very dear friends with Camilla."

Owen presented her with a bow. "Camilla mentioned you more than a few times, Mrs. Abbott. I believe she considers you a dear friend as well."

Adelaide's lips curved. "Of course she does, and I'm looking forward to speaking with you further regarding Camilla's stay in West Virginia, but for now, allow me to return to Camilla's case. I'm wondering, since you were with her when she was abducted, if you heard any pertinent information that may confirm our suspicions regarding who is currently holding Camilla for ransom."

"Since the attack was well organized, I'm going to say it was arranged by a criminal syndicate, perhaps run by one Victor Malvado, although I can't help thinking that Lord Shrewsbury is somehow involved," Owen said.

Gideon nodded. "We've been keeping a close eye on Victor and his operation, but he's slippery. Keeps himself surrounded with guards, and none of our agents have seen any suspicious activity that points a finger his way for this particular crime. Lord Shrewsbury, on the other hand, seems to be our most credible suspect at this point."

"Could it be that he's working in tandem with another criminal organization?"

"Given that the man is severely lacking in the morals department? Probably." Gideon nodded to Adelaide. "Adelaide and I began investigating Lord Shrewsbury after I had a talk with him in England when I encountered him at a gentleman's club I frequent. He was unaware of my close association with Camilla when I first asked if I could join him at his table, but he didn't hesitate to encourage me to sit down with him after I offered to buy him a bottle of his favorite wine. After Lord Shrewsbury gulped down a few glasses of that wine, and, even though he'd never met me before, he didn't hesitate to disclose that he'd divorced his wife and was intending on traveling to New York to reunite with a lady he claimed was the love of his life." Gideon's lips thinned. "I knew he was speaking about Camilla. I then revealed my close friendship with Camilla and told George that he wasn't to have anything to do with her—ever."

Adelaide caught Owen's eye. "Gideon and I knew, as we discussed that conversation, that Lord Shrewsbury was clearly pursuing another fortune, and who better to pursue than Camilla, a lady who'd fallen for him the year of her debut." She pursed her lips. "Camilla told me during this past winter Season that George, before he left New York, told her that although he was being forced to marry someone else, his heart would always belong to her."

"Sounds like George wanted to make sure he didn't burn any bridges where Camilla was concerned, just in case," Owen said, earning a bob of her head from Adelaide.

"Too right he didn't, but thank goodness Camilla came to her senses and hasn't been pining for the man all these years, especially since we've uncovered evidence that suggests George was slipping his wife, or rather ex-wife now, dangerous mushrooms."

Owen's mouth dropped open. "What?"

"You heard correctly," Gideon said. "From what we've been able to conclude, Lord Shrewsbury had grown weary of his wife being unable to provide him with an heir, and furthermore, had exhausted the considerable dowry Mr. Deerhurst, Eleanor's father, had settled on her. George must have been facing desperate financial straits, which is why we believe he began drugging poor Eleanor, then carted her off to an asylum when she became out of her mind, that state a direct result of consuming mushrooms that are known to cause hallucinations."

"Gideon and I took the liberty of getting Eleanor released from the asylum," Adelaide added. "We've since reunited her with her family, and interestingly enough, she hasn't shown any signs of being out of her mind for weeks—exactly around the time George stopped paying her visits. We've also learned from Mr. Deerhurst that George, before he committed Eleanor to an asylum, had been demanding money from him. Mr. Deerhurst, evidently having realized George was a fortune hunter, refused to send any, which he now sorely regrets because he knows if he'd capitulated, his daughter wouldn't have spent over a year in an asylum."

"It does sound as if George had the proper motivation to be behind Camilla's disappearance," Owen said.

"Unfortunately, though, he's also disappeared," Gideon said.

"He's disappeared?" Owen repeated.

"He hasn't," a voice said from the doorway before a woman

strode into the room, her features covered by the hood of her cloak, a hood she shoved back, revealing herself to be none other than Bernadette.

Owen frowned. "You told me you were going to stay behind in Wheeling to look after Gladys and El Cid."

"I lied, but I have a perfectly good reason for doing so, as well as a good reason for sneaking off to the train station and hopping on a train departing for New York before your train left, allowing me to arrive in the city a few hours before you—hours I've put to good use."

Before Owen could do more than narrow his eyes on a woman who'd clearly been holding some secrets from Camilla, and for some time if he wasn't mistaken, Lottie came striding into the room, stopping a mere foot away from Bernadette, bristling with animosity.

"I knew you had something to do with this, Bernadette, especially when I went looking for you to give you some last-minute instructions about Gladys and El Cid and couldn't find you anywhere."

"I'm afraid I'm guilty as charged," Bernadette admitted, taking a step back when Lottie took a step toward her. "And while I understand your urge to do me bodily harm, this is not the time for that, nor is it the time to discuss my horrendous behavior or the decision I made that will haunt me for the rest of my days. I'm here now to make amends for what I've done, but you, Lottie, out of anyone, should know that it's next to impossible to refuse a demand made by a criminal underworld boss."

"What criminal boss?" Owen demanded.

Bernadette shoved a strand of hair out of her face, not bothering to address the single tear running down her cheek. "Victor Malvado."

Gideon's gaze sharpened on Bernadette. "How long have you been working for Victor?"

"About three years," Bernadette admitted. "I had a break from him for a few months when he left for Chicago after Frank Fitzsimmons drew too much attention to the criminal set when he tried to extort that opera singer. Unfortunately, Victor returned to New York a few months ago. I heard through talk at the theater that he was back in the city and knew it was only a matter of time until he contacted me to do a job for him."

"What kind of jobs would you do for Victor?" Adelaide asked, stepping up beside Gideon.

"Just odd jobs here and there, such as ferreting out information from actresses who keep company with certain men of fortune."

"Why did he set his sights on Camilla?" Owen pressed.

Bernadette jerked her head toward Lottie. "Because of her. Victor wanted to acquire Lottie after Fitzsimmons was arrested, but Camilla got to Lottie first. Victor evidently got curious about a society lady who would take on a girl with a criminal past, and that curiosity led him to discover that Camilla's an heiress. I assume he began making plans to abduct her not long after that, needing me to help him fine-tune those plans when Camilla returned from Paris and took up residence at their Hudson manor."

"He asked you to get a job in the Pierpont household?" Adelaide asked.

"Victor doesn't ask, he demands," Bernadette countered. "He needed to learn Camilla's daily schedule, and who better to glean that type of information than a woman who aspires to become an actress and is perfectly capable of assuming the role of a maid? In my defense, though, I had no idea at the time why he wanted that information. All I knew is that Victor isn't a man you ever say no to."

Lottie released a snort. "It sounds to me as if you didn't even try."

"Of course I didn't," Bernadette shot back. "It would have been pointless, and besides that, Victor dangled a carrot in front of me—one he knew I wouldn't be able to resist."

"Let me guess," Lottie began. "He promised to arrange an acting job for you if you were successful, and you didn't hesitate to sell out Camilla because becoming an actress, as you've mentioned time and again, is your greatest goal in life."

"*Used* to be my greatest goal," Bernadette corrected. "And while I know I was disloyal to Camilla, know that I truly had no idea Victor wanted to learn her schedule because he intended to kidnap her."

Lottie's eyes flashed. "That might have initially been true. However, you would have been privy to what his plans were after Camilla and I were set upon by those men on the Hudson. Even realizing that, though, you had to have been the one who told Victor we'd gone to Wheeling."

"I won't deny I sent a telegram to Victor when we made a stop in one of those small towns on our way to West Virginia. But in my defense, he was expecting me to contact him on a daily basis. If I hadn't sent him word that we'd left town, I would have never been able to return to New York, and at that time, Wheeling sounded to me as if it might be the pit-of-the-earth type of place, not a town I'd ever care to remain in for good." Bernadette dashed a tear from her face. "I've regretted my actions for weeks, especially after I got to know Camilla and discovered she's nothing like I originally thought. I've always been jealous of those who have more than most of us, and I thought she was simply a rich, spoiled heiress who was going to want me to wait on her hand and foot after I became her lady's maid."

"She never expected you to wait on her hand and foot," Lottie snapped.

"I know that now, just as I know what I did was horrible." Bernadette drew in a shuddering breath. "That's why I'm here to rectify matters."

"How do you intend to do that?" Owen asked.

"I know where Victor's keeping Camilla, just as I know that he's going to send a lot of his men to pick up the ransom." She lifted her chin. "I went directly to Victor's from the train station.

As I mentioned, I arrived in the city before you. I knew he would expect me to show up there at some point, so off I went, arriving not long after Camilla did."

"Did you see her?" Owen demanded.

Bernadette shook her head. "I'm afraid not. I was shown directly to Victor's office, where he told me how pleased he was with the work I'd done. Before I had an opportunity to check on Camilla, Victor sent me off to claim my prize, which is where I'm supposed to be right now."

"You didn't bother to try and rescue her?" Lottie asked.

"I doubt I could have been successful with that, given how many men Victor has guarding his lair." Bernadette dashed another tear away. "I thought it would be more prudent if I came here, since I assumed this is the first place Owen would come. And if Owen wasn't here, I figured Camilla's parents would know how to contact agents from the Accounting Firm."

Bernadette caught Owen's eye. "Since you are here, know that I think a surprise attack might be possible while Victor's men are off to pick up the ransom, and I can help with that attack."

"How can you help?"

"I can tell you exactly where Camilla is being held, as well as give a detailed account of the layout of Victor's compound. I also know, since I made a point of stopping to talk to a few of the guards, how many men he's sending to collect the ransom, as well as how many men will be left behind. Victor is expecting me to return after I speak with the manager of the theater—my reward for doing this job—and when I return, I can then unlock one of the side doors for the surprise attack."

"And you think we should plan this surprise attack while Victor's men are off retrieving the ransom money?" Gideon asked.

"That's when he'll be the most vulnerable."

Gideon frowned. "How many men do you think will be left in Victor's compound during the pickup?"

"Around twenty, but that's better than the number he normally keeps on hand." Bernadette smiled. "He's sending a small army to collect the ransom because he thinks that'll make it more difficult for any of them to decide to grab the money and run."

"Twenty doesn't sound impossible to handle," Gideon began, "although given that Victor Malvado's rumored to have some of the most vicious criminals around on his payroll, it'll still be difficult to execute a rescue."

Owen caught Gideon's eye. "I've brought men with me who'll be more than happy to assist in the mission."

"And not just men," a far-too-familiar voice said from the doorway.

Swallowing a sigh, Owen turned and found Meemaw advancing into the room with Aunt Elma by her side, both women toting rifles, which had Margaret inching closer to her husband.

"You were supposed to wait at the Fifth Avenue Hotel until I sent for you," Owen said, which earned him a roll of the eyes from Meemaw.

"Don't be daft, Owen," she returned. "You know I'm not one to sit around and wait while the menfolk get down to the real business."

"Neither am I," Aunt Elma chimed in, pushing spectacles that were sliding down her nose back into place.

Owen frowned. "You're wearing spectacles."

"'Course I am. I'm blind as a bat without them, and I'm thinkin' my aim better be accurate today." Aunt Elma smiled. "I'd hate to be takin' out a person on our side."

"You always said you'd never get spectacles."

"As your meemaw said, don't be daft, boy. I've had these here spectacles for years, it's just that I ain't above playin' on everyone's sympathies to get the attention I feel I'm due by assumin' the role of some feeble ol' auntie."

"Who *are* these women?" Margaret whispered, her gaze fixated on Meemaw's rifle.

"I'm Beulah Chesterfield," Meemaw said before Owen could

get a single syllable out of his mouth. "I'm Owen's meemaw, and this here's my sister Elma. And now, with that out of the way, what say we go and get our Camilla? I heard Bernadette say she knows where Camilla's being held, so no use dilly-dallying."

Gideon cleared his throat. "I'm sorry, Mrs. Chesterfield, but you won't be accompanying us. Victor Malvado is holding Camilla, and he's not a man any lady should trifle with."

"You're apparently just as daft as my grandson if you think I'm going to be left behind" was all Meemaw said to that as Leopold and Charles strode into the room, Leopold flashing Meemaw a smile before he nodded to Gideon.

"Beulah and Elma would be an asset to us, Gideon," Leopold began. "And before you argue, know that both of them shoot better than I do, at least when Elma's wearing her spectacles. I can guarantee they'll come in handy with distracting Victor if it comes down to that because I highly doubt he'd expect two ladies who are somewhat advanced in years to be the threat they're perfectly capable of being."

Beulah smiled. "That was lovely, Leopold, and so, with that out of the way . . ." She caught Owen's eye. "What say we go and get your girl back?"

Owen didn't neglect to notice that Margaret's eyes widened directly after Meemaw called Camilla *his* girl, but since Aunt Elma was already heading out of the room, followed by Lottie and Bernadette, he decided now was hardly the moment to declare any intentions he might have toward Camilla to her parents, instead sending Meemaw a nod, which had her readjusting her rifle before she headed out of the room.

Annoyance was becoming Camilla's constant companion, a direct result of Victor neglecting to remove George from her near vicinity, which meant she'd spent the past hour listening to that irritating man list a variety of preposterous reasons why he was convinced she was still in love with him, and apparently thought she was only denying that love since he'd hurt her tender feminine sensibilities when he'd been forced to marry Eleanor.

"Forgive me, George, because this is going to come across as beyond rude, but would you please stop talking," Camilla finally said, unsurprised when George simply blinked owlishly back at her.

"Do you want me to stop talking because you're finally ready to admit you're absolutely delighted by the fact I've returned at long last to marry you?"

It took a great deal of effort to remain sitting with her hands folded demurely in her lap. "No. I want you to discontinue rambling on and on because I'm precariously close to giving in to the most compelling urge to throttle you, something I doubt you'd enjoy, although I'm sure Victor, who's most likely spying on us through one of those holes in the wall, is being vastly amused by your continued pontifications."

George blinked again before he smiled. "Ah, I believe I'm beginning to understand where your overly fraught emotional state is coming from. You're obviously concerned you'll come across as too eager to reclaim our long-lost love, and thus, lose my respect for you. Since I've never held any respect for the feminine set to begin with, there's no need for you to worry about that."

"I'm going to have to truly beg my father's pardon for ever arguing with him about his honest opinion of you," she muttered, which elicited another blink from George just as the door opened and Bernadette strode in, all but clinging to Victor's arm.

Camilla's sense of annoyance was immediately replaced with temper.

She'd been so certain she'd misjudged Bernadette, but instead, the woman had played her for a fool and was the reason she was now sequestered in Victor Malvado's lair, waiting for him to divest her father of a million-dollar ransom—not that her father couldn't afford it, given he was worth over a hundred million dollars, but still. It was inexcusable to think that a woman she'd employed, and then offered to set up in business, had turned out to be nothing more than an opportunist of the worst sort.

"Miss Pierpont," Bernadette trilled, "I bet you're not happy to see me, given that Victor has evidently apprised you of my role in this, well . . . distasteful business."

Camilla lifted her chin and merely stared back at the woman, unwilling to give Bernadette the satisfaction of an answer.

Her temper went from simmering to boiling when Bernadette laughed before she released her hold on Victor's arm and moseyed over to the coffee cart. "I see Victor's chef has provided you with a variety of delicacies. I daresay I'm famished, but . . ." She refocused her attention on George. "We haven't met. I'm Bernadette, and you are, of course, Lord Shrewsbury. Shall I make you up a plate before I launch into the many, many questions I have about you and Miss Pierpont?"

George waved the offer aside. "I don't make it a habit to converse with aspiring actresses."

"Suit yourself," Bernadette murmured before she took a second to plop some shrimp canapes onto her plate, then turned and settled a smile on Victor.

"I'm pleased to report, Victor, that the manager of the Eastern Theater Company was thrilled to offer me a position. He told me that you personally asked him ever so sweetly to give me a job. I truly must thank you for arranging such a sensational opportunity, as well as thank you because the manager also told me that you told him I possess remarkable acting skills."

"I would have to agree about those skills," Camilla grumbled.

"What's that?" Bernadette asked as she ambled Camilla's way.

"You heard what I said, and yes, your acting skills are quite extraordinary, as you were certainly able to deceive me."

"You have no—" was all Bernadette was able to say before she suddenly stumbled, the contents of her plate landing directly into Camilla's lap. "How clumsy of me," she exclaimed as she began plucking shrimp from Camilla's skirt, bending close to Camilla's ear in the process.

"Get ready," Bernadette whispered as something heavy plopped into Camilla's lap, something that turned out to be her derringer.

As she caught Bernadette's eye, who immediately sent her a wink, Camilla palmed the derringer as Bernadette straightened, set aside her plate of ruined shrimp, then sent a nod Victor's way. "I suppose I should get on my way, given that I know you'll be leaving just as soon as your men return with the ransom."

Victor inclined his head. "I certainly won't be lingering, but . . ." He reached into his pocket and pulled out his billfold. "I believe a bonus is in order before you go."

"A bonus?" Bernadette all but tittered.

"Let's say it's for putting your incredibly impressive acting skills to such lucrative use."

As Victor opened his wallet and began pulling out bills, Bernadette glanced over her shoulder, mouthed "Now," and then pulled a pistol from the pocket of her cape and pointed it at Victor, who froze and narrowed his eyes on her.

"What are you doing?" he demanded.

"Obviously putting those acting skills you complimented me on to good use," Bernadette returned. "I'm afraid I'm now going to have to insist you put your hands in the air and stay that way until reinforcements arrive."

"Have you lost your mind?" Victor countered, taking a step toward Bernadette but stopping when she cocked the hammer. "You know you'll never make it out of here alive, not when I have an entire brigade of men guarding me."

"You sent half your brigade out to fetch the ransom money. That left you vulnerable for the imminent attack I helped orchestrate." With that, Bernadette released a whistle Camilla knew Nems had taught her how to do.

A mere heartbeat later, Owen was racing into the room, his Colt Dragoons in hand, looking furious, as well as rather battered, given the two black eyes he was sporting.

Considering the current circumstances, it was an odd state of affairs when the thought flashed to mind that he'd never looked more appealing to her.

As the sound of gunshots rang out from outside the room, Camilla jumped from the chair, gripping her derringer, then found herself at a loss for what to do next when Owen launched himself at Victor.

"Don't just stand there acting like an imbecile," George screamed at her, his voice a few octaves higher than it normally was. "Shoot him, or if you're too squeamish for that, give me the gun and I'll do it."

"I can't shoot at Victor because I might hit Owen," Camilla said right as Victor's men rushed into the room, not because they were coming to Victor's defense, but because they were being pursued by Gideon, Leopold, Charles, and . . . Beulah.

A second later, Victor's men were rushing out the back door, Gideon, Leopold, and Charles in hot pursuit.

Beulah, after catching sight of Camilla, stopped in her tracks, her gaze traveling the length of her, and after apparently realizing she was unharmed, she turned her attention to Owen, who'd taken Victor to the ground and had already rendered him unconscious.

"Anyone have anything I can use to tie him up?" Owen asked.

"I've got a garter," Elma said, hobbling into the room, where she promptly propped her rifle against the settee, bent over and fumbled with her skirt, then looked up. "Might be better iffen you used my stockin's."

"Not something I ever thought I'd be speaking with you about, Aunt Elma, but stockings it is," Owen said, which earned him a grin from Elma, who, curiously enough, was wearing spectacles, ones that slid down her nose as she bent over and stripped a stocking from her leg.

As Elma went about the business of securing Victor's wrists, Owen shifted his attention to Camilla.

"Are you alright?" he asked.

She smiled. "As Nems and the boys would say, I'm fit as a fiddle."

He returned the smile. "Good."

Beulah released a snort. "That's it? That's all you've got to say to her? Just good?"

"It hardly seems the moment to launch into an in-depth conversation, not when there are probably still more criminals afoot."

"No need for you to go rushin' off to save the day, Owen," Nems said, pushing himself into the room in his wheeled chair, Andy walking behind him, nursing a bleeding lip but smiling all the same. "We done got them no-good 'nappers already nice and tidied up, so iffen you got somethin' to say to our darlin' Camilla, I say git on with it." Nems sent her a wink. "Nice to see ya, Miss Camilla, and know that I jist got the pleasure of meetin' your mama. I done told her that I can see now where'n you get your fine looks from."

"Nems told your mama she was done purtier than that there

queenie he saw holdin' court at the West Virginia state fair," Andy added.

Camilla blinked. "What did my mother say to that?"

Andy scratched his chin. "Not much, but I could tell she was real pleased about the compliment cuz she left the room, and me and Nems decided that was cuz she was overcome with ladylike emotions."

"I imagine she was overcome with something," Camilla muttered before she grinned and moved over to Nems, kissed him on the cheek, then did the same to Andy, leaving both men rather red in the face as she turned to Owen.

"I wasn't expecting you to be able to find me, but I'm certainly glad you did," she said.

"I shouldn't have had to come find you because I shouldn't have lost you to begin with."

"That wasn't your fault."

"Of course it was, and it was hardly a hero moment when you got carted away on my watch."

"It was certainly a hero moment because you were outnumbered, and yet you didn't hesitate to try and protect me. And if you must know, it's my fault I got nabbed because I wasn't able to outrun the man who succeeded in catching me."

"A lady should never have to resort to running from danger when there's a man around to protect her."

"Unless that man is, again, outnumbered, but . . ." She arched a brow at him. "Do you really want to stand here debating this with me right now?"

He raked a hand through his hair. "Not particularly."

She smiled. "I thought not, so what would you rather do instead?"

His gaze darted to her lips and lingered there until Elma hustled up to join them.

"This is your moment, boy. Time for you to get around to see iffen the two of you are compatible once and for all."

Owen's brow furrowed. "Not to be rude, Aunt Elma, but this is hardly the moment for another interruption."

"And to that I say hogwash. You've already lost this little lady once—not that it was your fault, mind you—but 'afore some other disaster strikes, you gotta get down to some serious business."

"I'm intending to."

Elma sent him a nod. "Well then, git on with it, but that gittin' on with it better not be havin' you doin' any proposin' just yet because you got another matter to attend to before that step."

"I bet that step has something to do with kissing again," Charles said, walking into the room with Luella by his side, Luella nodding even as she grinned.

"I bet you're right, Charles, so . . ." Luella turned her grin on Owen. "If you want to get on with matters, I think you're going to have to convince Aunt Elma that you adhered to her advice and stole a few kisses from Camilla, and that both of you are in accord that your kissing has made you realize you're incredibly compatible."

Owen narrowed his eyes on his sister. "I thought I told you to stay behind."

Luella batted her lashes at him. "Did you? I must have missed that as everyone got ready for the big rescue attempt, which clearly has been a rousing success. However, returning to the kissing situation, I have it on good authority, or rather, Lottie's authority, that the two of you almost kissed, until Lottie and Edward interrupted you."

"Why would they have gone and done somethin' like that?" Elma demanded.

Luella gave a breezy wave of her hand. "I'm sure it wasn't intentional, Aunt Elma, just as I'm sure Owen and Camilla got back to the whole kissing business at some point since Lottie mentioned it appeared to her as if they both seemed rather keen to kiss each other before they were interrupted." She turned and arched a brow Owen's way. "Am I right?"

"Ah . . ."

"I'll take that to mean there's been no kissing as of yet," Beulah said, stepping forward and sending a nod Owen's way. "That means you best get on with it now because you know Elma isn't going to let you get on with proposing until she's sure you and Camilla are compatible in the kissing department."

"This is really not how I thought any of this was going to unfold," Owen grumbled.

"It would've been unfoldin' a whole lot differently if you'd done kissed her already," Elma shot back.

Owen rubbed his jaw. "Undoubtedly, but in my defense, I didn't know if Camilla would be receptive to me trying to kiss her again until right before she got abducted."

Camilla frowned. "Why didn't you think I wanted you to kiss me?"

Owen frowned right back at her. "Because after that time I attempted to kiss you and we were interrupted, you gave me no indication you wanted me to try again." He took a step closer to her. "I figured, since you're the expert in matters of romance, that you'd give me some sort of sign that you wouldn't be opposed to some kissing—and with me, of course."

"I arranged for us to be alone together numerous times," she pointed out.

He blinked. "Those times were on purpose?"

"They were, but evidently you didn't realize that."

A hint of a smile curved his lips. "Further proof that I truly don't understand women."

She gave his arm a pat. "You're actually more astute about us than you realize and—"

"While I hate to interrupt this ridiculous conversation, I cannot remain silent another second," George said, striding over to join them from where he'd taken to hiding behind a large chair when gunshots had begun ringing out, proving himself to be, not only a cad, but an outright coward. He scowled at Camilla. "You cannot seriously be considering marrying this fool. Why, he looks like a farmhand, which means he's not good enough to even speak to you, let alone marry you."

Camilla's jaw took to clenching. "Owen's not the fool here, George."

"Surely you're not suggesting I am," George scoffed. "But again, you can't marry him, even if he might have impressed you by using all that brute strength of his to take out Victor. You're much too refined for someone like him, and you know you belong with me. You're simply being ridiculous, a trait of yours I realize I'll need to learn to live with, but . . ."

Camilla's temper took that moment to reach a boiling point, which resulted in her hand balling into a fist right before she took a step closer to George, drew back her arm, then punched the man directly in the nose.

George staggered back, righted himself, then stared at her with clear disbelief as he fished a handkerchief out of his pocket and began pressing it against a nose that was now bleeding somewhat profusely.

"I believe this is where I take Lord Shrewsbury off to have another little chat with him," Gideon, who'd just walked into the room, said, moving to take George's arm and then promptly pulling him across the room.

As they disappeared through the door, Camilla heard Gideon tell George that Eleanor had been sprung from the asylum and that Mr. Deerhurst was wanting to have a word with his ex-son-in-law, as well, something that was going to revolve around hallucinogenic mushrooms.

"What was all that about?" Camilla asked.

"We'll tell you later," Elma said, nodding to Owen. "For now, I think there's something of greater importance you need to get down to."

"I am not kissing Camilla in a room filled with people," Owen argued.

Beulah sent him a wink. "Then I suggest you and Camilla find yourself a more private spot before Elma decides to turn her rifle on you."

"That would be a memorable way for Owen and Camilla to remember this special day," Luella said cheerfully.

Owen leaned closer to Camilla. "Perhaps we should repair to the hallway to continue our discussion before Aunt Elma really *does* threaten us with her rifle if I don't get down to, ah, kissing you soon."

A sense of anticipation began thrumming through her. "Perhaps we should at that."

"But don't be doin' no proposin' until you find out about the kissin'," Elma warned, wagging a finger their way as Owen took hold of Camilla's hand and headed for the door, increasing their pace when Elma muttered something about hoping Owen was at least somewhat proficient in the kissing department.

Before Camilla knew it, she was all but barreling down the hall, Owen not stopping until they reached the very end of it. He turned and sent her a bit of a wince.

"I'm really sorry about all this," he began. "My family can be—"

"Adorable," Camilla finished for him.

"That's not the word I was going to use."

"Charming?"

"That's not it either."

She tilted her head. "What about loving?"

"I suppose that suits," Owen admitted with a smile before he blew out a breath. "And now, here we are, alone at last, although I have to admit that I could use some professional suggestions from a successful matchmaker who has probably coached gentlemen through these types of situations because I readily admit I have no idea how to proceed from here."

She smiled. "As a professional matchmaker, I would simply suggest you say whatever is on your mind."

"I know how to kiss."

"Not what I was expecting, but good to know."

He blew out another breath. "I wasn't saying that to, ah, brag, but I've never been pressured to kiss anyone before, and I definitely have never had a crowd of people expecting to learn the results of a kiss."

"What kind of results?" she asked.

"Well, the only one that probably matters is whether or not you enjoy my kisses, but I'm just going to admit that I'm thinking this isn't the most ideal moment to try out kissing in general since it seems like there's a lot of pressure for us to instantly decide if we're compatible in the kissing department or not." He ran his hand through his hair. "I mean, it's not really fair to you, is it? What if you don't like my kiss, but then don't want to hurt my feelings by telling me that, or if you tell everyone waiting for us that you found my kissing less than exhilarating?"

Clearly, it was time for the professional matchmaker to step in since Owen definitely seemed to be getting himself all worked up, and for no good reason, since she found simply being near him exhilarating.

She stepped closer, earning a slight widening of his eyes, his eyes widening even more when she wrapped her arms around his neck. She then pulled his head toward her and smiled. "I'm sure you're a more-than-exceptional kisser."

"Now you're just trying to make me feel better," he said as his gaze settled on her lips.

"I would hope that in a second, perhaps two, we're both going to be feeling something far more than . . . better."

Owen's lips began to curve right before he leaned closer, then settled his lips against hers.

Tingles immediately swept over her as he deepened the kiss, not drawing back for a good few moments, although since he immediately drew her against him and kissed her again, it turned into several minutes of being soundly kissed by a man who'd certainly been a bit modest when he claimed he knew how to kiss because . . . good heavens.

A sigh escaped her when Owen's lips finally left hers, and she opened her eyes to find him grinning back at her.

"I don't know about you, but I'm of the belief we're more than compatible," he said.

She returned the grin. "Too right we are."

"Perhaps we should triple-check," he suggested before he was cupping the sides of her face with his large hands, and then he was kissing her again, sending additional tingles rushing through her and leaving her feeling rather weak in the knees.

"He shore 'nuff is kissin' her," Camilla heard Nems call out, which had Owen's kiss stopping in a heartbeat as he drew back and caught her eye.

"You sure you're up for living amongst interfering people like Nems, Meemaw, and Aunt Elma?" he asked.

"I wouldn't want to live any other way."

"Could you tell if they was enjoyin' that kissin', Nems?" Elma yelled.

"Shore seemed like it to me, Miss Elma," Nems called back.

Owen turned his attention to where Nems had wheeled his chair into the hallway. "Could you go away?"

"Miss Elma and Miss Beulah done ordered me to come check on matters," Nems returned. "You know they turn terrifyin' if they're thwarted, so I'm stayin' right here until I can tell them the two of you is surely gettin' hitched."

Camilla took hold of Owen's hand. "I think the only way we're going to get through to the whole getting hitched part is if I take over."

"What does *taking over* mean? That you're going to ask me to marry you because . . . I wouldn't feel right about that," Owen said.

"I was only intending to tell Beulah, Elma, and Nems to stop interfering for a moment because I would think you'd want to propose to me without an audience, but . . ." Her eyes widened. "You were thinking about proposing to me just now, and before getting Elma's approval?"

"I'm a grown man, Camilla. I don't actually need my aunt's approval to ask you to marry me."

"Huh" was all Camilla could think to say to that.

Owen smiled. "Now you're starting to sound like me, but to return to proposing, maybe I should wait until I can do it properly."

"Define *properly*."

"I was thinking you might like it if I escorted you through a field of daisies, stopped right in the middle of them, got down on one knee, and asked you to marry me, but only after I told you I love you, of course."

"What in tarnation is keepin' the two of you so long?" Elma bellowed.

Camilla bit back a grin. "Clearly, Elma is getting restless, so I'm thinking your field-of-daisies option is probably not going to happen." She reached up and touched Owen's face. "I can picture that scene perfectly in my mind, though, and it is truly romantic, especially since we're surrounded by daisies, you're down on one knee, but more importantly, you've just told me you love me."

Owen took hold of her hand. "And what is your response to that declaration?"

"I love you as well," she didn't hesitate to say.

"You love me?"

She stood on tiptoe, pressed her lips to his, then smiled. "You, Mr. Owen Chesterfield, are the only man I would have ever abandoned my vow of spinsterhood for because you are my perfect match in every way, and with you, I know I will live that happily-ever-after I've always dreamed of living but never thought I'd experience . . . until I met my match in you."

EPILOGUE

TWO MONTHS LATER

"I must admit I never expected your mother to get along so well with Owen's family," Hubert Pierpont said as he and Camilla strolled around the lawn of the country house Camilla and Luella had decided was best left simply called Chesterfield Manor, since any other name they might come up with would undoubtedly be turned into something worse than Moonshine Manor. "I don't believe your mother, Beulah, or Elma have stopped talking since the wedding earlier this afternoon."

Camilla's gaze settled on where her mother was, indeed, chatting with Beulah and Elma, having been joined by Betty Lou, Owen's mother, who'd promptly moved home after Luella sent her a telegram telling her she didn't want to miss out on the excitement happening in Wheeling.

Ada Mae took that moment to join Betty Lou, taking a seat on the bench beside her and bending her head close to Owen's mother a second later, chatting away as if they were finally on their way to becoming friends.

Betty Lou had made a point of apologizing to Ada Mae directly after she returned home, and Ada Mae had responded by inviting Betty Lou to join the whist salon. She hadn't hesitated to accept the invitation and was beyond pleased to learn that, in her absence, the Chesterfields had become a most sought-after family, invited to all the society events in Wheeling and reciprocating with invitations to dinners held outside on the back lawn, ones where Nems, Andy, and a few other men would pull out their fiddles, banjos, and harmonicas and entertain guests for hours, especially when everyone started dancing—something that always lasted well into the night.

"Did I mention that your mother and I have decided to make plans to build a summer house down here?" Hubert asked, drawing Camilla's attention.

"You have not, but . . . don't you want to continue summering at your cottage in Newport?"

"We'd rather spend our summers with you. Besides, since you told your mother you've developed an interest in gardening, she knows you won't want to repair to Newport for the summers, which would leave you neglecting your plants."

"Won't the grandparents be upset when you don't make an appearance in Newport?" Camilla asked.

"Considering they told Margaret to make sure we build a house that'll be big enough to accommodate them for a month or so, I don't believe that'll be an issue."

"My grandparents—both sets of them—want to spend time in Wheeling?"

Hubert inclined his head. "I know, it surprised me as well, but I think they're feeling their age and have begun to realize, after seeing how close Owen's family is, that they've been missing out on what's really important in life. They're also apparently of the belief that since Leopold Pendleton, an esteemed Knickerbocker, believes Wheeling is a delightful place to live, seeing as how he'll be living here with Beulah after they get married in a few months, Wheeling is obviously now an acceptable location to summer."

"Huh" was all Camilla could think to say to that, unable to help but smile when her Grandmother Pierpont and Grandmother Rhinelander strolled into view, speaking to Bernadette, whom they'd been wanting to seek out to see if she could fit them into her very busy schedule at her new hair salon.

"You made a beautiful bride today, Camilla," Hubert said, drawing her to a stop and taking hold of her hand. "I don't believe I've ever told you this before, but I've always been incredibly proud of you."

"Even when I turned into a rebellious sort and insisted I was going to marry George?"

Hubert smiled. "I believe I was incredibly annoyed with you at that particular time. Although speaking of George, I'm more than pleased he's been sent back to England with his tail between his legs, as well as delighted that he'll never be welcome to mingle with the Four Hundred again, not after Gideon allowed it to be known what he'd done to poor Eleanor."

"Gideon told me George will probably have to resort to leasing out a few of his homes."

"And curtailing his spending, but thankfully George was never your financial problem."

Camilla released a sigh. "I'm sorry I ever doubted your judgment."

"There's no need to apologize, my darling girl. You were young, and even though I was disappointed over your decision to never marry, if you'd not made that decision, you would have most certainly ended up marrying a man within the Four Hundred. That would have been a shame because you wouldn't have met Owen, a gentleman who suits you in every way, as does this place that's quite unlike the world you grew up in."

Before Camilla could respond to that, Gladys zoomed past her, chased by Cleo and Calamity, El Cid following a few seconds later, although he stopped and rubbed himself against Camilla's skirt, which had her picking him up and giving him a hug, earning a purr in return.

"I'm still not accustomed to seeing a pig meandering about," Hubert said as Esmerelda waddled up to join Camilla, not because she'd become overly fond of her, but because El Cid was nestled in her arms.

Her father grinned when Esmerelda plopped down by Camilla's feet and released a bit of a snort. "It's definitely a different world," he said, shaking his head before he wandered off to join Andy and Nems, who were in the midst of telling Charles and Leopold another one of their tall tales.

"I told you I was right about you being a cat person," Adelaide said, strolling up to join her.

Camilla arched a brow. "Should I assume that statement is soon to be followed by you suggesting I need to make a home for a few additional little darlings of yours?"

"I bet Esmerelda would love to have more cats around," Adelaide said before her eyes took to gleaming. "And you know, I have a feeling that my Puff, a delightful little calico that loves to snuggle, would simply adore Esmerelda, which might improve Esmerelda's surly disposition, as well as leaving her not focusing all of her adoration on El Cid, who isn't what I would call the most affectionate of cats—except with you and Owen, of course."

Camilla gave El Cid another scratch. "Since I have a feeling you're going to turn relentless about the cats, I might as well graciously give in sooner than later." She smiled. "Besides, there are plenty of families around here who'd be happy to take in a few cats, and checking in on your cats would also give you a reason to visit more often."

"Gideon and I are taking on a case in Pittsburgh soon, something about industrial espionage in one of the steel mills, so you'll be seeing quite a bit of me, with or without the cats, although . . ." Adelaide took hold of Camilla's hand. "We've also been thinking, since we absolutely love Beulah's cabin, that we might buy some land around here and build our own summer cabin."

"That would be wonderful, especially when we can spend lots of time together, wading in creeks, helping Beulah with her garden, and I can teach you how to whitewash a fence."

Adelaide grinned. "We'll definitely be moving here for the summers now because I have a feeling I haven't truly lived until I've whitewashed something."

As Camilla returned the grin, Owen walked up to join them, taking El Cid before he handed her a bunch of daisies he'd clearly picked on his own. He then flashed her a smile before setting El Cid on the ground, which elicited a snort of obvious approval from Esmerelda before she lumbered after El Cid, who was now moving for tables that were groaning under the weight of the feast spread out on them, clearly in the hopes that someone would take pity on him and feed him his new favorite—fried catfish.

"Those are some lovely flowers, Owen," Adelaide said.

"I thought the bride would enjoy them."

Adelaide sent him a wink. "I'm sure she will, just as I'm sure she'd enjoy some alone time with her groom." With that, Adelaide sent Camilla a smile before she wandered away, saying she was off to find Gideon.

"Care to take a stroll with me, Mrs. Chesterfield?" Owen asked as he took hold of her hand and kissed it.

"I would love nothing more."

After tucking her hand into the crook of his arm, Owen began walking with her toward a grove of trees, drawing her to a stop once they were under a large maple, where he promptly leaned forward and kissed her.

The sound of their guests faded away, many of those guests having traveled to West Virginia from New York since Camilla had wanted to get married, not in her family's church in the city, but in Owen's church where everyone had welcomed her with open arms when she'd first arrived in Wheeling.

Reverend Braun had officiated the service and had surprised Camilla when he'd gotten to the part where he was supposed to ask if anyone had any objections to speak now or forever hold their peace. He hadn't asked anything at all, though, simply nodded to Beulah, who'd walked up to stand beside Camilla. She'd then turned to the guests assembled and done one of the sweetest things Camilla had ever seen.

Beulah had announced to everyone that, while she was originally supposed to have been given the final say regarding whether she'd found Camilla suitable to join the family, according to Elma, it was up to the whole family to decide the answer to that. She then went on to say that anyone related to the Chesterfield family was to retain their seat if they had an objection to the upcoming nuptials, but stand if they thought Camilla would be a most welcome addition to the family.

Everyone, even those not related to the Chesterfields, had risen to their feet.

"Why do I get the distinct impression you're thinking about something other than our kiss?" Owen asked, drawing back and smiling at her.

"I've always been a lady who can concentrate on more than one thing at a time."

"I've noticed that, but what were you thinking about?"

"The service and how wonderful it was."

"Did you notice that I got rather teary as I watched you walk down the aisle?"

"I did. It made me rather teary in return, although I found myself falling more in love with you at that moment than I was before."

He kissed her again, and this time, Camilla found herself unable to think about anything else because, clearly, Owen was determined to capture her full attention.

"That's better," he said a good few minutes later.

"Indeed."

He took hold of her hand and pressed a kiss to her fingers. "Did you tell your mother that Mr. Timken has decided he wants to stay here with us?"

"Mr. Timken already told her."

"And?"

"She says she's fine with that, although I believe she's probably going to want him to assume butler duties for her during the summer months after she and Father build a house here."

"Whatever will we do without a butler for a few months?" Owen asked with a grin.

"I imagine Mr. Timken will find a replacement for himself, what with how he's been busy with finding positions for numerous men who've been injured while working in the factories or mines. He's starting up a training program in a few weeks, one that'll teach these men how to take on roles such as valets, cooks, and even butlers."

"An excellent idea since Charles mentioned he'll be in need of a butler and full staff after he gets his house completed, especially when his mother, Petunia, has decided to move in with him and Luella once they get married."

"Charles told me he's intending on building a *very* large house, but speaking of parents moving in with their children, are you certain your mother and father are fine with living in the house on Wheeling Island instead of moving here to Chesterfield Manor with us?"

"Mother wants to be close to all the social activities she's now being invited to, and besides, she wants grandchildren and believes she'll get those sooner if we have more time to ourselves."

Camilla blinked. "I'm not even certain how to respond to that."

"Then I shall change the subject to . . . hmmm . . . nothing springs to mind except . . . I've been wanting to ask you something about matchmaking."

"Matchmaking?"

"I've been wondering if you've been missing that, given how many matches you were responsible for making over the past few months."

"I'm not sure I was solely responsible for all the matches, not when it turns out that Beulah managed to get that apple pie recipe into Charles's, Leopold's, and even my hands."

Owen's eyes began twinkling. "Did she really?"

The corners of Camilla's lips twitched. "Technically, no, since Charles just simply helped himself to her recipe box after he decided he was going to marry Luella, and then Leopold gained access to it by walking into the kitchen while Beulah was making the pie and volunteered to help." She grinned. "And you know how she got it to me—sneaky woman that she is."

"She had Elma sew it into the hem of that apron Lottie gave you before the family reunion."

Camilla smiled. "To give her credit, that was a master move since she knew Lottie would check the pockets and find the recipes there, while also knowing that my guard would be down, thinking Lottie had foiled her, and I wouldn't think to check the hem."

"Meemaw is convinced the recipe, and you taking possession of it, is what had us, as she puts it, coming to our senses and realizing she was right all along about us being perfect for each other."

"I think we would have realized that without the recipe, but since it is a Chesterfield tradition, it probably wouldn't hurt to make certain we always have some copies readily available since . . ." She nodded to where everyone was gathered on the back lawn. "There's a whole new generation of Chesterfields right over there. I'm thinking that recipe is going to come into play a lot over the next few years."

"And what about people who aren't Chesterfields and don't believe in the power of apple pie?"

Camilla glanced across the lawn to where Nems was speaking with Bernadette, then shifted her attention to Sally Murchendorfer, who was talking to five other Wheeling ladies, none of whom were married or even in the process of a courtship.

"I suppose it wouldn't hurt if I were to nudge Nems along a bit with Bernadette since they truly are well matched," she finally admitted. "And I can't help but think that Sally and her friends are still in need of a little guidance where gentleman are concerned."

Owen grinned. "I had a feeling you were going to say that, which is why . . ." He reached into his pocket, pulled out a wrapped box, and handed it to her.

"And this is?" she asked.

"Open it."

Biting her lip, she ripped off the paper and opened the box, drawing in a sharp breath when her gaze settled on calling cards, ones that read:

Mrs. Owen Chesterfield
Matchmaker Extraordinaire

Her arms were around Owen a second later as she stood on tiptoe and pressed her lips to his.

"I take it you like the gift?" he asked a good five minutes later as he kept his arm around her and they began wandering their way back to their wedding reception.

"You know I do."

"And you like the Mrs. Chesterfield part?"

"I *love* the Mrs. Chesterfield part," she corrected.

"And do you also love that you'll be living with me in West Virgina, which I know is a far cry from New York City?"

She stopped walking and smiled. "Beulah recently told me, when we were spending some time together on her front porch, simply rocking back and forth on the rocking chairs your grandfather made, that West Virginia is what she considers almost heaven. She was definitely right about that, because with you by my side, and with us surrounded by this little slice of heaven, I have a feeling the match we've made is only going to become sweeter with age, a match I'm sure you'll agree was always meant to be, and one that will allow us to enjoy this beautiful life we now get to live together."

With that, Camilla gave Owen's hand a squeeze, and together they moved to join their friends and family, Camilla realizing in that moment that she would never be plagued with ennui again, and all because she'd met the man who completed her and made her laugh, and a man who'd helped her discover where her place was meant to be in life—by his side and living in a paradise called West Virginia.

Named one of the funniest voices in inspirational romance by *Booklist*, **Jen Turano** is a *USA Today* bestselling author, known for penning quirky historical romances set in the Gilded Age. Her books have earned *Publishers Weekly* and *Booklist* starred reviews, top picks from *Romantic Times*, and praise from *Library Journal*. She and her family live outside of Denver, Colorado. Readers can find her on Facebook, Instagram, and at JenTurano.com.

FOR MORE FROM JEN TURANO,
READ ON
FOR AN EXCERPT FROM

When Gwendolyn Brinley accepted a paid companion position for the Newport Season, she never imagined she'd be expected to take over responsibilities as an assistant matchmaker. Tasked with finding a wife for the Season's catch, Walter Townsend, her assignment becomes increasingly difficult when she realizes his perfect match might be . . . her.

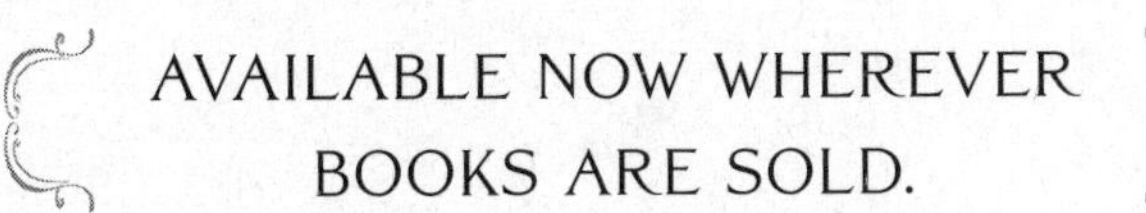

One

NEWPORT, RHODE ISLAND
JULY 1, 1888

One of the most curious discoveries Miss Gwendolyn Brinley had made during her brief sojourn as an unexpected and oh-so-reluctant assistant matchmaker was this—securing advantageous marriages amongst the socially elite was not for the faint of heart and, frankly, could be considered a blood sport.

She'd been in Newport a mere six days, and yet the events she'd attended leading up to this evening's official opening of the Season at Mrs. Astor's impressive Beechwood "cottage" had allowed her to observe underhanded tactics one didn't expect from young ladies of such illustrious social significance.

She'd witnessed an "accidental" punch spill at a pre-Season picnic, seen ladies edging other ladies out of their way with sharp elbows to the ribs, and then watched from the balcony of the esteemed Newport Casino as a lady took out an opponent she apparently saw as competition on the marriage mart by whacking a tennis ball directly at that opponent's head, which resulted in the young lady sporting a spectacular black eye a few hours later.

In retrospect, Gwendolyn's decision to accept a paid position for the summer to afford herself a respite from the drama that always surrounded her cousin, Catriona Zimmerman, whom she'd been a companion to for years, seemed ridiculous, given that she'd now landed in a most dramatic situation.

"Miss Brinley, would you be a dear and maneuver me and this dreadful chair to the other side of the ballroom?" Mrs. Parker, her employer, said, pulling Gwendolyn from her thoughts. "I'm having difficulties keeping track of our targets from this vantage point. If we want to succeed this summer, we must learn what the most eligible gentlemen desire in potential brides. I won't be able to point out the location of those gentlemen if I can't find them in the crush we're currently in."

Mrs. Parker's blue eyes began to gleam. "I'm determined to secure the best matches for the ladies I'm sponsoring this summer, Miss Elizabeth Ellsworth and Miss Hannah Howe. To accomplish that, we're going to have to throw ourselves wholeheartedly into reconnaissance work, which was delayed due to the unfortunate breaking of my leg."

"A leg that wouldn't have been broken if you hadn't entered a three-legged race," Gwendolyn said, taking hold of the handles on the back of Mrs. Parker's wheeled chair and pushing it slowly through the guests milling about the edges of Mrs. Astor's ballroom.

"In hindsight, the three-legged race was sheer foolishness on my part," Mrs. Parker admitted. "But how could I have refused to participate when my partner was Mr. Russell Damrosch? He's worth millions and is known to be searching for a wife. I'm quite convinced he'd be a perfect match for Miss Howe."

Gwendolyn stopped pushing the chair and leaned close to Mrs. Parker's ear. "Mr. Damrosch is the last gentleman you should consider for either of your young ladies. He's obviously a thoughtless man, what with how in his pursuit of winning the three-legged race he dragged you over the finish line after you stumbled and fell to the ground."

"I'm sure he didn't realize I'd fallen."

"It would have been difficult for him to miss, because one minute the two of you were galloping along and the next you were lying on the ground. It speaks volumes about his character, or lack thereof, that he was so determined to win two bottles of The Marsh and Benson from 1809, he didn't bother to notice the grievous injury he was causing you."

"You can't blame the man for being so earnest in his attempt to win the grand prize—1809 was an excellent year for Madeira."

"Considering Mr. Damrosch is a multimillionaire, he's capable of purchasing an endless supply of 1809 Madeira. He should have abandoned his desire to win the race the moment you fell."

Mrs. Parker bit her lip. "I suppose you have a point. It may be prudent to have you monitor his behavior to see if that inconsiderate nature you believe he possesses rears its ugly head again."

"It would be more prudent if you'd simply take him off your list of eligible bachelors. The last thing Miss Howe needs is to be shackled for life to an inconsiderate man."

"Miss Howe will be only too happy to overlook inconsideration if it means she'll have access to millions."

"That's a mercenary approach to marriage if there ever was one, and I haven't gotten the impression Miss Howe's a mercenary sort. I believe she may be interested in securing a love match over a profitable one."

Mrs. Parker waved that aside. "If she wanted a love match, she'd have convinced her mother to approach Miss Camilla Pierpont to sponsor her, not me."

"Miss Pierpont?"

Craning her neck, Mrs. Parker waved toward a beautiful lady with golden hair, dressed in the first state of fashion and surrounded by an entire brigade of gentlemen. "That's Camilla over there. She's a grand heiress, the only heiress, in fact, to the Hubert Pierpont fortune."

"And she's a matchmaker?"

"I know, she hardly fits the standard image of matchmakers, since we tend to be older matrons of society. Camilla's twenty-five, unmarried, and has allowed it to be known she intends to embrace her spinster state forever."

"It seems peculiar for a confirmed spinster to dabble in matchmaking."

"Indeed, but she's unusually successful with her matches, which makes her direct competition for me. I haven't heard a peep about a specific lady she may be sponsoring this Season, but even if she's decided to sit the summer out, she's surely sizing up the gentlemen surrounding her. It won't benefit us if she sets her sights on one of them for a match in the future. That means you need to get me settled and then get to the task I've given you this evening."

Mrs. Parker gestured to a spot next to the orchestra. "There's Mrs. Ryerson. You may deposit me beside her. I've been meaning to speak with her about her son, August. He's a quiet young man but may be a prime catch in the next few years because he's due to inherit a substantial fortune. He'll only be a catch, though, *if* he can learn to mingle more comfortably in society. I believe tonight is the night I'll present that concerning matter to his mother."

Gwendolyn opened her mouth, then swallowed the opinion she'd been about to broach. Mrs. Parker didn't appear to welcome unsolicited advice from a mere employee, but it was doubtful Mrs. Ryerson was going to enjoy listening to Mrs. Parker wax on about the deficiencies she saw in the lady's son. Pushing the chair into motion again, she kept to the edge of the ballroom floor as Mr. Nash, Mrs. Astor's cotillion leader, called out instructions to dancers weaving their way through a "German" known as the Hungarian.

She was forced to stop when she reached a gathering of young ladies dressed in lovely creations of soft-colored silk, the colors adding a festive atmosphere to an already splendid ballroom. Unfortunately, even though the ladies clearly saw they were blocking Gwendolyn's way, not one of them bothered to step aside to create a path for her. Instead, they continued chatting amongst themselves, acting quite as if Gwendolyn and Mrs. Parker were invisible.

Their lack of acknowledgment wasn't much of a surprise, because when she'd first arrived in Newport and accompanied Mrs. Parker to Mrs. Elbridge Gerry's pre-Season picnic, young ladies and their mothers had been only too keen to make Gwendolyn's acquaintance—until they learned she was in Mrs. Parker's employ. That information spread like wildfire, and after everyone realized she was not in Newport as competition, not one lady bothered to speak with her again.

At first, she'd been taken aback to find herself slighted, because she'd never experienced being labeled an outcast before. Truth be told, after spending the past several years traveling the world with Catriona, she'd grown accustomed to being well received by aristocrats, foreign leaders, and a variety of diplomats in whatever country they were visiting.

Granted, her reception in those far-off lands was directly connected to Catriona, who'd been a world-renowned opera singer before she'd fallen madly in love with Mr. Barnabas Zimmerman and left opera behind without a backward glance. Barnabas had been an industrial titan, and until his unexpected death after a short illness had showered Catriona with affection and love, leaving her despondent after he died, as well as a very wealthy widow.

When it became clear Catriona was becoming a shadow of her former self, Gwendolyn had taken matters into her own hands. She'd always considered herself an unconventional woman and, unlike most of her friends, had never longed to marry right out of the schoolroom and settle into wedded bliss. Because of that, she'd not hesitated to insist Catriona embark with her on a world tour, taking on the role of her cousin's companion—a position Catriona wholeheartedly approved of, because when she wasn't despondent, she knew full well she was capable of attracting trouble on a concerningly frequent basis.

Traveling the world had seen Catriona begin to heal from the devastation of losing her Barnabas, while Gwendolyn had been given the privilege of meeting fascinating people who genuinely seemed to enjoy spending time in her company.

But not once in her travels had she run across the blatant snobbery she was encountering in Newport. She'd been warned that Newport was one of the most pretentious summer retreats in the country, but not putting much stock in the warnings, she'd accepted Mrs. Parker's offer.

She'd believed summering in Newport as a paid companion would provide her with a much-needed rest from her travels, as well as a well-deserved reprieve from her cousin. Unfortunately, rest and relaxation seemed in short supply these days.

"Ladies, good heavens," Mrs. Parker barked, snapping Gwendolyn back to the situation at hand. "Have you failed to notice that Miss Brinley is trying to push me to the other side of the ballroom? She certainly can't be expected to plow through all of you, unless she doesn't mind taking out a few of your limbs, which I'm going to assume she *would* mind. You need to make a path for us—and quickly, if you please."

A chorus of apologies rang out before the young ladies glided out of the way, leaving Gwendolyn free to wheel Mrs. Parker across the floor. She maneuvered the wheeled chair into the spot directly beside Mrs. Ryerson, who didn't look overjoyed to be joined by the illustrious matchmaker. The lady's lips thinned before she began taking a marked interest in the orchestra—not that Mrs. Parker noticed, because she was squinting at something across the room.

"Ah, there he is," Mrs. Parker proclaimed. "And thank goodness, Miss Pierpont hasn't joined him yet. I'm not certain you're ready to go up against a matchmaker of her repute."

"I'm not up for going against *any* matchmaker, whether they're possessed of a wonderful repute or not. To remind you, yet again, I accepted a paid-companion position with you, not matchmaker."

"Assistant matchmaker, dear. You don't have the experience needed to be a true matchmaker."

"I'm not qualified to be an assistant matchmaker either. Frankly, I've been thinking I should do both of us a favor and bow out of your employ before I prove how unqualified I am. From what you've told me, you never fail with making splendid matches. I would hate to be responsible for your suffering a failure this Season."

"I have every confidence you'll rise magnificently to your assistant-matchmaking position," Mrs. Parker countered. "You, out of any of the candidates the agency sent me when my last companion left without notice, impressed me with your no-nonsense attitude and your air of competency. Add in the notion you were a paid companion of Catriona Zimmerman, a lady known for her temperamental nature when she was Catriona Sullivan, the opera singer, and I believe you'll find your summer as my assistant matchmaker downright successful."

"I beg to differ. I have no qualifications as a matchmaker and am doomed for failure. That will reflect poorly on you and is exactly why you should contact the employment agency again and have them send you actual matchmaker candidates."

Mrs. Parker waved Gwendolyn's declaration aside. "Matchmakers aren't a dime a dozen, Miss Brinley. I highly doubt the agency has any candidates qualified for the position I need fulfilled." She gestured across the ballroom. "With that out of the way, your first task awaits you underneath that chandelier—Mr. Walter Townsend."

A knot immediately developed in Gwendolyn's stomach before she settled a frown on Mrs. Parker. "Didn't you tell me Walter Townsend is considered *the* catch of the Season?"

"Indeed. And as such, it would be a true feather in my cap if we landed him for one of our young ladies." Mrs. Parker rubbed her hands together. "I adore my feathers, so off you go. And remember, I'm counting on you to not let me down."

Sign Up for Jen's Newsletter

Keep up to date with Jen's latest news on book releases and events by signing up for her email list at the link below.

JenTurano.com

FOLLOW JEN ON SOCIAL MEDIA

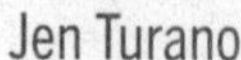

Jen Turano | @JenTuranoAuthor | @JenTurano